Praise for Patricia Davids and her novels

"Davids' deep understanding of Amish culture is evident in the compassionate characters and beautiful descriptions."
—*RT Book Reviews* on *A Home for Hannah*

"Davids' latest beautifully portrays the Amish belief that everything happens for a reason."
—*RT Book Reviews* on *The Christmas Quilt*

"A wonderful story."
—*RT Book Reviews* on *The Farmer Next Door*

Praise for Jo Ann Brown and her novels

"The story is rich with relatable...characters."
—*RT Book Reviews* on *Amish Homecoming*

"The characters demonstrate great perseverance."
—*RT Book Reviews* on *An Amish Match*

"Readers will be pleased."
—*RT Book Reviews* on *Her Longed-For Family*

After thirty-five years as a nurse, **Patricia Davids** hung up her stethoscope to become a full-time writer. She enjoys spending her free time visiting her grandchildren, doing some long-overdue yard work and traveling to research her story locations. She resides in Wichita, Kansas. Pat always enjoys hearing from her readers. You can visit her online at patriciadavids.com.

Jo Ann Brown has always loved stories with happy-ever-after endings. A former military officer, she is thrilled to have the chance to write stories about people falling in love. She is also a photographer, and she travels with her husband of more than thirty years to places where she can snap pictures. They live in Nevada with three children and a spoiled cat. Drop her a note at joannbrownbooks.com.

USA TODAY Bestselling Author

PATRICIA DAVIDS
A Home for Hannah

&

JO ANN BROWN
An Amish Reunion

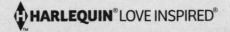

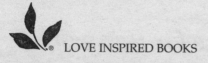

LOVE INSPIRED BOOKS

Recycling programs for this product may not exist in your area.

ISBN-13: 978-1-335-00874-9

A Home for Hannah and An Amish Reunion

Copyright © 2017 by Harlequin Books S.A.

The publisher acknowledges the copyright holders of the individual works as follows:

A Home for Hannah
Copyright © 2012 by Patricia MacDonald

An Amish Reunion
Copyright © 2017 by Jo Ann Ferguson

www.Harlequin.com

Printed in U.S.A.

CONTENTS

A HOME FOR HANNAH

Patricia Davids

In memory of Dave.
The one, the only, the love of my life.

But we are bound to give thanks always to God
for you, brethren beloved of the Lord, because
God hath from the beginning chosen you
to salvation through sanctification of the Spirit
and belief of the truth.
—*2 Thessalonians* 2:13

Chapter One

"**B**ella, what's wrong with you?" Miriam Kauffman pulled her arm from beneath the quilt to squint at her watch. The glow-in-the-dark numbers read one forty-five in the morning. Her dog continued scratching frantically at the door to her bedroom.

Miriam slipped her arm back under the covers. "I'm not taking you out in the middle of the night. Forget it."

Her yellow Labrador-pointer mix had other ideas. Bella began whining and yipping as she scratched with renewed vigor.

Miriam was tempted to pull her pillow over her ears, but she wasn't the only person in the house. "Be quiet. You're going to wake Mother."

Bella's whining changed to a deep-throated bark. At eighty-five pounds, what Bella wanted Bella usually got. Giving up in exasperation, Miriam threw back her quilt.

Now that Bella had her owner's attention, she plopped on her haunches and waited, tongue lolling with doggy happiness. In the silence that followed, Miriam heard a new sound, the clip-clop of hoofbeats.

Miriam moved to her second-story bedroom window. In the bright moonlight, she saw an Amish buggy disappearing down the lane.

When she was at home in Medina, such a late-night visit would mean only one thing—a new Amish runaway had come seeking her help to transition into the outside world. But how would anyone know to find her in Hope Springs? Who in the area knew of her endeavors? She hadn't told anyone, and she was positive her mother wouldn't mention the fact.

Miriam pulled a warm cotton robe over her nightgown and grabbed a flashlight from the top of her dresser. She patted Bella's head. "Good girl. Good watchdog."

Guided by the bright circle of light, she made her way downstairs in the dark farmhouse to the front door. Bella came close on her heels. The second Miriam pulled open the door, the dog was out like a shot. Bella didn't have a mean bone in her body, but her exuberance and size could scare someone who didn't know her.

"Don't be frightened—she won't hurt you," Miriam called out quickly as she opened the door farther. She expected to find a terrified Amish teenager standing on her stoop, but the porch was empty. Bella was nosing a large basket on the bottom step.

Miriam swung her light in a wide arc. The farmyard was empty. Perhaps the runaway had changed his or her mind and returned home. If so, Miriam was glad. It was one thing to aid young Amish people who wanted to leave their unsympathetic families when she'd lived in another part of the state. It was an entirely different thing now that she was living under her Amish mother's roof. The last thing she wanted to do while she was in Hope Springs was to cause her mother further distress.

Bella lay down beside the basket and began whining. Miriam descended the steps. "What have you got there?"

Pushing the big dog aside, Miriam realized the basket held a quilt. Perhaps it was meant as a gift for her mother. The middle of the night was certainly an odd time to deliver a package. She started to pick it up, but a tiny mewing sound made her stop. It sounded like a baby.

Miriam straightened. *There's no way someone left a baby on my doorstep.*

Bella licked Miriam's bare toes, sending a chill up her leg. She definitely wasn't dreaming.

She took a few steps away from the porch to carefully scan the yard with her light. "If this is someone's idea of a prank, I'm not laughing."

Silence was the only reply. She waited, hoping it was indeed a joke and someone would step forward to fess up.

The full moon hung directly overhead, bathing the landscape in pale silvery light. A cool breeze swept past Miriam's cheeks carrying the loamy scent of spring. The grass beneath her bare feet was wet with dew and her toes grew colder by the second. She rested one bare foot on top of the other. No snickering prankster stepped out of the black shadows to claim credit for such an outrageous joke.

Turning back to the porch, she lifted the edge of the quilt and looked into the basket. Her hopes that the sounds came from a tape recorder or a kitten vanished when her light revealed the soft round face of an infant.

She gazed down the lane. The buggy was already out of sight. There was no way of knowing which direction the driver had taken when he or she reached the highway.

Why would they leave a baby with her? A chill that had nothing to do with the cold morning slipped down her spine. She didn't want to be responsible for this baby or any other infant. She refused to let her mind go to that dark place.

A simple phone call would bring a slew of people to look after this child. It was, after all, a crime to abandon a baby. As a nurse, she was required by law to report this.

But that would mean facing Sheriff Nick Bradley.

"Miriam, what are you doing out there?" Her mother's frail voice came from inside the house.

Picking up the basket, Miriam carried it into the house and gently set it in the middle of the kitchen table. "Someone left a baby on our doorstep."

Her mother, dressed in a white flannel nightgown, shuffled over, leaning heavily on her cane. "A *boppli!* Are you joking?"

"*Nee, Mamm,* I'm not. It's a baby."

Miriam's first thought had been to call 9-1-1, until she remembered who the law was in Hope Springs. She'd cut off her right arm before she asked for his help. Who could she call?

Ada Kauffman came closer to the basket. "Did you see who left the child?"

"All I saw was a buggy driving away."

Ada's eyes widened with shock. "You think this is an Amish child?"

"I don't know what else to think."

Ada shook her head. "*Nee,* an Amish family would welcome a babe even if the mother was not married."

"Maybe the mother was too afraid or ashamed to tell her parents," Miriam suggested.

"If that is so, we must forgive her sins against *Gott* and against her child."

That was the Amish way—always forgive first—

even before all the details were known. It was the one part of the Amish faith that Miriam couldn't comply with. Some things were unforgivable.

Miriam examined the basket. It was made of split wood woven into an oval shape with a flat bottom and handles on both sides. The wood was stained a pale fruitwood color with a band of dark green around the top for decoration. She'd seen similar ones for sale in shops that carried Amish handmade goods. The baby started to fuss. Miriam stared at her.

Her mother said, "Pick the child up, Miriam. They don't bite."

"I know that." Miriam scooped the little girl from the folds of the quilt and softly patted her back. The poor thing didn't even have a diaper to wear. Miriam's heart went out to their tiny, unexpected guest. Not everyone was ready to be a parent, but how would it feel to be the child who grew up knowing she'd been tossed away in a laundry basket?

Stroking the infant's soft, downy cap of hair, she felt the stirrings of maternal attachment. She couldn't imagine leaving her child like this, alone in the darkness, depending on the kindness of strangers to care for it. Children were not to be discarded like unwanted trash.

Old shame and guilt flared in her heart. One child had been lost because of her inaction. This baby deserved better.

Putting aside her personal feelings, she called up the objective role she assumed when she was working. Carefully she laid the baby on the quilt again to examine it. As a nurse, her field of expertise was adult critical care, but she remembered enough of her maternal-child training to make sure the baby wasn't in distress.

Without a stethoscope to aid her, it was a cursory exam at best. The little girl had a lusty set of lungs and objected to being returned to her makeshift bed. Who could blame her?

Ada started toward the stairs. "A little sugar water may satisfy her until you can go to town when the store opens and stock up on formula and bottles. I have your baby things put away in the attic. I'll go get them. It's wonderful to have a child in the house again."

Miriam stared after her mother. "We can't keep her."

Ada turned back in surprise. "Of course we can. She was left with us."

"No! We need to find out who her mother is. She has made a terrible mistake. We need to help her see that. We need to make this right."

Ada lifted one hand. "How will you do that?"

"I… I don't know. Maybe they left a note." Miriam quickly checked inside the basket, but found nothing.

"*Vel,* until someone returns for her, this *boppli* needs a crib and diapers."

Miriam quickly tucked a corner of the quilt around the baby. "*Mamm,* come back here. You shouldn't go climbing around in the attic. You've only been out of the hospital a week."

A stormy frown creased her mother's brow but quickly vanished. "I'm stronger than you think."

That was a big part of her mother's problem. She didn't realize how sick she was. Miriam tried a different approach. "You have much more experience with babies than I do. You take her, and I'll go hunt for the stuff."

Her mother's frown changed into a smile. "*Ja,* it has been far too long since I've held such a tiny one. Why don't you bring me a clean towel to wrap her in first."

Miriam did as her mother asked. After swaddling the babe, Ada settled into the rocker in the corner of the kitchen with the infant in her arms. Softly she began humming an Amish lullaby. It was the first time in ages that Miriam had seen her mother look content, almost… happy. Miriam knew her mother longed for grandchildren. She also knew it was unlikely she would ever have any.

Ada smiled. "I remember the night you and Mark were born. Oh, what a snowstorm there was. Your *daed* took so long to come with the midwife that I was afraid she would be too late."

"But the midwife arrived in the nick of time." Miriam finished the story she'd heard dozens of times.

"*Ja.* Such a *goot,* quiet baby you were, but your brother, oh, how he hollered."

"Papa said it was because Mark wanted to be born first."

"He had no patience, that child." Ada began humming again, but her eyes glistened with unshed tears.

Miriam struggled with her own sadness whenever she spoke of her twin brother. Mark's death had changed everyone in the family, especially her, but the old story did spark an idea.

"*Mamm,* who is the local midwife?"

"Amber Bradley does most of the deliveries around Hope Springs."

"Bradley? Is she related to…him? Is he married to her?" Did he have a wife and children of his own? Thinking about him with a family caused an odd ache in her chest. Miriam had taken pains to avoid meeting him during her months in Hope Springs. She realized she knew almost nothing about his current life.

Ada said, "*Nee,* he's not wed. Amber may be a cousin. *Ja,* I'm sure I heard she was his cousin."

Nicolas Bradley was the sheriff, the man Miriam had loved with all her heart when she was eighteen and the man responsible for Mark's death. Would the midwife involve him? Miriam hesitated but quickly realized she had no choice. She didn't have any idea how to go about searching for the baby's mother. If Amber chose to notify Nick, Miriam would deal with it. She prayed for strength and wisdom to make the right decision.

"The midwife might have an idea who our mother is. She is certainly equipped to take care of a newborn. If nothing else, she will have a supply of formula and the equipment to make sure the baby is healthy."

Ada frowned at her daughter. "I have heard she is a good woman, but she is *Englisch,* an outsider. This is Amish business. We should not involve her."

"I'm no longer Amish, so it isn't strictly Amish business. Besides, she may feel like we do and want to keep this out of the courts. I'm going to call her."

"You know I don't like having that telephone in my house."

Her mother tolerated Miriam's *Englisch* ways, but she hated to allow them in her Amish home. It was a frequent source of conflict between the two women.

Irritated, but determined to remain calm, Miriam said, "I'm not giving up my cell phone. You are a diabetic who has already had two serious heart attacks. You could need an ambulance at any time. If you want me to stay, I keep the phone."

"I did not say you should leave. I said I do not like having the phone in my house. If I live or die, it is *Gottes wille* and not because you have a phone."

"It might be God's will that I carry a phone. Did you ever consider that?"

"I don't want to argue." Ada clamped her lips in a tight line signaling the end of the conversation.

Miriam crossed the room and dropped a kiss on her mother's brow. "Neither do I. I have said I'll only use the phone in an emergency and for work. I think this counts as an emergency."

When her mother didn't reply, Miriam quickly ran upstairs to her bedroom and pulled her cell phone from the pocket of her purse. A call to directory assistance yielded Amber Bradley's number.

When a sleepy woman's voice answered the phone, Miriam took a deep breath and hoped she was making the right decision. "Hi. You don't know me. My name is Miriam Kauffman, and I have a situation."

After Miriam explained what had transpired, Amber agreed to come check the baby and bring some new-born essentials. She also agreed to wait until they had discussed the situation before notifying the local law enforcement.

Miriam returned to the kitchen. Her mother was standing beside the kitchen table. She had taken the quilt out of the basket. Miriam said, "Amber Bradley is on her way. I convinced her to wait before calling the police, but I know she will. She has to."

Ada held up an envelope. "I told you not to involve the *Englisch*. I found a note under the quilt. The child's name is Hannah and her mother is coming back for her."

The farmhouse door swung open before Sheriff Nick Bradley could knock. A woman with fiery auburn hair and green eyes stood framed in the doorway glaring at him. "There has been a mistake. We don't need you here."

The shock of seeing Miriam Kauffman standing in front of him took him aback. He was certain his heart actually stopped for a moment before chugging ahead with a painful thump. He struggled to hide his surprise. It had been eight years since he'd laid eyes on her. A lifetime ago.

He touched the brim of his trooper's hat, determined to maintain a professional demeanor no matter what it cost him. How could she be more beautiful than he remembered? "Good morning to you, too, Miriam."

After all this time, she wasn't any better at hiding her opinion of him. She looked ready to spit nails. Proof, if he needed it, that she hadn't forgiven him. A physical ache filled his chest.

"Miriam, don't be rude," her mother chided from behind her. Miriam reluctantly stepped aside. A large yellow dog pushed past her and came out to investigate Nick's arrival. It took only a second for the dog to decide he was a friend. She jumped up and planted both front feet on his chest. He welcomed the chance to regain his composure and focused his attention on the dog.

"Bella, get down," Miriam scolded.

The dog paid her no mind. The mutt's tail wagged happily as Nick rumpled her ears. He said, "That's a good girl. Now down."

The dog dropped to all fours, then sat quietly by his side. He nodded once to Miriam and entered the house. The dog stayed outside.

His cousin Amber sat at the kitchen table. "Hi, Nick. Thanks for coming. We do need your help."

Ada Kauffman sat across from her. A large woven

basket sat on the table between them. The room was bathed in soft light from two kerosene lanterns hanging from hooks on the ceiling. The Amish religion forbade the use of electricity in the home.

He glanced at the three women facing him. Ada Kauffman was Amish, from the top of her white prayer bonnet on her gray hair to the tips of her bare toes poking out from beneath her plain, dark blue dress. Her daughter, Miriam, had never joined the church, choosing to leave before she was baptized. Tonight, she wore simple dark slacks and a green blouse that matched her eyes. Her arms were crossed over her chest. If looks could shrivel a man, he'd be two feet tall in about a second.

His cousin Amber wore jeans, sneakers and a blue T-shirt beneath a white lab coat. She served the Amish and non-Amish people of Hope Springs, Ohio, as a nurse midwife. Exactly what was she doing here? If Miriam's trim figure was anything to go by she didn't require the services of a midwife.

Amber wasn't normally the cloak-and-dagger type. He was intensely curious as to why she had insisted he come in person before she'd tell him the nature of the call.

He said, "Okay, I'm here. What's so sensitive that I had to come instead of sending one of my perfectly competent deputies? Make it snappy, Amber. I'm leaving in a few hours for a much-needed, week-long fishing trip, and I've got a lot to do."

"This is why we called you." Amber gestured toward the basket. He took a step closer and saw a baby swaddled in the folds of a blue quilt.

"You called me here to see a new baby? Congratulations to whomever."

"Exactly," Miriam said.

He looked at her closely. "What am I missing?"

Amber said, "It's more about what we are missing."

"And that is?" he demanded. Somebody had better start making sense.

Ada said, "A mother to go with this baby."

He shook his head. "You've lost me."

Miriam rolled her eyes. "I'm not surprised."

Her mother scowled at her, but said, "Someone left this baby on my porch."

"Someone abandoned this infant? When? Did you see who it was?" He pulled his notebook and pen from his pocket and started laying out an investigation in his mind. So much for starting his vacation on time.

"About three hours ago," Miriam answered.

Was she serious? "And you didn't think to call my office until thirty minutes ago?"

Miriam didn't answer. She sat in a chair beside his cousin. Amber said, "Miriam called me first. We've been discussing what to do."

"There is nothing to discuss. What you *do* is call your local law enforcement and report an abandoned child. We could have had a search for the parents started hours ago. Amber, what were you thinking? I need to get my crime scene people here. We need to dust for prints, collect evidence."

Miriam said, "No one has committed a crime."

He glared at her. "I beg to differ."

Her chin came up. She never was one to back down. He'd missed their arguments as much as he'd missed the good times they shared. If only they could go back to the way it had been before.

For a second, he thought he saw a softening in her eyes. Was she thinking about those golden summer days, too? Her gaze slid away from him before he could be sure. She said, "According to the Ohio Safe Haven Law, if a baby under one month of age is left at a fire station, with a law enforcement officer or with a health care worker, there can be no prosecution of the parents who left the child."

He didn't like having the law quoted to him. "This baby wasn't left with Amber or at a hospital. It was left with you."

"I'm a nurse."

She really enjoyed one-upping him. He had to admire her spunk. "But this isn't a hospital, it's a farmhouse. I still have to report this to the child welfare people. They will take charge of the baby."

"That's why we wanted to talk to you and not to one of your deputies." Amber had that wheedling tone in her voice. The one that had gotten him in trouble any number of times when they were kids.

Ada smiled brightly. "Would you like some coffee, Sheriff? A friend brought us cinnamon rolls yesterday. Perhaps you would enjoy a bite." She shuffled across the kitchen and began getting out plates.

The baby started to fuss. One tiny fist waved defiantly through the air. Miriam stood and lifted the child out of the basket. She sat down in the rocker beside the table. Holding and patting the baby, she ignored him.

He exhaled the frustration building inside him. The Amish dealt with things in their own fashion and in their own time. He knew that. Miriam might not have been baptized into the faith, but she had been raised in it. Intimidation wasn't going to work on her or her mother.

He crouched in front of Miriam and took hold of the infant's waving fist. The baby grasped his finger and held on tight. It was a cute little thing with round cheeks and pale blond hair. He smiled. "Is it a boy or a girl?"

Miriam wouldn't meet his gaze. "A girl."

He looked at Amber. "Is she healthy? I mean, is she okay?"

"Perfectly okay," Amber assured him.

"How old do you think she is?"

"From the look of her umbilical cord, a day at the most."

He looked around the room. "What aren't you telling me?"

Miriam finally met his gaze. Perhaps it was a trick of the lamplight, but he didn't see anger in their depths. She said, "I saw an Amish buggy driving away."

He wasn't expecting that. To the Amish, faith and family was the core around which everything was based. An abandoned Amish child was almost unheard of. It had never happened in his county.

"She's coming back for her child," Ada stated firmly.

Miriam stayed silent. She didn't take her eyes off the baby's face.

Amber laid a hand on Nick's shoulder. "The baby needs to be here when she does."

He rose to his feet and held up his hands. "Wait a minute. There are protocols in place for things like this. The child goes to the hospital to be checked out."

Miriam quickly said, "She's fine, but we'll take her into the clinic in Hope Springs for a checkup."

"Child Protective Services must place the baby with a licensed foster care provider or approved family member. I can't change that rule."

"I'm a licensed foster care provider," Miriam said and smiled for the first time. The sight did funny things to his insides. She should smile more often.

Surprised by a sudden rush of attraction, he struggled to regain his professionalism. "Good. Then you can offer your services to our child welfare people. If they agree, I don't see why you can't care for the baby. I would have brought a car seat with me if you'd told me I was coming to pick up a child. Now, I'll have to have someone bring one out. Unless you have one I can borrow, Amber?"

"I have one, but hear us out before you make a decision or call anyone else."

"I'm not breaking the law for you, cousin."

"Nor will you bend it, even if the outcome destroys a life." Miriam stood with the baby and moved away from him.

He'd been waiting for that. She knew exactly how to dig at the most painful part of their past. "Miriam, that's not fair. You know I would change things if I could."

"You can't. My brother is still dead."

"It was *Gottes wille,* Miriam. You must accept that. I forgave Nicolas long ago," her mother said quietly.

Miriam didn't reply. Nick knew a moment of pity for her. It couldn't be easy carrying such bitterness. It had taken him a long time to forgive himself for the crash that took her brother's life. With God's help, he had found the strength to accept what could not be changed and to live a better life because of it.

He caught Amber's questioning look. She had no

idea what was going on. He shook his head and mouthed the word *later.* His history with the Kauffman family had no bearing on this case.

"What is it you want me to do?" he asked.

Amber said, "The mother left a note. She's coming back in a week. We feel that technically she hasn't abandoned her child. She simply left her with neighbors."

"Why am I here at all?" he asked.

Ada withdrew the note from her pocket and handed it to him. It was written on plain notebook paper.

Please help us. I know this isn't right, but I have no choice. It isn't safe to keep my baby right now, but I'll be back for her. Meet me here a week from tonight. If I can't make it, I'll come the following week on Friday at midnight. I love my baby with all my heart. I'm begging you to take care of her until I return. I pray God moves you to care for her as you would your own. Her name is Hannah.

Amber said, "We called you because it's clear this young woman is in trouble. We want you to help us find her."

He glanced at Miriam. She was expecting him to deny their request. He could see it in her eyes and in the set of her chin. No matter what Miriam thought of him there was a woman in trouble and he couldn't ignore that. He said, "Ada, do you have a clean plastic bag?"

"Ja." She opened a cabinet door and withdrew a zip-top bag.

Nick said, "Hold it open for me." She did, and he slipped the note inside.

He glanced around at the women in the room. "What

I think should happen is irrelevant. I have to uphold the law. I'm not sure if we have a crime here or not. I need to speak with the county attorney before I can let this child stay here."

Miriam glanced out the window for the umpteenth time. Dawn was spreading a blanket of rose-colored light across the eastern sky. Nick had spent the past twenty minutes sitting in his SUV. Now, he held his phone to his ear as he slowly paced back and forth on the porch. Bella sat watching him, her normal exuberance totally missing. Miriam found it hard to believe that Nick hadn't rejected their request outright and whisked Hannah into protective custody.

He owed no allegiance to the Amish. They didn't vote him into office or elect any officials. While they were a peaceful, quiet people, many *Englisch* saw them as an annoyance. Their buggies slowed traffic to a crawl and even caused accidents. Their iron horseshoes damaged the roadways for which they paid no motor vehicle taxes to maintain. They often owned the best farmland and rarely sold to anyone who wasn't Amish. Many outsiders looked down on them because they received only an eighth-grade education. They were outdated oddities in a rapidly changing, impatient world.

"What's taking him so long?" she muttered.

Amber spread a fluffy white towel on the table and laid the baby on it. From her case, she withdrew a disposable diaper and a container of baby wipes. "Nick understands what is needed. He respects the Amish in this community. He'll help us, you'll see."

Miriam found her eyes drawn to Nick once more. He made a striking figure silhouetted against the morning sky in his dark blue uniform. He'd always been handsome, but age had honed his boyish good looks into a rugged masculinity that was even more attractive. He'd gained a little bulk in the years since she'd seen him, but it looked to be all muscle. He was tall with broad shoulders and slim hips. At his waist he wore a broad belt loaded with the tools of his trade: a long black flashlight, a gun and handcuffs among other things.

As she watched, he raked his fingers through his short blond hair. She knew exactly how silky his hair felt beneath her fingertips. His hat lay on the counter beside her. She picked it up, noticing the masculine scent that clung to the felt. In an instant, she was transported back to the idyllic summer days they had enjoyed before her world crashed around her.

Thinking of all she had lost was too painful. Quickly she put the hat down and clasped her hands behind her back. "What is taking so long? Surely, he could make a decision by now. Either the baby can stay with us or she can't."

The outside door opened and Nick came in. He looked around the room until his gaze locked with Miriam's. She couldn't read the expression on his face. Was it good news or bad?

Chapter Two

"**W**ell? What did you decide?" Amber demanded. "Do we have to involve social services?"

Nick couldn't take his eyes off Miriam. Emotions could cloud a man's judgment, and Miriam raised a whole bushel of emotions in him. She had since the first day they met when he was nineteen and she was an eighteen-year-old, fresh-faced, barefoot Amish beauty. Did she remember those wonderful summer days, or had her brother's death erased all the good memories of their past?

He brought his attention back to the present issue. "I've talked it over with the county attorney. He is willing to agree that the baby has not been abandoned, although the situation is certainly unusual. Hannah can remain in the custody of Ada and Miriam Kauffman for a period of seven days."

Miriam's eyes widened with surprise. "She can?"

"For *two* weeks," Amber said with a stubborn tilt of her chin.

Nodding curtly, Nick said, "However, if the family has not returned for her after two weeks, she becomes an abandoned infant, and I will call Child Protective Services."

"I'm sure someone will come forward before then." Amber's obvious relief eased some of his misgivings. She was more familiar with the Amish in the Hope Springs area than almost anyone. If she thought he was doing the right thing, he was willing to follow her recommendation.

Miriam didn't say another word. It was a struggle to keep from staring at her. He couldn't believe she still had such a profound effect on him. He had stopped seeing her the summer he turned twenty because he knew how strong her faith was and how important it was to her. He hadn't been willing to make her choose between her religion and his love.

The truth was he'd been afraid he would come out the loser. As it turned out, he had, only for a different reason.

He cleared his throat. "I've checked for reports of missing or abducted infants. Just because you saw an Amish buggy driving away doesn't automatically make this an Amish infant. Fortunately, there aren't any babies under one week of age that have gone missing nationwide. We'll go with your theory until there is evidence otherwise. If an infant girl is reported missing, that changes everything."

He paused. They weren't going to like the rest of what he had to say. "Now, I'm not willing to let someone who dropped a baby on your doorstep just waltz in and take her back. If they do show up, this will be immediately reported to Social Services."

Miriam glared at him. "I thought the point of us keeping the baby was to avoid that?"

"By letting you keep the baby, I'm making it easier for the mother to return or for her family to come forward when they might not do so otherwise. I'm sorry. I won't budge on this. Someone who is desperate enough to leave her child with you in the dead of night needs help—she needs counseling. I mean to see that she gets it."

The women exchanged looks. Ada and Miriam nodded. Nick breathed a mental sigh of relief. He said, "The note is too vague to open an official investigation into the mother's whereabouts. I see concern, but there is no evidence of a crime. 'It's not safe' could mean any number of things. However, I agree that we need to make an effort to find this young woman. The sooner, the better."

Amber threw her arms around him. "You're the best cousin I could ever ask for."

"That's not what you said when I wouldn't tear up your speeding ticket."

Amber blushed and cast a quick look at Miriam. "He's joking."

He rolled his eyes. "Right. Ladies, I don't want word of this baby getting out to the general public. Keep it in the Amish community and keep a lid on it."

Miriam frowned. "I would think public exposure is exactly what we want."

"When news of an abandoned baby surfaces, the nut cases come out of the woodwork. Women who desperately want children will claim it's their baby. Some are crazy enough that they will try to take legal action against you. People who want to adopt and simple do-gooders will come forward with offers to take the child. Trust me, it could become a media circus and a nightmare trying to sift fact from fiction."

"All right. Where do we start?" Amber asked.

"We can start by trying to tie the basket or the quilt to a specific family."

Ada spread the blanket open on the table so they could examine it. It was a simple quilt of patchwork blocks with a backing of blue-gray cotton. She said, "I don't see a signature or date, nor do I recognize the stitch work. It's fine work. Perhaps someone in the community will recognize it."

Nick put the basket on the quilt and snapped several pictures with his cell phone. "I'll email these photos to some of the shops that carry Amish goods. Maybe we'll get a hit that way."

Amber's cell phone rang. She opened it and walked away to speak to the caller.

"What else can we do?" Miriam asked.

"Do you recall what kind of buggy it was?"

"It was dark. I saw a shape, not much else."

"Did it have an orange triangle on the back, reflective tape or lights?"

"I couldn't tell."

"So we can't even rule out the Swartzentruber Amish families in this area. They don't use the slow-moving-vehicle signs. What about the horse? Could you recognize it again if you saw it?"

"No, I didn't see the animal, just the back of the buggy."

Amber returned to the room and said, "I'm sorry, but I've got to go. I have a patient in labor. Miriam, I'll leave the car seat with you. Nick, can you help me get it out of my car?"

"Sure." He followed his cousin outside to her station

wagon knowing she was going to grill him about his past relationship with Miriam.

Amber opened the door to the backseat. "It sounds like you have a history with the Kauffman family. Why don't I know about it?"

He leaned in to unbuckle the child safety seat. "It was years ago. You were away at school."

"Care to fill me in now?"

Lifting the seat out of the car, he set it on the roof and stared out across the fertile farmlands waiting for spring planting. He could hear cattle lowing in the distance and birds chirping in the trees. The tranquility of the scene was at odds with his memory of that long-ago night.

He closed his eyes. "The summer I turned nineteen, I started working for Mr. Kauffman as a farmhand. They lived over on the other side of Millersburg back then. It was our grandmother's idea. She thought I should learn how hard it was to work a farm the way the Amish do. She thought it would give me a better appreciation of the land."

"Grandmother is usually right," Amber said with a twinkle in her eye.

"She is. Anyway, I worked there for two summers. Miriam, her brother Mark and I became good friends."

"Why do I sense you and Miriam were more than friends?"

"We were kids. We fell in love with the idea of being in love, but she was strict, Old Order Amish. We both knew it wouldn't work. We chose to remain friends. It wasn't until a few years later that things changed."

"What happened?"

Nick took a stick of gum from his pocket using the

added time to keep his emotions in check. Even now, it was hard to talk about that night. He popped the gum in his mouth, deftly folded the foil into a small star and dropped it back in his shirt pocket.

"Ten years ago I was a brand-new deputy and a bit of a hotshot back then. I didn't go looking for trouble, but I didn't mind if I found it. One night, we got a report of a stolen car. On the way to investigate, I caught sight of the vehicle and put on my lights. The driver didn't stop. Long story short, a high-speed chase ensued. A very dangerous chase."

"What else were you supposed to do?"

"Protocol leaves it up to the responding officer's discretion. What I should have done was drop back and stop pressing him when I saw the risks he was willing to take. I should have called for a roadblock to be set up ahead of us. I didn't do any of those things. I kept after the car. It was a challenge to outdrive him, and I wasn't about to back down."

"It sounds like you were doing the job you'd trained to do. I know your father was killed during a traffic stop. I'm sure that made you doubly suspicious of anyone who tried to get away."

She was right. "That did factor into my decision, but it shouldn't have. I tried to get around the car, but we slammed into each other. The other driver lost control and veered into a tree. I'll never forget the sight of that wreckage. The driver was killed instantly. It was Mark, Miriam's twin brother."

Amber laid a comforting hand on his shoulder. "I'm sorry. I didn't mean to make you relive the whole thing."

"You want to know the really ironic thing? I'm the one who taught Mark how to drive. I never understood why he didn't just stop. He'd never been in trouble. I doubt he would have spent more than one night in jail. To have his life ended by a *rumspringa* stunt, a joy ride, it wasn't right."

"The Amish believe everything that happens is God's will, Nick. They don't blame you. That would be against all that they hold sacred."

"Miriam blames me. I tried to talk to her after Mark's funeral. Even months later she wouldn't see me. As you can tell, her feelings haven't changed."

"Then she needs our prayers. Finding forgiveness is the only way to truly heal from such a tragedy."

He lifted the car seat from the roof of Amber's car. "You should get going. You don't want the stork to get there ahead of you."

Amber grinned. "You're still planning on coming to my wedding, right?"

"Rats, when was that again? I might be fishing."

She punched his arm. "A week from this coming Saturday and you'd better not stand me up for a trout."

"Ouch, that's assaulting an officer. I could arrest you for that."

"Whatever. Phillip would just break me out of jail."

"Are you sure of that?"

"Absolutely—almost sure. Tell Miriam she can bring the baby into our office anytime tomorrow morning. I happen to know Dr. White has a light schedule. If the baby begins to act sick before then, she should take her to the hospital right away. She's a nurse. She'll know what to do."

"I'll tell her."

Her expression became serious once more. "Nick, Miriam had to know when she called me that I would involve the law. She might not admit it, but I think she reached out to you."

Nick considered Amber's assertion as she drove away. What if she was right about Miriam's actions? What if she was reaching out to him? Could he risk the heartbreak all over again if she wasn't? He glanced toward the house. She had left her Amish faith. That barrier no longer stood between them, but the issue of Mark's death did.

Nick was about to start a week's vacation. If he left town now, he might never have another chance to heal the breach with Miriam. He wanted that, for both their sakes. In his heart, he knew there was a reason God had brought them together again.

He shook his head at his own foolishness. He was forgetting the most important part of this entire scenario. Somewhere there was a desperate woman who needed his help. She and her baby had to be his first priority.

Miriam decided to ignore Nick when he came into the kitchen again. He held a car seat in his hands. The kind that could easily be detached from the base and used as an infant carrier. He said, "Would you like me to put it in your car?"

"I'll get it later."

"Is there anything else you ladies need?"

"We're fine," Miriam said quickly, wanting him out of her house. She'd forgotten how he dominated a room.

Ada spoke up. "Would you mind bringing the baby bed down from the attic for us?"

His eyes softened as he smiled at Ada. "Of course not."

"I'll get it later, *Mamm,* I'm sure the sheriff has other things to do."

"I've certainly got time to fetch the crib for your mother."

His cheerful reply grated on Miriam's nerves. She felt jumpy when he was near, as if her skin were too tight.

Her mother said, "*Goot*. Miriam, I'll take Hannah."

Miriam handed over the baby. Her mother smiled happily, then looked to the sheriff. "Nicolas, if you would give me the bottle warming on the stove, I'll feed her."

He lifted the bottle from the pan at the back of the stove. To Miriam's surprise, he tested it by shaking a few drops of formula on his wrist, and then handed it over.

Did he have children? Was that how he knew to make sure a baby's formula wasn't too hot? Had he been able to find happiness with someone else, the kind of happiness that eluded her?

He caught her staring when he turned and asked, "Which way to the attic?"

She all but bolted ahead of him up the stairs to the second floor. The attic was accessed by a pull-down panel in the ceiling of her bedroom. She rushed into the room, swept up her nightgown and the lingerie hanging from the open drawer of her bureau, stuffed everything inside and slammed it shut. She whirled around to see him standing in the doorway.

Her bed wasn't made. Papers and books were scattered across her desk. A romance novel lay open on her bedside table. The heat of a blush rushed to her face. For a second, she thought she saw a grin twitch at the corner of his lips. Her chin came up. "I wasn't expecting company in my bedroom today."

The heat of a blush flooded her face. She stuttered, "You know what I mean."

Stop talking. I sound like an idiot.

Nick pointed to the ceiling. "Is that the access?"

"Yes." She worked to appear calm and composed, cool even. It was hard when his nearness sent her pulse skyrocketing and made every nerve stand on end.

He crossed the room and reached the cord that hung down without any trouble. The long panel swung open and a set of steps came partway down. He unfolded them and tested their sturdiness, then started upward. When he vanished into the darkness above her, Miriam called up, "Shall I get a flashlight?"

A bright beam of light illuminated the rafters. "I've got one."

Of course he did. She'd noticed it earlier on his tool belt. Sheriff Nick Bradley seemed to be prepared for every contingency from checking baby formula to searching cobweb-filled corners. *Strong, levelheaded, dependable,* they were some of the words she had used to describe him to her Amish girlfriends so long ago. It seemed that he hadn't changed.

Miriam jerked her mind out of the past. This had to stop. She couldn't start mooning over Nick the way she had when she was a love-struck teenager. Too much stood between them.

He leaned over the opening to look down at her. "Any idea where the baby bed is? There's a lot of stuff up here."

"No idea. If you can't find a crib in an attic, you're not much of a detective." Her words came out sounding sharper than she intended. She was angry with herself for letting him get under her skin.

The sound of a heavy object hitting the floor overhead made her jump. It was quickly followed by his voice. "Sorry. I don't think it broke."

She scowled upward. "What was that?"

"Just an old headboard."

"Great-grandmother's cherrywood headboard, hand carved by my great-grandfather?"

"Could be." His voice was a shade weaker.

Miriam started up the steps. "Let me help before you bring the house down on our heads."

"It's tight up here."

"It might be for a six-foot moose," she muttered. She reached the top of the steps to find him holding out his hand to help her. Reluctantly, she accepted it and stepped up into the narrow open space beside him. They were inches apart. She wanted to jump backward but knew there was nothing but air behind her. It was hard to draw a breath. Her pulse skipped and skittered like a wild thing. She pulled her hand from his.

He said, "It's tight even for a five-foot-three fox."

She could hear the laughter under his words. Annoyed at his familiarity, she snapped, "It's not politically correct to call a woman a fox."

He cleared his throat. "I was referring to your red hair, Miriam. It's also not politically correct to call an officer of the law a moose."

Turning away, he banged his head on a kerosene lamp hanging from one of the rafters.

She slipped past him on the narrow aisle. "If the shoe fits… I think the baby stuff is down here."

Beneath the dim light coming through a dormer window, she spied a cradle piled high with old clothes and blankets. A wide-rimmed black hat and a straw hat sat atop the pile. She knew before she touched them that they had belonged to Mark.

Tenderly Miriam lifted the felt hat and covered her face with it. She breathed deeply, but no trace of her brother's scent remained. A band tightened around her heart until she thought it might break in two.

"Are they Mark's things?" Nick asked behind her.

She could only nod. Even after all these years, it was hard to accept that she would never see him again. He'd been her other half. She was incomplete without him. She could hear his laughter and see his face as clearly as if he were standing in front of her.

Nick lifted a stack of boxes and papers from the seat of a bentwood rocker and set them on the floor. He took the clothing and blankets from the cradle and laid them aside, leaving the flashlight on top of the pile. Picking up the cradle, he said, "I'll take this down. You can bring the baby clothes when you find them."

He didn't wait for her reply. When he was gone, she sat in the rocker and crushed her brother's hat against her chest as hot tears streamed down her face.

Nick descended the attic steps with the sound of Miriam's weeping ringing in his ears. He wanted to help, but he knew anything he offered in the way of comfort would be rejected. It hurt to know she still grieved so deeply.

After making his way down to the kitchen, he found Ada and the baby both asleep in the rocker. The bottle in Ada's slack hand dripped formula onto the floor. When he took it from her, she jerked awake, startling the baby who whimpered.

"Habe ich schlafe?" Ada peered at Nick with confusion in her eyes.

"Ja, Frau Kauffman. You fell asleep," he answered softly.

Childhood summers spent with his Amish grandmother and cousins had given him a decent understanding of the Amish language. While it was referred to as Pennsylvania Dutch, it was really Pennsylvania *Deitsh,* an old German dialect blended with English words into a language that was unique.

Ada sat up straighter and adjusted the baby in her arms. "Don't tell Miriam. She already worries about me too much."

"It will be our secret. Where shall I put the cradle?"

"Here beside me. I sleep downstairs now. Miriam insists on it. She doesn't want me climbing the stairs."

Taking a dishcloth from the sink, Nick mopped up the spilled milk. "I imagine Miriam gets her way."

Ada looked toward the stairs, then leaned closer to Nick. "Not so much. If I get well, she will leave again. I may be sickly all year."

He grinned. "That will be our secret, too."

"Goot. Where is she?"

Nick's grin faded. "She's still in the attic. She found some of Mark's things. I don't think she was ready for that."

"My poor daughter. She cannot see the blessings God has given her. She only sees what she has lost."

"She needs more time, that's all."

"No, it is more than that. I miss my son every day. I miss my husband, God rest his soul. I mourn them, but in God's own time I will join them in heaven. Until then, He has much for me to do here on earth. It will soon be time to plant my garden. With the weather getting nicer, I must visit the sick and the elderly. I have baking to do for the socials and weddings and I must pray for my child."

"I'll pray for her, too."

"Bless you, Nicolas. I accept that Miriam will never return to our Amish ways, but my child carries a heavy burden in her heart. One she refuses to share. I pray every day that she finds peace."

Ada struggled to her feet. Nick gave her a hand. *"Danki.* Take the baby, Nicolas."

"Sure." He accepted the tiny bundle from her amazed at how light the child was and how nice it felt to hold her.

"Sit. This cradle needs a good cleaning after more than twenty years in the attic. I'm so happy it is being put to use. It has been empty much too long."

Nick sat in the rocker and gave himself over to enjoying the moment. He hoped one day to have children of his own. Finding a woman to be their mother was proving to be his stumbling block.

He remembered how badly his mother had handled being a cop's wife. Even though he'd chosen small-town law enforcement over the big-city life his father craved, Nick wasn't eager to put a family into the kind of pressure cooker he knew his job could create. It would take a very special woman to share his life. Once, he'd hoped it would be Miriam, but that dream had died even before the wreck took her brother's life.

Chapter Three

Miriam had recovered her composure by the time she came downstairs. She saw Nick rocking Hannah while her mother was busy wiping down the dusty cradle. Miriam's eyes were drawn to the note still sitting in the plastic bag on the table. Somewhere, a young woman needed her help. She would concentrate on that and not on her tumultuous emotion.

She said, "It sounds like Hannah's mother is in an abusive relationship."

Nick said, "We're only guessing."

Miriam bit the corner of her lip. A young mother was having the worst day of her life. She'd done the unthinkable. She'd left her newborn baby on a doorstep. In her young eyes, the situation must have seemed desperate and hopeless. Miriam's heart went out to her. At least, she had chosen to give her child a chance. It was more than others had done.

Nick said, "The note raises questions in my mind about the mother's emotional state and about her situation but doesn't spell out a crime. I'll have it checked for fingerprints, but that's a long shot. If the person who wrote the note is Amish, I doubt we'll have his or her prints on file."

Miriam held up the bag to study the handwriting. "You think the father may have written this?"

"I think our mother had help. Do you believe a new mother could harness up the horse and buggy drive out here after she'd just given birth? That's one hardy woman if she did it alone."

Nodding, Miriam said, "You have a point."

Ada finished cleaning the cradle and covered the mattress with a clean quilt. "Amish women are tough. I know several who have had their child alone, and then driven to the home of a relative."

Nick handed the baby to Ada. "That may be, but I have to consider the possibility that she had help. Miriam, did you see which way the buggy turned after it reached the highway?"

"I'm sorry. I didn't." Miriam racked her memory of those few moments when the buggy had been in sight for something—anything that would help, but came up empty.

Somewhere a young woman needed help or she wouldn't have taken the drastic measure of leaving her baby on a doorstep. Miriam had spent too many hours with confused, frightened Amish teenagers not to know the signs. This was a deep cry for help. She had turned her back on one desperate mother years ago. Nothing but bitter ashes had flowed from that decision. She would not do it again. This time, she had to help.

Turning around, she grabbed her denim jacket from the peg by the door. "The lane is still muddy from the rain yesterday. We might be able to tell which way they turned."

"Good thinking." Nick pulled the door open and

held it for her. Bella was waiting for them outside. She jumped up to greet Nick with muddy paws. He pushed her aside with a stern, "No." Bella complied.

Miriam glanced over her shoulder. "*Mamm,* it's time to check your blood sugar. This added stress and lack of sleep could easily throw it out of whack."

"All right, dear. I'll get the baby settled and I'll check it." She rocked the baby gently in her arms and cooed to her in Pennsylvania Dutch.

"You know what to do if it's low?"

"*Ja.* I'll have a glass of milk and recheck it in thirty minutes. The honey is in the cabinet if it is too low, but I feel fine. Stop worrying."

"I'll be back in a few minutes." Worrying was what Miriam did best these days. Her mother didn't seem to realize how precarious her health was.

Outside, Miriam walked beside Nick down the lane. He asked, "How long has your mother been ill?"

"She had her first heart attack seven months ago. That's when they discovered she was a diabetic. She had a second heart attack three weeks ago. Thankfully, it wasn't as bad as the first one. She's been doing okay, but I think she should be recovering more quickly than she has. Her energy level is so low. Everything makes her tired, and that frustrates her."

"You've been here in Hope Springs for seven months?" He seemed amazed.

"Yes." She'd taken pains to remain under his radar. Coming face-to-face with Nick was the last thing she wanted. His presence brought back all the pain and guilt she'd worked so hard to overcome. Now, he was in her home and in her business with no signs of leaving. Why hadn't she followed her mother's advice and left the midwife out of this?

"I imagine you had to quit your job in order to stay this long." His sympathetic tone showed real compassion. It was hard to stay angry with him when he was being nice.

"I took a leave of absence from my job. My leave will be up in another month. I don't know what I'll do if I can't go back by then."

"That's got to be hard on both of you."

"She doesn't have anyone else." As soon as Miriam said it, she regretted pointing out the obvious.

A muscle in his jaw twitched, but his voice was neutral when he spoke. "We both know the Amish community will take care of Ada. She isn't alone."

"I know they will keep her fed and clothed, but she needs more than that. She needs someone to monitor her blood pressure and glucose levels and to make sure she takes her meds. She needs someone to make sure she eats the right things. If one more person drops by with a pan of cinnamon rolls or shoofly pie for her, I'm going to bar the door."

"Want to borrow my gun?" There was a hint of laughter in his tone.

"Don't tempt me," she replied, amazed that he could so easily coax a smile from her. Her anger slipped further away. They had both suffered a loss when Mark died, but their lives hadn't stopped. Nick had managed to move on. Perhaps she could, too.

He stopped and squatted on his heels to examine the ground. "My tires have erased any tracks the buggy might have left. I don't see anything distinctive about the horseshoe marks."

"Do you think the mother was coerced into leaving the baby?"

He rose and hooked his thumbs in his wide belt as he scanned the countryside. "Frankly, I don't know what to think. The whole thing doesn't fit. The Amish don't operate this way. It's so out of character."

"The Amish have flaws and secrets like everyone else." She would know. Flaws and secrets haunted her, every day and every night.

He must've heard something odd in her voice for he fixed her with an intense stare. She gazed at her feet.

He asked, "Who knows you are a nurse? Is it common knowledge?"

"I'm sure my mother has mentioned it to some of her friends."

"Did you notice the note said 'Meet me here a week from tonight.' Did that strike you as odd?"

"A little. Why?"

"I don't know. It just didn't seem to fit. What about someone from your past? An Amish friend who might know you're here with your mother."

"No, there's no one like that."

"How can you be so sure?"

"We were Swartzentruber Amish, remember? They are the strictest of the Old Order Amish. When I refused to join the faith, my parents had to shun me. My friends did the same. It wasn't until after my father died that my mother chose to become a member of a less rigid order."

"Didn't that mean she would be excommunicated by her old bishop?"

"Yes. She gave up her friends and the people she'd known all her life. It was very hard, but she did it so that she could see me again. She was accepted into Bishop

Zook's congregation about a year ago. They are more progressive here. Unlike my old congregation, Bishop Zook's church believes a person has the right to choose the Amish faith. Those who don't are not punished."

He said, "Bishop Zook is not the only bishop who believes that. Amber's mother and my mother are sisters who both chose not to join the faith. They have siblings who remained Amish. My grandmother embraces all her family, Amish and English alike."

"Some districts are that way, some are more strict, some are rigid in their beliefs and don't tolerate any exceptions. People hear the word *Amish* and they think the Plain People are all the same. There are enormous differences."

Miriam cocked her head to the side. "Wait a minute. If your mothers are sisters, why do you share the same last name with Amber?"

He grinned and started walking again, scanning the ground as he went. "Our mothers are sisters who married two brothers. Got to love small-town romances. Where did you live before you moved in with your mom?"

"Medina, Ohio."

Bella left Miriam's side and went hunting through the old corn stubble of the field beside them. It would soon be time for the farmer who rented her mother's land to begin planting new crops.

"What kind of nursing do you do?" Nick asked, slanting a curious glance her way.

Was he really interested? "I work in adult critical care."

"That's a tough job."

"Overdoses, strokes, trauma, heart attacks, we see it all."

"And car accidents." He looked away, but she saw the tension that came over him.

"Yes, car accidents," she replied softly.

She expected him to drop the subject, but to her surprise, he didn't. "Do you like it? I mean, not all the outcomes can be good."

"Every patient deserves the chance to reach their full potential. I'm part of a team that works to make that happen. Sometimes, what they regain isn't as much as they had before their event, but it's not for lack of trying on our part. For every loss of life, we see a dozen recoveries." It struck her as odd to be talking about her work with Nick, but she wanted him to know she was about making a difference in people's lives and she loved her work.

"When do you find the time to foster little kids?"

"I don't. I foster teens."

"Really?"

She met his gaze. There was a new respect in his eyes that she hadn't seen before. Lifting her chin, she said, "They are mostly Amish runaways."

He stopped in his tracks. "Today has been chock full of surprises."

"You don't approve? They are kids with nothing but an eighth-grade education. They don't have driver's licenses or social security cards. They are completely ill prepared for life in the outside world."

"I know that."

"If by some stroke of luck they can find work, they have to take low-paying jobs. Most get paid under the table from employers happy to take advantage of them.

Without outside help, leaving the Amish is almost impossible for some of them."

"You left."

She started walking again. "Don't think it was easy."

"When did you start hating the Amish way of life?"

Stunned, she spun to face him. "I don't hate it. It's a beautiful way to live. The Amish believe in simplicity. Their lives are focused on faith in God and in keeping close family and community ties."

Quietly, he said, "They believe in forgiveness, too, Miriam."

"It sounds easy to say you forgive someone. Actually doing it is much harder. Did they ever catch the man who shot your father?"

He looked away. "No."

"It's tough when there's no justice in life, isn't it?"

Meeting her gaze, he nodded. "Yes. That's why I trust that God will be the ultimate judge of men."

She waited for the boiling anger to engulf her, but it didn't materialize. Maybe she was just too tired. She wanted to stay angry at him, but it was easier when she couldn't see the pain in his eyes. He knew what it was to lose someone he loved.

Nick started walking again. "If you admire the Amish, why help kids leave?"

"Because there are other ways to live that are just as important and as meaningful. You can't be a doctor or a nurse if you are Amish. You can't create new medicines or go to college, build dams or explore the oceans. You can't question the teachings of your church leaders. That said, two-thirds of the teenagers who come to me wanting a taste of *Englisch* life go back to their Amish families. Why? Because it's what they desire in their hearts. My job is to help them sort out what they truly want."

"Okay, I get it. That's cool." He walked to the edge of the highway and sank to his heels again as he examined the ground.

Did he get what she did and why? Or was he simply trying to placate her? She stopped a few feet away from him. Her shifting emotions made it difficult to stay focused on the task at hand.

He looked at her. "Could your efforts to help Amish youth be the reason someone brought this baby to you?"

"I don't think so. No one here knows what I do in Medina. My mother doesn't approve. While I'm living under her roof, I have to respect her feelings. Most people know me only as a driver for hire. I needed some kind of income while I'm here, and I can't spend the long hours away from Mom that a nursing job would require."

He gestured toward the road. "Our buggy went toward Hope Springs. See the way the impression of the wheels turn here and carried the mud out onto the highway."

"I do." She gazed at the thin tire track disappearing down the winding roadway. She could see half a dozen white Amish farmhouses along either side of the road before the road vanished over the hill. How many Amish families lived in that direction or on one of the many roads that branched off the highway? Fifty? A hundred? Where would they start looking for one scared, desperate young woman?

"Ah, now this is useful." Nick took a step closer to the roadway. A small puddle had formed after the rain. The imprint of the buggy wheel was deep where it rolled through the mud.

"What is it?" she asked.

He pointed to the print. "The buggy we are looking for has a jagged crack in the steel rim of the left rear wheel. If it breaks all the way through, someone is going to need a new rim put on."

"It looks like a crooked *Z*. It should be easy enough to spot."

He stood and rubbed a hand over his jaw. He took another stick of gum from his pocket, unwrapped it and popped it into his mouth. Carefully he folded the silver foil into a star. He noticed her stare and said, "I quit smoking a few years ago, but I can't kick the gum habit."

He had his share of struggles like everyone else. It made him more human. Something she wasn't prepared to see.

She looked away and asked, "How do we begin searching for Hannah's mother?"

"Even if I had the manpower to launch a full-scale investigation, I couldn't check every buggy wheel in the district. Most Amish families have three or four buggies, depending on how many of their kids are old enough to drive. It could take months."

"And Hannah has only two weeks before her mother's rights are severed if she doesn't return."

"Time may not be on her side."

"That's it? You're going to give up before we've started? I'm sorry I let Amber call you. I can tell you aren't going to go out of your way to save this family. I don't know why I thought you would."

Nick studied the myriad expressions that crossed Miriam's face and wondered where such passion came from.

He said, "I'm not sure I know what you want me to do?"

"We have a letter asking for help. We can't ignore it. This young girl's life may be ruined by a rash decision. I don't think we should wait for her to come back. I think we should go find her."

"Is there something you aren't telling me?"

It was as if his question had caused a mask to fall over her face. Her expression went completely neutral. Instead of answering his question, she said meekly, "I want to help, that's all."

Miriam's abrupt switch triggered his cop radar. She was hiding something. By her own admission few people knew she was a nurse. Fewer still would know that she aided Amish youth looking to leave their faith and go out into the world. Was accepting an unwanted baby part of her plan to help an unwed Amish girl escape into the *Englisch* life?

He didn't want to believe she would lie to him, but did he really know her? They hadn't spoken in years. People changed.

Maybe it wasn't a coincidence that Hannah had been left on Miriam's doorstep. If the mother knew Miriam, would she be able to stay away? He figured she would need to know how her little girl was doing. The sight of Miriam with the child just might draw that woman out if she were still in the Hope Springs area. He wanted to be around when that happened. It would mean spending time, lots of time, in Miriam's company.

Could he keep his mind on his job when she was near? At the moment, all he wanted to do was run his fingers through her gorgeous hair. The early morning sun brought fiery highlights to life in her red-gold, shoulder-length mane as it moved like a dense curtain around her face and neck. It was the first time he'd seen her without the white bonnet the Amish called a prayer *kapp*. In his youth, he'd fantasized about what her hair would look like down. His imaginings paled in comparison to the beauty he beheld at the moment.

He realized he was staring when she scowled at him. Forcing his mind back to the task at hand, he asked, "Are you sure you can't think of anyone who might be Hannah's mother? Maybe you gave a ride to her or to her family recently and mentioned you were a nurse."

"No one stands out. Believe me, I've been racking my brain trying to think who she might be."

"I need to get back to the office and have our note and the hamper run for prints. Why don't you make up a list of the families who might know you're a nurse? We can go over them later. Something may click in the meantime. If it does, give me a call."

They returned to the house, covering the quarter mile in silence. When they reached his SUV, Miriam whistled for the dog. As Bella ambled up, she stopped to give Nick a parting lick on the hand. He patted her side. "She's a nice dog."

"Thank you."

"When did you rescue her from the pound?"

Miriam paused. "How did you know that?"

"It seems to be your MO."

"My what?"

"Your modus operandi, your mode of operation. Runaway teens, sick people, foundling babies—it just makes sense that your dog would be a rescue, too."

Her frown turned to a fierce scowl. "Don't think you

know me, Nick Bradley, because you don't. You don't know me at all."

She turned on her heels and marched toward the house.

At the porch, she stopped and looked back. "My mother was right. This is Amish business. We will handle it ourselves. Have a great vacation."

Chapter Four

Miriam stopped short of slamming the door when she entered the house. Nick infuriated her. How dare that man presume to know anything about her? She didn't want him to know anything about her. She didn't want him to read her so easily.

She was scared of the way it made her feel. Like she could depend on him.

She balled her fingers into fists. She couldn't decide if she was angrier with him, or with herself. For a few minutes, she had forgotten what lay between. Somehow, after everything that happened, Nick still had the power to turn her inside out, as he'd done when she was eighteen and a naive country girl.

Well, she wasn't a teenager anymore. She wouldn't fall under his spell again. She had too much sense for that. There was too much that stood between them.

How could she have forgotten that even for a second? She had gone months without running into him. Why now? How much more complicated could her life get? Perhaps in the back of her mind she knew this would happen. That Nick would use his charm to make her forget her anger and forgive him.

If she forgave Nick, she would have only herself left to blame for Mark's death. She was the one who had sent her brother on his panicked flight that night. The guilt still ate at her soul. If only she'd had the chance to beg Mark's forgiveness, perhaps she could learn to live with what she'd done.

When Mark's *Englisch* girlfriend, Natalie Perry, had come begging for a word with him, Miriam had been only too happy to inform her Mark wasn't home. When the tearful girl explained that her parents were making her leave town the following evening, Miriam had been relieved. It was God's will. Without this woman's influence, her brother would give up worldly things and be baptized into the faith. Miriam had given up Nick's love for her faith. She had passed that test. Mark would, too.

Natalie had scrawled a note and pressed it into Miriam's hand, pleading with her to give it to Mark as soon as possible. At the time, Miriam had no idea what the note contained, but she didn't give it to Mark until late the next day. Only afterward did she understand what harm she had caused.

Mark had flown out of the house, stolen a car and tried to reach his love before it was too late. Nick had stopped him, and Miriam never had the chance to beg her brother's forgiveness.

The front door opened, and Nick came in looking as if he expected a frying pan to come sailing at his head. The idea of doing something so outrageous made her feel better. Slightly.

When he saw that he didn't need to defend himself,

he said, "Ada, is there anything you need me to do before I leave? I can chop some kindling if you need it."

"*Nee,* I reckon we'll be fine."

He nodded. "You let me know if you hear anything from the baby's family."

Ada nodded toward the baby sleeping in the newly washed bassinet. "Do not worry, Nicolas. The mother, she will come for her babe."

"I pray you are right. Miriam, I'd appreciate knowing what the doctor has to say about Hannah."

He waited, as if he expected Miriam to say something. When she didn't, he nodded in her direction. "Okay, I've got to get back to town."

When the door closed behind him, Miriam took the first deep breath she managed to draw all morning. "I thought he would never leave."

"It was *goot* to see him again. I remember him as such a nice boy."

"It's too bad he turned out to be a murderer."

"Do not say such a thing, Miriam!" Her mother rounded on her with such intensity that Miriam was left speechless.

Ada shook her finger at her daughter. "You are not the only one who has suffered, but you are the only one who has not forgiven. The more you pick at a wound, the longer it takes to heal. I don't know why you refuse to see that. I'm tired of your selfish attitude. Maybe it is best that you go back to your *Englisch* home."

Dumbfounded, Miriam stared at her mother in shock. Not once in her life had her mother raised her voice in such a manner.

Miriam struggled to muster her indignation. "That

man caused the death of your only son. Have you really forgiven him for that?"

"It was *Gottes wille* that Mark died. I can't pretend to understand why such a thing had to happen, or why your father was taken before me, too. I can only try to live a good life and know that I will be with them when it is my time." Ada turned her back on her daughter and began to wash the coffee cups in the sink.

Miriam's anger slipped away. She wanted to punish Nick, but she'd wound up hurting her mother instead. "Do you really want me to leave?"

Her mother seemed to shrink before her eyes. Ada heaved a deep sigh. "I want what I cannot have. I'm tired. I'm going to lie down for a while. Can you watch the baby?"

"Of course." Miriam fetched her mother's cane from beside the table and watched her head toward the hallway. Ada moved slowly, leaning heavily on her cane for support.

Overcome with guilt, Miriam said, "I'm sorry if I upset you."

Her mother paused at the doorway and looked over her shoulder. "I forgave you the moment you spoke. We will talk no more about your stubborn, willful ways and the bitterness you carry. I leave it up to *Gott* to change your heart."

After her mother disappeared into her room Miriam sat down beside Hannah. Bella had staked out her new territory beneath the crib. She looked up at Miriam with soulful eyes and gave a halfhearted wag of her tail.

Miriam leaned down to pet her. "You love me no matter what I do or say. Thank you. That's why I have a dog."

* * *

The following morning, Miriam sat in the waiting room of the Hope Springs Medical clinic with Hannah in her borrowed car seat on the floor beside her. They were waiting to be seen for Hannah's first well-baby appointment.

Miriam was starting to wonder if she *was* a well baby. How soon did colic set in? If Hannah wasn't sick, she was certainly a fussy baby. It had been a long night for both of them. Miriam's eyes burned with lack of sleep. A headache nagged at the base of her neck. The baby had fallen asleep in the car on the way to the clinic, but she was starting to fidget now that the car ride was over.

"The doctor will be with you shortly. Would you like some tea or coffee while you wait?" Wilma Nolan, the elderly receptionist, asked with an encouraging smile.

Miriam shook her head. What she wanted was a few hours of uninterrupted sleep. The outside door opened. She looked over and saw Nick walk in.

He was out of uniform this morning. He'd traded his dark blues for worn, faded jeans, Western boots and a wool sweater in a soft taupe color that made his tan look even deeper. No one could deny he was a good-looking man. She struggled to ignore the sudden jump in her pulse.

The elderly receptionist behind the counter sat up straight and smiled. "Sheriff, how nice to see you. I'm afraid you will have quite a wait if you need to see the doctor this morning. Dr. White isn't feeling well, and Dr. Zook is the only one seeing patients."

"Not to worry, Wilma, I'm not sick. I just came to check on Ms. Kauffman and…the baby."

Wilma's eyebrows shot up a good two inches as she glanced between Miriam and Nick. "I see. Is this official business?"

Mortified by what she knew the receptionist was thinking, Miriam wanted to sink through the floor. Nick obviously came to the same conclusion because he quickly stuttered, "It's…it's personal business, Wilma."

"Oh, of course." A smug, knowing smile twitched on her thin lips as she blushed a bright shade of pink.

Nick took a seat beside Miriam. "Hi."

"What are you doing here?" she snapped under her breath, keeping a bland smile on her face for Wilma's benefit.

He leaned down to gaze at Hannah in her carrier. "I wanted to make sure she is okay. Amish babies have a higher incidence of birth defects, you know."

"Of course I know that. I thought you were going to wait for me to call you with an update."

"I wasn't sure you would call me."

He was right. She had no intention of involving him any more than she absolutely had to. "You didn't have to come in person. You know what Mrs. Nolan is thinking, don't you?"

"I'm not responsible for what people think."

"'It's personal business, Wilma.' Oh, you're *so* going to be responsible if word gets out that *we* are a couple with a new baby."

Nick shifted uncomfortably in his chair. "She's known me for years. We go to the same church. Even if she thought it, she would never repeat it to anyone."

"Hannah Kauffman?" A young man with thick-rimmed black glasses stood at the entrance to the hallway. He had two pens in the top pocket of his lab coat and a manila folder in his hands.

"It's not Kauffman, Dr. Zook," Nick stated as he picked up Hannah's carrier and walked toward the young doctor.

Miriam took the carrier away from Nick. "It is for now."

The doctor turned and walked down the hall ahead of them. "Let us know what you put on the birth certificate and that will be her legal name."

"Legally, she's a Jane Doe." Nick stood close behind Miriam. The warmth of his breath on the back of her neck sent shivers rippling across her skin.

Dr. Zook stopped and looked at him in surprise. "She's a foundling?"

Miriam nodded. "Someone left her on my mother's doorstep two nights ago. I caught a glimpse of a buggy going down the lane. A note said her name was Hannah, but that's about all."

"I see now why you are involved, Sheriff. This is very odd."

Nick said, "I'm hoping you can help us."

Dr. Zook's eyes narrowed behind his glasses. "You do understand that I can't reveal any information about my patients."

"Even if you think you know who the mother might be?" Nick asked in a tone of voice that made Miriam glad she wasn't the one he was questioning.

Dr. Zook drew himself up to his full height, which was a good four inches shorter than Nick's six feet. "Not even then."

Miriam expected this roadblock. "I'm a nurse, so I

understand how it works. We won't ask for confidential information."

The young doctor relaxed. "Good. Let's take a look at this little girl and make sure she is healthy."

He held open the door to an exam room. Miriam walked in and set the carrier on the exam table. Carefully, she unlatched the harness and lifted the baby out. Hannah began fussing but soon settled back to sleep as Miriam soothed her with rocking and quiet words.

Nick took the carrier and put in on the floor, making room for Miriam to lay the baby on the exam table. She took a step to the side, but kept one hand on Hannah. Dr. Zook quietly and thoroughly went about his examination.

Miriam had met him a few times before. She preferred Dr. Harold White, but the older physician was well into his eighties. Dr. Zook had taken over a small part of Dr. White's practice, and his involvement had grown in the past year until he oversaw almost half of the patients.

Miriam had been impressed with his handling of her mother's health issues and had no qualms about letting him see Hannah. She said, "I've always meant to ask, are you related to our Bishop Zook?"

The young doctor smiled. "All Zooks are related in one way or another, but in the case of Bishop Zook and myself, it's not a close connection. My family comes from near Reading, Pennsylvania."

Nick spoke up. "Can you tell if Hannah has any birth defects associated with being Amish?"

"I can rule out dwarfism and Troyer Syndrome, which is a lethal microcephaly or small head, and several others diseases just by looking at her. Only blood tests or time will tell us if she suffers from any inherited metabolic defects such as glutaric aciduria, PKU, maple syrup urine disease or cystic fibrosis. I'll draw her newborn screening blood tests today. That will check for many of the things I've mentioned and more. Do you want me to draw blood for DNA matching, as well?"

Nodding, Nick said, "You read my mind. If someone shows up claiming to be her parent or grandparent, I want to make sure they are related before I release her."

Miriam said, "The mother's note did say she would be back for Hannah, but she also said it wasn't safe to have the baby with her. Can you think of anyone in a situation like that?"

The doctor rubbed the back of his neck. "I honestly can't."

Miriam laid a hand on his arm. "I know the Amish are reluctant to go to outsiders with their problems, Doctor. If you hear of anyone in a difficult situation, please let us know."

Dr. Zook stared at her hand. She withdrew it hoping she hadn't made a mistake.

He looked into her eyes and said, "I do understand the reluctance of the Amish to become involved with Social Services and the legal system in general. They have not always been treated fairly. I respect the way they take care of each other. I deeply admire their faith in God. I will let you know if I hear of anything like this."

Miriam blew out a sigh of relief. "Thank you, Doctor."

"Not at all." He was actually blushing.

Nick gave Miriam a funny look, then said, "Thanks, Doc."

"I'll draw some blood for those tests and I'll have Amber follow up with this little girl just as she would one of her home deliveries. If you have any questions, feel free to call me. Day or night."

He took a card from his pocket and scrawled a number on it. He handed it to Miriam. "This is my personal cell phone. Don't hesitate to use it."

She smiled at him. "I won't hesitate for a minute."

"Is there anything else?"

Miriam said, "She's very fussy, Doctor, especially after she eats. I'm wondering if I should switch her to a soy-based formula."

"You can certainly try that, but don't make an abrupt switch. Mix the two together a few times until you gradually have all soy in her bottles."

"All right. We'll try that."

"Fine. I'd like to see her again in two weeks. Sooner, if you have any concerns," he added.

When the appointment ended, Nick scooped up Hannah's carrier and held the door open for the doctor and Miriam to go out ahead of him. Outside the clinic, he handed the baby over to Miriam. She opened her rear car door and leaned in to secure the carrier.

He knew he shouldn't say anything, but as usual, his good sense went missing where Miriam was concerned. "Doctor Zook seems quite taken with you."

She popped up to gape at him. "What has that got to do with anything?"

"Nothing. It was a simple observation. I assume he isn't married?"

"No, he isn't, and I'm sure that is none of your business."

He liked the way her eyes snapped when she was angry. If only her anger wasn't always directed at him. He took a step back and raised his hands. "Don't get all huffy."

"I have every right to get huffy. What if I suggested Wilma had a crush on you?"

"Since she is old enough to be my grandmother, I'd say that would be weird."

"There's no talking to you. Now that you've been re-assured Hannah is in good health, please go away. The less I see of you the better."

He hid how much her words hurt and gave her an offhand salute. "As you wish."

She rolled her eyes and turned her back on him to finish fastening Hannah's car seat. She struggled to get the last buckle fastened.

He didn't want to leave on a sour note, but he knew when he was butting his head against a brick wall where she was concerned. In spite of his best intentions, he couldn't help making one parting comment. "That chip on your shoulder isn't doing you any good, you know."

She backed out of the car with a growl of exaspera-tion. He nudged her aside, leaned in and deftly secured the baby. Straightening, he looked at Miriam and calmly said, "It isn't going to do Hannah any good, either. We have a better chance of finding her mother if we work together."

"I thought you were leaving town for a fishing trip?"

He gazed at her intently. "The fish can wait. Hannah shouldn't have to."

He wanted Miriam's cooperation. He didn't believe in coincidences, he still believed whoever left the baby with her knew she was a nurse. "Did you put together the list of families who know you're a nurse, the way I asked?"

"Yes." She dug into her purse and pulled out a handwritten sheet.

It was a short list. There were only seven names on it. It wouldn't take long to interview these families. He looked at her. "I appreciate your cooperation."

Miriam considered carefully before she spoke again. If Hannah's mother didn't come forward, there would be little she could do on her own to find her. Nick, on the other hand, had an entire crime-solving department at his beck and call. If he was willing to put some effort into finding the baby's mother, Miriam shouldn't be discouraging him. In the end, finding the young woman who needed her help took priority over her feelings for cooperating with Nick.

She said, "I have an idea how we can check lots of buggy tires in one place."

He looked at her sharply. "How?"

"The day after tomorrow, Sunday preaching services will be held at Bishop Zook's farm. Every family in his congregation will be there. Including all the people on that list. The younger men usually drive separately so they can escort their special girls home afterward. Why go farm to farm when there will be dozens of buggies in one place? It's a start."

"A good start. Still, his isn't the only Amish church in the area. I can think of at least five others. I can try to find out where the other congregations are meeting. Tuesday is market day. That will be another opportunity for us if she hasn't come forward by then."

The thought of working with Nick should have left

Miriam cold, but it didn't. Instead, a strange excitement quickened her pulse. What was she getting herself into?

"I'll see you Sunday," he said and walked away.

When he reached his vehicle, he glanced back. She was still standing by her car watching him. An odd look of yearning crossed his face. It was gone so quickly she wondered if she imagined it.

What was he thinking when he gazed at her like that? Was he remembering happier days? She licked her lips and tucked her hair into place behind her ear. Did he think she had changed much? Did he still find her attractive?

The absurdness of the thought startled her. Why should she care what he saw when he looked at her? Impressing him should be the last thing on her mind. She walked around her car, got in quickly and drove away.

But no matter how fast she drove, thoughts of Nick stuck in her mind. She couldn't outrun them.

Chapter Five

Sunday morning dawned bright and clear. Miriam knew that because her mother was clanging pots and pans around in the kitchen before any light crept through Miriam's window. The sounds echoed up the stairwell into her room because she had the door open to hear Hannah when she cried. She needn't have bothered. Each time the baby fussed, Bella was beside Miriam's bed five seconds later, nosing her mistress to get up.

Miriam's mother had put a cot in the kitchen to sleep beside the baby's crib, but Miriam had been the one to get up and feed the baby through the night. Her mother's intentions were good, but she needed her sleep, too. Tonight, Miriam would insist on taking the cot. That way she might get a little more sleep.

The soft sound of her mother humming reached Miriam's ears. Ada was delighted her daughter was taking her to the Sunday preaching. Her mother might say she accepted that Miriam had left the Amish faith for good, but for Ada, that door was always open. Any former Amish who sought forgiveness would be welcomed back into the Amish fold with great joy.

Her mother hollered up the stairs. "You should feed the horse, Miriam. She will have a long day."

Miriam groaned. Arriving at a church meeting in a car was unacceptable to Ada. Amish people walked or drove their buggies. End of discussion.

To keep her mother from trying to walk the six miles to Bishop Zook's farm, Miriam would have to feed, water and hitch up their horse. She might be out of practice at harnessing the mare, but she hadn't forgotten how to do it.

After dressing in work clothes, Miriam walked through the kitchen. At the front door, she waited for Bella to join her. "Come on, the baby's not going to wake up for another two hours. I just fed her. This might be your only chance to spend time with me today because you are not coming with us to church."

Bella reluctantly abandoned her post beneath the crib and trotted out the door Miriam held open. Her mother, looking brighter than Miriam had seen her in weeks, was mixing batter in a large bowl. "You'd best get a move on, child. I'll not be late to services at the bishop's home. Esther Zook would never let me live it down."

"I can't understand why such a sweet man married that sour-faced woman."

Ada chuckled, then struggled to keep a straight face. "It is not right to speak ill of others."

"The truth is not ill, *Mamm,* it is the truth. There is only one reason I can think of why he fell for her."

The two women looked at each other, and both said, "She must be a wondrous *goot* cook!"

Laughing, Ada turned back to the stove. "How many times did your father say those very words?"

"Every time he talked about his brother's wife, Aunt Mae."

"She was a homely woman, God rest her soul, but your *onkel* was a happy man married to her." Ada spooned the batter into a muffin tin.

Miriam's smile faded. "I miss Papa. He was a funny fellow."

"*Ja.* He often made me laugh. God gave him a fine wit. You had better hurry and get the horse fed or these muffins will be cold by the time you get back." Ada opened the oven door and slid the pan in.

Miriam walked outside into the cool air. Even after six months, she was still amazed by the stillness and freshness of a country morning. She scanned the lane for any sign of a returning buggy. It remained as empty as it had all night. She knew because she'd looked out her window often enough. Perhaps Hannah's mother wouldn't return. What would become of the baby then?

Had Nick had any luck lifting fingerprints from the note or hamper? Surely, he would have called if he had. She still found it hard to believe that he had agreed to leave the baby with them. Was he trying to make amends? Did he care that she hadn't forgiven him?

Annoyed with herself for thinking about Nick once again, she hurried across the yard to finish her chores. In the barn, she quickly measured grain for the horse and took an old coffee can full to the henhouse. Opening the screen door, she sprinkled the grain for the brown-and-white-speckled hens. They clucked and cackled with satisfaction. She didn't bother checking for eggs. She knew her mother had gathered them already.

By the time she returned to the house, hung up her jacket and washed up, her mother was dumping golden brown cornmeal muffins into a woven wooden basket lined with a white napkin. The smell of bacon filled the air and made Miriam's stomach growl. A few more years of eating like this and she would be having her own heart attack.

"What was your blood sugar this morning?" Miriam snatched a muffin and bit into the warm crumbly goodness.

"104."

Miriam fixed her mother with an unwavering stare. "Have you taken your medicine?"

"Ja."

"Checked your blood pressure?"

"Ja."

"What is your blood pressure this morning?"

Ada's eyes narrowed. "Before or after my daughter began badgering me?"

Miriam didn't blink. "Before."

Ada rolled her eyes. "110 over 66, satisfied?"

Smiling broadly, Miriam nodded. *"Ja, Mamm dat* is very *goot."*

"And we will be very late if you don't hurry up and eat." Her mother carried the empty muffin tin to the sink and then returned to the table. After bowing their heads in silent prayer, the woman began eating.

Ada asked, "Have you decided what to tell people about Hannah?"

"The truth is generally best. I will tell people she was left with us to care for until her mother returns."

The baby began to fuss. Miriam reached over to her cradle, patted her back and adjusted her position.

Ada smiled. "She is such a darling child. I dread to

think we might never see her again when her mother does come for her."

Miriam remained silent, but the same concern had taken root in her mind, too. Hannah was quickly working her way into Miriam's heart and into her life. Letting go of her wasn't going to be easy.

Nick stopped his SUV near the end of the lane at the Zook farm. He knew the church members wouldn't appreciate his arrival in a modern vehicle on their day of worship. He wasn't here in an official capacity, so he wasn't wearing his uniform. It was almost noon, so he figured the service would be over and he would be in time for the meal.

Most Amish Sunday preaching lasted for three or four hours. The oratory workload was shared between the bishop and one or two ministers, none of whom had any formal training. They were, in fact, ordinary men whose names were among those suggested by the congregation for the position and then chosen by the drawing of lots. It was a lifelong assignment, one without pay or benefits of any kind.

Following the services that were held in homes or barns every other Sunday, the Amish women would feed everyone, clean up and spend much of the afternoon visiting with family and friends.

Approaching the large and rambling white house, Nick looked for Miriam among the women standing in groups outside of the bishop's home. Their conversations died down when they spotted him. It was unusual to have an outsider show up in such a fashion. Although many people knew he had Amish family members, he was still an outsider and regarded with suspicion by many.

He gave everyone a friendly wave and finally spotted Miriam sitting on a quilt beneath a tree with a half dozen other young women. Hannah lay sleeping on the blanket beside her. He caught Miriam's eye and tipped his head toward the house. He needed to pay his respects to Bishop Zook and the church elders before speaking with her. She nodded once in agreement and stayed put.

Inside the house, several walls had been removed to open the home up for the church meeting. The benches that had arrived that morning in a special wagon were now being rearranged to allow seating at makeshift tables. The bishop sat near the open door in one of the few armchairs in the room.

A small man with a long gray beard, he looked the part of a wise Amish elder. Nick knew him to be a fair and kind man. He rose to his feet when he saw Nick. Worry filled his eyes. "Sheriff, I hope you do not come among us with bad news."

More than once, Nick had been the one to tell an Amish family that their loved ones had been involved in a collision with a car or truck. He often asked the bishop to accompany him when he brought the news that the accident had been fatal.

"I don't bring bad news today, Bishop. I'm here to speak with Miriam Kauffman, and to give you greetings from my grandmother."

"Ah, that is a relief. How is Betsy? I have not seen her for many months."

"She's well and busy with lots of great-grandchildren, but not enough of them to keep her from trying to marry off the few of us who are still single."

Bishop Zook chuckled. "She always did fancy herself something of a matchmaker. I believe Miriam is outside with some of our young mothers. The case of this abandoned babe is very troubling. I cannot think any of our young women would do such a thing."

"I understand, but we have to ask."

"We have several families who would be pleased to take the child into their homes."

"Where the child is placed, if her mother doesn't return, will be up to Social Services."

"I feared as much. We would rather handle this ourselves. If the mother returns, the child will remain with her, *ja?*"

Nick didn't want a string of hopeful women showing up and claiming to be Hannah's mother. He needed to be very clear it wouldn't be that easy. "Once we have proof, by a blood test, that she is the mother, and we can see that she is in a position to take care of the child, then yes, it is likely that Social Services will agree to her keeping the child. If you do come across information about the mother, please get word to Miriam or myself."

"This is the Lord's working. We offer our prayers for this troubled woman and for her child."

"Thank you, Bishop."

Nick glanced again to where Miriam sat surrounded by young Amish mothers with their babies. Except for a slight difference in her dress, Miriam could have been one of them.

She had been one of them. It had taken a lot to drive her away. What would it take to make her return? If she found it in her heart to forgive him for Mark's death, would she return to the life she'd left behind?

The bishop said, "You will stay and eat with us this fine day, *ja?*"

Nick pulled his troubled gaze away from Miriam. "I would be honored, Bishop Zook. I hear your wife makes a fine peanut butter pie."

"She made a dozen different pies yesterday, and chased me away with a spoon when I tried to sample one."

"I hope for your sake there will be leftovers."

There was never a lack of food at an Amish gathering. The makeshift tables were laden with home-baked bread, different kinds of cheese and cold cuts. There was *schmierkase,* a creamy, cottage cheese-like spread, sliced pickles, pickled beets, pretzels and, Nick's favorite, a special peanut butter spread sweetened with molasses or marshmallow cream. He liked the marshmallow cream version the best. There were also a variety of cookies, brownies and other baked goods as well a rich black coffee to dunk them in.

A rumble deep in his stomach reminded Nick that breakfast had been hours ago. He had already visited two other church groups that morning and looked at dozens of buggy wheels. There was no way to keep his examinations quiet. The community would be abuzz with speculation, but it couldn't be helped.

Nick thanked the Bishop for his invitation to eat and walked toward the lawn where Miriam was sitting. She caught sight of him and rose to her feet. She spoke to Katie Sutter who was sitting beside her. At Katie's nod of agreement, Miriam left Hannah sleeping on the quilt.

Before he could say good morning, she said, "I expected you hours ago. Hannah got fussy so I took her out of the house during the service and I was able to check all the buggies that are parked beside the barn. I didn't get a chance to check those parked on the hillside."

He smiled. "Good morning, Miriam. How are you this fine morning? How is Hannah? Is she keeping you up at night? I hope your mother is feeling well."

Miriam planted her hands on her hips. "Do you really want to waste time on pleasantries?"

"It's never a waste of time to be civil."

"Fine. Good morning, Nicolas. Of course Hannah is keeping me up at night. She's a baby and she wakes up wanting to be fed every three hours. My mother is on cloud nine because I came to church with her, and Bella was pouting because she couldn't come along. Now can we go find the buggy I saw leaving Mom's place?"

"That's the plan." He started walking toward the pasture gate. Several dozen buggies and wagons were parked side by side on the grassy hill. The horses, all still in harness, were tied up along the fence dozing in the morning sun or munching on the green grass at their feet.

Miriam tipped her head toward Nick and asked quietly, "How are you going to do this without attracting attention?"

He glanced around and leaned closer. "Under the cover of bright sunshine, I'm going to stroll along the hillside with you, stopping beside every buggy. If anyone happens to look our way, I hope they think we're just having a Sunday stroll."

Her scowl vanished and she tried to hide a grin. Glancing over her shoulder, she said, "News flash, Sheriff. *Everyone* is looking at us."

"I guess our cover is blown. Did you know your eyes sparkle when you smile?"

She blushed bright red, folded her arms over her chest and stared at her feet. He could have kicked himself for making such a foolish, but true statement.

He once again became all business. "If anyone asks, which they won't, I'll say it's official police business and that's all I'll say. It's my best line. I use it all the time. The Amish are so reluctant to involve themselves in outsider business that they will politely pretend they don't see anything out of the ordinary."

She nodded. "You're right. They won't ask you questions, but they will ask my mother questions."

"Ada can tell them I said it's police business."

They stopped at the first buggy on the hill. Nick did a quick check of the wheels. There were no marks similar to the one he'd seen on Miriam's lane. When he looked up, Miriam was studying the farmhouse.

She said, "If the mother is here and she sees us looking at buggies together, she may put two and two together and come forward."

"Or, she could put two and two together and redouble her efforts to keep hidden. Did anyone appear particularly interested in Hannah today?"

"Nothing more than the usually flurry of interest a new baby generates. There was a lot of disbelief when I said I found her on my doorstep."

"I imagine."

"I didn't notice any young woman deliberately avoiding me, either. If she saw the baby, she's really good at hiding her emotions."

"Aren't we all?" he said with a wry smile. He was hiding the fact that he was falling for her all over again.

Nick quickly moved from buggy to buggy without discovering the one he hoped to find. At the end of the line, he said, "It's not here. I don't know what else to do except try again on Tuesday when people go to market. The problem with that is I'm going to end up checking most of these same ones all over again. It's not like I have a way to tell them apart."

"Wait a minute." Miriam slipped her purse strap off her shoulder, reached in and withdrew a tube of lipstick. Looking around to make sure no one could see, she dabbed a spot in the lower corner of the orange triangle on the back.

From a few feet away, it didn't show, but when Nick moved closer he could see the mark because he was looking for it. "Nice. Now, if it just doesn't rain."

They made their way back along the line of buggies as Miriam unobtrusively added a dot of lipstick to each one. When they came out the pasture gate, he held out his hand. "Mind if I borrow that? I've got two other congregations to visit today."

She handed it over. He turned the tube to read the label. "Ambrosia Blush. I like that."

"It's not your color, Sheriff. It's a shade made for redheads."

He tucked the tube in his pocket. "I'll keep that in mind. Have you eaten yet?"

"No, we were waiting for the elders to finish, but I'm not hungry. Mom insists on making a breakfast fit for a farmhand."

By this time they had reached the quilt where Katie Sutter sat holding a fussy Hannah. Miriam reached for the baby. "I'll take her."

Katie handed her over. Hannah quieted instantly.

Katie smiled at Nick. "Hello, Nick, it's good to see you again."

"You, as well, Katie. Where is Elam?" He looked around for her husband.

Katie had gone out into the world and returned to the Amish several years ago. She was happily married now with two small children. She understood the challenges of both worlds.

"Elam is out in the barn with Jonathan talking horses. Jonathan was just saying the other day that he hadn't seen you in weeks. He was wondering if you'd forgotten where he lived."

Nick laughed aloud. Hannah, who had quieted in Miriam's arms, started crying again. He cupped her head softly. "I'm sorry, sweet one, did I scare you?"

The baby quieted briefly, then began protesting in earnest. Miriam said, "I think she's just getting hungry. Who is Jonathan?"

Nick recounted the story. "The Christmas before last, Jonathan Dressler was found, beaten and suffering from amnesia on Eli Imhoff's farm. I investigated the case and eventually solved it, but not until after Jonathan recovered his memory."

"And fell in love with Eli's daughter Karen," Katie added. "He is *Englisch,* but he will be baptized into our faith soon and then everyone expects a wedding will follow. Quickly."

"Not quick enough for Jonathan." Nick knew his friend was counting down the days until he could marry the woman who saved his life.

Miriam had taken a bottle of formula from her purse. Nick held out his hand. "Let me take it up to the house and see if the bishop's wife can warm it up for her."

"Thanks." She held it up for him.

Her fingers brushed against his as he took the bottle. Her touch sent a jolt through his body and sucked the air from his lungs.

Miriam gaze flew to Nick's face. She saw his eyes widen. Just as quickly, his jaw hardened and he looked away. He said, "I'll be back in a couple of minutes."

When Nick was out of sight, she drew a shaky breath. How was it possible that the chemistry still simmered between them?

The answer was simple. Because it had never died.

Katie said, "We like Nick Bradley. He is a good man. He cares about the Amish. His cousin Amber delivered both my babies. Are you going to her wedding?"

Miriam was delighted to talk about anything except Nick. "I didn't know she was getting married. When is it?"

"This coming Saturday. She is marrying Dr. White's grandson, Phillip. He is a doctor, too. When they first met, no one imagined they would end up together. He had the whole community in an uproar when he put a stop to Amber doing home deliveries."

Since the vast majority of Amish babies were born at home with the help of midwives, a doctor trying to stop home deliveries would not be popular. "If they are getting married, they must've come to terms somehow. Is she still delivering babies at home?"

"Oh, yes. I think it took a lot of soul-searching and compromising on both their parts. Isn't it wondrous how God sends love into our lives? Not when we are expecting it, even when we think we don't want it or deserve it. He has His own time for everything if only we open our hearts to His will."

Miriam had closed her heart to love after Mark died. She had filled her life with caring for others. In spite of the good works she did, and she knew they were good works, there was still a measure of emptiness inside her. Opening her heart to love would mean forgiving herself. Was she ready to do that? She studied the baby in her arms. It would be so easy to fall in love with this child. What if she opened her heart to love Hannah and had to give her away? Wasn't it better not to love than to feel the pain of another loss?

"Elam and I are going to Amber's wedding. You could come with us."

"I don't know."

Nick came walking back with a mug in one hand. The formula bottle sat warming in it. In his other hand he carried a bundled napkin. He sat down and placed the mug carefully between them. He held the napkin out to Miriam. "Your mother put together something for you to eat."

"I can't believe she thinks I need to be fed. I'm still stuffed from breakfast."

"Are you sure? Because if you're not hungry, I am."

"Help yourself. Is Hannah's bottle warm enough?"

Laying his lunch aside, he checked the milk. "I think it's good. Don't babies drink formula at room temperature? My sister never heated up her baby's bottle."

"I've tried, but Hannah seems to like it better if it's warm. Otherwise, she gets fussy and doesn't eat as much." Miriam positioned the baby in her arms and gave her the bottle. It was exactly what Hannah wanted.

The only sounds she made were contented sucking noises.

Katie said, "I was just telling Miriam that she should come to your cousin's wedding. I know Amber would be delighted to see her there."

Miriam shook her head. "I would feel funny showing up without an invitation."

Nick took a bite of his sandwich and mumbled around his full mouth. "I've got you covered."

He leaned to the side and pulled an envelope out of his hip pocket and held it out to her.

Miriam's hands were full. "What is it?"

Grinning, he said, "Your invitation to the wedding. I asked Amber to invite you. There will be plenty of room in the church, and it's not like there's going to be any shortage of food at the dinner afterward. Half our family is Amish. Believe me, there will be food." He laid the envelope beside her and took another bite of his sandwich.

"See, now there is no reason not to come," Katie said with a bright smile.

Miriam still wasn't sure it would be a good idea. It was one thing to work with him as they tried to locate Hannah's mother. It was another thing to spend time with him at a social occasion. She opened her mouth to decline but ended up saying, "I'll think about it."

Katie got to her feet. "I see the elders have finished eating. I must go and help Elam feed the children. It was nice talking with you, Miriam. I will pray that Hannah's mother comes for her soon."

As Katie walked away, Nick said, "You know, she may not be coming back. The letter could have been a ruse. We may never learn who she is."

"I know that."

"Are you prepared to accept it?"

Miriam gazed at the baby in her arms. "I won't have any choice in the matter, will I?"

"I guess not, but you do have a choice to attend a fun-filled wedding or to stay home and mope about not having fun."

"What makes you think I would mope?"

The teasing grin left his face. His eyes grew serious. "It would mean a lot to Amber, and to me, if you come. Will you?"

"I said I'll think about it." It was the best that she could until she figured out how she felt about spending more time with Nick.

Chapter Six

Hannah was crying at the top of her lungs. The dog was whining and pawing at Miriam and the kettle was whistling madly. With only four hours of sleep out of the past twenty-four, Miriam reached the end of her rope at ten o'clock Monday morning. As she struggled to get an irate baby into a clean sleeper for the third time in as many feedings, she shouted at the dog, "Bella, stop it! Mother, will you *please* take the kettle off the fire."

Her mother had gone to her room to read and seemed oblivious to the pandemonium in the kitchen. Miriam finally got Hannah's flailing fist through the sleeve and quickly tied the front of the outfit closed. She lifted the baby to her shoulder to calm her. Nudging Bella aside with her knee, Miriam reached for clean burp rag. She threw it over her shoulder, but before she could switch Hannah to that side she felt something warm and wet running down her back.

Miriam closed her eyes and gritted her teeth. "You did *not* just throw up on me."

From the doorway, a man's amused voice said, "Oh, yes, she did."

Great. Why did Nick have to show up when she was too tired to keep up her defenses? "Don't you knock?"

"I did. Several times."

He crossed the kitchen and pulled the kettle from the heat. The whistling died away, but Hannah was still crying at the top of her lungs, and Bella was still whining and dancing underfoot, upset that her baby was unhappy.

Nick returned to the door, held it open and said, "Bella, outside."

The dejected dog trotted out the door, and he closed it behind her. Then, he crossed the room to Miriam and lifted the baby away from her soggy shoulder. "Come here, sweet one, and tell me what's the matter."

It wasn't the first time in the past few days that Miriam felt inadequate as Hannah's caretaker, but it was the first time she'd had her shortcomings displayed to an audience.

Nick took the clean burp cloth from Miriam, tossed it over his shoulder and settled the baby with her face nuzzled into the side of his neck. She immediately stopped crying. Why she couldn't throw up on him was beyond knowing.

In the ensuing silence, Miriam dropped onto a chair and raked a hand through her hair. "Where were you eight hours ago?"

"Eight ago I was sleeping like a baby."

"Babies do not sleep. They fuss, they spit up, they make the dog crazy and they keep everyone else from sleeping, but they do not sleep."

Miriam didn't want to look at his face because she knew he would be smiling, amused at her expense. It was kind of funny now that she thought about it. She met his gaze and they both chuckled.

"Rough night?" he asked.

"Killer."

"Why don't you go change? I'll take care of her for a while."

"I had things under control, you know."

He smirked. "I saw that."

"What are you doing here, anyway?"

"I just wanted to check on the two of you. No sign of the mother I take it?"

Miriam stood up. The streak of warm formula down her back was quickly growing cold and sticky. "No sign of her or the father. At the moment, I'm beginning to think she was smarter than I gave her credit for."

"You don't mean that," Nick chided.

Miriam glanced at him and the little darling in a pink sleeper curled into a ball against his chest. The soft smile on his face as he looked down at the baby did funny things to Miriam's insides. There was something endearing about a man who held a baby so easily. "No, I don't mean it. I just need some sleep."

Ada walked into the room. "Nicolas, what a surprise. How nice to see you. Miriam, did the kettle boil? I didn't hear it. I'm afraid I fell asleep. A strong cup of tea will perk me up."

"Yes, mother, the kettle boiled. Nick just took it off the heat so it should be perfect for your tea. If you'll both excuse me, I'm going to go change my shirt, again. I hope this spitting up settles down when she is switched all the way over to soy formula."

Her mother said, "All babies spit up a little. You did. How your papa hollered when you spit up on his Sunday suit just as we got to the preaching. I tried so hard not to laugh at him. Is he home yet?"

Miriam exchanged a startled glance with Nick. She studied her mother closely. "Is who home yet?"

Ada's shoulders slumped. "That was silly. I know my William is gone. I must have been dreaming about the old days."

She turned and gave Nick a bright grin. "Would you like some tea?"

"Sounds great. Do you need any help?"

"*Nee,* you sit and hold our pretty baby. She's so *goot.* She barely made a peep last night. Miriam, would you like tea?"

Not a peep, but a whole lot of crying. Miriam was amazed her mother had slept through it. "No tea for me, *danki.*"

"That's right. You're a coffee drinker like your papa. Mark was the one who liked tea." She smiled sadly and turned back to the stove. "What was I going to do?"

"*Mamm,* are you okay?" Miriam stepped closer.

"I'm fine. I need another cup, that's what I was going to do." She pulled a second mug from the cabinet and placed a tea bag in it.

Miriam gave her mother one more worried look, then hurried upstairs. When she came downstairs five minutes later, Hannah was sound asleep in her crib. Bella was curled up on the rag rug beneath it. Her long tail thumped twice when she saw Miriam, but she didn't move. Ada and Nick were chatting over tea and oatmeal cookies at the kitchen table. Miriam joined them, but she couldn't stifle a yawn.

Her mother patted Miriam's hand. "Why don't you take a nap, dear. Nicolas and I will watch the baby."

"I'm sure the sheriff has other things to do besides babysit."

"I have a few errands to run, but I'm not in any hurry. I'll stay for a while. At least until the cookies run out." He bit into the one he was holding.

Ada grinned. "Miriam made them. They are sugar-free. She can be a *goot* cook when she sets her mind to it."

"Sugar-free doesn't mean calorie-free, so only two for you, *Mamm*," Miriam reminded her.

"How many can I have?" He slipped another one from the plate on to his napkin.

"None," she teased.

"You mean none after this one." He filched a fourth cookie and added it the stack in front of him.

Miriam shook her head. "Whatever."

Nick gave Ada a sympathetic look. "She's cranky today, isn't she?"

Ada glanced at the crib. "*Nee,* she is a sweet *boppli.* I wish she could stay with us forever."

He said, "I was talking about Miriam."

Ada glanced at Miriam and leaned closer to Nick. "She gets that way when she is tired."

Straightening in her chair, Ada gave Miriam a stern look. "Go lie down. We will be fine."

Miriam knew if she didn't get some rest she was going to fall down and sleep on the floor. "All right, but get me up if she gets fussy again."

"I will," Ada promised.

Miriam wondered if she would be the topic of conversation once she was out of the room. At this point, she really didn't care. She climbed the steps, walked into her bedroom and fell down on her bed fully dressed.

The next time she pried her eyes open, her watch told her she been asleep for four hours. She ran her fingers through her tangled hair and made her way back downstairs. The kitchen was empty. Hannah wasn't in her crib.

Frowning, Miriam was about to check the rest of the house when she heard a sound coming from the front porch. She walked to the window and looked out. Nick sat in her mother's white rocker. She couldn't see if he had Hannah, but she assumed he did because Bella sat quietly beside him watching him like a hawk.

Nick was singing softly in a beautiful baritone voice that sent chills up her spine. It was the old spiritual, "Michael Row the Boat Ashore." She stood listening for several stanzas, captured by the beauty of his voice and the healing words of the song. Death was not an end, merely a river to be crossed.

Mark and her father waiting for her on a shore she couldn't see yet, but someday she would. If only she could be sure she could gain their forgiveness.

How could she if she hadn't forgiven Nick? She pushed the screen door open and walked out onto the porch.

Nick looked over his shoulder as Miriam came out of the house. Her hair was tousled and her eyes were puffy, but she looked more rested than when he arrived. "Did you have a nice nap?"

"Better than you'll ever know. Where's my mother?" She paused to gaze lovingly at the baby.

"She went to take a nap shortly after you did."

"And she just left you with the baby all this time?"

"I didn't mind." He looked down at the baby nestled

in the crook of his arm. She was so sweet and so innocent. In his line of work he often saw the seedy side of
humanity. It did his soul good to realize how healing
and calm holding a baby made him feel.

"I thought you had errands to run?" Miriam rubbed
her hands up and down her arms as if she were cold.

It was warm on the porch. He knew it was his presence, not the temperature that made her uncomfortable.
He wished it could be different. Would he ever be able
to break through the barrier she had erected between
them? He prayed to God that it was possible. They had
been good friends once. He would settle for that again
if were possible.

Miriam said, "I can take her now."

Reluctant to give Hannah up, he said, "I don't mind
holding her. She's asleep. If I give her to you, she may
wake up and start fussing."

Taking a seat in the other rocker on the porch, Miriam
smothered another yawn. "I honestly don't know how
new mothers do this."

"Beats me. I'm pretty much a wreck if I don't get
eight hours."

He hesitated, then asked, "Has your mother been
confused and forgetful before today, or is this something new?" Miriam had a lot on her plate at the moment. How well would she hold up under the strain?

"It's something new. I hope it's just the excitement of
the past few days and not something serious."

"Don't take this the wrong way, but are you sure
you're up to this?" He knew the moment the words left
his mouth that he had made a mistake.

She scowled at him. "Exactly how should I take your

inference that I can't take care of my mother and a newborn?"

"What I wanted to say was you have enough to worry about with your mother's health. It's understandable that you would have difficulty managing a new baby on top of that. Never mind. I can see by the look in your eyes that you don't want sympathy and you don't want help. No need to bite my head off. I'm sorry."

To his surprise, she took a deep breath and leaned back in her rocker. "I'm the one who is sorry. My mother is right. I get cranky when I don't get enough sleep. I may not want help, but I need it. You have no idea how much I needed this break. Thanks for sticking around today."

"You're welcome. Did you know your mother is talking about wanting to keep Hannah?"

"I do."

He could tell from the tone of her voice that she harbored the same wish. Nick looked down at the sleeping child in his arms. "It is easy to become attached to her. When she isn't spitting up or crying, she is adorable."

"Did she spit up again?" Quick concern flooded Miriam's face.

Nick smiled. Miriam was no different than his sisters or any other new mother. It was all about the baby. He raised the burp rag he had on his shoulder to reveal a damp stain. "It wasn't too much."

Miriam relaxed. "I was beginning to think it was just me. I'm happy to know she's willing to share."

He smiled at the baby and stroked her hair with the back of his fingers. "She seems to be an equal opportunity spitter, but she sure knows how to wrap a guy around her little finger."

"All babies can do that. You seem to have a knack for handling her."

"I've had lots of practice with a half dozen nieces and nephews. What can I say, I like babies."

"It shows." There was a softening in her tone that pleased him. He was glad now that he had stayed.

Miriam couldn't take her gaze off of Nick's face. There was such compassion and wonder in his eyes as he gazed at the baby.

Painting him as a heartless villain had been easy when she didn't have to see him. Face-to-face with him now, she didn't see a villain, just a man in awe of the new life he held.

Did it change anything? She wasn't sure.

He said, "I meant to tell you earlier that I drew a blank for fingerprints on the basket and note. It was a long shot at best. We recovered several prints but they were too smudged to be of any use. Which is rotten luck if she doesn't come back. It will leave us almost nothing to go on."

"I believe she'll come back for Hannah. I just wish we could locate her and find out what kind of trouble she is in."

"You're a practical woman. You have to know that women who leave their babies in a safe haven are unlikely to return for them. I don't know of a single case in Ohio where custody was returned to the biological mother."

"How many of those women were Amish?"

"No one knows. The point of the Safe Haven Law is to give mothers anonymity. Frankly, while the intention is good, I think the law has one big flaw."

"Fathers?"

"Exactly. Hannah's father has the same rights as her mother does. We don't know if he knew about this decision or not. I don't like the idea that a mother can give away her child without the father's consent."

"The world is full of deadbeat dads who couldn't care less what happens to their kids. Many of them can't be bothered to pay child support."

"There are many, many more men who would give anything to see that their children have good lives."

Nick would be one of those men, she decided. Mark would've been one if he had lived. Thinking about him made her sad but she didn't feel angry anymore. It was odd, because the anger had consumed her for so long. She felt empty without it. What would she find to replace it?

Nick said, "At least we know that Hannah will go to a loving family, even if her mother doesn't return. There are good people waiting to adopt a baby like her."

"I will be sorry to see her go."

"But you'll be able to get a decent night's sleep when she does," he said with a grin.

"There is that." She tipped her head to the side and stared at her dog. "Bella is the one who's going to be brokenhearted."

"You'll have to adopt a puppy for her."

"Ha! You do want to punish me, don't you? What makes you think a new puppy would be any less trouble than a baby? I could always adopt two and leave one on your doorstep."

"It wouldn't work."

"Why not? Don't tell me you'd take a helpless puppy back to the pound."

"No. However, among all my nieces, nephews and cousins, I wouldn't have any trouble finding a better home than my apartment."

Miriam knew that Nick was the oldest in his family. He had three younger sisters. She'd never met them, but he used to talk about them—make that complain about them—the way teenaged boys talked about their sisters. She was suddenly curious about his life. She asked, "What are the three terrors up to these days?"

Nick gave a bark of laughter that disturbed Hannah and made her whimper. He soothed her with a little bouncing, and she settled back to sleep. "I haven't heard them called that in years. They were the bane of my existence when I was growing up. Fortunately for me they didn't like the country or Amish living and refused to spend summers with Grandma Betsy. Summers were my great escape."

Miriam raised her foot to rest it on the rocker seat and wrapped her arms around her knee. She remembered waiting for him to return, eager to see him again and hear about everything he'd done in the strange *Englisch* world. "You never had much good to say about your sisters."

"True. Happily, I've learned to like them a lot better now that they have their own homes and aren't keeping me out of the only bathroom for hours on end. I never did understand why it takes a girl so long to get ready in the mornings. Multiply that by three, and you know I had like six seconds to get ready for school every day."

Miriam hesitated before asking her next question. Nick's home life had been difficult after his father's death. He had confided many things to her when they had been friends. Before she heaped all her anger and guilt on him. "How is your mother doing?"

"Better some days, worse other days. I know Dad loved her, I know she loved Dad, but they couldn't make it work. She wasn't cut out to be a big city cop's wife. She hated his job. After he was killed, she couldn't stand the guilt. She believed it was her punishment for leaving the Amish."

"I know you once said she was abusing prescription drugs. Is she still?"

"I don't think so, but I'm not there every day. My youngest sister lives close by. She seems to think Mom is doing okay. I know that having grandchildren has been good for her."

Miriam gazed at Hannah. "My mother would love grandchildren. That's why I'm worried she is getting too attached to Hannah. I don't want it to break her heart when the baby has to leave."

"As much as you love kids, I'm surprised you haven't married and had children."

She cocked her head at him. "Don't think it's because I haven't had offers. I just haven't found the right guy."

Hannah began fussing and squirming in his hold. He said, "I think she's getting hungry. It's been almost three hours since she last ate."

Miriam sprang to her feet. "I'll go get her bottle ready."

She entered the house with a sense of relief. Their conversation had taken a personal turn that she wasn't quite ready for. It was one thing to have him talk about himself, it was another thing to expose her own life to his scrutiny.

Nick adjusted Hannah's position to his shoulder and patted her back gently. "Did you see how quickly she shot out of here when I started asking personal questions? Note to self—no matter how much I would like to know about Miriam's life, don't press, wait for her to volunteer that information."

At least she wasn't glaring daggers at him every chance she got. Something was different this afternoon. Her mood had softened. Perhaps having a baby in the house brought out her gentler side. Whatever was going on, he hoped it didn't change soon. He liked being able to spend time in her company without feeling like he was barely tolerated.

He glanced up as she came out of the house with a bottle in her hand. She self-consciously tucked her hair behind her ear and smiled slightly as she held out the formula.

The trouble with spending time with Miriam was that it made him wish for more. More of her time, more of her smiles, more of everything she cared to share.

"I can feed her if you want," she offered.

"That's okay, I'm already damp." He took the bottle from her hand and tried to shift the baby into a more upright position. Miriam bent down to help just as he leaned. Her face was inches from his. Close enough to kiss if he leaned forward a bit more. And he wanted to kiss her.

The timing was all wrong, the situation was all wrong, but he wanted to kiss her. It took all of his self-control to hand her the bottle, adjust the baby in his arms and lean back. He glanced at her to see if she had noticed his interest. Color bloomed in her cheeks. She gave him the bottle and took a step back.

Keep it casual. Don't blow it.

He could give himself good advice but he wasn't sure he could follow it. He cleared his throat. "I hope we have better luck finding our mystery buggy during the farmers market tomorrow."

Miriam took a seat in her chair and stared straight ahead. "I think we'll see a lot of the same ones. If I knew when the next singing was being held we could check out more of the young men's buggies."

"I know a lot of them like the open-topped buggies for courting. You saw a closed-top buggy."

"I'm sure what I saw was a standard variety, black, Ohio Amish buggy."

"It's too bad there isn't something to help us tell them apart."

"That's the point of all the Amish driving the same style. Uniformity, conformity, no one stands out above their neighbor."

"I understand that, but I can still wish for license tags."

"Well, unless the numbers had been three feet tall and could glow in the dark, I wouldn't have been able to see them, either. It was dark and the lane is a quarter mile long."

"I'm not faulting you for a lack of description. I'm frustrated by the fact that I can't do more."

"Are you sorry that we let you in on this?"

"Yes, and no. I know that Hannah is being well cared for. I just wish I could bring the power of my office into the hunt. If I considered this a straight child abandonment, my office could offer a reward for information. We could have law enforcement officers going door to door. We could make it hard for this young woman to hide. While I've alerted the local hospitals and clinics to be on the lookout for a woman with postpartum complications and no baby, all I'm really left with is checking buggy wheels. It's not high-tech police work."

"You like your job, don't you?"

"I do, but it's not for everyone." Hannah had finished her bottle. Nick sat her up to burp her. She gave a hearty belch for such a tiny baby, but all of her formula stayed down.

Miriam got up and reached for her. Nick handed her over reluctantly. He had no more reasons to hang out on Miriam's front porch.

"I'm glad we let you in on this, and I'm glad you came by today. Thank you."

"You're welcome. Why don't I pick up you and your mother tomorrow? We can cruise the market together." He waited, hopeful that this new, softer Miriam would agree.

"That sounds fine." She hesitated, as if she wanted to say more, then simply nodded goodbye and walked into the house.

Nick walked out to his vehicle. He opened the door of his SUV but hesitated before getting in. He knew it was a selfish thought, but he hoped Hannah's mother stayed out of sight a little longer.

Without Hannah to bring them together he'd have no excuse to spend time with Miriam.

Chapter Seven

A heavy morning shower didn't put a damper on the first market day of the spring. The small town of Hope Springs was bustling with wagons, buggies, produce buyers and tourists. Nick turned off Main Street onto Lake Street.

The regular weekly market had been held on Friday afternoons in a large grassy area next to the town's lumberyard. After a recent meeting of the town council, the day had been changed to Tuesday in an effort to draw in tourists from the other area markets held on the same day. The striped canopies of numerous tents were clearly visible, as were dozens of buggies lined up along the street.

Nick had been to the market numerous times. It was one way to meet and get to know the often reclusive Amish residents of his county. Today, he wouldn't be looking over homemade baked goods or cheeses. He'd be watching for anyone with a marked interest in Hannah as well as for their mystery buggy.

After he found a parking place, he got out of the vehicle and opened the door for Ada. She had been in good spirits on the ride to town, as was her daughter. Amish families looked forward eagerly to the weekly trip to town. Much of the day would be spent visiting and shopping with friends and family.

Ada said, "*Ach,* there is Faith Lapp with one of her alpacas. They are such cute animals. I must get some of her yarn to make Hannah a blanket."

Nick looked to see if her nephew Kyle was with her. He wanted speak to the boy and find out how he was adjusting to his new Amish family. Nick had had the unhappy duty of removing Kyle from his aunt's home when an overzealous and uninformed social worker insisted Faith's plain home was an unsafe environment. Fortunately, Judge Harbin, the family court judge, was familiar with the Amish and knew that Kyle would be raised with every care.

It took Nick several long moments to locate the boy. He was dressed in a wide-brimmed straw hat, dark pants and a white shirt beneath a dark vest. He was standing in a group of boys in almost identical clothing. They were laughing and patting the young black alpaca that Kyle had named Shadow. From the look on the young boy's face, Nick knew he was settling in well.

Miriam had Hannah out of her car seat and was settling her into a baby carrier that kept her snuggled against Miriam's chest. Nick said, "That's a nice little rig."

"She seems much more content when she is being held or carried upright. Amber brought it by yesterday after you left. It works wonders, and it lets me keep my hands free."

Nick surveyed the field. "Which end of the street do you want to start on?"

"First, I'd like to visit the tent where the quilts are being displayed."

Nick frowned at her. "There won't be any buggies in that area."

"I know, but I brought the quilt Hannah was wrapped in. I'm hoping someone will recognize it. I also wanted to say hello to Rebecca and Gideon Troyer. You know Rebecca's story, don't you?"

"Sure. I was one of the people bidding on her quilt last November when she was trying to raise enough money to have her eye surgery. Of course, Gideon outbid us all and ended up with a wife as well as a fine quilt. We are all thankful for God's mercy in restoring Rebecca's sight."

Ada said, "I think the bigger miracle was Gideon's return to the Plain life after being out in the world for so many years. It was a blessing to his family and our community."

Miriam couldn't get the strap of the snuggle harness to fit comfortably. Nick said, "Here, let me help you with that."

She turned her back to him. He swept aside her hair to see where the strap was twisted. Her hair whispered across his wrist and bunched like the softest silk in his hand. He paused, captivated by the sensation.

"Can you get it?" she asked.

"Yup. Just a second." He straightened the strap and let her hair slide through his fingers. If he lived to be an old, old man, he wouldn't forget the softness of it.

"Why don't we split up? Nick, you can take mother to buy yarn, and I'll go say hello to Rebecca and Gideon. We can meet back here and start checking buggy wheels."

"I think it would be better to stick together," he said.

Miriam gave him a funny look. "What difference does that make?"

"I want to be able to watch the people watching you

and Hannah." He wanted to walk by her side and pretend they were friends again.

"Okay, alpaca yarn, quilts, once through the market and then buggy wheels?"

"Sounds fine. It's too bad it rained. Your lipstick marks will have been washed off all the slow-moving-vehicle signs. We'll end up rechecking dozens of the same ones."

Miriam giggled, a light, free sound that made his heart beat faster. "It's waterproof lipstick. It should still be there."

He shook his head. "Waterproof. A man learns something new every day."

Nick kept a close watch on Miriam as she moved through the crowds. There were a number of people who stopped to admire Hannah, but no one seemed overly interested, or out of the ordinary, except for a pair of Amish teenage boys who followed them but never approached her.

Nick said to Ada, "Do you know those boys?"

She looked to where he indicated the pair looking at hand-carved pipes. "Do you mean the Beachy twins?"

"Beachy? Which family do they belong to?" Since almost all Amish were descended from a small group of immigrants, there was very little diversity in their names. There were dozens of families with the same last name in his county.

"They are Levi Beachy's younger brothers. He is the carriage maker in Hope Springs. He rented the business from Sarah Wyse's husband shortly before he passed away."

"Yes, I remember that."

Nick said to Miriam, "I believe I'll have a word with the twins. Walk on and I'll catch up with you."

As Miriam and her mother made their way down the row of tents, Nick dropped back and approached the boys from behind, taking care to keep out of their line of sight until he was standing only a step away. "You two seem awfully interested in Miriam Kauffman's baby. Care to tell me why?"

The boy spun around, their eyes going wide at the sight of the sheriff towering over them. One stammered, "W-we don't know what you mean."

"I'm asking what is your interest in that baby? Is one of you the father?"

He doubted they could look more surprised if he'd suggested that they could fly. "*Nee,* we're no one's *daed,*" they exclaimed together.

"Are you willing to take a DNA test to prove that?"

The boys looked at each other. One said, "We're not so good at taking tests. We'd rather not."

Nick folded his arms and clapped a hand over his face to hide his grin. "What are your names?"

The one on the right said, "I'm Moses, and this is my younger brother, Atlee."

Atlee elbowed him. "Younger by five minutes ain't hardly enough to mention."

Nick put a stop to what was clearly an old argument. "Why are you following Miriam?"

"Is that the baby that was left on the porch step?" Atlee asked.

"You answer my question first." Nick used his most intimidating tone.

"We were wondering what she would charge to drive us to Cincinnati," Moses said.

Atlee looked at him quickly, but then nodded. "Yeah, Cincinnati."

Nick considered their story. They looked to be about the right age to be on their *rumspringa,* the time following an Amish teenager's sixteenth birthday when they were allowed to experience the forbidden outside world prior to taking their vows of faith. Many learned to drive cars, but those who couldn't afford them would hire drivers to take them into the cities. "So why not just ask her?"

Moses looked at his feet. "She's so pretty."

Puppy love—that was all Nick needed. "Samson Carter will quote you a fair price on a trip that far."

The boys nodded. Atlee said, "But he ain't so pretty. Is that the baby that was left on the stoop?"

"It is. What do you boys know about it?"

"Only what we heard. Is the baby okay?" Atlee asked. Moses looked as if he'd rather be anywhere else.

Nick relaxed. "She's fine as far as we can tell. If you boys hear anything about a girl people thought might be pregnant but then didn't have a baby, I'd sure like to know about it. Now, beat it."

He didn't have to say it twice. The boys dashed away without a backward glance.

After coming up empty at the quilt tent and spending another fruitless hour of searching through the buggies, they called it quits. Nick, Miriam and Ada returned to his vehicle. With Hannah secured in her car seat, Nick started the vehicle and headed toward Miriam's house.

At the edge of town his radio crackled to life. He pulled over to listen. The dispatcher was asking for a unit in the Hope Springs area to respond to a domestic disturbance call. A neighbor had called in a report that a woman was being beaten. As each of his deputies replied, Nick realized he was the only one in the vicinity. The address the dispatch gave was only a few blocks away.

He glanced at Miriam. "I have to respond to this."

"What can I do to help?"

"Just stay in the car." He shared his intentions with his dispatcher, turned his SUV around and flipped on his lights and siren. In a matter of minutes, he was pulling up to a ramshackle house on the far edge of town.

The clapboard structure had been white once, but peeling paint and bare boards had turned it a dull gray. The yard was devoid of grass, but a tricycle and several toys leaned against the rusting chain-link fence. Several of the windows were covered with aluminum foil. Two others boasted broken shades but no curtains.

A young woman in jeans and a blood-spattered yellow T-shirt sat on the steps with a towel pressed to her face. There was no sign of her attacker. Nick handed the keys to Miriam. "If anything happens, if you feel unsafe at all, I want you to get out of here. There are deputies on the way for backup, so don't worry about me."

She grasped his arm. "I'm not leaving you here alone."

He opened the door and got out of the vehicle. Turning to her, he said, "Lock the doors and do as I say."

Miriam's first impulse was to assist the young woman. She couldn't sit by and do nothing when someone was so clearly in need of medical assistance. She took the keys from Nick. "I'm a nurse. I can help."

He shook his head. "Not until I know it's safe."

The words were no sooner out of his mouth than the screen door of the home banged open. A thin man with slicked-back hair started yelling at the woman. "Look what you've done now. You brought the cops down on us. How could you do this to me?"

The woman scrambled out of his way. Nick closed

the vehicle door and approached the scene. "Stop right there, sir. I'm Sheriff Nick Bradley, and I just want to talk to you."

The man threw his hands up in disgust, spun around and reentered the house before Nick could stop him. The woman collapsed on the bottom step still weeping. Nick approached her and asked, "Are you all right?"

"Don't take him to jail. My husband is just upset because he's been out of work so long. He's been drinking today, but he almost never drinks. I'll be okay. Honest, I cut my head when I fell."

Nick didn't take his eyes off the door. "Does he have any weapons in the house? Does he have a gun?"

"We don't have anything like that. I'm sorry someone called you. I'm fine, really I am." She tried to stand, but her legs gave out and she plopped back. She tried a second time and succeeded, but she wobbled. Nick reached out to help steady her.

From along the corner of the house, Miriam saw the husband approaching with a long thick piece of wood in his hand. He was out of Nick's line of sight.

In that instant, she saw a terrifying scene beginning to unfold. The man rounded the corner of the house with the club raised over his head. Nick was in danger. Miriam pushed open the door and yelled, "Nick, watch out!"

Nick caught sight of the man an instant before it was too late. From his crouching position, he launched a sideways kick that landed square in the middle of the man's chest. His heavy boot connected with a sickening thud. The husband tumbled backward, the board dropping from his hand.

Seconds later, Nick straddled him using an arm lock

to hold him down while he snapped on a pair of hand-cuffs.

Miriam's heart started beating again. Nick was safe. The emotions she'd kept bottled inside exploded into her mind. She pressed a hand to her mouth to keep from crying out. She cared about Nick. Deeply.

The wife started screaming hysterically for Nick to let her husband up. It was clear Nick had all he could handle. Miriam had to help. She jumped out of the car and rushed to the wife, placing herself between her and Nick. She grasped the woman's arms and held on.

"It's all right. He's going to be all right. Don't make things worse for him. Calm down."

Nick growled, "Miriam, get back in the car."

"Everyone take a deep breath. This doesn't have to end badly if everyone keeps their cool."

A movement at the window shade in the house drew Miriam's attention. The frightened faces of two small kids looked out on the scene. She forced the woman to focus on her. "You're scaring the children. You don't want that, do you?"

It was the first thing that seemed to get through to the distraught wife. "No, don't let them see this." She turned her face away from the house.

"Miriam, get back in the car, or so help me, I'll arrest you, too."

She ignored him. Concentrating on keeping the wife calm, Miriam spoke quietly to her. "The children have already seen this. They are going to need you to reassure them. You can't do that if you end up in jail for assaulting a police officer. Do you have someone you can call? Do you have a family member or a pastor who can come over and help take care of the children?"

The woman shook her head and started sobbing again. "Danny and the kids are all the family I have. Please don't arrest him."

Miriam glanced toward the car, where her mother was watching with wide worried eyes. Looking at the young mother, she asked, "What is your name?"

"Caroline. Caroline Hicks."

"Caroline, my mother is here. Is it all right if she goes inside and stays with the children for a little bit?"

Caroline nodded, but she couldn't take her eyes off her husband. Miriam motioned to her mother. When Ada reached her carrying Hannah, Miriam said, "*Mamm,* would you please go into the house and stay with the children. Caroline, what are their names?"

"Danny Jr. and Mary Beth."

Her mother nodded. "*Ja,* I will see to the *kinder.*"

"*Danki.* We won't be long."

Knowing that her mother would be able to soothe and calm the frightened children, Miriam focused her attention on Caroline. This woman wasn't much different than the confused and frightened teenagers who showed up at Mariam's door in the middle of the night.

Nick lifted Danny to his feet and led him to the steps, where he allowed him to sit and regain his breath. Danny looked up at his wife. "I'm sorry, Caroline. Please forgive me. I'll never do it again, I promise."

Caroline reached toward him. "I know you didn't mean it, Danny."

Miriam held back her opinion of men who hit women, and women who stayed with men who hit them. She knew the situation was never as black-and-white as it seemed. The best thing to do was to separate Caroline from Danny and get her to concentrate on what was best for her and for the children.

Taking her by the arm, Miriam led her down the block to a neighbor's vacant front porch. She stayed with Caroline until Nick's backup arrived. With a second and then a third officer on the scene, Miriam felt comfortable leaving Caroline in the hands of people who had been trained for exactly that type of situation. She walked toward the house and saw her mother putting Hannah's carrier in the SUV. Looking around, she asked, "Where is Nick?"

"In the house. He said we were to go home, and he would have someone bring him by to pick up the truck later."

Miriam glanced toward the house. She didn't feel right abandoning him. "All right. I'll let him know we are leaving now."

She walked up the steps and entered the shabby, run-down building. She spotted Nick sitting on the stairs and talking to Danny Jr. The boy looked to be about five years old. Both he and Nick had their hands clasped between their knees. Neither one noticed her. The little girl sat with a female deputy on the sofa.

Nick said, "This sure was a scary day, wasn't it?"

The little boy looked ready to burst into tears again. He nodded quickly.

Nick drew a deep breath and let it out slowly. "There is no way I can make it un-scary for you. Sometimes bad things happen and it's nobody's fault."

"It might be my fault," the boy whispered.

"I'm pretty sure it wasn't, but why don't you tell me why you think it might be."

It was a good response. Miriam waited to see how Nick was going to handle the child.

"I was making too much noise with my dump truck."

"I used to have a dump truck when I was a kid. Is yours yellow?"

Little Danny shook his head. "It's red."

"But the back tips up, right? So you can dump your load of blocks or dirt?"

"Yup. I was dumping rocks on the stairs."

"I've done that."

Danny slanted a questioning gaze at Nick as if he wasn't quite sure he couldn't believe him. "You have?"

"More than once. And sand, too. My mom wasn't very happy with me when I did. Can I see your truck?"

Danny nodded and tromped upstairs. He came down in a few moments with the red plastic truck in his arms. He sat on the floor near Nick's feet and began rolling the truck back and forth, picking up the gravel scattered across the floor. Nick said, "I imagine you could carry a ton of rocks in that thing."

"Yeah. I dumped my load on the stairs, but they rolled down and Dad stepped on one with his bare feet. He got real mad about it. Mom started yelling at him to leave me alone, and then…" His voice trailed away to nothing.

"And then something bad happened, didn't it?" Nick waited patiently for the child to speak. He wasn't rushing the boy or trying to put words in his mouth.

Danny Jr. rolled his truck back and forth for a while, then he rolled it into the stair step. He looked up at Nick. "Dad pushed Mom. She fell and hit her head on the step. There was blood everywhere."

Nick laid a reassuring hand on the boy's small shoulder. "Your mother is okay, Danny. It wasn't a bad cut. Does your dad get mad often? Does he hit your mom?"

Danny Jr. shook his head. "No, so I know this is my fault. I wish he could get a job again. He was happier then."

"Has your dad hit you? Has he hit your sister?"

"No."

Nick nodded. "Danny, I'm going to tell you something that I want you to remember. It is never okay to hit someone, especially a woman or girl, or a boy like you. It doesn't fix things. It only makes things worse."

"Yeah, I kind of knew that."

"I could see you were a pretty smart kid as soon as I met you. Your dad is going to need some help. He needs help dealing with his anger. I'm going to see that he gets that help."

Miriam was impressed with Nick's compassionate handling of the situation. This was a new side to him, one she was glad she had a chance to see.

"Are you going to lock my dad up?" Danny Jr. asked.

"I'm afraid so. It's the only way we can get him the help he needs. Your mom is going to need you to be strong for her."

"She's going to jail, too?" He was close to tears once more.

"No. I don't want you to worry about that. A friend of mine who is a social worker will come and talk to your family about how to deal with being angry without hurting anyone. Now, your mom is pretty upset. She's going to be crying, but I want you to be brave for her and show her that you aren't scared. Can you do that?"

"Maybe." Uncertainty filled his voice again.

"If you don't feel brave, that's okay, too. There are lots of times when I don't feel brave."

"But you are a cop."

"Even cops get scared." Nick rose to his feet and held out his hand. Danny Jr. took it. They crossed the room to where Mary Beth was sitting holding a doll clutched to her chest. Danny Jr. offered his hand. She took it and jumped off the sofa. Nick led them outside.

Miriam held open the screen door for him. "Are you sure you don't want me to wait for you?"

He shook his head. "I'll have a lot of paperwork to do after this. It's best if you take your mother and the baby home."

"All right. I'll see you later." She started down the steps toward his SUV.

He handed the children over to their mother, who was waiting by the squad car. As Nick had predicted, she burst into tears and hugged them both tightly. Inside the squad car, her subdued husband fought back tears as he said goodbye to his family.

Nick followed Miriam to his SUV. He stood beside the door as she got in. "The next time I tell you to stay in the car, Miriam, you'd better do it."

His stern tone rankled. It wasn't as if she had been a liability. Maybe she had overstepped the bounds, but she hadn't been able to stand by and do nothing. She didn't want to respect Nick's authority or his abilities, but she couldn't deny how well he'd handled himself and the child just now. There was a maturity to him that was both calming and attractive. His compassion for the young boy touched her deeply. Nick had become the kind of man she could admire.

Alarm bells started going off in her head. There was

no way she was going to fall for him again. She couldn't let that happen. It was easier to go back to being mad at him than it was to face the slew of new emotions churning in her brain. She scowled at him. "Fair enough, but the next time I see somebody about to swing a two-by-four at your head, I just might keep my mouth shut."

He pressed his lips into a thin line. "Okay, I owe you a debt of thanks for that one."

"Don't mention it," she snapped back.

Nick blew out a deep breath. "I'm sorry if I sound edgy. You may not want to believe this, but I still care about you. I don't know how I could have lived with myself if something had happened to you because I brought you here."

He was right—she didn't want to hear that he still cared about her.

When she didn't reply, he nodded in resignation. "Okay, thanks for your help and now get out of here so I can worry about my job without worrying about you and your mother's safety."

Miriam sketched a brief salute, started his truck and drove out of town. As he did, his words kept echoing in her mind. He still cared about her. What did that mean? Did it change anything? Oddly enough, it did. A small part of her smiled in satisfaction at the thought that Nick still had feelings for her.

They hadn't driven very far when Ada spoke. "There is so much sorrow in the world. Will those children be okay?"

"It's hard to say. If the family accepts and benefits from the counseling, then yes, I think they'll be okay."

"Do you think Hannah could have come from such a home?"

"I hope not, Mother."

Chapter Eight

Miriam didn't know if she was disappointed or relieved when Nick didn't come by the following day. Although he called several times to check on Hannah, Miriam was left to sort out her feelings about Nick without having to face him. No matter how she tried, she couldn't see a clear path ahead of her.

That she was still attracted to him was becoming increasingly clear. That she told herself she didn't want to revive those feelings didn't help. It was as if her body was waking up after a long sleep. She had been moving through life, but the texture had been missing. When Nick was near, she noticed everything, from the brilliant color of the sky to the deep timbre of his voice. She was becoming aware that her life was lonely.

After having destroyed her brother and Natalie's chance at happiness, she hadn't believed she had a right to reach for that same kind of happiness. So why was she suddenly thinking about what it would be like to love and be loved in return?

Miriam's emotions stayed in a state of turmoil over the following two days, but at least Hannah was doing better. Her episodes of fussiness and spitting up had passed. She began sleeping up to four hours at a stretch and woke up alert and eager to interact with anyone who would spend time talking to her. She was well and firmly on her way to embedding herself in Miriam's heart.

When Thursday evening rolled around, Miriam wasn't surprised when Nick's SUV pulled into the yard. Tonight was the night the note said Hannah's mother would return. Miriam knew Nick wanted to be here.

She was on her knees planting rows of black-eyed Susans along the front of the porch. Her mother was watering the rows she had finished on the other side of the steps. Miriam sat back on her heels.

Nick rolled down his window. "Can I park in the barn? I don't want my presence to scare anyone away."

"Go ahead. There should be room beside the buggy."

"Thanks." He strode to the wide barn doors, pulled them open and then drove his truck inside. After closing the door, he walked across the yard. He wasn't wearing his uniform.

Miriam's heart beat a quick pitter-patter when he smiled at her. She sternly reminded herself he was only being friendly and only here because of Hannah. She asked, "Do you think she will show?"

He stuffed his hands in the front pockets of his jeans. "Your guess is as good as mine. I've ferreted out the time and place of a local hoedown if she doesn't. It will give us a chance to ask around among the teenagers and check more buggy tires."

Hoedowns were gatherings of *rumspringa*-aged teenagers that involved loud modern music, dancing and sometimes drinking and even drug use. Amish parents often turned a blind eye to the goings-on, but their children were never far from their prayers. Until a child had a taste of the outside world, he or she could not understand what temptations they would have to give up to live orderly, devout Christian lives in their Plain community.

Ada said, "Supper is almost ready, Nicolas. I hope you like chicken with dumplings."

He patted his stomach. "It's one of my favorites, but you remembered that, didn't you?"

She grinned. "*Ja,* I remember that you and Mark could put away a whole chicken between the two of you and leave the rest of us nothing but dumplings."

Chuckling, she went into the house. Miriam rose to her feet and pulled off her gloves. Now that the time was finally here, she didn't know if she could let Hannah go.

Nick tipped his head to the side. "Another killer night?"

She shook her head and smiled. "No, the new formula is working wonders. She actually slept for five hours last night. I'm just worried, I guess."

"Worried her mother won't come, or worried that she will?"

"Both."

"I know what you mean."

She nodded toward the door. "Come in. I'll get washed up and we can eat. It may be a long night."

During supper, Ada happily reminisced with Nick about the days when he had worked on their farm. Her mother's chatter was unusual. Most Amish meals passed in silence. Nick cast several worried glances at Miriam when her mother brought up Mark, but Miriam kept silent. For some reason, listening to talk of her brother no longer brought her the sharp pain it once had. She missed Mark dearly, but listening to her mother's and Nick's stories about Mark's life brought Miriam a measure of comfort. Mark was gone—he would never be forgotten. Not by Miriam and her mother and not by Nick.

When the meal was over and the table cleared, Ada went to bed leaving Nick and Miriam alone in the kitchen. He said, "It's a nice night, shall we sit outside for a while?"

Miriam glanced at the baby. "Sure. Hannah will make herself heard if she needs anything."

When they were both seated in the rockers on the front porch, silence descended between them. It was a comfortable silence broken only by the sounds of the night, the creaking of the windmill, insect chirpings and the distant lowing of cattle.

Nick said, "I'm sorry if Ada talking about Mark upset you."

"She needs her good memories. It's okay."

From inside the house, Hannah began making noises. Bella came to the door and barked. Miriam rose from her chair and moved past Nick, but he reached out and grasped her hand. "We all need to hold on to good memories," he said quietly.

Was he talking about Mark or about his memories of her? How would things have turned out between them if Mark had lived?

It was foolish to wonder such things, yet she did wonder.

His hand was warm and strong as he held her cold fingers. They quickly grew heated as a flush flooded her body. Bella barked again.

"Is there a chance we can be friends again?"

"I don't know," she answered quietly. She pulled her hand away and went inside, grateful that she had a few minutes to marshal her wild response to his touch. The simple contact of his hand had sent her reeling with a flood of memories. She remembered holding hands with him as they crossed the creek on the way to their favorite fishing hole. Once, he'd taken her in his arms to show her the way the *Englisch* teenagers slow danced together. Mark had been there, making fun of her awkward attempts to dance, laughing with them when Nick slipped and fell in the creek and his big fish got away.

They were good memories of a better time. Could she and Nick be friends again? She didn't see how. Too much stood between them, but seeing Nick every day was helping her heal—something she'd never thought would happen.

After feeding Hannah, Miriam retreated to the cot in the kitchen. She slept in snatches, waking at every creak or groan from the old house. Nick, if he slept at all, lay sprawled on the sofa in the living room. Twice Ada came into the kitchen to check on Hannah and to scan the lane but no buggy appeared. When dawn finally lit the sky, Nick came into the kitchen and began to stoke the coals in the stove. After that, he fixed a pot of coffee.

When he had it brewing he took a seat at the table. Miriam pushed her hair out of her face and joined him. "Now what?"

"We are back where we started from."

As much as Miriam wanted to help Hannah's mother, she was secretly glad the woman hadn't shown up. She didn't want to give Hannah back. If only there was a way to keep her.

* * *

"Nick tells me you are coming to my wedding tomorrow. I'm so glad." Amber had arrived for Hannah's checkup on Friday afternoon. After she had weighed, measured and examined the baby, she turned her full attention to Miriam.

"I didn't say yes. I said I'd think about it. Mother hasn't been feeling well, and I don't like to leave her alone with the baby."

"Please come. I'll stop by the Wadler Inn and ask Naomi Wadler to come and keep your mother company. She mentioned wanting to drop in for a visit. Tomorrow would be the perfect time. If someone can stay with your mother will you come?"

"I really don't have anything to wear." Miriam still felt strange about her last-minute inclusion. She didn't know Amber that well, and she didn't know Dr. Philip White at all.

"That is absolutely the lamest excuse I've ever heard. You know that I have Plain relatives. My wedding is going to be far from fancy and as long as you don't come in a bathing suit, I'm okay with what you wear."

Miriam grinned. "I was just thinking how nice I would look in my teeny-weeny bikini."

"Is it yellow with polka dots?" Amber's eyes sparkled with mirth.

"How did you guess?"

"No, you can't wear that. I don't want Phillip's eyes on anyone but me. Nick, on the other hand, will be sorely disappointed when I tell him what you had in mind."

Miriam looked down at Hannah in her crib. "I'm sure that Sheriff Bradley couldn't care less about what I wear."

Amber tipped her head to the side. "I'm not so sure about that. Have the two of you overcome your differences? I had hoped that this situation would help. I pray that you can find it in your heart to forgive Nick for his part in your brother's death. I know Nick as well as anyone can. I know he would never willingly hurt someone."

Miriam wasn't ready to discuss her feelings for Nick. "Can we talk about something else?"

"I'm sorry. I was out of line, wasn't I? Phillip tells me I get carried away in my quests to right the wrongs of the world. Please don't let my foolish mouth keep you from coming to the wedding. You have to come, if for no other reason than to meet the most wonderful man in the world. I won't take no for an answer." Amber gave Miriam one of her endearing smiles.

"If you can find someone to stay with Mother and the baby, I'll come."

Amber squealed with delight and hugged her. Later that night, Amber called to tell Miriam that Naomi was thrilled to come and visit with Ada.

The following morning, Miriam picked through the clothes in her closet with disdain. She hadn't been lying yesterday. She didn't have a thing to wear that was wedding appropriate. A stay in an Amish household didn't lend itself to fancy attire.

Although she was sure the bride wouldn't notice what she had on, Miriam was afraid Nick would notice. He had a way of looking at her that made her sure he could see all the way through her.

After choosing a simple green skirt with a white blouse, Miriam slipped on her favorite high-heeled sandals and went downstairs. Her mother was rocking the baby and humming an Amish lullaby.

"Are you sure you will be okay while I'm gone?" Miriam asked.

"I'll be fine. Naomi Wadler will be here. She and I will have a nice visit. Do not worry your head about us."

"I won't be gone long." Miriam gathered her purse and car keys from the small table by the front door. Should she leave? She didn't want to disappoint Amber.

And Nick was going to be there.

The prospect didn't fill her with alarm the way it once had. Nick was a good man, not the monster she had tried to make him out to be.

"Are you leaving, or are you going to stand there staring off into nothing?"

Her mother's comment dispelled Miriam's sober thoughts. "I'm going. My cell phone will be right here on the table. Nick's number is in it. He will be at the wedding, too. If you need anything, he will get ahold of me."

"You know that I don't like that thing."

Miriam crossed the room and dropped a kiss on her mother forehead. "I know you don't like it, and I also know that you know how to use it. I'm not worried about you, I'm worried about Hannah."

The frown left Ada's face. "She hasn't been fussy in days. We will be fine."

"Maybe I should stay home. I don't know that Amber will miss me at her own wedding."

"You told her you would come so you must go. Hurry now, or you will be late. There will be a lot of buggies on the road. Amber is very well liked among our people and many will want to celebrate with her on this blessed day."

"Okay, I'll go, if only to see what her future husband looks like."

On her way out the lane, she met Naomi in her buggy coming in. That gave her one less worry. Her mother's prediction proved true. There were almost as many buggies lining the streets and in the church parking lot as there were automobiles. Inside the white clapboard structure of the Hope Springs Fellowship Church, she signed the guest book and took the arm the usher offered her. She allowed him to escort her to the bride's side of the aisle.

The church was nearly full. Many of the guests were wearing Amish dress and children were everywhere. Soft organ music filled the air. To her dismay, the usher stopped and indicated a seat next to Nick Bradley.

She looked around quickly, but there wasn't another empty spot close at hand. Unless she wanted to make a scene by cutting Nick directly, she would have to endure the ceremony seated beside him. Would he be able to tell the way her heart beat faster when he was close?

He scooted over slightly to make more room. There was no hope of finding a seat elsewhere. She graciously thanked the usher, sat down, gave Nick a friendly smile and proceeded to ignore him. What she couldn't ignore was the rapid rush of blood to her skin. She opened her collar slightly and fanned herself.

He leaned close. "Hot?"

His breath stirred the hairs on her temple and sent her temperature up another notch.

"A little. I had to rush to get here." *Please don't let him think it's because of his nearness.*

"I was afraid you wouldn't come. You look nice, by the way. Those are cute shoes."

Cute shoes? What man noticed a woman's shoes? She gave him a sidelong glance.

"Three sisters," he said in answer to her unspoken question.

He turned to speak to the person on the other side of him. It gave Miriam the chance to gather her composure and survey her surroundings.

It was her first time attending a service at the Hope Springs Fellowship Church. The inside of the church was simple and elegant with dark, rich wood paneling and brilliantly colored stained-glass windows. Off to one side of the altar, a young woman continued playing the organ. It felt good to be back in church. She had avoided going for fear of running into Nick. Now that her fear was no longer a factor, she was free to worship as she normally did. The soothing sounds of the beautiful melody began to ease the tension from Miriam's body. It was then she noticed the sound of muffled crying.

Looking across the aisle, she saw a woman in her late sixties crying softly into a lavender lace hanky that perfectly matched her lavender suit and hat.

Overcome with curiosity, Miriam whispered to Nick, "Who is the weeping woman?"

Nick leaned forward to look around her. He sat back with a grin on his face. "That is Gina Curtis. She is something of a town character. She is very attached to Dr. Phillip. When everyone else considered her a hypochondriac, he correctly diagnosed her fibromyalgia. I think she has been in love with him ever since, but she cries at everyone's wedding so it's hard to tell."

Miriam nodded, and then sat in awkward silence. *Please, Lord, let this be a quick ceremony.*

The organ music suddenly stopped as the minister

and three men entered from a door behind the pulpit. As they arranged themselves at the front, the organist began the familiar strains of the "Wedding March."

The congregation rose and turned to see a pair of bridesmaids in plum dresses carrying small bouquets of pink roses. Amber, a vision in a simple A-line satin gown with lace cap sleeves and a short veil, started down the aisle on the arm of a short stout man that Miriam assumed was her father. As she approached the front of the church, Miriam saw she had eyes for only one person in the building—the tall man waiting for her beside the minister.

Phillip looked a great deal like his grandfather, Dr. Harold White, but where Dr. Harold looked distinguished with his high cheekbones and white hair, Dr. Phillip looked downright delicious. He was movie-star gorgeous with a deep tan, sun-streaked light brown hair that curled slightly above his collar and eyes so blue they looked like sapphires.

She glanced at Nick beside her. He was a good-looking man, too, but in a rugged way that she preferred to the young doctor's suave features. When the music stopped, Miriam listened to the preacher's sermon about the way love allows us to accept the faults of others and how that same love makes us strive to mend our own faults for them.

Amber and Phillip then faced each other for the exchange of vows. When it came time for Phillip to slip the ring on Amber's finger, he fumbled and dropped it. The ring went rolling across the floor. The minister stopped its flight by stepping on it.

He picked up the golden circle and held it aloft. "My grandmother used to say that something had to go wrong in the wedding or it will go wrong in the marriage. Not that I believe in such superstitions, but let's all be glad that Amber and Phillip are off to the best start possible."

The congregation laughed. The minister gave the ring back to Phillip and this time he placed it on Amber's hand without incident. Everyone applauded when he kissed his bride.

Miriam glanced at Nick. He was smiling—not at Amber, but at Miriam. She looked away quickly, but not before her heart did a funny little flip-flop in response. If things had been different, it could have been them standing together in front of their family and friends. Was he thinking the same thing?

After the wedding service, Miriam descended the steps of the church. Around her, families and friends were gathered in small groups, catching up on the latest news and events of the week. People surrounded Amber and Phillip. Words of congratulations and well-wishes flowed around them. Every one, including Miriam, was happy for them. It was clear they were very much in love.

Rather than join a group, she turned aside and walked along the path that led behind the church to a small footbridge that spanned a brook at the edge of the church property. The source of the clear, small stream lay a short way uphill—the gurgling spring from which Hope Springs had derived its name.

When she reached the secluded bridge, she saw she wasn't the only one seeking solitude. Nick stood at the far end of the bridge staring upstream. His brow was furrowed in concentration. She started to turn away, loath to disturb him, but he spoke suddenly.

"Do you ever wonder where the water comes from? I

mean, I know it comes out of the earth, but before it was trapped underground, it had to come from somewhere."

"I never thought about it."

"When I was a kid, I thought the gurgling of the water was laughter, delight at being out in the sun and the air again. It still sounds like that to me."

She leaned against the opposite railing and looked down at the water slipping over and around stones as it raced away downhill. "I think about where the water is going. It's just starting its journey. Imagine all the places and people it will pass on the way to the sea."

The silence lengthened between them. The sounds of the birds in the trees and the gurgling brook were soothing. It didn't surprise her that Nick was so introspective. He was someone who heard laughter in the sounds of a brook and truth in a little boy's worried words.

Silence was making her more aware of Nick's presence even though he stood a good six feet away and outside her line of sight. "It was a nice wedding," she said at last.

"All weddings are nice, aren't they? They mark the beginning of what everyone hopes will be a blessed union. To bad it doesn't always work out that way."

"You sound like you're speaking from personal experience."

"I've never taken that plunge. I was thinking about my folks."

"I'm sorry."

"It was what it was. Mom couldn't reconcile herself to living the life of a cop's wife. One day, after one of their ugly fights, she told him she wished he would leave and never come back. After he was killed, she couldn't deal with the guilt she carried."

"I've been told guilt is a useless emotion." Useless but so hard to put away.

"It's also a very powerful emotion."

"Yes, it is." Reuniting Hannah with her mother would be Miriam's way of making up for the tragedy she had instigated so many years ago.

More than anything, Nick wanted to know what Miriam was thinking. He had hidden his surprise when she sought him out. He didn't want to break the tenuous thread that kept her from running away again. So instead of moving closer, he stayed put, allowing her to control the situation.

His heart ached to gather her in his arms and hold her close. He'd once dreamed of asking Miriam to marry him. Seeing the love and joy in Amber's and Phillip's eyes had driven home just how much he wanted to resurrect that sweet dream. Did he dare hope that Miriam was softening toward him? Didn't her presence here prove that? He prayed God would show him the way to heal Miriam's heart. His every instinct told him that if he moved one step closer she might flee.

"The sound of the water is soothing," Nick said, quietly.

"Yes, it is."

She didn't leave, but stood listening to the water with him. It gave him a reason to hope, a reason to believe they could repair the love they had once shared. He wanted that more than anything, because he was once more falling in love with Miriam Kauffman.

Chapter Nine

Miriam gave Hannah a kiss on the top of her head before laying the baby in her crib late Monday morning. She had slept for five hours during the night and Miriam was feeling like a new woman after that much sleep. Ada, stirring a kettle of soup on the stove, said, "You are taken with her, aren't you?"

"Who wouldn't be? She's so precious."

"*Ja,* I feel it, too. The love for a child is a powerful thing."

"I know I said I wouldn't get too attached to her, but it's already too late." Hannah was firmly embedded in her heart. Giving her up was going to hurt terribly.

Ada came and wrapped one arm around Miriam. "She has crept into my heart, too."

"I think we made a mistake trying to keep her until her mother came back. All we did was set ourselves up for a big heartache."

"Heartaches are part of life, child. God brought this baby to us for a reason. We can only pray that He shows us His will."

Miriam's cell phone rang. She stepped outside on the

porch to answer it to avoid her mother's disapproving glare. It was Dr. Zook on the other end.

"Miriam, I need you to bring Hannah into the office today."

A knot of worry formed in Miriam's stomach. "Why?"

"We need to repeat some of her blood tests. I'm afraid her MSUD screen has come back positive."

"MSUD? Hannah has Maple syrup urine disease?" Miriam sank onto the porch steps. Bella came from beneath the porch and sat beside her.

Dr. Zook said, "Let me stress that this may be a false positive. We need to double-check before we assume the worst."

"How often do you have a false positive?"

He hesitated, then said, "Not often but it does happen. I'm sorry to worry you but there is treatment now for this disorder if the test is correct."

"Treatment, but no cure."

"I'm afraid not. We'll repeat the test to be doubly sure, but in the meantime, you need to make a formula change right away. We have cans of a special powdered formula that you can start using today."

"I'll be there as soon as I can." Miriam closed her phone and stared at nothing. Her beautiful little baby might have a genetic disorder that in worst-case scenarios could lead to mental retardation and complete paralysis of her body, even death. The unfairness of it overwhelmed her.

Wasn't it enough that Hannah's mother had given her away? Why did God laid this burden on a helpless child? She wrapped her arms around Bella and burst into tears.

An hour later, she helped her mother out of the car and lifted Hannah from her car seat. As they approached the front door of the clinic, Nick's SUV spewed gravel as he turned into the parking lot and pulled up beside them.

He jumped out of his vehicle and slammed the door. His hair was still damp and he had one missed button on the front of the shirt. "Dr. Zook just called me. I could tell from his voice that this is serious, but how serious?"

"That's what we have to find out. There are variations of the disease. Some types are not as serious as others."

"Do we know what type she has?"

"They aren't sure she has it. That's why she needs further testing."

He pulled the clinic door open so that she could go in. Wilma rose from behind the desk and came forward to meet them. "Dr. White and Dr. Zook are waiting for you in Dr. White's office. I'll show you the way."

Miriam followed her down the hallway with growing dread. She prayed as she had never prayed before. *Please let this be a false alarm, Lord.*

When Wilma held open a door, Miriam froze, unable to move forward. She felt a comforting hand on her shoulder and turned to look at her mother but it was Nick who stood beside her. He said softly, "We can bear all things with God's help. He is with us always."

She nodded, drew a deep breath then walked in.

Dr. White was seated at his desk, his head of snow-white hair bent over a book laid open on his desk. Dr. Zook stood beside him. As soon as he saw Nick was with them, he said, "I'm glad you could all make it. Miriam and Ada, please have a seat. I'll get another chair for you, Nick."

He shook his head. "I'd rather stand."

Dr. White closed his book and laced his fingers together. "I'm sure hearing that Hannah may have MSUD is very disturbing news."

Nick said, "You're going to have to use plain English, Doc. I don't know what your medical terms mean. I'm sure Ada doesn't, either."

"My apologies, Sheriff. MSUD, or maple syrup urine disease, is an inherited disorder. It's a rare disorder in the general population, only about one in every 185,000 births worldwide. Unfortunately, in the Amish and Old Order Mennonite communities the incidence is much higher. Almost 1 in every 380 Amish children will have some form of this disease."

"What type does Hannah have?" Nick asked.

"Let me stress that we aren't sure she does have it. However, in the most severe cases, a child's body is unable to properly process certain protein building blocks called amino acids. The three essential amino acids a child can't break down are leucine, isoleucine and valine. They are often referred to as the branched-chain amino acids or BCAAs. The condition actually gets its name from the distinctive sweet odor of affected infants' urine."

"I haven't noticed that," Miriam said quickly, hoping to prove their diagnosis was wrong.

Dr. Zook said, "Not all babies will show that symptom until they are in crisis. It used to be that babies with this condition showed poor feeding, frequent vomiting, a lack of energy and finally developmental delays before anyone knew what was wrong with them. Fortunately, in recent years all babies in the state of Ohio began being tested for this condition because if untreated, maple syrup urine disease can lead to seizures, coma, paralysis and death."

Nick looked from Dr. Zook to Dr. White. "If left untreated. That means there is treatment available, right?"

"Yes." Dr. White extended a pamphlet toward Nick and Miriam. "Treatment of MSUD involves a carefully controlled diet that strictly limits dietary protein in order to prevent the accumulation of BCAAs in the blood. The cornerstone of this diet is a special formula that does not contain any leucine, isoleucine or valine but is otherwise nutritionally complete. It contains all the necessary vitamins, minerals, calories and the other amino acids needed for normal growth."

"How soon do we start it?" Miriam asked. This shouldn't be happening. It wasn't fair, but then how often was life really fair? Without Hannah's family in the picture it would be up to Miriam to give the baby the best possible start in life.

Dr. Zook gave her a sympathetic smile. "Initially, Hannah will need the MSUD formula to be supplemented with carefully controlled amounts of the protein-based baby formula she is on now until we know for certain that the test is correct. It if is, I'm afraid Hannah is going to become a frequent flyer here. She will need frequent monitoring of her blood levels."

"Will she grow out of this?" Nick asked. He was grasping at straws. Miriam knew better.

Dr. White shook his head. "No. Lifelong therapy is essential. Typically, the MSUD diet excludes high protein foods such as meat, nuts, eggs and most dairy products."

Dr. Zook said, "Children can gradually learn to accept the responsibility for controlling their diets, however, there is no age at which diet treatment can be stopped."

Ada had remained silent until now. "What does this mean for her mother and father?"

Dr. Zook and Dr. White exchanged glances. Miriam said, "If the test is correct, it means they both carry the MSUD gene. If they have more children together, there is a strong possibility that those children will have the same disease."

A strange look came over Ada's face. "It is *Gottes wille* if their children are sick or if they are healthy. Perhaps that is why He brought the child to you, Miriam. So that your knowledge can help her."

It was the first time her mother had even come close to admitting that Miriam's education was a good thing.

Dr. White sat back in his chair. "What is really important is that we make sure we have correct test results. Let's not panic until we know for sure she has this thing. In the meantime, we don't allow Hannah to develop a BBCA crisis. High fever, vomiting or diarrhea, not eating, these can all trigger an elevated level of BBCA in her blood, and that can lead to brain damage. She is going to require close medical supervision."

Nick asked, "Should she be hospitalized now? What kind of further testing does she need?"

Dr. White rose to his feet and came around the desk. He perched on the corner and reached for Hannah. Miriam handed the baby over to him. He lifted her to his shoulder and bounced her gently. Looking at Nick, he said, "You are wondering if you made a mistake by allowing Amber and these women to talk you into keeping the baby out of child care services."

"Did I?"

"I don't believe so. There's no reason to hospitalize

Hannah at this point. We can draw the additional blood we need for testing here."

Miriam saw the tension ease in Nick's shoulders. Dr. White continued, "No one has more respect for the Amish than I do, Sheriff. They welcome and lovingly accept children with any kind of disability as a gift from God. Fewer and fewer people in the general population feel the same way. If her mother doesn't return for her, I would hope that she can be adopted by an Amish couple here in this community."

Miriam stood and took the baby from Dr. White. "How can I get the formula that Hannah needs?"

Dr. Zook smiled at her. "We have some that we can give you. I will also give you the number of our formula supplier so that you can order all you need."

"Thank you."

Dr. Zook moved to open the door. "If you'll come with me, we can draw her blood. We should have the final test results back in about twenty-four to forty-eight hours. Hopefully, all this worry will be for nothing."

Nick stayed behind as the women left. Folding his arm over his chest, he spoke to Dr. White. "I wish I could compel you to reveal all you know about Hannah's mother."

"Sheriff, I wish I had something to reveal. Sadly, I don't know any more than you do."

"But you have seen this disorder in families around Hope Springs."

"I have. Too many times, as a matter of fact."

"I don't suppose you could give me a list of those families' names. I don't mind looking for a needle in haystack, but if I could have a smaller haystack to search, that would be better."

Dr. White chuckled. "I can imagine it would. I'm sorry I can't be more help. The baby is in good hands now, and that is what's important. I hear that you've been checking buggies all over the county."

"The buggy that left Hannah at Miriam's had a crack in the left rear wheel in the shape of a long Z. It's all we have to go on. I must have looked at over a hundred buggies, and I haven't been able to locate it."

"Levi Beachy is here waiting to get stitches taken out of his hand. He's the local buggy maker. It's possible he might know who owns a rig with a wheel like that. I'll tell him you'd like to speak to him."

"Thanks, Doc."

Nick left the office and saw Miriam waiting outside by the car. She looked tearful and worried. All he wanted was to hold her close and reassure her.

No, he wanted much more than that. He wanted to tell her that he loved the color of her hair. That he loved the way her eyes sparkled when she was happy. That he wanted to spend the rest of his life making her eyes sparkle.

A dozen ways to tell her how much he cared about her ran through his mind. None of them seemed like the right thing to say at the moment. Soon, he would find a way to tell her how he felt and pray that she might return his affection. Soon, but not now.

He didn't see Hannah or Ada as he left the clinic and stopped beside Miriam.

"At least it's a treatable disease," she said before he could say anything.

"That's right and she may not even have it. Where is your mother?"

"She's changing Hannah. I needed some fresh air." She pressed a hand to her mouth. Her eyes filled with unshed tears. "I'm so scared for her, Nick. Any illness she gets could result in permanent brain damage. A bad cold, the flu..."

Nick wrapped his arms around her and pulled her close. He pressed a kiss to her forehead. "I know you're scared. I'm scared, too."

Her arms crept around his shoulders. To his surprise, she returned his hug. "How is a teenage Amish mother going to handle this if I'm terrified and I'm a critical care nurse?"

"Maybe we should stop looking for her." Nick held his breath as he waited for Miriam's reply.

Softly, she said, "I've thought of that. Hannah is so easy to love. The longer she stays with me the harder it's going to be to give her up. Now that I know she may be sick, I can't bear to let her go."

Nick stepped back and held Miriam at arm's length. "There may be a way for you to keep her. Have you heard of being a treatment foster parent?"

"Of course I've heard of it. They are foster parents that provide medical care to children with emotional or serious medical problems."

"Right. There is an agency called The Children's Haven, Incorporated. They cover foster children in Ohio and Indiana. I might be wrong, but I would think a registered nurse, who's already a foster parent in Ohio, would have an easy time becoming one for them. If I were you, I'd start making phone calls."

"How do you know about this?"

"It's called the internet. Ten minutes with a search engine was all it took."

"And when did you do this search?"

"Last Monday after I left your place.

"We didn't know about Hannah's condition then."

"I've watched you with her. You looked at her the way other mothers look at their babies. I can see that you love her, even when she's throwing up on you. Since I knew you were already a foster parent, I wanted to see if there was a way for you to keep her. It seemed worth a shot to do some research."

"I'm stunned."

"The Children's Haven was one of the sites I ran across. Now that she may have this disorder, it makes me believe that God intends for you to take care of her."

Nick's revelation was a stunning one. Miriam wanted to believe she might be more than a temporary part of God's plan for Hannah. "Do you really think so, Nick?"

"He had some reason to lead Hannah's mother to your house."

The clinic door opened and a young Amish man came out. He wore dark trousers and a pale blue shirt and sported a straw hat on his head of curly brown hair. He was clean shaven. Only married Amish men wore beards. He had a thick dressing around his left hand.

He stopped in front of Nick, but wouldn't meet his eyes. It took him a moment to speak. "I'm Levi Beachy. The doctor said…ya wanted to know about a buggy with a broken rim."

Miriam and Nick exchanged a quick glance. Nick said, "Yes."

"It was my buggy. I replaced the wheel rim two days ago." His face grew beet-red as he spoke.

"Did you visit Miriam Kauffman's farm a week ago on Thursday night?"

"*Nee,* I did not." The man looked up at last. Miriam realized he was painfully shy. He took a step back and tried to hurry away, but Nick called out, "Do you have twin brothers about sixteen years old?"

He stopped, but he didn't meet Nick's gaze. "I do."

"Could they have taken your buggy without you knowing it?"

"What night did you say that was?"

"It would have been a Thursday night."

Levi rubbed the back of his neck. "My best mare came up lame on Friday morning for no reason. I mentioned it to the boys, they didn't say anything, but I did wonder if they'd taken her out and driven her hard. I don't like to pry."

Nick said, "I need to talk to those boys."

"They're at home." Levi nodded to the Sheriff and walked away down the street.

Miriam said, "I should come with you."

"I can handle it."

She said, "I know you can handle it. I also know that I am less intimidating than you are. They might be more willing to confide in me."

He considered it for a moment and said, "All right, we'll go out there together, but let's take Hannah and your mother home first."

"What shall we tell Mom?"

"The truth. That we're checking a lead, but it could be a wild-goose chase."

Miriam agreed. After taking her mother and the baby

back to the farm, Miriam climbed into Nick's SUV for the trip back.

"I had a feeling those two boys knew more than they were saying." Nick sped up to pass a wagon pulled by two large draft horses.

"When did you talk to them?"

"The day of the market, I saw them following you and I asked them what their interest was. They said they wanted to find out how much you would charge to drive them to Cincinnati. I don't think either one of them is the father. You should've seen their faces when I asked them point-blank if they were."

Miriam said, "I believe the buggy shop is on the east side of town."

"I know where it is. It used to belong to Sarah Wyse's husband before he died."

A few minutes later, they pulled into a lot with buggies ringing the perimeter. They were in all stages of construction and repair.

Miriam saw a young woman sweeping the front steps of the office. She stopped work, and waited until Nick and Miriam approached. "Good day. I'm Grace Beachy, how may I help you?"

Nick said, "You can tell us how to find Atlee and Moses."

"My brothers are chopping wood behind house. Shall I get them for you?"

Nick shook his head. "I'll find them."

Miriam remained silent and followed his lead. Behind the small house, the twins were splitting logs at such a rapid pace than Miriam knew it had to be a contest.

One of them, she couldn't tell them apart, caught

sight of her and stopped swinging. A wary look crossed his face. He spoke to his brother who instantly stopped working as well.

Nick surveyed them closely. "Afternoon. Which one of you is winning?"

"I reckon we're about tied."

Nick pointed to the ground. "I want both of you to put your axes down and answer a few questions."

One rolled his eyes at his brother. "Told you that you didn't fool him, Moses."

"You should hush, Atlee." They both laid their axes aside.

Nick stepped closer and towered over the two of them. "No, I want you to keep talking. A week ago on Thursday night, a buggy with a cracked rim on the left rear wheel drove up to Ada Kauffman's place and left a baby on her doorstep. I don't think you know how much trouble you are in. You had better tell me everything I want to know."

Atlee looked at Miriam. "The baby was all right, wasn't it?"

"Where is her mother?" Nick demanded.

The two boys looked at each other. Atlee said, "I told you it was a bad idea."

"Like you wanted to bring it home and say, Levi, look what we found while we was over to Millersburg without you knowing it? We'd be chopping wood until Christmas."

Nick growled, "Anything your brother would do or say will pale in comparison to spending time in jail. Where is the mother?"

Atlee spread his hands wide. "We don't know. We sneaked out after Levi went to bed and took the buggy into Sugarcreek. We left the buggy there and went to see a movie in Millersburg with some *Englisch* friends."

"Friends?" Nick arched one eyebrow.

Atlee said, "Girls we met a few weeks ago at a hoe-down. One of them has a car."

Moses said, "After the movie we came straight back to the buggy and home."

"Well, we meant to come straight home," Atlee conceded.

"We didn't know the baby was in the buggy until we were almost to the Kauffman place."

Miriam held up one hand. "Wait a minute. Someone put the baby in your buggy while you were at the movies?"

The twins nodded. Miriam tried to wrap her brain around what they were saying. "You don't know who did it?"

"No, honest we don't," Atlee insisted.

"How did you boys know that I was a nurse?" She glanced between their faces.

They looked at each other and shook their heads. Moses said, "We didn't."

Nick stepped closer with a fierce scowl darkening his face. "I don't believe you."

Atlee's eyes widened in fear. "It's true. We left the buggy in the parking lot at the convenience store. On the way home, we stopped when we heard the baby crying. Who would give us a baby? We didn't know what to do. We couldn't take it home with us, 'cause then Levi would know we'd been sneaking away. Moses knew Ada Kauffman didn't have grandchildren. We thought she might like a baby, and her farm was the closest."

Nick turned away and ran a hand through his hair. "This is unbelievable."

"It's the truth." Atlee looked ready to cry.

Nick paced across the grass and came back. "Hannah's mother didn't choose a safe place for her. She stashed her in the back of a buggy in a parking lot. We're lucky she didn't pick a trash can instead. These two just dropped her at the closest farm. This is child abandonment and child endangerment with reckless disregard for the baby's safety. I've wasted more than a week of investigation time."

Miriam pressed her hands to her mouth. "Oh, that poor, poor woman. She must be dying inside since no one returned with her child. How terrible it must have been to wait for someone who never came, and now she has no idea where her baby is or even if she is safe."

Chapter Ten

Nick struggled to rein in his anger and frustration. He had no one but himself to blame for the situation. He had allowed his feelings for Miriam to override his sense of duty and his better judgment.

Atlee Beachy and his brother Moses fidgeted as they waited for him to say something. He let them wait. All he had to show for a week of investigative work was a pair of scared sixteen-year-olds worried that they were going to jail or that their brother would be mad.

They had every right to worry. He did, too. They had all helped cover up a crime, but he was the one who should've known better.

"What do we do now?" Miriam asked.

He looked into her beautiful green eyes so filled with concern. Any second now, she was going to realize that Hannah had to go into protective custody. She was an abandoned child in need of care. The law was very clear on what he had to do.

He said, "We can't keep waiting for her Amish mother to reappear. Unless she reports her baby as missing, our hands are tied."

Her eyes widened and he knew the reality of the situation was sinking in. He would have to take Hannah away from her and her mother.

His heart ached for the pain he knew she was going through. The pain he was causing.

He laid a hand on her shoulder. "We don't know that Hannah's mother is even Amish. The note didn't say that. We only assumed it."

He had a crime scene that spread from one end of his county to the other. After so long, he could only pray he'd find some leads to follow.

"Are we in trouble?" Moses Beachy's voice cracked when he spoke.

"Yes!" Nick snapped as he spun back toward them. He was tempted to haul them down to the station just to make himself feel better, but it probably wouldn't help.

He said, "I am going to impound the buggy and have a forensic team go over it with a fine-tooth comb. Hopefully, there is still some evidence left. Are you sure you didn't see who left the baby?"

They shook their heads. "All we saw was a bad movie," Atlee said.

Glaring at the boys, Nick said, "I should take you both in for child endangerment. Did it even cross your minds that you should notify the authorities when you found her?"

"We did think about taking her to Bishop Zook," Atlee admitted.

Miriam laid a hand on Nick's arm. "It won't do any good to arrest them."

"It will make me feel better."

"But it won't get us any closer to finding Hannah's mother."

"The odds of us locating her now are next to nothing. Even if she came back, as she said she would, her baby wasn't there and she didn't report her as missing. Atlee, Moses, go tell your brother that someone from the sheriff's office will come to pick up the buggy. And tell him why."

They took off leaving him alone with Miriam. She said, "This is all my fault. I should've let you start an investigation right away."

"There is enough fault to go around." He headed toward his truck. She followed behind him. Opening the driver's-side door, he picked up his radio and started giving instructions to the dispatch desk. When he finished, he looked up to see Levi Beachy striding toward him with two chastened boys at his heels.

Levi stopped beside Nick. "My brothers have told me what they did. They wish to help in any way they can."

"I want them to separately write out what went on the entire time they were gone from home. One of my deputies will be out later to question them. If they think of anything else that might help, I want you to call me."

"*Ja,* it will be as you say." Levi spoke to his brothers in quick Pennsylvania Dutch. Nick didn't understand all the words but he recognized the tone. The twins were going to be chopping wood until long past Christmas.

When they left, Nick turned to Miriam. With a sinking feeling in his stomach, he said, "I need to go pick up Hannah."

"No. Isn't there something you can do? Some way she can stay with us?" Her eyes pleaded with him to agree. He was going to give her one more reason to hate him.

"I've got no choice in the matter, Miriam. I'm sorry."

* * *

Miriam could see that it would be useless to argue with Nick. She'd opened her heart to Hannah and now she was paying the price. Why had she done something so stupid when she knew how much it hurt to lose her?

Nick said, "Get in. I have to get rolling on this."

He was angry and he had every right to be upset. He loved Hannah, too. This couldn't be easy for him.

Miriam went around the SUV and climbed in. As soon as she clicked her seat belt, he sped out of the parking lot and onto the highway. He didn't slow down until he reached her mother's lane.

When he stopped in front of her house, she hesitated to get out. "Mother is going to be upset. She's become so attached to Hannah. That baby has become the grandchild she never had."

He bowed his head and closed his eyes. "I know. I don't want to do this."

"Is there a chance she could be returned to us?" Miriam was ready to grasp at straws.

He shifted in his seat to face her. "Now that we know her mother abandoned her, she won't be put up for adoption anytime soon. Efforts have to be made to locate family and see if there is anyone suitable to take her. Her placement will be up to Child Protective Services and Judge Harbin."

"I'm sorry, Nick."

He looked toward the house. "We should go in."

"I know." She didn't move.

Miriam sat beside him in silence for a few more minutes. He finally opened his door and put an end to their procrastination. Miriam followed him to the house with lagging steps.

Inside, Ada was rocking Hannah and singing a lullaby. She looked up with a happy grin. "She is such a charmer. She smiled at me. I don't believe she is sick. The doctors are wrong about that. They are wrong about things all the time."

Miriam crossed the kitchen and knelt beside her mother's chair. "*Mamm,* there is something we need to tell you."

Ada's grin faded. "What is it, Miriam? You look so serious."

Nick stepped up. "We went to see Levi Beachy, the buggy maker."

Ada held Hannah closer. "Does he know something about our baby's mother?"

Miriam nodded. "It was his buggy that left the mark on our lane. His brothers took the buggy without his knowledge."

"Boys will be boys. The twins are in their *rum-springa.* So why did they come here?"

Nick said, "They drove to Sugarcreek and met some friend who took them to see a movie. While they were there, someone left Hannah in their buggy. They don't know who it was. When they realized what had happened, they were near your lane and decided to leave Hannah with you."

Miriam laid a hand on her mother's arm. "Hannah's mother may not be Amish. She won't be coming for her. She doesn't know where she is."

"That is *goot.* Hannah can stay with us, *ja?*"

"No, *Mamm.* Hannah can't stay with us anymore. She has to go with Nick. She must go with the *Englisch.* It is the law. They will find a wonderful home for her with parents who will love and care for her."

"I can love and care for her." Ada pressed the baby against her chest so tightly that Hannah began to fuss.

Nick dropped to one knee beside the rocker. "I'm sorry, Ada. She must come with me. Please let me have her. Don't make this any harder."

"No. You can't take my boy away from me and then take this baby, too. It isn't right." She began to sob.

"It's all right, mother. It will be okay." Miriam gently took the baby from her mother's arms. She rose to her feet and carried the baby to her crib.

"Ada? Ada, what's wrong?"

Miriam turned around when she heard the panic in Nick's voice. Her mother was slumped in her chair holding her left arm across her chest. Her face was ashen colored, and twisted into a grimace of pain. Miriam hurried to her side. "*Mamm,* are you all right?"

"I can't…get my breath," Ada gasped.

Nick jerked his phone from his pocket. "I'm calling 9-1-1."

Miriam laid a hand on her mother's forehead. Her skin was cool and clammy. Grasping Ada's wrist, she felt a weak irregular pulse. It wasn't good. She looked up at Nick. "Tell them to hurry."

Miriam felt her mother's pockets until she located a small vial of pills. Pulling it out, she shook one into her palm. "Take one of your nitroglycerin. It will help with the pain."

When her mother had done as she asked, Miriam jumped to her feet and raced into her mother's bedroom. She grabbed the oxygen canister and mask from closet and returned to the kitchen as quickly as she could. Turning on the oxygen, she placed the mask gently over her mother's face. "Try to take deep slow breaths."

Nick snapped his phone shut. "The ambulance is on its way. They should be here in twenty minutes."

This was her worst nightmare coming true. She was going to watch her mother struggling for breath and die waiting for an ambulance to reach their rural home.

Nick said, "It will be quicker if we take her and head toward them."

Without waiting for her to agree, he lifted Ada from her chair. Galvanized into action, Miriam grabbed the oxygen tank and followed behind him as he carried her mother to his SUV. Miriam opened the door to the backseat and climbed in. Nick gently laid her mother on the seat with her head pillow on Miriam's lap.

He said, "I'll get Hannah."

Miriam cupped her mother's face. "You're going to be fine, mother. We'll get you to the hospital in no time."

Ada tried to speak. Miriam had to pull the mask away from her face to hear what she was saying.

"I am in God's hands. His will be done. I love you, child."

"I love you, too."

A few minutes later, Nick raced out of the house with the baby in her carrier. As he opened the passenger's side front door, Miriam said, "She can't ride up front."

"She can in this vehicle. I can turn the passenger side airbag off. Don't worry, Miriam, I won't let anything happen to her."

He slammed the door, raced around and got in behind the wheel. The engine roared to life as he sped out of the yard and down the lane with Bella running behind them barking madly.

Chapter Eleven

It was the longest ride of Miriam's life. Nick tore down the highway with lights and siren blazing. There was nothing she could do but hold her mother's head, keep the oxygen mask on her face, tell her that everything was going to be okay and pray that she wasn't lying.

Please, God, please let her be okay. She loves you so much, but please don't take her away from me.

They met the ambulance ten minutes after leaving the farmhouse. The paramedics were efficient, competent and sympathetic. The roadside transfer went smoothly. Miriam tried to summon her nursing expertise, but she couldn't. At the moment, she wasn't a critical care nurse, she was a terrified woman whose mother might be dying.

Once her mother was inside the ambulance, hooked up to an IV and on a heart monitor, Miriam was able to relax a little. She could read and analyze the information the equipment provided. Not knowing what was happening was the hardest part.

It wasn't until the ambulance crew started to close the doors that she realized Nick was standing outside with Hannah in his arms.

Tears sprang to Miriam's eyes. Was this the last time she would ever see the baby? She prayed, not for herself, but for the child she loved.

Please, Lord, if it is Your will that she go away from me, hold her in Your hand no matter where she goes in her life.

She met Nick's gaze. "Can you follow us to the hospital?"

"Of course." He nodded to the driver who closed the door blocking them from her sight.

The remainder of the trip to the hospital was a blur for Miriam as she concentrated on her mother's pale face, her ragged breathing and the green blip steadily crossing the surface of the portable monitor.

In the emergency room, her training started to kick in again. She shared her mother's recent cardiac history with the attending physician and was pleased when he immediately consulted her cardiologist. Her mother was transferred to the coronary care unit after her doctor arrived at the hospital. It wasn't until Ada was taken for a heart catheterization procedure that Miriam had time to think about Nick and Hannah.

She found them in the waiting room outside the intensive care unit. Nick was feeding the baby and didn't see Miriam. Her carrier sat on the floor at his feet. He was alone in the room except for the infant he held.

His monologue of baby talk had Hannah enthralled. The baby couldn't take her eyes off him. Miriam smiled at his antics. He was so cute. Parenting seemed to come naturally to him.

He tipped Hannah's bottle to give her the last drops, then set it aside. Lifting her to his shoulder, he patted her back gently until a loud unladylike burp was heard.

"That's my girl," he cooed as he settled her in the crook of his arm and dabbed at her chin.

"I leave you alone for thirty minutes and already you've taught her to belch like a sailor." Miriam walked into the room and took a seat across from him. The minute she sat down she realized how tired she was.

"How's your mother?" Nick asked.

"She's stable for the moment, they've taken her downstairs for a heart catheterization. Her doctor suspects that one of the blood vessels in her heart has closed off. He's going to try to put a stent in to keep it open. I knew this might happen, I thought I was prepared for it, but I wasn't."

"You did everything you could."

Looking back, she realized it was true. She'd done everything she could under the circumstances. The outcome was up to God and Ada's doctors. Miriam held out her hands for Hannah. "May I?"

Nick gave the baby over. "She finished her bottle, but I haven't changed her yet."

"Leave the tough stuff for me, that's so like a guy."

"Hey, if you had shown up five minutes later, it would have all been done."

"Sure. Sure."

"That's my story, and I'm sticking to it." His teasing was just what she needed. He had a knack for reading her mood and finding a way to lighten it. She loved that about him.

The thought startled her. She gazed at him intently. He was focused on Hannah and didn't seem to notice her scrutiny. He had changed a lot from the young man she once knew. His eyes were bracketed with small crow's-feet, and laugh lines were carved into his cheeks. He smiled a lot. She loved that about him, too.

He had a small scar on his chin that was new, or at least she didn't remember it. His eyes were the same intense blue, but there was a weariness behind them that told her life wasn't always easy for him. How could it be for a law enforcement officer?

"You'd better take this." He held out the burp cloth.

She took it, kissed Hannah's head and settled the baby in her arms with the burp cloth under her chin just in case.

If only it could be like this forever, the two of them taking care of the most beautiful baby in the world. It couldn't be, but just for a moment, she could imagine what it would be like. Much as she wanted to, she couldn't keep reality at bay. "How soon do you have to notify Child Protective Services?"

"Soon."

"Can you wait until I know that Mother is going to be okay?"

"Yes. I'm so sorry, Miriam. I didn't realize she would take it so hard."

Miriam saw the regret in his eyes and heard it in his voice. He wasn't to blame for her mother's condition. Even if the stress of the situation had triggered this episode, none of it was his fault. He didn't need to carry that guilt.

"Nick, Mother could have had another attack at any time. I don't blame you for this, and you shouldn't blame yourself."

"I appreciate that."

There was so much she needed to tell him about Mark and about the days leading up to his death. Some of what she had to say would reflect poorly on her, but Nick needed to know the truth. Even if it changed what he thought of her.

"Nick, I need to talk to you."

"I have things I've been wanting to say to you, too."

She opened her mouth to speak just as his phone began ringing. He gave her an apologetic glance and pulled his cell phone from his pocket. "Sheriff Bradley."

As he listened, his expression hardened. "I'm already at the hospital. How soon will she be here?"

He glanced at his watch and then rose to his feet. "I'll meet you in the emergency room."

Nick snapped his phone shut and gave a deep sigh. "I'm sorry, Miriam. There are a lot of things I want to talk to you about, but they're going to have to wait."

"What's going on?"

"EMS is bringing in a suicide attempt. An eighteen-year-old girl has slashed her wrists. Apparently, her boyfriend is the one who found her. I need to interview both of them and sort out what happened."

"Eighteen. That is way too young to feel life has nothing to offer."

"Amen to that. I don't know how long I'll be."

"What about Hannah?"

"As far as I'm concerned, she's in the best possible hands."

She smiled in relief. At least she would have a chance to say goodbye. "Thank you."

"If you want, I'll make arrangements for someone to take you home in case I'm tied up later."

"I'm staying here until I know Mother is doing okay."

"All right, keep me informed. You have my cell phone number, right?"

"I do. Don't worry about us."

She could tell he was reluctant to leave. Suddenly, he crossed the room and bent to kiss her. She was so astonished that for a second she didn't respond. The firm pressure of his lips on hers sent her heart soaring. Then the warmth drew her in and she kissed him back as joy spread through her, making her ache to have his arms around her.

He drew back and said, "When this mess is over and your mother is better, we need to talk."

"Yes, we do," she muttered as she came down to earth with a thud.

He nodded and headed toward the door. She accepted that conversation needed to wait until they could have some uninterrupted time together, but she hoped it wouldn't be long before she could ask him exactly what the kiss meant.

When he was gone, she gazed at Hannah's face. It was amazing how a baby changed things. With God's help, Miriam had come to understand that forgiving Nick was her first step on the journey to forgiving herself. For the first time since Mark's death, she was able to believe in the possibility. And the possibility of a future with Nick.

Nick was waiting in the emergency room when the ambulance carrying the girl who had attempted suicide arrived. As they wheeled her past him, he thought how small, pale and alone she looked. Her eyes were open, but they were empty of emotion.

One of the nurses stopped a young man from following the gurney into the exam room. She directed him to the information desk and told him someone would be with him shortly. Nick had a chance to observe the man wondering if he was the boyfriend. He looked a lot older than eighteen. Nick would've pegged his age closer to thirty. He was unkempt with dirty clothes and greasy hair.

Nick saw his deputy's cruiser pull in behind ambulance. Lance Medford got out and came inside the building. When he caught sight of Nick he stopped. "I was surprised to hear you were already here. I hope everything's okay?"

"I was out at Ada Kauffman's place when she had a heart attack."

"That's a shame. How's she doing?"

"I'm not sure yet. They're still working on her. Is that the boyfriend?" Nick nodded toward the nervous man standing in front of the reception desk.

"That's him. Said he found her in the bathroom when he got home tonight. He claims the cuts were self-inflicted."

Nick gave Lance a sharp look. "You don't believe his story?"

"I do, but I'm running the name he gave us, anyway. I suspect it's an alias. He has conveniently misplaced his ID. Our crime scene tech was pulling some fingerprints from the apartment when I left. My guess is that we'll get a hit and it won't be on Kevin Smith."

Lance pulled out his notebook and opened it. "He says she's eighteen years old. To me, she doesn't look older than sixteen. He's twenty-eight and claims he was just giving her a place to stay."

"Does he have an idea why she might have wanted to kill herself?"

"Yeah, he said she had a miscarriage a little over a week ago and she hasn't been the same since then."

Another woman who'd lost a baby. He couldn't help

but think of Miriam waiting to have Hannah taken away from her. Life wasn't fair. "What about the girl's family?"

"He says she doesn't have any. She wouldn't talk to me at all. As far as I know, she hasn't said a word to anyone."

"All right, you sit with Mr. Smith until we can figure out if we need to hold him or cut him loose. I'll check with the doctor to see how soon I can talk to her."

After speaking to a nurse in the emergency room, Nick learned it would be at least two hours before he could interview the young woman. She was in serious condition and on her way to surgery to have her lacerations repaired.

He no longer had an excuse to put off making his call to Child Protective Services. With lagging steps, he went back inside the hospital to search out Miriam. He found her sitting beside her mother in the intensive care unit. Hannah was asleep in her carrier on a chair beside Miriam. When he entered the room, he met Miriam's eyes. She raised a finger to her lips, and came to the door to speak to him. By mutual and unspoken consent, they stepped outside of the room before speaking.

"How is she?" he asked.

"The procedure went well. They were able to get the stent in place and increase the blood flow to her heart. The doctor is optimistic that she will make a good recovery."

He let out a breath of relief. "That's the best news I've heard all day."

"How is your suicide attempt doing?"

"She's in surgery. I'm still waiting to talk to her."

"I hope she's okay."

He cupped her cheek and stroked it softly with his thumb. "How are you doing?"

"I'm tired. I'm sad. I'm angry."

"At me?"

"At the universe. At God. Why bring Hannah to me only to tear her away? Why make my mother suffer with a bad heart? Hasn't she suffered enough already? Life is so unfair, it makes me want to scream."

"Come here." He pulled her close in a comforting hug. For a second she resisted, then she settled against him with a weary sigh.

"Thank you. I needed a hug."

"I will always have one for you if you need it." It was the least he could do after the grief he'd brought into her life.

Miriam pulled away and folded her arms over her chest. "Have you talked to Child Protective Services?"

He pulled out his cell phone. "I was just about to make the call."

She nodded, but there were tears in her eyes. He had no choice in what he was about to do, but it didn't make him feel any better. Miriam didn't deserve this. She deserved happiness and so much more. He noticed the sting of tears at the back of his own eyes and knew he wasn't doing any better than Miriam at letting go of the child they had both grown to love. He dialed the number of Child Protective Services and swallowed back his grief when a social worker came on the line.

When he explained the circumstances of Hannah's abandonment, he was surprised to find Hannah's new case worker was sympathetic. She was familiar with the Amish and understood the reluctance of the Kauffman family to report an abandoned child. She wasn't quite so understanding of Nick's part in the affair, but as the baby had received adequate care and medical attention, she didn't intend to make an issue of it.

At her direction, Hannah was to be admitted to the hospital for observation. Once they were certain her condition was stable, she would be placed in foster care. He arranged to meet the social worker shortly and turn the baby over to her.

He closed the phone and shoved his hands in his pockets to keep from reaching for Miriam again.

"Are they coming?" she asked.

"Yes. A case worker named Helen Benson is on her way here. I know her. She's a good woman. She wants Hannah admitted to the hospital until the pediatrician here is certain her condition is stable. After that, Hannah will go to foster care."

"They'll be good to her, won't they? I've heard so many horror stories about children in foster care."

"I'll keep an eye on her and her new family, whoever they are."

"Thank you, Nick. I know this is difficult for you, too."

"The social worker will be here soon. Do you want to come with me when I turn Hannah over to them?"

Miriam opened the door to glance into the room. She whispered, "I should be here in case Mother wakes up."

From the bed, Ada said, "You can stop whispering. I'm not asleep and I hear just fine."

Nick and Miriam reentered the room. He said, "I'm sorry for disturbing you, Ada. You gave me quite a scare earlier today."

She chuckled. "Could be it was well earned, but I imagine I should be sorry for upsetting everyone."

"I'm certainly sorry for upsetting you," he said as he leaned on the bed rail.

"Old women get foolish sometimes. We think of things we should have done differently and we wish for chance to do them over. The baby is not ours to keep. *Gott* will take care of her."

"She has to come with me now," he whispered. He could barely get the words past the lump in his throat.

"Let me give her one more kiss before you take her."

Miriam lifted the baby from her carrier and placed her in Ada's arms. She spoke to the child softly in Pennsylvania Dutch and then kissed her on each cheek. "All right, Nicolas, you may take her now."

He picked up the baby and glanced at Miriam. She said, "I already said my goodbyes."

After settling the baby in her carrier again, he left the room without another word.

Miriam willed herself not to cry. If she broke down it would only upset her mother.

Ada said, "I know it is a hard thing for you, but rely on God for strength and you will get through this."

"Is that how you did it when Mark died?"

"*Nee,* I railed against *Gotte* for taking my son. Grief is a human thing. No mother should have to lose her child, but we must accept *Gottes wille* for we cannot change it."

"I'm not sure I can do that. I'm not sure I can accept that the sorrowful things in life are God's will."

"Understanding his ways are not possible for us. Our faith must be as the faith of a child."

"That is easier said than done."

"Don't you think it's time you told me what is really troubling you?"

Miriam's defenses shot up. She wasn't ready for this. "I don't know what you mean."

"Yes, you do. You know exactly why you ran away from your faith and your family. Whatever fear you carry in your heart, it is not a burden you must carry alone."

Ada grimaced and shifted in her bed. Miriam moved to help adjust her pillow. "You should rest now."

Ada closed her eyes and sighed deeply. "I think you're right."

Miriam thought her mother was asleep until a few moments later, when Ada said, "I saw your brother in a dream, earlier."

"That's nice." In Miriam's dreams she searched for Mark but could never find him. She smoothed a few strands of hair away from her mother's forehead.

"He loves you, and so do I." Ada's voice trailed off. Her mother's breathing grew regular and Miriam knew she was sleeping at last.

A nurse peeked into the room and asked quietly, "How is she doing?"

Glancing at the monitor over the bed, Miriam was satisfied with the numbers it displayed. Her mother's color was definitely better and her heart rhythm was normal. The heart cath and stent placement had done wonders. "She's resting comfortably."

"Sleep is the best thing for her. Let us know if she needs anything."

Miriam nodded. "I will."

The nurse left, closing the door softly behind her. One more crisis averted.

Miriam sat down and glanced at the empty chair where Hannah had been only a short time ago. The tears she tried so hard to hold back began to slide down her cheeks.

Chapter Twelve

Helen Benson was waiting for Nick when he arrived in the hospital lobby. A petite woman with a short bob of white-blond hair, she was wearing a business suit and carrying a large briefcase. Her smile when she saw him was warm and welcoming. It eased some of his fears.

He set Hannah's carrier on the floor between them. "This is the baby I was telling you about."

She squatted in front of Hannah and said, "You are a cute one."

"Careful, she'll steal your heart before you know it." Nick stuffed his hands in his front pockets.

Helen rose. "Don't worry, Sheriff, we will take good care of her."

"Will I, or the family who has been caring for her, be able to see her here in the hospital?"

"I'm afraid not. I will keep you updated on any changes in her condition and let you know when she is ready for discharge. Other than that, don't expect to hear from me until we've found a placement for her. How is the investigation into finding her parents going?"

"At this point, there's little to go on. Just a blue-and-white patchwork quilt and a wooden laundry basket with green trim and a note saying she would be back. Since no one has reported a missing baby in the area, I have to wonder if it was a ruse to give her more time to get away."

"Placing the baby in an Amish buggy might indicate she wanted the child raised by Amish parents."

"Or, it might have been the first handy place she saw. I've already had the buggy impounded. We'll check it for prints and trace evidence. We'll be expanding the search tomorrow and focus on the store in Sugarcreek. I'm hoping they have a surveillance camera in their parking lot. Either way, we'll do door-to-door interviews in the area. Finding the woman who discarded this baby is going to be my top priority."

Helen picked up the carrier. "I understand. And making sure the baby is happy and well cared for is going to be mine. How are your friend and her mother doing?"

"Things are looking hopeful for Mrs. Kauffman. Miriam is coping with a lot right now, losing Hannah and having her mother so ill."

"I'd like to visit with her in the next day or two. I understand she has a foster care license in our state."

"Yes, but she fosters teens in Medina."

"It wouldn't take much for us to do a home study of her new residence."

"Are you saying it is possible she could keep Hannah?"

"Finding willing and skilled foster parents to take children with medical issues is an ongoing problem for our agency. Encourage her to go ahead with her application. Who knows, it may be possible to place Hannah with her eventually. So much depends on finding the child's parents."

It was a small ray of hope, but it was better than nothing. Hannah had succeeded in bringing Miriam back into Nick's life. Her arrival had opened a door he thought was closed forever. He would always be grateful for that. "I'll relay your information to Miriam. Thank you."

"I'm sorry this didn't turn out as you had hoped."

"You and me, both. How are Danny Jr. and his sister doing?"

"The family has agreed to counseling. I'm hopeful that we won't need to intervene. Both parents realize it was an unhealthy situation, not only for them, but for the kids, too. The dad says he is willing to do whatever it takes to keep the family together, including anger management classes. I hope he follows through with it."

"I have a friend who works in construction. He's going to see about getting Mr. Hicks a part-time job. He understands the man's out on bail, but I think he'll get community service rather than jail time. It was his first offense."

"That would take a tremendous amount of strain off the family. Thank you."

Helen bid him goodbye and walked toward the admissions desk carrying Hannah. Nick watched her leave with a heavy heart. He missed the little girl already. What was life going to be like without her?

He made his way back to the emergency room and found his deputy selecting a candy bar from the vending machine just outside the doorway of the waiting room. "Any word on the girl, Lance?"

Shaking his head, Lance pulled his selection from the bin. "We're still waiting for her to come out of surgery."

"Is the boyfriend talking?" Nick looked inside the room and saw Kevin Smith pacing back and forth by the windows.

"He hasn't said much, but he sure is nervous. I'm not sure how much longer he'll stick around."

"Do you want me to question him?"

"It's your call, Boss, but I'd really like to take another crack at the guy. Besides, I figure you'll do better with the girl."

As they spoke, a woman in blue scrubs came to the doorway. "Family of Mary Smith?"

Kevin came across the room. "Friend, not family. She doesn't…she doesn't have any family."

"I'm afraid I can only give information to family members. There is a form that Mary will have to sign before I can give you any information."

She turned to leave but Nick stopped her. "How soon can I speak to her?"

The nurse said, "She's being moved to her room now. If you officers will come with me, I'll have the doctor speak to you."

Kevin objected. "Hey, how come they get information and I can't?"

"Because they are officers of the law," she said and walked away.

Lance laid a hand on Kevin's shoulder. "As soon as we find out anything, I will let you know. These hospital rules and regulations are for the birds. Have a seat, I'll be back in a jiffy."

Nick and Lance followed the nurse down the hall and around the corner. They waited outside the recovery room doors until the doctor emerged until the doctor emerged.

Nick asked, "How is she?"

"She is stabilized but she is still in serious condition. She's already had two units of blood. We're going to give her another two. The lacerations were deep. She was serious about killing herself. We're giving her something for pain. She will recover from her injuries, but she's going to need counseling."

Nodding, Nick asked, "How soon can I interview her?"

"You can talk to her now, although she may be a bit groggy."

"Did she say why she tried to kill herself?"

"She hasn't said anything. I think we're dealing with a lot of factors, and one of them may be postpartum depression."

"The boyfriend mentioned a miscarriage." Lance frowned deeply

The surgeon shrugged. "She has certainly had a baby. If something happened to the infant, that might well have triggered the suicide attempt."

Nick held out his hand. "Thanks, Doc. I think we'd like to get a little more information from the boyfriend before we see her."

"Very well. She's not going anywhere."

Nick and Lance returned to the waiting area. Kevin Smith jumped to his feet. "How is she?"

Lance took the lead. "The doctor says she'll be okay but she's gonna be here for a while. Any idea what might've made her do this?"

"I guess it must've been the baby. She miscarried a while back."

"I'm sorry for your loss." The compassion in Lance's voice was real. Taking Kevin's arm, Lance led him to a sofa in the middle of the room.

"Yeah, well, I wasn't into being a dad, so I'm not exactly torn up about it."

Nick was pacing back and forth behind Kevin. "Dad? I thought she was just staying at your place. Now you're the father of her child. Which is it?"

Kevin craned his neck to see Nick behind him. "Um, both I guess."

"What doctor did your girlfriend see after her miscarriage?"

"Nobody, as far as I know."

Nick planted his hands on the back of the sofa on either side of Kevin neck. "Your girlfriend had a miscarriage, and you didn't take her to the hospital?"

"I was out of town for a couple of days. When I came back, she told me she'd lost the baby. She didn't seem broken up about it at the time."

"Was it a boy or girl?" Lance asked gently.

"I didn't ask. I mean what's the point?"

This guy was some piece of work. Nick hoped he could find a reason to haul him to jail since being a jerk wasn't against the law.

The man glanced between Nick and Lance. "Can I see her or what? 'Cause if I can't see her, then I have things to do."

The buzz of his cell phone caused Lance to pull the device from his pocket. He read the text, held it out so that Nick could read it and then tucked it back in his pocket.

He clamped a hand on the man's shoulder. "You're not going to see her just yet, Kevin Dunbar, wanted for check fraud over in Wayne County. First, we're going to take a ride downtown, and then you're going to see the inside of our lovely jail. Put your hands behind your back."

"There's been some kind of mistake."

"You'll get to tell it all to the judge."

Once Lance had him handcuffed, Nick walked out with them and waited until Lance had their prisoner secured in the backseat of the cruiser. He said, "Make sure you do a real thorough job of running a background check on this guy. Something tells me he's been doing more than writing hot checks."

"You got it, Boss. If I had my way, I'd lock him up and throw away the key. Didn't even ask if it was a boy or a girl. What kind of father is that?"

"The worst kind. I'm going to have a talk with the girlfriend now."

Lance walked around to the driver's side of his car "The poor kid. She's too young to be involved with a loser like him."

After Lance drove away, Nick went back into the hospital and learned that Mary Smith had been taken to a room on the fourth floor. He took the elevator to the ward and asked at the nurse's station to speak to the charge nurse. After a brief conversation with her, he was relieved to learn that Ms. Smith would have a sitter with her through the night.

When he entered her room, he saw a middle-aged woman sitting in a recliner with a book open on her lap. She looked up and asked, "Would you like me to step outside, Sheriff?"

"No, it's best if you stay."

He pulled a chair up to the side of the bed where Mary lay curled up beneath the covers. Sitting down, he leaned forward with his elbows propped on his knees. "My name is Sheriff Bradley, and I'm going to have to ask you some questions."

"Where's Kevin?" she asked in a tiny, hoarse voice. She didn't make eye contact but stared at the wall instead.

He decided it was best not to share the fact that Kevin was on his way to jail. He needed this girl's cooperation. "He's fine. You'll be able to see him later. I need you to tell me what happened tonight."

She sank farther beneath the covers. "You know."

"I'm not sure that I do. Why don't you tell me?"

Glaring at him, she raised her bandaged arm.

"You cut your own wrists? Are you sure that Kevin wasn't holding the knife? It's all right. You can tell me if he hurt you. I'll see that he never hurts you again."

"Go away."

"I'm only here to help, Mary. Why don't you tell me what happened."

She gingerly tucked her arm back under the sheet. "Go away."

She picked up her call light and pushed the button. When a nurse answered, she said, "I need something for pain."

Nick could see he wasn't going to get anywhere with her, but he made one last try. "Was your baby a little boy or little girl?"

Tears filled her eyes. She rolled over and turned her back to him.

Discouraged, he left the room and stopped at the nurse's station. Speaking to the woman at the desk, he gave her his card with instructions to call him if anything changed with Mary Smith.

* * *

Dawn was breaking outside the hospital window as Miriam sat up and stretched sore muscles. A night spent in a hospital-grade recliner was a sure way to earn a stiff neck. Her mother's condition hadn't changed much through the night. She was on the mend, but her blood pressure had been all over the place.

Miriam rose and moved to the side of the bed. Ada's eyes snapped open. "It's about time you got up. It's been light for almost an hour. The horse will be wondering where her breakfast is."

"Good morning, *Mamm*. How are you feeling?"

"Better. Can I go home now?"

"I doubt your doctor will let you go home today, but it's good to see you are on the mend."

Ada moved to sit up in bed. "I'm hungry. Where is Hannah?"

The reminder brought a sharp pain to Miriam's chest. "Hannah is upstairs in the nursery."

"Oh, dear. I was hoping that part was a bad dream. She isn't coming back to us, is she?"

"I'm afraid not, *Mamm*."

"You look tired, dear."

"I am."

There was a knock at the door and a young woman in blue scrubs looked in. "Mrs. Kauffman, are you ready for some breakfast and a bath?"

"I am. Miriam, why don't you go get something to eat while I get *redd-up*."

The nurse's aid was setting a tray on the bedside table. She glanced at Ada. "What does *redd-up* mean?"

"To get ready or cleaned up," Ada said with a smile.

She made shooing motions to Miriam. "Go get some-thing to eat and find out how soon I can leave."

Miriam left the room and headed toward the eleva-tors. As she passed the small waiting room beside them, she glanced in and saw Nick sprawled on one of the chairs. He was wearing the same clothes he'd had on yesterday. His cheeks bore a shadow of stubble, and his hair was sticking up on his head. She smiled as comfort-able warmth filled her heart. She wanted to comb his hair and find out exactly how rough his cheeks would feel beneath her fingers.

He opened one eye. "What are you smiling at?"

"You look like I feel."

"How's that?" He sat up with a grimace.

"Like you've been pulled through a cornfield back-ward."

"That about sums it up. The social worker in charge of Hannah's case wants to meet with you later."

"I imagine I'll be here. She's welcome to stop in."

"She also said to go ahead and apply for a home study here. It's possible—now, I said possible, so don't hold your breath. It's possible that you could foster Han-nah once you get the go-ahead from the state."

"Oh, Nick, really?" Miriam's heart surged with re-newed hope. There was a chance Hannah could come back to her.

"Really, but try not to get your hopes up too much. It all still depends on finding her family. How's your mother?"

"Bossy."

"That's good to hear. How are you?"

"I'm tired and I'm hungry."

He rose to his feet. "The hungry part I can fix. Would you care to join me for breakfast?"

She did want to join him. He understood how much his news meant to her. "If you'll let me buy."

"Sorry, no can do. I invite, I pay."

"That is very old-fashioned of you."

"Yes or no? Breakfast with an old-fashioned man or go hungry?"

"I'm not likely to go hungry. I'm sure the cafeteria serves a great breakfast."

He glanced at his watch. "Not for another hour and ten minutes. However, there is a vending machine behind you."

She glanced over her shoulder and wrinkled her nose. "No, a candy bar or pretzels will not do it for me."

He shoved his hands in his pockets. "I know a place where you can get great scrambled eggs and bacon."

"All right, you win. Since I'm without a car, are you driving or are we walking?"

"I'll drive."

Miriam walked beside him as they left the hospital and climbed into his vehicle. Five minutes later, he pulled up in front of a duplex. He said, "It's not much to look at from the outside, but I promise you the food is good."

"It looks like an apartment." She frowned at the building.

"Actually, it is my apartment. But there are farm-fresh eggs in the fridge along with a new slab of bacon. I have bagels, English muffins or Texas Toast, and gourmet coffee just waiting to be brewed."

"Okay, you won me over at gourmet coffee. Lead on, let's see if you are all talk or if you can cook."

His eyebrows shot up and he slapped a hand to his chest. "I wasn't planning to cook. I thought you would."

"Are you serious?"

"Ha! Gotcha. Of course I can cook." He grinned as he unlocked the door and pushed it open.

Miriam stepped inside what was clearly a bachelor pad. An oversize TV took up most of the wall along one side of the living room. It was flanked by bookshelves filled with an assortment of movies and novels. Opposite the TV was a well-worn brown leather sofa and a low coffee table. Beyond the living room was a small dining room with a glass-top table and two café-style chairs.

Nick gestured to the table. "Have a seat, or you can freshen up if you want. The bathroom is down that hall, first door on the left."

Miriam decided she needed to freshen up more than she needed coffee. It wasn't as good as a shower, but she was able to wash off and run a comb through her hair. Nick's bathroom, like the rest of the house, was spotless. Was he that good a housekeeper, or did he have someone come in?

By the time she returned to the dining room, the smell of frying bacon filled the air. Her stomach rumbled, and she pressed her hand to her midsection to quiet it.

"It smells good," she said, feeling odd to be in his home. It was nothing like she had imagined. She wasn't sure what she thought it would be like, but not once had she pictured Nick cracking eggs in a bowl.

"How do you like your eggs?" he asked without looking up.

"Over hard, break the yolks. It's the only way my mother ever fixes them."

He chuckled. "I do remember that, now. I asked her

for a sunny-side up egg the first morning I came to stay with you. She looked at me like I had asked for rat poison."

"I remember. We call them dippy-eggs."

She remembered a lot about that summer, and there were things she needed Nick to understand, but not now. For a little while, she wanted to enjoy his company and pretend her secret didn't exist.

Smiling too brightly, she asked, "Where is the coffee you promised me?"

He pointed over his shoulder with the spatula. "On the counter behind me."

She entered the small kitchen and brushed past him. "And the cups?"

"If you can't find a cup in a kitchen this size, you're not much of a detective."

"Ha! Ha! You've been wanting to say that for days, haven't you?"

She could feel his shoulders shaking with suppressed laughter behind her. *"Ja, Fräulein."*

"Your Amish accent is terrible." She got a cup and elbowed him in the ribs in the process.

He ignored her puny attempt to rile him. "You've managed to get rid of yours. Most of it, anyway."

"It took some work."

"Diction classes?"

"Yes. I didn't want to sound like a hick from the sticks when I applied for jobs. I encourage all the kids who stay with me to take the classes."

She filled a cup and returned to the table. She knew her cheeks were flushed. Would he think it was caused by the hot coffee, or did he realize it was because of his proximity? When they had been close years ago she had fantasized about what it would be like to be married to him, to wake up with him, to have breakfast, just the two of them, in his *Englisch* house. Her girlhood daydreams didn't do justice to the reality of sharing a meal with him. How could she know that the intimate setting of his kitchen would be every bit as alluring as dinner in a fine restaurant? She took a quick sip of her coffee and scalded her tongue.

"Is that how you think of the Amish? Hicks from the sticks?" He brought a plate of crispy bacon to the table and set it in front of her.

She blew on her cup. "It's not my opinion that counts. I know Amish kids are naive, unused to worldly things and curious, but they aren't stupid. They simply can't make informed decisions because they lack knowledge, not intelligence. People have learned to take advantage of that. By sounding less Amish, they have a better chance at fair treatment."

He returned to the table with his plate and her eggs on his spatula. He slid them on to her plate and sat down. He bowed his head and silently prayed. Miriam waited until he was finished to ask for the salt. Smiling, he pushed it toward her.

It was a simple meal, but it had an intimate feel to it. It was a feeling she wanted to cultivate and enjoy more often. The thought had barely crossed her mind when his phone rang.

He looked at the number and shook his head. "I knew it."

"Work?" she asked. Was this cozy interlude destined to end early?

"It's my deputy. He's investigating our suicide attempt. I have to take this." He rose from the table and walked into the other room.

* * *

"This had better be important, Rob," Nick growled into the phone. His morning had been going so well.

"Hi, boss. The crime scene people are wrapping up."

"You called to tell me that?" Nick frowned. Rob Craiger was one of his most experienced deputies. He normally let his written reports do the talking.

"No, I just finished interviewing the woman who lives in the trailer next door. She didn't get home from work until thirty minutes ago."

"Did she give us anything useful?"

"She didn't have anything good to say about the boy-friend, but here is the odd thing. She swears that she heard a baby crying over here two weeks ago on Thursday. She remembers the night because someone stole a laundry basket off her back porch and a quilt off her clothesline that same night. There's no sign of a baby inside the Smiths' trailer. No diapers, no baby bottles, no crib."

All the pieces came together with a snap in Nick's mind. Mary's baby hadn't died. She'd left it in a buggy two blocks away at the Shop and Save Grocery Mart.

He asked, "Was the quilt blue patchwork and the laundry basket wooden with green trim?"

He could hear Rob thumbing through the pages of his notebook until he found the one he wanted. He said in surprise, "Yeah. How did you know that?"

"Never mind. Come back to the station. I'll be over at the courthouse as soon as it opens."

"Why?"

"To get a court order for DNA testing. I think I know where the baby is."

Nick looked over his shoulder at Miriam buttering a

piece of toast. There was no way he wanted to tell her that Hannah was once again out of her reach. Still, if things were to go as he hoped, she had to see how difficult his job could be.

When he walked back to the table, she looked up and her smile faded. "Nick, what's the matter?"

"We think we've found Hannah's parents."

"Oh." Her shoulders slumped.

"Her mother is the girl who tried to commit suicide and the man we think is the father is in jail for writing hot checks."

"Will Hannah be returned to someone like that?"

"They aren't the best parents, but I've seen the courts give children back to worse."

"What do we do?"

"Wait until we have DNA evidence to prove who they are. If the mother is up to a visit, I'd like to try and interview her again. She wouldn't talk to me last time. You've had a lot of experience with girls this age. Would you like to give it a try?"

"Sure. Have you got time to finish your breakfast? Your eggs are getting cold."

He sat down but had taken only two bites before Miriam's cell phone began ringing. She flipped it open but didn't immediately answer.

"Who is it?" he asked.

She looked at him with a new fear in her eyes. "It's the Hope Springs medical clinic."

Chapter Thirteen

Miriam answered the phone. Dr. White's craggy voice boomed in her ear. "I won't keep you in suspense. Hannah's tests have come back negative."

"Negative?" Miriam could barely breathe the word as relief flooded her.

"All negative. She shows no signs of maple syrup urine disease. It was a simple lab error. It seems her report was mixed up with another baby with the same last name."

Miriam turned to Nick. "Hannah is fine. Her tests came back okay. She isn't sick."

Nick closed his eyes. "Thank you, God."

Miriam smiled through tears of joy. "You have no idea how much we needed some good news this morning, Dr. White. Thank you."

"My pleasure." He hung up before she could tell him that Hannah was no longer in her care.

Knowing that social services would take care of those details, Miriam put her cell phone back in her purse. "If you're finished, we should get back to the hospital. Let me wash these dishes and we can go."

"What are the odds that I'll get a second date if I make you wash dishes?"

"Slim, since I wouldn't call this a first date," she teased.

Some of the tension returned to his shoulders. "What would you call it?"

"I'd call it an interrupted meal."

He shrugged. "That is the lot of a county sheriff. I've had more interrupted meals than I can count."

"What you need to do is learn how to take your food with you." She took two pieces of bacon and rolled them in a piece of bread.

She handed the concoction to Nick, took his keys from where he'd set them on the counter and headed for the door. "I'll drive while you finish eating."

"Yes, boss." He gave her a quick salute.

Once he was in the truck, he ate and lapsed into silence. She glanced at him several times on the way to the hospital, but he simply stared out the window. He was deeply concerned by the thought of Hannah having such troubled parents.

She said, "Thanks for breakfast."

"Egg peppered with good and bad news. It could have been better."

"I'm a big girl, Nick. I understand that sometimes the job has to come first. It's the same in my profession."

He smiled a real smile. "I appreciate that. Let's check on how your mother is doing."

When they got back to her mother's room, they found her mother's doctor making his rounds. Miriam was glad she hadn't missed him. At least one good thing had come out of her rapid exit from Nick's place.

The doctor spent a few minutes going over Ada's

X-rays and lab reports. Although he was generally pleased with her progress, he felt it was necessary to keep her a few more days. Ada disagreed, but he had an ally in Miriam.

She was concerned about her mother's poor blood pressure control. She didn't want her mother going home only to have to turn around and come back again. Or worse.

When the doctor left the room, Ada said, "I don't know why you had to agree with him. This is costing too much money."

Miriam knew her mother's church would help cover the costs of her medical care. "Don't worry about that. Concentrate on getting better."

"I'm better enough," Ada grumped, but she couldn't hold back a yawn.

Nick pushed the bed control to lower it. "A little nap will do wonders for you. Miriam and I have some errands to run, but we'll be back soon."

Once the bed was down, Ada pulled the covers up to her chin. "Seeing Hannah would do wonders for me."

Miriam tucked the covers around her mother's shoulders. "I know. It would do wonders for us, too."

Ada said, "I miss her. I pray the Lord finds a loving home for her."

"So do I," Miriam replied with a deep ache in her heart as she met Nick's gaze. She didn't know how she would bear it if it turned out otherwise.

Nick had no trouble getting the court order he needed. Since both Hannah and Mary Smith already had blood in the hospital laboratory, the process of obtaining a DNA match was simplified to some degree, but it would still take at least forty-eight hours before he would know if they were mother and child.

Kevin Dunbar refused to allow a DNA swab, claiming he wasn't the father and he didn't want to be forced to pay child support for a kid who wasn't his. By noon, he made bail. As he jogged down the steps on his way out of the building, Nick stood with Miriam at the door to his offices. "I doubt he will stay in town long enough to visit Mary. He has the look of a man who is going to skip out on his bail."

"How can you tell?"

Nick gave her a wry grin. "I've seen enough small-time crooks to know how they behave."

He needed to concentrate on this case, but all he could think about was how natural it had seemed to fix breakfast for Miriam and how good it had been to see her smiling at him from across his table.

He wanted to see her again. Not just at his table, but in every aspect of his life. He'd fallen head over heels in love with her and he still had no idea how she felt about him.

"Excuse me, Sheriff."

Nick looked over his shoulder to see his secretary standing in the doorway. "Do you need something?"

"Just to deliver this file from Child Protective Services."

"Thanks. I'll take it." He held out his hand.

She left the file with him. He walked into his office with Miriam and closed his door. He sat in his chair and stared at the folder in his hand.

"You're going to have to call Ms. Benson and tell her what you suspect," Miriam reminded him gently.

He smiled at her. Perhaps she would be able to get

through to Mary Smith and get the young woman to open up about what had happened to her baby and why she'd tried to kill herself.

"If Hannah isn't Mary's child, then I have another missing infant somewhere in Sugarcreek."

The thought made his blood run cold. After nearly two weeks, he wouldn't be looking for a live child.

If Mary would just admit she'd left the baby in the Beachys' buggy it would save him a lot of time and effort. He picked up the phone to call her doctor. He needed to know when he could interview the girl again.

When he had her psychiatrist on the line, he asked, "Has Mary Smith started talking to anyone?"

"No. I have her on a strong antidepressant medication, but it takes a while for it to build up in the body. It may be several days before we see improvement. All she has done is to ask for pain meds. Other than that, she hasn't said anything."

"I have some information you may find useful. We have a baby that was found abandoned around the same time that Kevin Dunbar says Mary's baby was stillborn. A neighbor reports hearing a baby crying at the Smith address a few hours before the abandoned infant was found. It's possible Mary got rid of her baby by placing it in an Amish buggy at a nearby parking lot."

"I see. That is disturbing news. This may be a case of postpartum psychosis rather than depression. Mary may not even realize what happened to her child. Thank you for the information."

"I'd like to question her again and mention what I just told you. I'd like to see what kind of response I get."

"I don't think that's a good idea at this point, Sheriff.

I have to be careful. She is very fragile. I don't want her to regress into a more serious state of mind."

"This is a police investigation into a missing child, Doctor. I hope you understand the seriousness of it."

"I do, but I have to keep the best interest of my clients in mind when making these kind of decisions. Until I think she is strong enough, I won't allow you to question her."

"I can get a court order to interview her."

"Fine. When you have one in hand, I'll comply with it. Until then, good day, Sheriff."

The line went dead in Nick's hand. He hung up in frustration.

"Well?" Miriam asked.

"He says I can't see her."

"Can you get a court order to do so?"

"I doubt it. I don't believe any of the local judges would go against the recommendation of a patient's doctor."

"So what now?"

"We're back to waiting." It was something he didn't do well.

Miriam convinced Nick to run her home so that she could collect a few of her mother's things and get her own car. She knew he was frustrated and impatient with waiting.

Bella was delighted to see them and practically knocked her down with affection. There was still food in Bella's dish and water in her bowl, so Miriam knew the dog hadn't suffered anything but loneliness while they'd been gone. Nick took care of the outside chores while Miriam took a shower and changed into fresh clothes.

When she came downstairs, she found Nick staring into Hannah's empty cradle. There was so much sadness in his eyes that she went into his arms without thinking. She whispered, "I miss her, too."

He sniffed and wiped at his eyes. "I should put this back in the attic."

"Not yet. Leave it down here a little longer."

"All right. What's next?"

"I'm not sure how long mother will be in the hospital. I want to let Bishop Zook know so that he can arrange for people to come and take care of the animals."

"I could take Bella back to my place," he offered.

"That would be great."

Bella jumped into Nick's backseat, happy to be going for a ride. Miriam waved goodbye as Nick headed back to work. The moment he was out of sight she began to miss him. When had he become the person she depended on? Perhaps he had always been that person, she just couldn't see it until now. Within a few minutes she was pulling into the Zook farm.

The bishop was working on his corn planter, hammering a bent blade back into shape. He looked up, wiped the sweat from his brow with the back of his sleeve and came to speak to her.

"Good day, Miriam Kauffman, what brings you here on this fine afternoon?"

"I came to let you know that my mother is in the hospital in Millersburg. She had another heart attack."

"We shall pray for her recovery and ask for God's mercy."

"Thank you, Bishop Zook."

"Do not be concerned about the farm," the bishop added. "It will be taken care of until you and your mother return."

Miriam smiled with gratitude. An Amish person never had to worry about what would happen if they were unable to continue their farm work or provide for their family. The entire community would pitch in at a moment's notice to see that everything was taken care of.

No one went hungry. No one was left alone. The Amish took care of each other. When her mother came home, there would be fresh chopped firewood, kindling in the stove and a table full of things to eat.

As she headed back toward the hospital, Miriam couldn't help thinking about Nick. Before their relationship went any further, she needed to tell him about the day Mark died. There might not be a relationship after her confession.

Nick had shouldered the blame alone for years when she could have eased his guilt by admitting her part. Would he forgive her when he learned the part she had played? She prayed that he would. She no longer blamed him for the accident that took her brother's life. Nick needed to hear her say that. She needed to tell him.

Back at the hospital, Miriam found her mother was once again having chest pain with a spike in her blood pressure. This time it was so high that Miriam feared she would have a stroke. When the staff was finally able to bring it under control, Miriam took a seat near the window.

"Miriam?" Her mother raised a hand as if seeking her.

"I'm here." Miriam moved her chair to the bedside and took her mother's hand between her own.

"We should go visit your brother."

Gently, Miriam said, "Mark is gone. We can't visit him."

"I meant visit his grave. I want to plant new flowers there. You can do that for me, can't you?" Ada drifted back to sleep saving Miriam from having to answer. She hadn't been back to Mark's grave since his funeral.

Ada slept through most of the day. Miriam catnapped in the chair, watched some senseless afternoon talk show on TV and waited for Nick to call. When he finally did, she couldn't stop the happy leap of her heart. "Hi, there. I was beginning to think you didn't want to talk to me."

"I'm sorry. I've been busy. Hopefully, things will be wrapped up soon and I can get back to the hospital. Maybe we could try for dinner together?"

"I'd like that," she answered, amazed at just how much she wanted to spend time alone with him.

"How's your mother?"

"She had a bad spell right after I got back. She was talking about going to see Mark's grave. It has me worried."

"She's always been such a strong woman. I'm sure she'll be fine." His assurance rang hollow. He was worried, too.

"How's Bella?"

"She's hiding out under my desk after stealing my secretary's lunch."

"My poor baby. This has been rough on her."

"You couldn't tell it by looking at her. She's eyeing my cheese-covered pretzel as we speak."

Miriam chuckled. "Call me later. There are things I need to say to you."

"Can't you tell me now?"

"No, not on the phone. When I see you in person."

"Now you have me worried."

"Don't be. I have a feeling that you may already know what I have to say."

Throughout the day, Miriam divided her time between caring for her mother and waiting to spend a few stolen minutes with Nick. His promise of dinner turned into a late-night burrito that he carried into her mother's room in a greasy, brown paper bag long after visiting hours. It was the best burrito Miriam had ever eaten. Unfortunately, he couldn't stay.

The next evening she had a short, to the point meeting with Hannah's social worker. Mostly, the woman wanted to know about Hannah's schedule, her feeding issues and any type of history Miriam could provide. It wasn't much, but it felt good to be doing something that might help Hannah.

The woman was leaving when Nick showed up. They spoke briefly, but the woman again said she couldn't share any information about Hannah.

Miriam turned to Nick after she was gone. "Come on. I need a lookout."

He followed her into the hall. "What are we doing?"

"We are taking matters into our own hands. I want to know how Hannah is doing."

Miriam entered the elevator and pushed the button for the maternity floor. They walked down the halls listening to the sound of infants crying. None of them were Hannah. Miriam was sure she'd recognize her cry. She stopped beside the viewing window that looked into the special care section of the nursery and tried to get a glimpse of Hannah.

There was only one baby in the nursery. It had to be Hannah. Nick would have been notified if she had been dismissed.

Miriam tapped on the window and then noticed a sign that said to go to the door and not to knock on the window. The young nurse inside looked over and smiled. She gestured toward the door.

Miriam looked at Nick. "Keep an eye out for anyone who might know me."

"Is this illegal?"

"Can I take the Fifth on that?"

"No." He scowled at her.

"Then it isn't illegal." She waited as the nurse opened the door.

The young nurse asked, "Are you a relative?"

Miriam smiled. "No, I'm a critical care nurse and I'd love to tour your unit. I've often thought about working in pediatrics."

It was the truth. She had considered changing fields more than once.

"Actually, there is an opening on the night shift, but it's only part-time. This really is a great place to work. You should consider taking the job. Our charge nurse has stepped out, but she'll be back in about ten minutes. She knows more about what goes on here. I've only worked here a few months."

Miriam smiled at Nick and walked inside. "You don't have a very high census. I only see one baby, is that right?"

"Normally we run between three and five occupied

beds, but right now all we have is a baby that is a police hold."

"I thought only sick babies were admitted here."

"The child was in to rule out MSUD but that came
back negative. The baby has been spitting up a lot. She
didn't seem to care for our regular soy formula."

"Have you tried holding her upright and rocking her
for thirty minutes after her feedings instead of laying
her down afterward? I once knew a baby with spit-up
problems and that worked wonders."

"Funny you should say that. The social worker on
the case came in a few minutes ago with the same suggestion."

Miriam stepped forward enough to see Hannah was
sleeping quietly. Her color was pink and she looked perfect. "Can I sneak a peek at her?"

"I'm afraid not. Hospital policy and all that."

Miriam took a step back. "Sure. Thanks for letting
me look around your unit."

Miriam turned to leave. The young nurse quickly
asked, "Don't you want to talk to the charge nurse?"

Miriam shook her head. "I need a full-time job, but
I'm sure you'll find someone who likes to work with
babies."

She went out the door, gestured to Nick to follow
her. He said, "If you want to take up police work, I can
get you a recommendation."

"No, I'm happy being a nurse. We should get back
to Mother."

"I'm going to stop and check on Mary Smith. I want
to find out if I can talk to her soon. I'll catch you later."
To Miriam's delight, he pressed a kiss on her lips. The

thrill was over all too quickly when he pulled away. She longed for more.

She took the elevator back to her mother's floor. When she walked into her mother's room, she found Ada trying to get out of bed. Miriam rushed to help her.

"Mom, you should call for help before you get up."

"I called and I called, but no one came."

"I'm sorry, I went to see Hannah for a few minutes."

Her mother gave her a puzzled look. "Who is Hannah?"

"The baby that was left on our doorstep."

"Mark's baby?"

Miriam's heart sank to her feet. How had her mother learned about Mark's child? "No, Mother, it wasn't Mark's child. His baby was never born. His *Englisch* mother didn't want him."

Ada sighed heavily. "Have you been to plant flowers on Mark's grave? I wish you would. I can't go home until that is done."

Before Miriam could reply, her mother's eyes rolled back in her head and she collapsed into Miriam's arms.

Yelling for help, Miriam lowered her mother to the floor. A quick check of her pulse showed she was still alive. Relief flooded Miriam, but it was quickly thrust aside as the room filled with people. Miriam repeated what had happened to five different people including the nurses, a new resident and finally her mother's doctor.

He reviewed Ada's chart and listened to her heart for a long while before he turned to Miriam. "Her blood pressure is too low at the moment. I believe that's what caused her to faint. We're having so much trouble getting this medication regulated that I'm going to try her on something else. I know this is frustrating for you."

"*Scary* is the word I would use." Low blood pressure meant a sluggish flow of blood through the brain. That would account for her mother's confusion. Still, her mother's words haunted her. "I can't go home until that is done."

Had she meant home as in the farm, or home as in her heavenly home?

The thought chilled Miriam. It was time, long past time, for her to face her mistakes and admit them.

She left word with the nursing staff to call her if her mother's condition changed. In the hospital parking lot, she got in her car and headed toward the other side of town. It wasn't long before she was in the country she recognized from her childhood.

The highway wound through low hills and past pristine farms. Everywhere, signs of spring were turning the landscape green. In the pastures, tiny black-and-white calves frolicked together while their mothers grazed nearby.

After ten minutes, she reached the fork in the road that led to a small Amish cemetery.

She pulled her car to a stop beside the white-board fence that surrounded the property. For a long time she sat in the car not moving. It was the first time she had been back to visit Mark's grave since his funeral.

Opening the car door, she stepped out into the bright sunshine. The smell of new grass brought back memories from her childhood. With barely a thought, she kicked off her sneakers and stepped barefoot into a thick, cool green carpet.

Like all Amish children, she had spent her childhood barefoot. Not until frost hardened the ground each fall had she and Mark put on shoes. It felt right to visit him barefoot.

She made her way between the rows of nearly identical white headstones to his gravesite. When she came upon his name, tears welled up without warning as emotion choked her throat. With a moan, she sank to her knees and covered her face with her hands.

"I'm so sorry," she wailed as she rocked back and forth with grief. "I'd change it all if I could. I'm so sorry."

She had no idea how long she knelt there, but finally her sobs subsided. Weak and spent, she put her hand on the face of his marker. Would he forgive her? As she gazed at the stone, she brushed aside a small bit of moss growing on the edge of the stone. The clump fell to the grass and exposed something glittery. Reaching down, she picked up a silver star made of foil.

Instantly she knew where she had seen one before. Nick made one every time he put a piece of gum in his mouth.

Chapter Fourteen

Miriam spread the thick grass aside and saw more silver stars. Dozens of them lay around Mark's tombstone. Some were bright and new, others were old and dull, still others were mere flakes, having disintegrated from their time out in the elements.

"I started leaving them when I made sheriff."

Startled, she twisted around to see Nick standing behind her. She hadn't heard him approach.

Stepping forward, he laid a new star on the headstone. The breeze quickly blew it into the grass. "I put one out every time I come to visit."

Miriam rubbed at her tearstained face. "You've been here a lot."

"I have." He thrust his hands into the front pockets of his jeans. His shoulders were rolled forward as if he was expecting a blow across his back.

Was he waiting for her to say something? What words could convey the depth of what she was feeling? She looked up at his face. His hat cast a shadow across his eyes.

So much heartache. So much pain. Where is it all to end, Lord?

She knew the answer. It had to end with her. It was time for her confession. It was time to start healing. It might not happen today, or even tomorrow, but unless she spoke now, true healing would never happen for her.

"I'm glad you've come to his grave. I never could." She placed the star she held in her hand on her brother's stone. The wind died away and the star remained in place.

Nick squatted on his heels beside her. "Why haven't you come, Miriam? You were closer to him than anyone."

Sighing, she gripped her hands together until they ached.

Now or never. It was now or never.

"Because it was my foolish jealousy that led to his death and to the death of his child."

Nick's hand closed over her arm in a viselike grip. "What do you mean? What child?"

She looked into Nick's eyes. "Did you know he was in love with an *Englisch* girl?"

"No."

"All my life I thought I knew what I wanted, Nick. I wanted to grow old as a member of the Amish community. I thought Mark wanted the same thing. From the time we were little we talked about the day we would be baptized into the faith. That all changed the day *she* came into his life."

"Who was she?" Nick asked. He eased his grip on her arm but didn't take his hand away.

"A girl who lived in Millersburg. Her name was Natalie Perry. I don't know how they met—he never told me that. He stopped telling me almost everything after they began going out. What he did talk about was leaving the faith."

"Miriam, it's not unusual for young Amish men and women to have their doubts."

She shook her head. "You don't understand, Nick. I don't think he had any doubts at all. I was so mad at them, both of them, for disrupting our lives."

"That's understandable."

She shrugged off his hand and rose to her feet. "Maybe, but what happened that last day was inexcusable."

Walking to the fence, she braced her hands on the white-painted boards, feeling the roughness of the planks against her skin. She couldn't face Nick or her brother's memory.

"I've already said I'm sorry a hundred times, Miriam. How many more ways can I say it?" The anguish in his broken voice made her turn around. He stared at her with regret and pain etched in every feature.

Closing her eyes, she blocked the vision of yet one more life she'd damaged. "I wasn't talking about you, Nick. I was talking about what I did that forced Mark to steal a car and drive to his death."

Nick wasn't sure that he had heard Miriam correctly. "I don't understand. Are you saying that it wasn't a joy ride?"

She shook her head. "He was desperately trying to save his child's life."

"You keep talking about a child. What child?"

"Mark's unborn child. I promise you that I wouldn't have interfered if I had known about the baby."

He wanted to grab her and shake the truth out of her.

All these years, he'd wrestled with the reason for Mark's behavior. It had never made sense. His death had been so meaningless. Nick forced himself to remain calm. "Tell me what happened."

"I know now that he must've loved her deeply, but he loved our family, too. I argued with him over and over that it was a mistake to go out into the world with her. I threatened to tell our parents and the bishop about them if he continued seeing her. Mark knew our family would be shunned if he ran off. I made him see he would break our parents' hearts—my heart, too. I convinced him it was God's will that he stay away from her."

Nick had been close to the Kauffman twins when they were all teenagers, but he had stayed away when he realized his feelings for Miriam went beyond friendship. Maybe, if he had hidden his own feelings better, Mark might have confided in him.

"Mark didn't see her for several weeks. The day before he died, she came to the farm. Mark had gone to visit some family with our parents. I could see Natalie was distraught, but I didn't have any sympathy for her. She had come close to destroying our family."

Miriam folded her arms across her chest and shivered. "Natalie told me her family was leaving the next day. She scrawled a note for Mark and thrust it into my hands. She begged me to give it to him as soon as possible."

"And did you?"

Tears ran unchecked down Miriam's face. "If only I had."

"Do you know what was in the note?"

"I gave it to him the next evening after supper. His face turned white when he read it. The look in his eyes frightened me to death. He dropped the note and ran out of the house. That was the last time I saw him alive."

"You said he dropped the note. You read it, didn't you, Miriam? Tell me what it said."

"It said she had just found out that she was pregnant and she didn't want the baby. I think her exact words were, 'I can't go through this alone. If you love me, come for me. I'll be waiting at the train station until nine o'clock. If you don't come, I will know you have made your decision, and I will have made mine. I'm not going to have this baby without you.'"

Miriam covered her face with her hands. "She was going to get rid of Mark's baby. That's why he stole our neighbor's car and wouldn't stop when you came after him. He was desperate to reach Natalie before she left town. The terrible accident was all because of me."

Miriam pressed a hand to her mouth and moaned. Her legs folded and she sank toward the ground. Nick caught her and held her against his chest as she cried.

Nick led Miriam to a small bench beside the caretaker's shed and sat beside her, holding her close as he'd always dreamed of doing. When her crying slowed, he lifted her tear-streaked face with a finger beneath her chin.

"Miriam, you can't keep blaming yourself for a mistake, no matter how serious you believe it is. We are human. We all make mistakes. Some of those mistakes have terrible consequences, but you have to forgive yourself. I know you thought you were protecting your brother."

She nodded. "I stopped seeing you because of my faith. I thought Mark should be able to do the same.

I was jealous that his love for her was stronger than mine for you."

Nick pulled her close again. "I believe that Mark forgave you. He had to know you'd never willingly harm him or anyone. He was your brother. He loved you."

"I believe he has forgiven me, too. But can you forgive me? I let you carry the blame when I was the cause of it all. I'm so sorry for the harsh things I said and for the way I treated you."

"Of course I forgive you. Now that I understand Mark's motives for trying to outrun me it all makes sense. I respect what he was trying to do."

She cupped his face with her hand. "I'm glad I have given you some peace."

He turned his face to kiss the palm of her hand. "You have given me much more than peace. You've given me back one of the best friends I ever had. You."

And now he was going to give back pain. Taking her hand, he held it between his palms. "Miriam, I have something I need to tell you. We got the DNA report back. I know who Hannah's mother is."

Her eyes widened. "Are you sure?"

"Yes, her mother is the young woman who tried to commit suicide. Her name is Mary Smith, but we think it's not her real name. The father has skipped town, but we're looking for him. There's a good possibility that he never knew Mary gave the baby away."

"But why would she do it?"

"The doctor feels she may be suffering from a case of postpartum psychosis. If so, she wasn't responsible for what she did. She may not even be aware of what she did. With treatment, she can recover and be a good mother."

Miriam's eyes softened. "I know that you love Hannah, too. I can only imagine how hard this must be for you."

"I appreciate that you understand. We can hope and pray for her, but little else."

"Life is so unfair."

"Amen to that."

She drew back a little. "How did you know where to find me?"

"I stopped by the hospital and your mother told me you'd come here."

"Mother told you? I never told her I was coming here."

"Then she made a good guess. Or maybe she knows you better than you think."

Worry creased Miriam's brows. "I need to tell her about Mark and his baby."

"It can wait until she is stronger."

"I guess you're right about that. Now that I've told you, it's as if the weight of the world has been taken off my shoulders." Her smile was bright and genuine.

"I'm glad." He wanted to know where he stood in her life now, but he sensed it wasn't the time for such questions. It was a time for healing. What Miriam needed was a supportive friend and he could be that.

He asked, "Are you okay to drive back to town?"

"I am. I don't want Mother to start worrying."

"She seemed fine when I was there. She was eating a piece of peanut butter toast."

"Are you kidding me? She passed out cold this morning and scared me out of three years of my life."

"Like I said, she's a strong woman. You are, too, by the way. I hope you know that." He loved her strength and so much more about her. He prayed he'd have the chance to tell her exactly how he felt one day soon.

Miriam stared into Nick's eyes. She read more than friendship in their blue depths, but was she fooling herself?

He rose to his feet and offered her a hand up. She took it, cherishing the warmth that flowed from his hand to hers. He was a very special man, and she was going to do her level best to make up for the pain she'd caused.

He held her hand a moment longer than he needed to. "I'll let you know if I find out anything else about Hannah's father."

"It's an open case? I thought you couldn't talk about those."

"You've been involved from the beginning. I'll make an exception for you."

"Thanks. I guess I should get back."

"I've got to leave. Why don't you stay a little longer and visit with your brother? I think you need that."

"I think you're right. I'll see you later."

"Count on it." He tipped his hat and walked away.

Miriam followed his suggestion and spent a little time sitting by Mark's grave, talking about her life and about Hannah. In a way, she felt connected to him again—something that had been missing for far too long in her life.

When she returned to the hospital, she found her mother sitting up in a chair and professing to feel great. It was a relief to see the new medication was agreeing with her.

"*Mamm,* how did you know I went to visit Mark's grave?"

"I couldn't think of any place else you would go without telling me if you weren't with Nick. And you've been talking a lot about your brother, lately."

Miriam frowned. "You are the one who has been mentioning him."

"Have I? I don't recall. I think the medicine has made me *narrisch.*"

"You're not crazy, Mother. You've had some bad side effects, that's all."

"I wish I could go home. I'll get well much quicker there."

"If you do well on this new blood pressure medicine, I think you'll be home before you know it."

"How is Hannah? Have you heard anything about her?"

Miriam hesitated. Her mother looked so much better, but would the news of Hannah's situation cause a relapse? She chose to err on the side of caution. "Hannah is still here in the hospital and she is fine."

"I do miss that child. Who knew a person could fall in love with a baby so fast? I reckon Nick will have to carry the baby bed back up to the attic. At least it got used for a little while. Perhaps I should sell it."

"That's something we can talk about later. For now, you need your rest."

"You need some rest, too, child. You look all done in."

"It's been an emotional day. Even that recliner isn't going to keep me awake tonight."

Later that night, Miriam woke with a start in the darkness of her mother's room. She had been dreaming about Hannah. She sat up in the chair to check her mother. Ada was sleeping peacefully. The monitor displaying her vital signs showed they were all normal.

Miriam sat back and closed her eyes, but she couldn't get Hannah out of her mind. There was no use trying to sleep when seeing the baby was the only thing that would make her feel better.

Miriam softly closed her mother's door as she left the room. It was after 2:00 a.m. and the hospital corridors were quiet. She took the elevator down one floor and turned left toward the nursery. As she approached the viewing window, she saw a young woman wearing a hospital gown standing in front of the glass. Her hair hung in a long blond braid down her back. She was barefoot and barely looked old enough to be a mother.

When she noticed Miriam approaching, she turned away quickly. Something in her posture made Miriam take a closer look. This wasn't a new mother happily looking in the window at her baby. This was a girl hoping not to be noticed.

The girl glanced over her shoulder. When she saw Miriam was watching her, she began walking away.

Miriam followed her and called out, "Wait a minute."

The girl walked faster. Miriam was practically running by the time she caught up with her. Reaching out, Miriam grasped her arm. The girl jerked away with a hiss of pain. It was then Miriam noticed the bandages on each of her wrists.

"I'm so sorry. *Ist es vay?*" Miriam asked with deep concern. The words meant, does it hurt? She wanted to know if what she suspected was true.

Shaking her head, the girl whispered, "Only a little."

"So you are Amish. I thought so. You must be Mary

Smith, although Smith is hardly an Amish name. Why don't you tell me your real one?"

The girl froze, a look of fear in her eyes. She was so young. Little more than a child herself.

"Don't be afraid. I'm Miriam Kauffman. I'm sorry if I hurt you."

Staring at the floor, Mary remained silent.

"I saw you looking in the nursery window. She's in there, you know."

Mary raised her face a fraction. "Who?"

"Hannah. She ended up on my doorstep. Of course, you couldn't know that."

"I don't know anyone named Hannah. I don't know what you're talking about." Mary began backing away. "I don't want to get in trouble. I have to go."

"I'm talking about your baby, Mary. I know you told your boyfriend your baby was stillborn and that's why people think you tried to commit suicide, but that's not true."

"It is true—she's better off without me." Mary's voice was little more than a harsh whisper.

"I understand if you wanted her to have a better life, but I don't understand why you thought those Miller boys would make good parents. Between the two of them, they don't have enough sense to come in out of the rain."

Mary remained silent, but she didn't move away. Miriam began to hope she was getting through to her. "The only bright thing the twins did was leave the baby on my porch. Luckily, we found her before she got too cold."

"She shouldn't have been cold. I wrapped her in a quilt."

Miriam smiled. "The workmanship is quite lovely. Did you make it?"

"I stole it." The girl looked ready to bolt.

"With good reason." Miriam laid a hand on her shoulder in an effort to comfort her. The girl shrugged it off.

"I have to get back." She turned away and started to open the stairwell door.

"Don't you want to see her?" Miriam asked. "She's just down the hall in the nursery."

Mary froze. After a long moment, she closed her eyes. "I don't want to see her."

"Because you know if you do, you'll never have the strength to leave her again."

Mary's chin quivered but she didn't speak.

Miriam tried once more to comfort her. She gently brushed a strand of hair behind Mary's ear. Mary flinched, but allowed the touch. "I feel the same way about her. I had no idea how quickly I could fall in love with that little girl. I had no intention of loving her, but she has a way of looking at you that goes straight to your heart."

Mary looked up with angry eyes to glare at Miriam. "What do you want?"

"A long time ago, there was another young woman who didn't want to face being pregnant alone. I stopped her baby's father from helping her. I was never able to tell them how sorry I was and ask their forgiveness. Helping you and Hannah may just make up for that mistake."

"You can't help me."

"Oh, but I can. I do it all the time. I help young Amish people just like you to go out into the world."

"I've been out in the world. It's a bad place."

"Yes, it can be. Are you hungry?" Miriam glanced at her watch.

Mary looked perplexed, as if she couldn't follow Miriam's reasoning. "A little."

"Good. I believe the cafeteria is open for another half hour."

"I'm not supposed to leave the floor where my room is."

"You already have. I say we eat before we're caught. Sometimes it's better to beg forgiveness than to ask permission. I also need to check on my mother before I go. She's a patient here, too."

"What's wrong with her?" Mary glanced back toward the nursery as Miriam led her away.

"She has heart trouble. Having to give up Hannah brought on an attack. She's better now."

"Why didn't they let you keep the baby?"

Miriam pushed the elevator button. "*Englisch* law is a funny thing. It is designed with the best interest of the child at heart. They think Hannah belongs with her mother."

"But I gave her away. Doesn't that prove I'm a bad mother?"

The doors opened and Miriam stepped inside. "I guess that would depend on why you left her in an Amish buggy."

Mary didn't say anything, but she did enter the elevator.

Miriam breathed a sigh of relief. One small step at a time.

When the doors opened on her mother's floor, Miriam led the way, giving Mary a chance to follow or leave as she chose. At her mother's room, she opened the door softly to peek inside. To her surprise, the lights were on and her mother was sitting up in bed with a black knit shawl around her shoulders and her hair done up beneath her crisp white *kapp*.

She smiled at Miriam. "Come in. I've been waiting for you to come back. Esther Zook hired Samson Carter to bring her for a visit while you were gone yesterday. She brought us a shoofly pie and I feel like having a piece. How about you?"

She leaned forward to see behind Miriam. "Would your friend like some?"

Chapter Fifteen

Nick glanced from the tearstained face of the night nurse to the furious, red face of Dr. Palmer, the shrink in charge of Mary Smith, to the bulked-up security guard standing with his massive arms crossed. They were all trying to talk at once. Nick held up his hand to stop them. "You're saying she just walked out of this building and no one saw her leave?"

First he finds Hannah's mother and then he loses her again. This was starting out to be a bad day, and it was only four in the morning.

The nurse said quickly, "I can assure you, Sheriff, this has never happened before on our floor. The sitter staying with Mary Smith says she only nodded off for a few seconds. When she looked up, Mary was gone."

"She vanished from the entire hospital in seconds. I doubt that," Dr. Palmer grumbled.

"Either way, she's missing. What about Hannah?" Nick asked quickly.

The security officer said, "The nursery says she's fine. I called them first thing."

Relieved, Nick nodded. "I'll get an APB out on Mary

Smith right away." He spoke into his radio and ordered the all points bulletin for a white female, approximately five foot tall with long blond hair, wearing a hospital gown when last seen.

There was little else he could do at the moment. He looked to Dr. Palmer. "Did you tell her that we have her baby?"

"I did."

"And what did she say?"

"Nothing. She still won't speak to me or to the staff."

"Any idea what would make her cut out? Was her boyfriend in to see her?"

The nurse shook her head. "No one has been to see her."

"That you know of," Dr. Palmer snipped.

Nick turned to the security officer. "Organize a search of the entire building, every broom closet and storage room. I want the security camera footage of the doors reviewed to see if she actually left."

"Will do." The burly man walked away, talking into his radio.

Nick said, "I'll be in the cardiac care unit if you need me." Miriam would want to know what had happened. She dealt with runaway teenagers all the time. Maybe she would have some insight that would be helpful in locating Mary Smith.

And maybe he just needed to see her again.

When he reached Ada's room, he paused outside the door. He didn't want to wake her or frighten her. He eased the door open to see if he could catch Miriam's attention. Instead of a dark room, he saw all the lights were on and the sound of Amish chatter filled the air. He stepped inside.

Ada was propped up in bed and involved in telling a story. Mary Smith sat cross-legged at the end of Ada's bed, a bright smile on her face. Miriam sat in a chair beside her mother and a nurse's aide sat in the recliner with a piece of pie on a paper plate.

Mary Smith saw him first. Her eyes went wide with fright. Miriam, seeing her distress, turned around. She waved at him. "Hi, Nick. Care for some shoofly pie? We have one piece left, but I'm afraid it's a small one."

Miriam turned back to Mary. "Don't worry, he's one of the good guys."

"Flattering as it is to hear you admit that, Miriam, can I ask what's going on here? Do you know that I have every officer in the county on the lookout for Ms. Smith?"

"Don't be silly, Nick. How could we know that? We've been in here since two-thirty."

"Having a party?"

Mary slid off the bed and spoke to Miriam in Pennsylvania Dutch. Miriam shook her head. The nurse's aide finished her last bite of pie and said, "I've got to get going. Thanks for the pie. It was great."

She had a faint German accent and Nick took her to be another ex-Amish. He stepped aside so she could slip out the door with a sheepish look on her face. He flipped the switch on his radio and canceled the APB, then he took a seat in the recliner. "What have I missed?"

Miriam brought him a thin slice of pie and said, "Mary Smith is really Mary Shetler, she's fifteen, not nineteen and Kevin isn't her husband or Hannah's father. Hannah's father is a married man in Canton. Hannah was working as a maid there and he seduced her. She ran away because she couldn't go back to her family. Her mother had passed away and her stepfather wasn't happy about having another mouth to feed. Mary hooked up with Kevin because he promised to take care of her, but he's into drugs and not a nice man. Mary thinks he's a drug runner. Each week he makes a trip to Canada."

Miriam paused to look over at Mary for confirmation. Mary nodded and fixed her gaze on her bare feet.

"That's a very interesting story. What I want to know is why Mary left her baby in the back of a buggy?"

Miriam scowled at him, but returned to her chair and waited for Mary to speak.

"Kevin wanted to sell the baby." Mary's voice trembled with fear.

"We told you he wasn't a nice man," Ada added. "That's all right, child. Tell your story."

Mary smiled at her and stood straighter. "He said we could get a lot of money for a baby like mine. I was scared he would go through with it and I wouldn't be able to stop him."

"He can't hurt either of you now," Ada assured her.

Mary nodded. "I took the baby and put her in the Amish buggy because I didn't want her to grow up in the *Englisch* world. I knew she would be safe with a good Amish family if I couldn't return. I left a note to tell them I'd be back for her. I needed time to get enough money to get away."

She fell silent and Nick said, "When they didn't return with her the next week, what happened?"

"I… I tried to be strong, but I knew I'd never see her again. Not knowing where she was, if she was safe—I couldn't stand it."

"Did you slash your own wrists?" Miriam asked gently.

She nodded as tears ran down her cheeks.

Nick couldn't begin to understand what this girl had been through. He was only grateful that she had survived. One thing was certain. He'd make it his business to see that Kevin was brought to justice. "Will you testify to Kevin's intentions in a court of law? Can you give me the names of the people he was working with?"

Ada said, "We must forgive him. It is up to God to judge."

Miriam laid a hand on Mary's shoulder. "We do forgive, but we must also care for those who can't take care of themselves. Kevin may try to do this to another woman and her baby."

Mary looked at Nick and nodded. "I have names. I'll testify."

Miriam hugged her. "Now, you must grow strong because your baby is going to need you."

It took a long, hard week of police work, but Kevin Dunbar was finally behind bars in Nick's jail, and there wouldn't be any bail this time. It was with intense satisfaction that Nick closed and locked the cell door.

He returned to his office and started to pick up the phone. He hadn't seen Miriam since her mother was dismissed from the hospital the day after Mary Shetler told her story. It had been far too long as far as he was concerned.

His secretary came in. "Sheriff, I took a message from Helen Benson. She wanted you to know that Hannah has been returned to the temporary custody of her mother. Hannah's case will remain open and the mother has to continue with her counseling but Helen is hopeful that Mary Shetler will be granted full custody in the future."

"Thanks. That's good news." It was for Mary and Hannah, but not for Miriam and Ada. Instead of the phone, he picked up his car keys. He'd rather deliver this news and his other news in person.

It took him thirty minutes to reach the turnoff to the Kauffman place. When he did, he saw Bishop Zook coming down the lane in his black buggy. Nick pulled to the side of the lane and waited.

When the bishop drew alongside, Nick rolled down his window. "Afternoon, Bishop. I hope all is well at the Kauffman place."

"All is better than well, Nicolas, for a lost sheep has returned to the fold. I performed a baptism this day. There is nothing but rejoicing in our hearts when such an event is brought about by God's mercy. I can't remember the last time I saw Ada so happy. I must get going, Sheriff, for I have cows that need milking and I have good news to spread." He tipped his hat and slapped the reins on his horse's rump. The mare trotted away, leaving Nick staring after the bishop in shock.

Miriam had been baptized into the Amish faith? Perhaps he should have seen it coming, but he hadn't. Not now, not when he was so certain they had a chance to be together.

He drove slowly up to the house thinking of all the lost chances he'd had to tell her how much he loved her.

He spotted Miriam hanging laundry on the clothesline beside the house. His heart turned over at the sight of her the way it always did and probably always would. He'd gained her forgiveness and opened the door for her to return to her Amish roots. He wanted to be happy for her, but he wasn't ready for that. The pain of loving her and losing her all over again was too new and two raw.

She waved when she spotted him and walked toward him with a laundry hamper balanced against one hip. She wore a dark blue dress with the long sleeves rolled up and an apron tied around her waist. A white kerchief covered her gorgeous hair. Her smile was bright and open, the way he remembered it when she was young. It was good to see her happy.

One of them deserved to be happy.

He got out of the car and waited with his hands thrust into the front pockets of his jeans.

"Nick, I was hoping to see you. I have so much to tell you that I hardly know where to begin." She stopped a few feet away. When he didn't respond, her smile faded, as if she was uncertain of her welcome.

He couldn't wish her happy when she was breaking his heart.

"I just stopped in to say goodbye and see how your mother is doing."

She frowned slightly. "What do you mean you stopped in to say goodbye?"

"There are some trout waiting patiently for me to toss my hand-tied flies close enough to bite." Maybe wading in the swirling waters might help him forget the way she felt in his arms. The way he wanted to kiss her, even now, when he knew it was wrong.

Relief filled her eyes. "I forgot, you have a vacation pending. You deserve some time off after all you have done for us."

"How is your mother?"

"The stent has helped enormously with her energy level and her new medication is working. She is happy as a lark and bossing everyone around again."

"I'm glad." He braced himself to say what he didn't

want to say. "I'm glad, too, that you have found your heart's desire, Miriam. It means a lot to me to know that you are happy and at peace. I wish only the best for you."

"You sound so serious. Is something wrong?" Worry crept into her eyes once more.

Didn't she know how he felt? "Did you think this would be easy for me? I wish you had told me yourself instead of letting me hear it from the Bishop Zook."

"I thought you would be happy with my decision."

He took a deep breath and tried to disguise the hurt in his voice. "I will try to be happy for you, Miriam. Goodbye."

He turned back and started to open the car door. She dropped her laundry basket and stopped him by grabbing his wrist.

"Okay, I really didn't expect you would jump for joy, but I thought you'd be a little more enthusiastic. Tell me why you're unhappy about this?"

The warmth of her hand on his bare skin crumbled his defenses. "Do you really need to ask that?"

She stepped closer. "Apparently I do. Talk to me, Nick."

He closed his eyes. "I have loved you since I was twenty years old. I have never stopped loving you. I kept silent back then because I knew how much your faith meant to you. I could not ask you to choose me over your relationship with God. After Mark's death, it was almost a relief to realize how much you hated me. It made it easier to stay away from you. I'm glad you have returned to the Amish life, Miriam, but it will never be easy for me to stay away from you."

He felt her hands cup his face. Years of pent-up longing broke free and tears squeezed out from beneath his lashes. "I love you so much, Miriam."

"And I love you, Nicolas Bradley. I don't know where you got the idea that I have returned to my Amish roots, but you are grossly mistaken. I have no plans to leave my *Englisch* life."

His eyes popped open and he focused on her face so close to his. "Bishop Zook said everyone, particularly your mother, is rejoicing because the lost lamb has been returned to the fold. I thought he was talking about you."

"He was not talking about me. He was talking about Mary Shetler. She is the one who has returned to the fold. Yes, my mother is happy because she has a new daughter and a new granddaughter to help rear. That's the news I wanted to tell you. Mary and Hannah have moved in with me and my mother."

Unable to contain his joy, Nick pulled Miriam against his chest in a crushing hug. "Oh, thank you, God, for taking pity on this man. Thank you, God."

Miriam pulled her arms free of his grip and then slipped them around his neck. "I thank God daily for bringing you back into my life. I have been so blessed." Rising up on tiptoe, she kissed him as he had dreamed she would one day.

When she drew away, he saw love glowing in her eyes and his heart expanded until he thought it would break, not with sorrow, but with joy.

She smiled at him and he knew he would never tire of seeing that smile. "Nick, I have cared deeply for you since I was a teenager, but I never realized that I loved you until the day I found you rocking and singing to Hannah on the front porch."

He still couldn't believe he was holding her in his arms. "I love you. I don't care when you fell in love with me, only that you did."

"I didn't think I deserved to find love. Now I know God wants all his children to love and be loved in return. So maybe what I need is a little more practice at loving you." She lifted her face inviting his kiss. He was all too happy to comply.

As his lips closed over hers, the world narrowed to the softness of her skin and the taste of her lips, the way they fit his perfectly. His pulse hammered in his ears. He never wanted to lose her again.

When she finally broke away, he pulled her head forward and tucked it against his neck. "I think you're getting the hang of it."

Miriam smiled, breathing in the wonderful scent that was uniquely Nick's own. Resting in his arms, she was happier than she had ever been in her life. She loved him, and he loved her in return. God was indeed good.

She couldn't resist teasing Nick a little more. "You're lucky I'm something of a perfectionist. I'll keep trying until I get it right."

"Oh, you have it right, sweetheart. But if you want to keep practicing, I'm going to be available for the next seventy years."

She pulled back to look up at him. "Careful, Sheriff, that sounded surprisingly like a proposal."

He cleared his throat and held her at arm's length. "I've always believed that good communication is the key to any relationship. So let me be clear about this. Miriam Kauffman, will you do me the honor of becoming my wife?"

She stared at him in stunned surprise. "Nick, are you serious?"

"I've never been more serious in my life. We have wasted enough time."

"Two weeks ago I didn't even like you."

"If you've come this far in two weeks, I can only imagine how good things will be in two months or two years. I understand that this was rather sudden because, believe me, I didn't come here intending to propose. So if you want some time to think it over, I understand completely, but I couldn't stop myself from offering you my heart. I thought I'd lost you."

"Yes."

He eyed her intently. "Yes, you want some time to think it over? Or yes, you will marry me?"

"In an effort to improve the communication in our relationship, let me be perfectly clear. Yes, Nicolas Bradley, I will marry you."

"Are you sure?"

"Are you trying to make me change my mind?"

He pulled her close once more. "Not at all, darling. I just can't believe that I've attained my heart's desire."

She snuggled closer. "I'm good at helping people discover what it is that they really want."

He chuckled and she felt the sound reverberate in his chest beneath her ear. She would never grow tired of being held in his arms. He lifted her hand and placed a kiss on her palm. "When?"

"When what?" she asked with dreamy happiness.

"When can we get married?"

From behind Miriam, Mary said, "It looks like it had better be soon."

Miriam twisted in Nick's hold but she didn't move out of his embrace. "I think I would enjoy a long engagement. What do you think, Nick?" She gave him a saucy glance.

"I will wait for as long as it takes. As long as it doesn't take more than two months."

"Two months!" Ada had come out onto the porch with Hannah in her arms.

Nick said, "I can take her off your hands faster if you need me to, Ada."

"Bah, no one can get ready for a wedding in two months. We shall need at least six months."

"Is that what you want?" Nick whispered into her ear. His warm breath sent a chill of anticipation sweeping across her body.

"I want to stay here, wrapped in your arms for the rest of my life."

"My thoughts exactly." He pressed a kiss on her temple. It was nice, but she wanted more. She turned and raised her face. His lips found hers and she gave herself over to the magic of his touch.

Hannah began to fuss. Ada said, "Enough with the kissy-kissy. The baby wants to be fed, and we have many plans to make. Come inside, everyone."

Nick stopped kissing Miriam long enough to say, "We'll be along in a little bit, Ada. Your daughter and I have a lot of lost time to make up for."

Mary laughed and shook her head. She took Hannah from Ada's arms. "Kids today, they never listen to their elders."

As she followed Ada back inside the house, Miriam gazed up at Nick. She would never grow tired of seeing the love shining in his eyes. "Before we get hitched, there is one thing you should know."

"Only one?"

"This is an important thing. I intend to adopt Mary. Both she and my mother are in favor of it. That way, if anything happens to my mother, or to me, Mary and Hannah will always have a place to live."

Nick raised one hand to rub his jaw. "You mean in addition to getting a bride, I'm also going to be getting a teenage daughter—with the baby."

"That's right, Grandpa."

He groaned. "Grandpa? I thought I'd have twenty-five or thirty years before I got stuck with that label."

"Well?"

"Well what?" he asked as he pulled her close and settled her against his hip.

"We come as a package deal. Take all of us or take none of us."

He kissed the tip of her nose. "You drive a hard bargain, Miriam Kauffman. I'll do it as long as you include Bella in the deal."

"Done." She smiled at him with all the love in her heart.

"What do you think Mark would say about this?" His question held an odd edge.

"I think Mark is glad. He loved both of us."

"How do you think your mother would feel about having an English grandchild?"

Miriam rolled her eyes. "You are getting a little ahead of yourself, Sheriff. You haven't walked down the aisle with me yet."

"I wasn't talking about us. I've been debating whether to tell you this or not, but I think I should. I did some digging, and I found Mark's girlfriend, Natalie Perry. She lives in St. Louis now, with her eight-year-old son."

Miriam blinked hard. Had she heard Nick right? "She kept Mark's baby?"

"Yes, she did."

"Nick, that is wonderful. Oh, my goodness, how I agonized over the thought that I was responsible for two deaths. I'm so glad."

"I knew you would be—that's why I came here today. I wanted to give you some good news, and to tell you Kevin Dunbar has been arrested. Will you tell your mother about Mark's child?"

"I have already told her about my part in Mark's death. I told her the reason he was on the road that night. She will be as thrilled as I am that Natalie kept the baby. Do you think there's any chance that we could meet her and see him? Do you know his name?"

"His name is Mark."

Tears welled up in her eyes as words failed her. Nick slipped a finger beneath her chin and tipped her face up. "Please, don't cry."

"They are happy tears, Nick. Come inside and give *Mamm* the news."

She started toward the door, but he caught her hand and pulled her back. "Not so fast. We have unfinished business."

She grinned at him. "What business would that be?"

"You haven't said *when* you will marry me. I'm not leaving this spot until I have an answer."

Miriam wrapped her arms around his neck. "In that case, we could be here all night."

"I'm in favor of that." He lowered his head. Miriam had a moment to thank God for His mercy and goodness before Nick's kiss made her forget everything but the wonder of his love.

* * * * *

AN AMISH REUNION

Jo Ann Brown

For Janet Jones Bann
Thanks for all you do for all of us,
especially being my friend.

Then said he unto me, Fear not, Daniel:
for from the first day that thou didst set
thine heart to understand, and to chasten thyself
before thy God, thy words were heard,
and I am come for thy words.
—*Daniel* 10:12

Chapter One

Paradise Springs
Lancaster County, Pennsylvania

The knock came at the worst possible moment.

Hannah Lambright had her *grossmammi* partway to her bed where she could look out, through the cold rain, at the covered bridge over Hunter's Mill Creek until she fell asleep for her afternoon nap. *Grossmammi* Ella depended on Hannah to help her. She refused to use a cane, not wanting to be considered old, though she'd recently celebrated her 90th birthday.

Smoothing the blanket over her *grossmammi*, who'd already closed her eyes, Hannah hurried from the room. She wiped her hands on her black apron and pushed loose strands of hair under her white *kapp*. The impatient rapping continued. She opened the door. Words fled from her mouth and her brain as she stared at a handsome face she'd never expected to see at her door. She couldn't be mistaken about the identity of the man with sleek black hair beneath his dripping straw hat and deep blue eyes set below assertive brows. Her momentary hope that she was looking at his twin brother vanished when she noticed the cleft in his chin.

"Daniel Stoltzfus, why are you here?" she asked.

"Is she yours?"

Only then did she realize Daniel held a wicker container about the size of a laundry basket. A little girl, her golden hair in uneven braids sticking out like a bug's antennae, was curled, half-asleep in the basket. Chocolate crumbs freckled her cheeks. The *kind* wore an *Englisch*-style pink overall and a shirt with puffy sleeves. She couldn't have been more than eighteen months old.

"Mine?" she choked.

The little girl's dark brown eyes opened. Her chubby, adorable face displayed the unmistakable characteristics of Down syndrome.

"I was on my way to the covered bridge when I saw her in your side yard," he replied. "By the time my buggy stopped and I could get out, she'd disappeared behind the house."

"My honeybees are out there! Did she get stung?"

"I don't think so. Is this *kind* yours?"

She recoiled from the strong emotions darkening his blue eyes. Behind his question, she heard unspoken accusations. An answer of *ja* would mean not only was she an unmarried woman with a *kind*, but she let the toddler wander near her beehives.

After the five months she and Daniel had walked out together three years ago, did he know so little about her? Didn't he know she was the dependable one? As she'd been since her *mamm* died when she was ten years old. When she dared to trust someone again, she'd chosen Daniel Stoltzfus, who'd broken her heart.

"I don't know who she is," Hannah said, determined

to keep her thoughts to herself. "Just because she was in my yard—"

"And this basket was on your porch. She must have crawled out of it."

"Why would someone leave her on my front porch?"

"I've got no idea." He glanced over his shoulder. "It's raining. Can we come in?"

Hannah could think of a dozen reasons to say no, but nodded. She couldn't leave a young *kind* out in the cold and damp...nor Daniel.

He set the basket on the well-worn sofa and squatted beside it. When the little girl sat and began to whimper, he said, "It's okay, *liebling*. You're safe."

She didn't know if the little girl knew the word meant sweetheart, but the *kind* began to calm as she gazed at him, trying to figure out who he was.

Hannah bit back a sad laugh. After months with him, she'd been shocked when he turned out not to be the man she'd thought he was. She shook those thoughts aside. The *kind* should be her sole concern.

The little girl moved, and Hannah heard a crackle. A crumpled and wet envelope was stuck in the basket. Hannah took it and removed a single piece of wet paper. How long had the basket and the toddler been in the rain? She peeled the damp edges apart and was relieved the writing hadn't been smudged.

"What does it say?" Daniel asked.

She read aloud, "Shelby is your sister. Take care of her." Looking at the *kind*, she asked, "Are you Shelby?"

The little girl blinked.

"I guess Shelby *is* her name." He began to make faces at the little girl. "Does it say anything else?"

Hannah gasped when she saw the signature.

Daed.

In the fifteen years since he'd left after her *mamm*'s death, her *daed* hadn't written her a single letter. At first, she'd thought it was because he'd been placed under the *bann* when he abandoned his faith along with his only *kind*. Later, he'd sent postcards from the places around the United States and Canada. Nevada and Florida. California and Mississippi. Manitoba and Texas. Never anywhere near Paradise Springs. And never with any message other than *Daed.*

Until now.

What was going on?

"Is it signed?" Daniel asked.

She nodded, unable to speak. Had her *daed* been right outside the door? Why hadn't he knocked? Did he think she'd turn him away? She sighed as she realized he might have been afraid she wouldn't take the basket from him. The rules of the *bann* were clear—she could speak with him, though her words should be focused on persuading him to confess his sins and return to their plain life. She couldn't eat at the same table or take a piece of paper from his hand. The whole community hoped a shunning would convince an offender to repent; then family and friends would welcome him into the fold as if the *bann* had never happened. As God forgave, so should those who loved Him.

"Who signed it, Hannah?" Daniel's voice was as gentle as when he'd spoken to the little girl.

She gulped, trying to swallow past the lump in her throat. How could *Daed* have left without seeing her again? Feeling as hurt as the day she'd discovered he'd jumped the fence into the *Englisch* world, she whispered, "My *daed.*"

Daniel's eyes widened. He was as stunned as she was. More than once, while they'd been courting, she'd talked about her hope to see her *daed* again.

Under a stained blanket, she saw a lump. She lifted out two plastic bags. The handles were tied together. She hooked her finger in the top of one and pulled. The bag tore, and tiny clothing, most in shades of pink, scattered across the floor.

"Her clothes, I'd guess," Daniel said as he picked up the little girl. He bounced the *kind* and tried to keep her from pulling off his straw hat at the same time.

The sight was so endearing Hannah smiled in spite of herself. When a chuckle escaped, he looked at her in astonishment.

"Are you okay?" he asked.

"I don't know." That was the most honest answer she had. One minute, she'd been going about her daily routine. The next, the man she'd once believed wanted to marry her was standing on her porch with a *boppli* in a basket. "I don't know what to do or say."

"You could start by holding your sister."

Sister! She'd never had a sister...or a brother. Her extended family lived in northern New York, too far away except for an occasional visit when one of her cousins married. It'd been her and *Grossmammi* Ella since her *daed* left. She'd dreamed of having a sibling. As a *kind*, she'd prayed night after night for one. Had God answered her prayer like this?

She held out her arms, and Daniel shifted the *kind* so Hannah could take her.

With a cry, Shelby clung to him. She buried her face in his shoulder, rubbing chocolate into his coat, and wrapped her tiny arms around his neck. Her sobs trembled along her.

"Give her a minute," Daniel said before murmuring in *Englisch*, "Shelby, look at Hannah. She likes little girls."

She shrieked as if caught in a swarm of bees.

Hannah yanked her hands away. Her little sister, the blessed gift she'd yearned for, wanted nothing to do with her. And Shelby cuddled against the man who'd wanted nothing to do with her either.

Daniel watched the flurry of emotions sweep across Hannah's face. Frustration. Uncertainty. Regret. Pain. He'd seen the last when she'd found him flirting with other girls. The memory of that evening had lurked in his thoughts for three years, a constant reminder that if he let someone else come as close to his heart as she had, he could wound that person as badly. Better to keep things light and laugh with every girl instead of making a marvelous one like Hannah cry. He wasn't going to take a chance of that happening again. He'd learned his lesson the hardest possible way.

He wouldn't have come to the stone-end farmhouse where she lived with her great-grandmother and her bees if he'd had another choice. But he needed to ask for a favor. A big one, and he wasn't sure if Hannah would agree when they hadn't spoken in three years.

He should look away from her pretty face, but he couldn't. How was it possible that Hannah had become even more beautiful? He hadn't seen her since that evening she'd walked out of his life. His older brother Amos had occasionally mentioned Hannah bringing honey from her hives to sell at his grocery store. Each time,

Daniel had changed the subject. He didn't want to think about how he'd ruined everything between him and Hannah.

In the rainy day's dim light, her hair was the shade of her honey. Drawn under a green bandana that matched her dress, her hair framed her oval face. Her chocolate-brown eyes displayed her feelings. She'd never been able to hide her thoughts. Now she was upset because the *kind* refused to go to her.

"It's okay, Shelby," he said in *Englisch* because he suspected she didn't understand *Deitsch*, the language the Amish spoke. "You don't have to go anywhere you don't want to."

The *kind* tilted her head; then she gave him a big grin, showing off tiny teeth. Her eyes crinkled closed, and he saw the striking resemblance between the little girl and Hannah. The shape of their faces, those dark eyes and the shiny, honey-gold hair were almost identical.

"Is your great-grandmother here?" he asked.

"She's taking a nap." Hannah continued to stare at Shelby with distress.

"With all this noise?"

"*Grossmammi* Ella takes a nap every day from one until two-thirty. Even if she's awake, she won't come out until two-thirty." Her lips quirked. "No matter what."

"That's weird."

"It's her way."

His nose wrinkled. "Someone could use a diaper change." He ran a finger along the *kind*'s tiny arm. "And she's cold. What she needs is a *gut*, warm bath."

"She won't let me give her one." Again the dismay filled her voice.

"I'll help." He hesitated, then said, "If you'll let me."

She glanced toward the front door. As clearly as if she'd shouted, he knew she wanted him to leave.

"This isn't about what happened to us, Hannah. It's about what's happened to your little sister."

Her face blanched, but she squared her shoulders. He recognized the motion. Whenever Hannah set her shoulders, she was ready to take on a disagreeable task. He'd prefer not to think she saw him as that.

"The bathroom is this way." She gathered the scattered clothes and bags before leading him into the simple kitchen. She opened the door next to the woodstove and motioned for him to enter.

He couldn't ignore how Shelby tightened her arms around him when he passed Hannah. He wanted to tell the *kind* she was making a big mistake. Hannah would do anything for anyone. Everybody knew they could depend on her.

He, on the other hand... He frowned. Trying to explain to Hannah why he'd done what he did would be a waste of breath. He'd failed her three years ago, and he doubted he'd do better now. He couldn't find the words to tell her how important it was for him to own a business as his older brothers did. He couldn't admit how scared and worried he'd been to try to handle the challenges of that along with a wife and family. He'd wanted to be honest, but how could he tell the most dependable person he knew he wasn't sure she could depend on him? And then he'd proved that by flirting with someone else. He couldn't remember which girl it'd been.

Pushing aside self-recriminations, he carried Shelby into the bathroom as Hannah put the clothes on a counter by the sink. It was a small room. The big bathtub

must have been installed for Hannah's *grossmammi*.
The tub had a door in the side and held a chair where
someone could sit while bathing. Hannah made sure the
door was locked and lifted out the chair. She shoved it
as far toward the window as she could. After turning
on the faucet and testing the water to make sure it was
neither too hot nor too cold, she faced him.

"Will she let me take her?" she asked.

"Let me get her started, and we'll see how she does.
Can you get a towel and washcloth while I put her into
the tub?"

"*Ja*. They're right behind you. I'll get—"

He put out an arm to halt her from reaching past
him. When her hand touched his arm, she flinched as
if he were connected to an electric circuit and she'd
gotten zapped.

Pulling down a towel, she shoved it into his hand.
"Why are you here?"

He set the little girl on the floor and knelt to unhook
the straps on her overalls. That gave him an excuse not
to look at Hannah while he asked for her help. Shelby
wiggled as he drew off her wet clothes. Once she was
undressed and her braids undone, he rinsed off her bottom before placing her in the tub. She slapped the water
and giggled when it flew everywhere, including the front
of his shirt.

Taking a washcloth and soap from Hannah, he began
washing the *kind*'s face and arms. He kept one hand
on Shelby's shoulder as he said, "I've been hired to
strengthen the Hunter's Mill Creek Bridge so it can be
used for heavier traffic again, and I need your help."

"I'm not much *gut* with a hammer."

Was she jesting? He didn't dare take his eyes off the

little girl to see. Deciding it'd be better not to respond to her comment, he said, "I can't begin work until something is done about the beehive in a rotting board beneath the bridge."

"Bees? What kind?" Excitement sifted into her voice.

"I think they're honeybees."

"You're not sure?"

He risked a quick glance at Hannah who sat on the chair she'd taken from the tub. She watched how he cleaned the toddler. "You're the expert. Not me. I can't tell one kind of bee from another. They need to be moved so nobody gets stung while we're working on the bridge. I considered spraying them, but I've heard there aren't as many honeybees as there used to be."

"*Ja*, that's true. Pesticides and pests have killed them."

"That's why I decided to check with an expert—with *you*—before I contacted an exterminator." He cupped his hand and poured warm water over Shelby's head, wetting it so he could wash her hair. He kept his other hand above her eyes to prevent water from flowing into them.

"*Danki* for checking, Daniel. Many people don't. They spray the hive, never stopping to think we need honeybees to pollinate our crops." She held out a bottle of shampoo. "You're *gut* with her."

"Practice. My sister Esther was a lot younger than the rest of us, and I used to help *Mamm*. And I've got a bunch of nieces and nephews." He edged back. "Do you want to put the shampoo on her hair?"

"Do you think she'll let me?"

"One way to know." Keeping his right hand on Shelby's arm, he stepped aside.

Hannah eased past him, making sure not an inch of her brushed against him, not even the hem of her apron or *kapp* strings. She bent over the tub and smiled. "Let's get your pretty hair clean, Shelby."

The *kind*'s lower lip trembled, and thick tears rolled down her cheeks.

Her face falling, Hannah edged away. She wrapped her arms around herself as Shelby returned to her playing when Daniel stood by the tub again.

"How am I going to take care of her when she hates me?" Hannah murmured.

"She doesn't hate you. She's scared, and she's known me longer."

"Two minutes! That doesn't make sense."

"Just as it doesn't make sense she doesn't like you. Who knows what goes on in the heads of *bopplin*?" He shampooed Shelby's hair, taking care not to get suds in her eyes. He'd stop at his brother's grocery store and get some shampoo made for *boppli* before he returned to work on the bridge tomorrow.

At that thought, he said, "I'll make you a deal, Hannah." He began to rinse Shelby's fine hair. "You help me by moving the bees, and I'll help you learn how to take care of Shelby. In addition, I'll do all I can to find your *daed*."

"How will you find *Daed*?"

"I can ask the police—"

She shook her head. "It's not our way to involve *Englischers* in our business."

"It may need to be if you want to know the truth about your *daed*."

"I don't know." She dragged the reluctant words out.

"If the bishop says it's okay, will you?" He hated backing her into a corner, but she must see that they needed help in the extraordinary situation.

Hannah nodded, but didn't speak.

Knowing he shouldn't push her further, he lifted the *kind* out and wrapped her in a towel before her wiggling sent water all over the bathroom. He watched Hannah's face, knowing she wished he'd walked away as he had before. But she needed his help. And he needed hers. None of the men he'd hired would get close to the bridge supports while the bees were there.

Putting Shelby on the floor, he grabbed for the unopened bag. He couldn't reach it.

"What do you need?" Hannah asked.

Your agreement to move the bees, he wanted to say, but didn't. She was upset, and he didn't want to make her feel worse. "A diaper."

She opened the bag and frowned. "Um…"

"Let me look." He took the bag, and with a smile, he pulled out a disposable diaper. He diapered the toddler and pulled a warm shirt and trousers from the counter to dress her.

Hannah handed him a pair of socks. "I'm sorry. I've only seen cloth diapers before."

"It's okay." He hesitated, then said, "If you want, I can take her to our house. My *mamm* will watch her."

"No!"

"Are you sure?"

"*Ja.* My *daed* could come back. She needs to be here when he does."

Daniel didn't argue, though he had his doubts any man who abandoned two daughters would return. "Did you see how I put the diaper on her?"

"*Ja.* It's easy."

"It is. As you're going to need my help with her, what do you say? Do we have a deal? I'll help you with

Shelby as well as try to find your *daed*, and you'll move the bees for me. Do we have a deal?"

"All right, Daniel," she said as if agreeing to a truce with her worst enemy. He flinched, hoping she didn't consider him that. He knew he'd have time to find out when she went on, "It's a deal."

Chapter Two

As soon as the words agreeing to the plan with Daniel left her lips, Hannah wanted to take them back. But how could she turn aside his help? Looking at the little girl perched on Daniel's knee while he sat on the edge of the tub, Hannah knew she needed his assistance. Her great-grandmother might want to help, but the elderly woman was fragile. *Grossmammi* Ella couldn't chase an active toddler. Though nothing had ever been said, Hannah often wondered if her *grossmammi* resented having a ten-year-old dumped on her to raise.

"Gut," Daniel said as he shifted Shelby into his arms as he stood.

He avoided Hannah's eyes, and she couldn't meet his either. Suddenly the bathroom seemed as small as a phone shack.

It seemed to shrink farther when he went on, "I'm glad you're willing to be sensible about this, Hannah. After all, what happened in the past is best left there."

"I agree." That wasn't exactly the truth, but she wanted to put an end to this strained conversation. She couldn't imagine how their "deal" would work. Daniel might be able to leave the past in the past, but she wasn't sure she could. A heated aura of humiliation surrounded her whenever she thought of how he'd dumped her without an explanation.

Shelby chirped and tugged at his hair, interrupting Hannah's bleak thoughts. A *kind* depended on her. For that reason—and to protect a hive of what she hoped were healthy honeybees—she would work with Daniel. She wouldn't trust him. She'd learned her lesson.

Hearing a soft chime from the timer on the kitchen stove, Hannah gathered the wet towel and washcloth. She tossed them in the tub and ignored Daniel's surprise when she left them there.

"Do you have something in the oven?" he asked.

"No. My great-grandmother sets the timer every afternoon before going to rest in her room. About fifteen minutes after it chimes, she'll come out. I try to have a cup of tea ready for her."

"I should get going then."

"But the bees—"

He pointed toward the window where water ran down the glass. "Let's put that off until the rain stops. We can go tomorrow morning."

"That makes sense." At least one thing had today. Everything else, from Daniel's appearance at her door to the idea her *daed* might have been there moments before, had been bizarre and painful. Why hadn't *Daed* knocked on the door?

A fresh wave of grief struck her as hard as the rain battered the window. Had *Daed* thought she wouldn't want to see him? Or did he think *Grossmammi* Ella would refuse to let him in? Hannah would have talked with him on the porch. She wouldn't have been able to hug him while he was under the *bann*, but she would have welcomed him home and asked him why he'd left her behind. Why hadn't he come home? And, when he did, why did he leave Shelby without letting Hannah know he was there?

"If you need anything before I come back," Daniel said, "let me know."

She frowned. "How? I can't leave a toddler and my great-grandmother here alone."

"My brother has a phone in the barn. I'll give you the number."

"Danki." She regretted snapping at him. She couldn't let dismay with her *daed* color her conversations with others. Maybe Daniel was right. Leaving the past in the past was a *gut* idea. "Our *Englisch* neighbors let me use their phone when it's necessary. We should be okay. There are plenty of diapers and clothing in the bag for tonight."

"Gut." He left the bathroom.

Suddenly there seemed to be enough oxygen to take a breath, and Hannah sucked in a quick one. She needed to get herself on an even keel if Daniel was visiting for the next few days. How long would it take to learn how to take care of Shelby? Not that long, she was sure.

Her certainty wavered when Daniel paused in the living room and held out Shelby to her. Smiling and cooing at the *kind*, Hannah took her.

The room erupted into chaos when the toddler shrieked at the top of her lungs and reached out toward him, her body stiff with the indignity of being handed off to Hannah.

"Go!" Hannah ordered.

"Are you sure?" Daniel asked.

"*Ja.*" Stretching out his leaving would just upset everyone more.

Shelby's crying became heartbreaking as Daniel slipped out and closed the door behind him. She squirmed so hard, Hannah put her down.

Teetering as if the floor rocked beneath her, Shelby rushed to the door. She stretched her hand toward the knob, but couldn't reach it. Leaning her face against the door, she sobbed.

Hannah was tempted to join her in tears. The sight of the distraught *kind* shattered her heart. When she took a step forward, wanting to comfort Shelby, the toddler's crying rose in pitch like a fire siren. Hannah jumped back, unsure what to do. She silenced the longing to call after Daniel and ask him to calm the *kind*. As soon as he left once more, Shelby might react like this all over again.

Hating to leave the little girl by the door, Hannah edged toward the kitchen. She kept her eyes on Shelby while setting the kettle on the stove to heat. The *kind* didn't move an inch while Hannah took out the tea and a cup for her great-grandmother. Nor when Hannah set a handful of cookies on a plate and poured a small amount of milk into a glass.

The first thing to put on her list of what she'd need for the *kind*: plastic cups. Maybe she could find some with tops so Shelby could drink without spilling. Or was Hannah getting ahead of herself? She didn't know if the little girl could drink from a cup.

The door to the downstairs bedroom opened. Her great-grandmother, Ella Lambright, leaned one hand on the door frame. She'd left her cane in the bedroom. Her steps were as unsteady as Shelby's. Unlike the *kind*, her face was lined from many summers of working in her garden. She wore a black dress, stockings and shoes as she had every day since her husband died two years before Hannah's parents had wed.

Hannah rushed to assist her great-grandmother to the kitchen table. The old woman took a single step, then paused as another wail came from beside the front door.

"Who is that?" *Grossmammi* Ella said in her wispy voice. The strings on her *kapp* struck Hannah's cheek as she turned her head to look at the sobbing toddler. The elderly woman's white hair was as thin and crisp as the organdy of her *kapp*. She actually was Hannah's *daed*'s *grossmammi*.

"Her name is Shelby."

"That isn't a plain name." Her snowy brows dropped into a scowl. "And she isn't wearing plain clothes. What is an *Englisch kind* doing here?"

"Sit, and I'll explain."

"Who was that I saw driving away? What did he want here?"

"One thing at a time." Hannah had grown accustomed to *Grossmammi* Ella's impatience. In many ways, her great-grandmother's mind had regressed to the level of a toddler's. Impatient, jumping from one subject to another and with no apparent connection of one thought to the next, focused on her own needs. "That's what a wise woman told me."

"Foolish woman, if you ask me," *Grossmammi* Ella muttered.

Hannah assisted her great-grandmother to sit. Now wasn't the time to mention the wise woman had been *Grossmammi* Ella. Saying that might start an argument because the old woman could be quarrelsome when she felt frustrated, which was often lately.

Hoping she wouldn't make matters worse, Hannah went to Shelby. She knelt, but didn't reach out to the toddler. "Shelby?" she whispered.

The little girl turned toward her, her earth-brown eyes like Hannah's. Heated trails of tears curved along her full cheeks, and her nose was as red as the skin around her eyes. Averting her face, the *kind* began to suck her thumb while she clung to the door.

Hannah waited, not saying anything. When Shelby's eyes grew heavy, the toddler slid to sit and lean her face against the door. The poor little girl was exhausted. Hannah wondered when the *kind* had last slept.

When Shelby's breathing grew slow, Hannah slipped her arms around the toddler. Shelby stiffened, but didn't waken as Hannah placed her on the sofa. Getting a small quilt, Hannah draped it over the little girl.

Straightening, Hannah went to sit beside her great-grandmother. Patting *Grossmammi* Ella's fragile arm, she began to explain what had happened while the old woman was resting. The story sounded unbelievable, but its proof slept on the sofa.

When her great-grandmother asked what Hannah intended to do now, Hannah said, "I don't know."

And she didn't. She hoped God would send her ideas of how to deal with the arrival of an unknown sister, because she had none.

Reuben Lapp's place wasn't on Daniel's way home to the farm where he'd lived his whole life, but he turned his buggy left where he usually turned right and followed the road toward where the sun was setting through the bank of clouds clinging to the hills. It was growing chilly, a reminder winter hadn't left. At least, the rain hadn't turned to sleet or snow.

He'd promised Hannah that he'd help her find out where her *daed* was. Hannah had been willing—albeit reluctantly—for him to speak with Reuben and get the bishop's advice.

Why didn't she want to use every method possible to find her *daed*? Daniel was sure she was as curious as he was about why Shelby had been left on the porch. Yet, she'd hesitated when he mentioned locating her *daed*. Why?

You could have asked her. His conscience refused to let him ignore the obvious, but he had to admit that Hannah had her hands full when he left. As he closed the Lambrights' door, he'd heard Shelby begin to cry in earnest. He'd almost gone back in, stopping himself because he wanted to get the search for her *daed* started as soon as possible.

Propane lamps were lit in the bishop's large white house when Daniel arrived. He drove past the house and toward the whitewashed barns beyond it. Odors of overturned earth came from the fields. Reuben must be readying them for planting, using what time he had between storms.

Stopping the buggy, Daniel jumped out and walked to the biggest barn where the animals were stabled on the floor above the milking parlor. Through the uneven floorboards, he could hear the cows mooing. The bishop's buggy team nickered as he walked past. Several mules looked over the stall doors, their brown eyes curious if he'd brought treats. He patted each one's neck, knowing they'd had a long day in the fields spreading fertilizer.

He didn't slow as he went down the well-worn steps to the lower floor. The cows stood in stanchions, and the rhythm of the milking machine run by a diesel generator in the small, attached lean-to matched his footsteps.

Reuben, a tall man who was muscular despite his years, stood up from between a pair of black-and-white cows. He held a milk can in each hand. The bishop's thick gray beard was woven with a piece of hay, but Daniel didn't mention it as he greeted the older man.

"You're here late," Reuben said in his deep voice.

"I'd like to get your advice."

The bishop nodded. "I need to put this milk in the dairy tank." He motioned for Daniel to follow him through a doorway.

"Let me take one."

"*Danki*, but they're balanced like this." He hefted the milk cans with the strength of a man half his age.

Reuben had been chosen by the lot to be their bishop before Daniel was born. His districts were fortunate to have his gentle, but stern wisdom as well as his dedication to his responsibilities as their bishop. It wasn't an easy life for a man with a family to support, because those selected by the lot to serve weren't paid.

When Reuben went to the stainless steel tank where the milk was kept cold by the diesel engine, Daniel opened the top and checked that the filter was in place. He stepped back so Reuben could pour the milk in. As soon as both cans were empty, Reuben lifted out the filter and closed the top. He set the filter in a deep soapstone sink to clean later.

Wiping his hands on a ragged towel, Reuben said,

"I hear you've got a new job. Fixing the Hunter's Mill Creek Bridge."

"Word gets around fast." He chuckled.

"The Amish grapevine is efficient."

Daniel had to smile. For people who didn't use telephones and computers at home, news still managed to spread through the district. He wondered how long it would take for his neighbors to learn about Shelby. News of a *kind* being left on the Lambrights' front porch was sure to be repeated with the speed of lightning.

"I went out to the bridge today," Daniel said. "No work can be done until some bees are removed."

"Bees?" The bishop leaned against the stainless steel tank. "Doesn't Hannah Lambright keep bees? The bridge is close to her house, ain't so? Maybe she'll be willing to help."

"I've already spoken with her. She'll take care of the bees if I help her with a few things."

"Sounds like an excellent solution." Reuben folded his arms over the ends of his gray beard. He shifted and plucked out the piece of hay. Tossing it aside, he went on, "But from your face, Daniel, and the fact you want to talk with me, I'd guess there's more to the story."

"A lot." In terse detail, Daniel outlined how he'd found the *kind* after she escaped from the basket. He told the bishop about the note from Hannah's *daed*. "Hannah will take care of Shelby, of course, until her *daed* can be found."

"Hannah already carries a heavy load of responsibilities with her great-grandmother. Some days, the old woman seems to lose her way, and Hannah must keep a very close watch on her."

"I offered to help with Shelby."

The bishop nodded. "A *gut* neighbor helps when the load becomes onerous."

"And I also told Hannah I'd come to ask you about whether we should contact the police to get help in finding her *daed*. If you're all right with her talking to the police, she agreed that she will."

Reuben didn't say anything for several minutes, and Daniel knew the bishop was pondering the problem and its ramifications. It was too big and important a decision to make without considering everything that could happen as a result.

Daniel wished his thoughts could focus on finding Hannah's missing *daed*. Instead, his mind kept returning to the woman herself. Not just her beauty, though he'd been beguiled by it. No, he couldn't keep from thinking how gentle and solicitous she was of the *kind* and her great-grandmother.

Some had whispered years ago Hannah was too self-centered, like her *daed* who hadn't spared a thought for his daughter when he jumped the fence and joined the *Englisch* world. Daniel had never seen signs of Hannah being selfish when they were walking out. In fact, it'd been the opposite, because he found she cared too much about him. He hadn't wanted her to get serious about him.

Getting married then, he'd believed, would have made a jumble of his plans to open a construction business. That spring, he'd hoped to submit the paperwork within a few weeks, and he thought being distracted by pretty Hannah might be a problem. In retrospect, it'd been the worst decision he could have made.

He hadn't wanted to hurt Hannah. He'd thought she'd turn her attention to someone who could love her as she deserved to be loved. But he'd miscalculated. Instead of flirting with other young men, she'd stopped attending gatherings, sending word she needed to take care of her great-grandmother. At the time, he'd considered it an excuse, but now wondered if she'd been honest.

But whether she'd been or not, he knew one thing for sure. He'd hurt her, and he'd never forgiven himself. Nor had he asked for her forgiveness as he should have. Days had passed becoming weeks, then months and years, and his opportunity had passed.

"I thought we'd seen the last of Isaac Lambright," Reuben said quietly as if he were talking to himself.

"That's Hannah's *daed*?"

The bishop nodded. "Isaac was the last one I guessed would go into the *Englisch* world. He was a *gut* man, a devout man who prized his neighbors and his plain life. But when his wife sickened, he changed. He began drinking away his pain. After Saloma died, he refused to attend the funeral and he left within days."

"Without Hannah." He didn't make it a question. "But Isaac has come to Paradise Springs and left another daughter behind."

"So it would seem." The bishop sighed. "I see no choice in the matter. The *Englisch* authorities must be notified. Abandoning a *kind* is not only an abomination, but a crime. Has the *kind* said anything to help?"

"Shelby makes sounds she seems to think are words, because she looks at you as if you should know what she's saying. It's babbling."

He nodded. "That was a foolish question. A *kind* without Down syndrome uses only a few words at her age. An old *grossdawdi* at my age forgets such things." His grin came and went swiftly. "But that doesn't change anything as far as going to the police." Again he paused, weighing his next words. "Waiting until tomorrow to contact them shouldn't be a problem. I'd like to take tonight to pray for God's guidance."

"Hannah may be hesitant about talking to the cops because she doesn't want to get her *daed* into trouble."

Reuben put his hand on Daniel's arm. "We must assume Isaac is already in trouble. I can't imagine any other reason for a *daed* to leave another one of his daughters as he has." He sighed. "We'd hoped when Isaac was put under the *bann* that he'd see the errors of his ways. He told me after Saloma's death he'd never come back, not even for Hannah. Now he's done the same thing with another daughter."

"If Shelby is his daughter and not someone's idea of a cruel prank."

"And that, Daniel, is why I'll be talking with the police tomorrow morning. They'll know be the best way to find out what's true and what isn't."

"What will happen if Shelby isn't Hannah's sister?"

The bishop clasped Daniel's shoulder and looked him in the eye. "Let's not seek. The future is in God's hands, so let's let Him lead us where we need to go."

Daniel nodded, bowing his head when the bishop asked him to join him in prayer. He wished a small part of his heart didn't rebel at the idea of handing over the problem to God. That part longed to do something *now*. Something he—Daniel himself—could do to make a difference and help Hannah.

After all, he owed her that much.

Didn't he?

Chapter Three

As the sun rose the next morning, Hannah wondered how she was going to survive the coming day…and the ones to follow. During the night, which had stretched interminably, Shelby had been inconsolable. Her cries from the room across the upstairs hall from Hannah's had kept *Grossmammi* Ella awake, too, on the first floor. Hannah had spent the night trying to get them—and herself—back to sleep. She'd managed the latter an hour before dawn.

Then she'd been awoken what seemed seconds later by the sound of her neighbors working in the field between her house and theirs. The Jones family were *Englischers*, which meant Barry Jones used rumbling tractors and other mechanized equipment in his fields. Usually Hannah was up long before he started work, but not after a night of walking the floor with an anguished toddler and calming her great-grandmother who was outraged at the suggestion her beloved grandson had left another *kind* on her doorstep.

Hannah dressed and brushed her hair into place. She reached for a bandana to cover it, then picked up her *kapp.* Daniel had said he was going to talk to Reuben Lapp before he came back this morning. It was possible the bishop might visit to discuss Shelby's situation. She hoped he would have some sage advice to offer her.

Lots of sage advice…or any sort of advice. She could use every tidbit to raise a toddler who screamed at the sight of her.

"Keeping my eyes open instead of falling asleep on my feet is the smartest thing I can do," she murmured as she slipped down the stairs.

Passing her great-grandmother's bedroom door, she was relieved it was closed. *Grossmammi* Ella had been soothed about Shelby's arrival because Hannah assured her great-grandmother the *kind* wouldn't be with them long. She let *Grossmammi* Ella believe that Hannah's *daed* would return straightaway to collect Shelby.

The situation wasn't made easier because the elderly woman's hearing was failing as fast as her memory. The toddler's cries could slice through concrete, so the noise must be extra jarring for *Grossmammi* Ella who missed many quieter sounds. No wonder her nerves were on edge.

Hannah whispered an almost silent prayer of gratitude that *Grossmammi* Ella and the *kind* were still asleep. She doubted the peace would last long, and she needed to figure out what she absolutely had to do that day. She guessed most of her day would be focused on her abruptly expanded family. For the first time in a week, it wasn't raining, so Daniel would want her to check the hive.

She sighed. That would be difficult because she couldn't leave either her great-grandmother or the toddler alone. Though the covered bridge was down the road only a couple hundred feet, going would mean taking *Grossmammi* Ella and Shelby with her unless someone was at the house to keep an eye on them. She'd ask Daniel to do that while she went to figure out what she'd need to move the bees.

Maybe Daniel would have answers about her *daed* when he returned. His brother Amos ran the grocery store, and he may have heard something. It was even possible *Daed* had stopped at the store at the Stoltzfus Family Shops. No, that was unlikely. Why would he go where someone might recognize him?

Oh, Daed, why didn't you knock on our door? I would have listened to you, and perhaps Shelby wouldn't be distressed with me if she'd seen you and me together.

There weren't answers, which was why, during the night while she walked the floor with Shelby, trying to get the little girl to go to sleep, Hannah had known Daniel's suggestion to get Reuben's advice about contacting the police was *gut*. The police had ways of obtaining information no plain person did. She had to concentrate on what was best for Shelby.

With a sigh as she put ground *kaffi* into the pot on the propane stove, she reminded herself, until she learned how to take care of the toddler and removed the bees from the covered bridge, Daniel would be part of her life. That should last only a few days; then he'd be gone again. *Gut*, because she didn't want to let herself or her great-grandmother or Shelby become dependent upon him. She'd do as she promised Daniel, and then she'd go on with her life without him.

As she had before.

A cup of fresh *kaffi* did little to wake Hannah. She

was halfway through her second one when she heard faint cries upstairs. Putting the cup on the counter, she hurried to the toddler's room.

Shelby was standing in the crib Hannah had wrestled down from the attic last night. *Grossmammi* Ella kept everything, and Hannah was glad the old crib was still in the house. Shelby's diaper was half-off, and big tears washed down her face. The sight of the forlorn *kind* made Hannah want to weep, too. Again she had to fight her exasperation with her *daed*. Being angry wouldn't help her or Shelby.

"Hush, little one," she crooned as she gathered the *kind* into her arms, hoping Shelby would throw her tiny arms around Hannah's neck.

Instead the toddler stiffened and screeched out her fury. Hannah longed to tell her everything would be okay, but she wouldn't lie to her little sister, though she doubted the toddler understood her. So far, it seemed Shelby comprehended simple words and phrases in *Englisch*. Nothing more, and Hannah hadn't been able to decipher her babblings.

Daed probably wouldn't have spoken to her in *Deitsch*, and it was unlikely Shelby's *mamm* knew the language. Or would she? Who *was* Shelby's *mamm*?

In the chaos of yesterday, Hannah hadn't given the toddler's *mamm* much thought. Where was she? Did she know her *kind* had been left alone on the front porch? Most important, Hannah thought as the little girl leaned her face against her shoulder, would Shelby's *mamm* want her back?

All questions she couldn't answer. What she could do was get Shelby cleaned and fed.

Hannah soon had the little girl, despite Shelby's attempts to escape, in a fresh diaper and clothes. Another pair of pink overalls. She wondered if those were all Shelby wore. Her white shirt today had pink and blue turtles on it. Hannah needed to make clothes for the little girl, but the pressing matter was diapers. She had only about a half dozen on the dresser.

She came down the stairs with Shelby and saw *Grossmammi* Ella was awake and in the kitchen waiting for her breakfast. Exactly as she did every morning, but this day was different.

Putting Shelby in the high chair she'd found in the cellar, Hannah handed the toddler some crackers to keep her busy while she scrambled eggs for them. That seemed to quiet the *kind* who focused her attention on breaking crackers into the tiniest possible pieces.

Hannah gave her great-grandmother a kiss on her wizened cheek. "*Gute mariye, Grossmammi* Ella," she said with a smile. "I hope you got some sleep."

"Some." She stared at the table.

"Let me get you some *kaffi* and toast while I make a *gut* breakfast for us."

The old woman frowned at Shelby who was dropping minuscule pieces of cracker on the floor. "How long will that *kind* be here?"

"I told you last night. I'm not sure. I'm sorry she kept you awake." She went to the stove and pulled a cast-iron frying pan from beneath the oven.

"She doesn't belong here."

"What?" Hannah turned, shocked. *Grossmammi* Ella had always been fond of *kinder*. Many church Sundays, her great-grandmother was the first to volunteer to hold a fussy *boppli* on her lap or watch over a little one so older siblings could join in a game after the service. "She may be my sister."

"I don't believe you! Your *daed* would never cast away his daughter like that."

"He did me." The words came out before she could halt them.

Her *daed* was a sore subject between her and *Grossmammi* Ella. The old woman believed Isaac Lambright would return someday and confess his sins before the congregation. Hannah wondered how her great-grandmother could continue to believe that after fifteen years. Hannah's anger and grief at being left behind herself had been brought to the forefront by Shelby's abandonment.

Dear Lord, show me the way to forgive my daed *as You taught us. I can't find a way in my heart to grant him forgiveness after what he's done.*

"Don't forget what's in God's Ten Commandments. A *kind* should honor her *daed* and *mamm*." Her great-grandmother's scowl deepened.

"Ja." She broke eggs into the frying pan and took out her frustration on them by stirring them hard. She did her best to keep the commandments, but her *daed*'s selfish actions made respecting him difficult.

I'll try harder, Lord. Help me remember what's important. She glanced over her shoulder as Shelby flung out her hands. A shower of cracker crumbs went everywhere, into the little girl's hair, onto the floor, onto the table…onto *Grossmammi* Ella who abruptly smiled and handed the toddler another cracker. That delighted Shelby who babbled with excitement.

Hannah wanted to wrap her arms around them both and hold them close. The days to come wouldn't be easy, but for her family, she'd try her hardest.

* * *

"*Komm* in, young man," called a wavering voice when Daniel peeked around the front door of the Lambrights' house after no one responded to his knock. "Don't just stand there." The voice took on a reproving tone. "*Komm* in."

Daniel did, giving his eyes a moment to adjust to the interior after the bright early morning sunshine. Unbuttoning his coat, he didn't take it off. He doubted he'd be staying long. He shifted his hold on the bag holding the shampoo and diapers he'd bought at his brother's store.

A very old woman sat by the window. She was almost gaunt, and her white hair was so thin he could see her scalp through her *kapp*. Her bony fingers looked like talons as she clasped them on her black apron over her dress of the same color. But her eyes drilled through him as if he were a naughty boy standing in front of his teacher.

"I'm Ella Lambright," she said, "but you can call me *Grossmammi* Ella. Who are you?"

"Daniel Stoltzfus."

She eyed him up and down. "You have the look of Paul Stoltzfus about you."

"He was my *daed*."

"No wonder you look like him then. Why are you here? Are you courting our Hannah?"

Before he could reply, he heard a quick intake of breath beyond the old woman. Glancing toward the kitchen, he saw Hannah wiping her hands on a dish towel. Shelby was sitting in a high chair and eating what looked like toast covered with honey. The toddler would need another bath as soon as she was finished, because honey was smeared all over her face.

Hannah flipped the dish towel over the shoulder of her dark purple dress as her gaze locked with his. She didn't move or look away. He found he couldn't either when he saw the deep wells of sorrow in her emotive eyes. Had she believed he'd return with her *daed* this morning? No, she hadn't believed that, but she'd hoped. How could he fault her for her faith that all would turn out well in the end? Now wasn't the time to tell her he'd learned that, though God was a loving Father, He didn't have time to take care of details. Daniel had decided years ago to handle those on his own.

"Gute mariye," he said into the strained silence. Pulling out the shampoo bottle from among the packages of diapers, he added, "My sister-in-law uses this on her *boppli* because it's gentle on little ones' hair and doesn't sting their eyes."

"Danki." Her hand trembled as she took the bag without letting her fingers brush his. Setting it on the counter by the sink, she said nothing when he came into the kitchen.

Shelby stretched out sticky fingers toward him. She began to chatter in nonsense sounds. She bounced on the hard high chair, excited to see him again. Honey dripped off her chin, and bits of bread were glued to her face and her hands.

He kissed the top of her head. "How are you doing, Shelby?"

Giggling, she offered him a tiny piece of toast. He ate it, pretending he was going to eat her fingers, as well. That made her laugh louder. He was astonished how deep and rich the sound was.

The toddler's high spirits vanished when Hannah approached her with a washcloth to clean her hands and face. Shelby screwed up her face and opened her mouth to cry.

Daniel yanked the wet cloth from Hannah's hand. When she protested, he said, "Let me do it. There's no reason to upset her again."

"All right." Resignation filled Hannah's voice.

As he cleaned honey and bread crumbs off the little girl's hands, he stole a glance toward her older sister. He almost gasped aloud at the pain and despair on Hannah's face. Every instinct told him to toss aside the cloth and pull Hannah into his arms and console her. When they were walking out together, he wouldn't have hesitated, but everything was different since the night he decided he had to be single-minded in the pursuit of his dream of running a construction company.

"While you're getting the stickiness off her, I'll get my beekeeping equipment." Her voice was muffled, and he guessed she was struggling to hold back the tears he'd seen in her eyes when she wasn't aware he was looking in her direction.

Again he'd had the chance to say something comforting, but he couldn't think of anything that wouldn't upset her. What a disaster he'd made of what had been a *gut* friendship! To be honest, he was surprised she even talked to him after he'd avoided her during the past three years.

The back door closed behind her, and Daniel focused his attention on Shelby who slapped the high chair tray, getting her fingers sticky again. Picking her up, he sat her on the edge of the table. He succeeded in getting most the honey off her, but some stuck in her hair.

"She's a *gut* girl," said *Grossmammi* Ella from her chair by the window.

"*Ja*, she is." He grinned at Shelby. "And she's washed."

"Not that one! Our Hannah is a *gut* girl."

Daniel wasn't sure what the elderly woman was trying to convey to him. Did she want him to leave her great-granddaughter alone so he didn't have a chance to hurt her again, or was *Grossmammi* Ella hoping he'd court Hannah? He thought about assuring her that he had no plans to do either. Nothing had changed for him. He was working toward his goal, and it required every bit of his attention.

The door opening allowed him to avoid answering the old woman. In astonishment, he saw Hannah was dressed as she'd been when she'd left. Didn't beekeepers wear protective suits to keep from getting stung? She held a small metal container with a spout like an inverted funnel on one side and small bellows on the other. The odor of something burning came from it.

"Is that all you're bringing?" he asked.

"The smoker is all I need."

"What does it do?"

She looked at the container and squirted some smoke into the air between them. "It baffles the bees. The smoke masks the chemical signals bees use to communicate with each other. They can't warn each other I'm near. Otherwise, they'd believe the hive is in danger, and they'd attack. It's an easy way to get close to a hive without getting stung."

"A *gut* idea. I'm not fond of bees."

"They'll leave you alone if you leave them alone."

"But we aren't going to leave them alone." He reached to take Shelby's tiny jacket off a nearby peg. It was bright red, and the front closed with a zipper and was decorated with yellow ducklings, something no plain *kind* would wear.

"What are you doing?" Hannah asked.

"Getting Shelby's coat on her. I'll let you help your great-grandmother."

"What? I'm not taking a toddler or *Grossmammi* Ella near the bees."

"They could stay by the road and—"

"Don't be silly." She pushed past him and strode toward the front door. "You stay here with them, and I'll go to the bridge." Turning, she smiled, and something pleasant—something he remembered from when they spent time together—rippled through him. "I don't need you to point out where the bees are. I can find them." She left.

Daniel went out onto the porch with Shelby in his arms, her coat half on. Behind him, he heard *Grossmammi* Ella asking where everyone was going. He saw her struggling to get to her feet. He didn't hesitate as he rushed back into the house, not wanting the old woman to fall.

Making sure Hannah's great-grandmother was seated again and the door closed, he stared out the window as Hannah stepped over the stone wall beside the guardrail. She hurried down the steep hill toward the creek.

He wasn't worried about her falling in. The current was sluggish because the water behind the dam upstream beside the remnants of the old mill was still partially frozen. Daniel wanted to get as much work as possible done before the water rose when the ice melted. Once the failing joists were replaced, he could complete the interior work even if it rained. Discovering the hive had threatened to destroy his timetable.

He had to make this job a success. The bridge was one of the few in the area not washed away by Hurricane Agnes in 1972. The wear and tear on the bridge couldn't be ignored any longer. The original arched supports and the floor joists needed to be strengthened. Most of the deck boards would have to be replaced. The walls were rotted. Work he knew how to do, and he'd been pleased when the highway supervisor, Jake Botti, asked him to take over the project. It was the first step toward his long-held dream of becoming a general contractor.

Suddenly Shelby began chattering in his ear and wiggling. He set her on the floor. Once he took off her coat, she waddled to a chair and began to try to pull herself onto it.

Daniel's eyes shifted between the toddler and Hannah who was standing by the bridge and staring at the beam where he'd found the bees. She squirted smoke at the opening several times. She paused, then squeezed the bellows on the side of the smoker again. The wisps of smoke swirled around her, making her disappear; then she emerged from the gray cloud and retraced her steps to the house.

He opened the door before she could. "Did you see them?"

"Ja." She left her smoker on the porch, then came into the house. Motioning with her head toward the kitchen, she walked past Shelby who was focused on climbing onto the chair.

Grossmammi Ella didn't acknowledge any of them as she continued to gaze out the window. Unsure if she'd notice if Shelby fell, Daniel grabbed the toddler before he went into the kitchen.

"Would you like some tea while we talk?" Hannah

asked as she opened the cupboard and reached in for two cups.

"Sounds *gut*. I'll put Shelby in her high chair, if you'd like."

She shook her head. "Let her play on the floor. Next to the sewing machine, there's a small box of toys I found in the attic. Will you get them out for her?"

He complied, trying to curb his impatience. He wanted to ask about the bees again. If Hannah couldn't move them, work would have to be delayed until an exterminator could come to the bridge. Having promised he'd get the project done in six weeks or less, losing precious time might make the difference between finishing on time or being late.

Hannah didn't speak again after she'd placed two steaming cups on the table. Sitting, she waited for him to pull out the chair across from her. She took a sip from her cup, then said, "You're right. It's a hive of honeybees."

"Can you move it?"

She nodded as she wrapped her hands around her cup. "I'll have to move it twice."

"Why?"

"If we lived farther away from the bridge, I could move your hive once. Because I keep my own hives so close to the bridge, if I move those new bees to a new hive behind the house, they'll simply return to the bridge and rebuild their hive. I'll keep them in the cellar in the dark for the next couple of weeks or so. Then, when I put the new hive outside, the bees will have lost their scent trails to the bridge. They'll become accustomed to the new location and stay here."

He watched her face as she continued speaking of

relocating the bees as if they were as important to her as her great-grandmother. Her voice contained a sense of authority and undeniable knowledge about how to execute her plan. The uncertain girl he'd known three years ago had become a woman who was confident in her ability with bees.

When she smiled, an odd, but delightful tremor rushed through him again. He dampened it. They were in the here and now, not the past.

"Daniel, I'll need you to do one more thing for me as part of our bargain."

"What's that?"

"The hive is going to need a new home. I don't have any extra honey supers, and it will take at least a week or two for some to arrive from my supplier."

"Honey supers?"

"The boxes stacked to make a hive."

He wasn't sure what she was talking about, but he said, "Show me what you need, and I'll build it. Anything else?"

"No. I've got the rest of the materials I need."

When Hannah went to the back door, he scooped up Shelby and followed. Somehow he was going to have to persuade these two stubborn Lambright women they could trust each other. He wasn't sure how.

Daniel faltered as Hannah walked to two stacks of rectangular boxes set off the ground on short legs. She glanced back as if wondering why he'd stopped, but she halted, too, when her gaze settled on Shelby. Hannah explained what size the four stackable boxes she'd need for the new hive must be as well as describing the cross braces that supported the frames for the honeycomb.

"Sounds simple enough," he said when she finished.

A raindrop struck his face, then another. He glanced up as rain pelted them. Together they rushed into the house. Shelby giggled as she bounced in his arms.

Hannah closed the door behind them. "It looks as if the sky is going to open up. You're going to get wet."

If you don't head out now. He finished the rest of her sentence, which she hadn't spoken. She couldn't make it any clearer he was overstaying his welcome.

He'd take the hint, but not until he got the information he needed. "When will you be able to move the bees?"

"It can't be a rainy day or a warm one. The rain can hurt the bees when I cut the comb out of the old hive, and, if it's warm, they'll be flying about looking for nectar. A lot of the bees could be lost that way." She looked past him to where rain splattered on the window over the sink. "As soon as you have the supers built and the weather cooperates, I'll move them. Looks like rain tomorrow, so I can do it the day after if everything's ready."

"Sounds *gut*." He slapped his forehead. "No, day after tomorrow won't work. You've got to take Shelby to Paradise Springs that day."

"What?"

"On my way here, I stopped at the health clinic and made a *doktor*'s appointment for Shelby."

"You did what?" Her brown eyes darkened with strong emotions. "Shelby is my responsibility, not yours."

"*Ja*, but, when I told my *mamm* about finding Shelby, she insisted the *kind* be seen by the *doktorfraa* as soon as possible." He grinned, hoping she'd push aside her anger. "I learned many years ago not to argue with my *mamm* when she speaks with that tone."

Hannah's eyes continued to snap at him, but she took a deep breath and released it as he set the toddler beside the box of toys again. He pulled out the appointment card with the time on it and handed it to her.

In a calmer tone, as she put the card in the pocket of her apron, she said, "I'm sorry. I should have thanked you for making the appointment, Daniel." Before he could relax, she hurried on, "But from this point forward, making appointments for Shelby has to be my responsibility and mine alone. If the note's right, she's my sister. If she's not, she was left on my porch. But I do appreciate your *mamm* being concerned about her. Please tell her."

"I will, and, Hannah, if you'd like, I'll go with you and Shelby to the appointment." He glanced at the *kind*. "I can see she's not cooperating with you."

"That's a *gut* idea."

Surprised at her quick acceptance of his help, when she'd resisted at every turn before, he said, "I'll pick you up about a half hour before the appointment, if that works for you."

"That should be fine."

When she didn't add anything else, he knew he needed to leave. Something he couldn't name urged him to stay, but he ignored it, unsure what would happen if he lingered an extra minute more.

Ruffling Shelby's hair, he bid Hannah and her great-grandmother goodbye. He heard the toddler cry out in dismay as he closed the door behind him. The sound chased him across the grass and toward his buggy on the road alongside the creek. As he climbed in, a motion inside the house caught his eye.

A shadow moved in front of the living room window. Was Hannah watching him leave? He was surprised when he realized he hoped she was.

He sighed. Hannah Lambright was as unpredictable as the bees she loved, and he was going have to be extra careful around her.

Extra, extra careful.

Chapter Four

Daniel kneaded his lower back as he got to his feet. He'd already worked a full day and had decided to use a few hours after supper to work on his special project. He stretched out kinks and looked around the living room of the house he was building in the woods on his family's farm. Nailing floor molding was a time-consuming job, especially when he wasn't using a nail gun as he did when he worked for *Englisch* contractors. He could have borrowed an air compressor to power his tools, but he'd decided he wanted to build the house as his ancestors had. Now he was paying for his pride.

Hochmut. One of the most despised words among the Amish, because plain folks found pride contemptible. But he'd had a *gut* reason for his decision. He intended to use the house as a showcase for his skills when he solicited clients. He needed to stick with the choice he'd made. His family considered him too frivolous already because he took a different girl home from each singing.

Mamm had mentioned more than once—some days—it was time he considered starting a family as his other brothers were doing. She'd been delighted as each of her *kinder* married. Both of his sisters were wed as well as three of his six brothers, not including Isaiah who was a widower. His oldest brother Joshua remarried last year, surprising Daniel who'd wondered if Joshua would recover from his grief at the death of his first wife.

Leaning one shoulder against the kitchen doorway that needed to be framed, Daniel appraised what else wasn't done. The rest of the molding, painting, appliances in the kitchen, furniture. A year ago, he'd thought the idea of having a showcase for what he could do was an inspired idea, but now he just wanted to be done. Once he had projects completed for clients, he could use them as examples, and he'd give this house to his twin brother, Micah, when he married.

Micah was in love with Katie Kay Lapp, the bishop's daughter, but Katie Kay couldn't know because his twin brother, Micah, hadn't asked to take her home. Not once. Instead, he'd stood aside month after month, mooning over the vivacious young woman while others courted her. That Katie Kay seemed to have no steady suitor had convinced Micah he had a chance with the woman who was at the center of every gathering.

If Micah did get up his gumption and walked out with Katie Kay other than in his imagination, the house in the woods would be the perfect wedding gift. Maybe it was a *gut* thing Micah continued to hesitate because the house was taking longer to finish than Daniel had expected.

On other jobs, Daniel was accustomed to working with a crew. He'd had to do the work of different trades as he poured a foundation, raised walls and put on the roof. When he hadn't known how to run the propane lines to power the refrigerator, the range and the stoves that would heat the cozy house, he'd watched and learned from a plumber at a project where Daniel was doing the roofing. With each unfamiliar task, he was able to correct any mistakes he made on his house, so he wouldn't have to do the same for his clients.

The door opened with a squeak. Daniel added oiling the hinges to his to-do list as his brother Jeremiah walked in.

Like the rest of the Stoltzfus brothers, Jeremiah was tall and unafraid of work. His hair was reddish-brown and a few freckles remained of the multitude that once covered his face and hands. His hands were often discolored with the stain and lacquer he applied to the furniture pieces he built. He wasn't shy, but could never be described as outspoken either. He stayed quiet when he didn't have anything to say.

"You wanted to borrow my miter box," he said in lieu of a greeting. He held out the tool that would allow Daniel to cut the corners for the supers he planned to make for Hannah tonight.

"Danki."

Jeremiah squatted to appraise Daniel's work. "Are you painting the molding white or staining it?"

"I haven't decided." He grinned at his older brother. "I know you'd stain it. You hate painted wood."

"Paint hides the beauty and imperfections in the wood." Glancing over his shoulder, he said, "I hear you're involved with Hannah Lambright again."

"Involved? Not really. I'm helping her take care of a toddler, and she's helping me move a beehive off the bridge."

"That sounds like involvement to me."

Daniel picked up his hammer and moved across the room. Kneeling, he drove another nail into a section of molding. "Not in the way you're insinuating. Hannah treats me as if I'm a necessary evil."

"That can't be a surprise to you."

It wasn't, but he didn't intend to admit that to his brother. Jeremiah was the one who was most like their *daed*. Paul Stoltzfus had been calm, taking each challenge as it came. Jeremiah, on the other hand, was calm almost to the point of appearing passionless for anything but his work. If his brother had recently taken a girl home from a youth gathering, Daniel hadn't heard of it. Jeremiah wouldn't walk out with a girl without planning every detail and considering every ramification. He wouldn't have made the mistakes Daniel had with Hannah.

"I'm pleased," Daniel said, "she can remove the bees. I wasn't looking forward to getting stung." He gestured with his head toward the boards on the far side of the room. "I'm making her a hive, and she'll make sure the bees are out of our way."

Jeremiah didn't say anything for several minutes, and the only sound was the hammer driving nails into the wood.

Daniel waited, knowing his brother must have something else to say if he'd come over to the house.

"When are you seeing her again?" Jeremiah asked as if there hadn't been a break in the conversation.

"I'm seeing her *and* Shelby the day after tomorrow. Shelby has an appointment for a checkup at the clinic in town, and the little girl refuses to cooperate with Hannah."

"And she does with you?"

He gave his brother a wry smile. *"Ja."*

"That doesn't make sense." Jeremiah held up his hands to forestall Daniel's reply. "You don't need to answer. I know what you're going to say. When did any woman, no matter her age, make sense to a man?"

"I wasn't going to say that."

"No?" His brother laughed, at ease in the unfinished house in a way that he wasn't around a crowd of people. "If so, it's the first time you *haven't* said that."

Daniel wanted to shoot back a sharp reply, but he couldn't. Not when Jeremiah was right. He'd said those words more times than he could count. Each time, he'd meant them.

So why wasn't he saying them tonight?

Two reasons: Hannah Lambright and her little sister, Shelby. They'd invaded his thoughts, and he couldn't shake them loose. He shouldn't feel responsible for Shelby because he'd discovered her on the Lambrights' porch, but he did. And, as for Hannah, he shouldn't feel…however he felt. He wasn't sure what to call the morass of emotions bubbling through him whenever he thought of her or spoke with her.

But he was sure of one thing. He needed to get those feelings sorted out before he saw her again.

Hannah sat at the kitchen table and worked on the equipment she'd need for moving the bees. She'd thought about doing a load of laundry before Shelby and her great-grandmother woke, but rain was falling steadily.

She hoped the day after tomorrow would be dry and cool. If the bees on the covered bridge were cold, they'd cling to the center of the hive and be unlikely to swarm.

She must prevent a swarm. Once the queen took it in her mind to leave, the rest of the bees would follow. They might fly to the next opening in the boards beneath the bridge. The current hive wasn't difficult for her to reach, but farther out along the bridge would make it impossible. And it must not be raining when she moved the bees. Removing them from the safety of their hive in the rain could mean some drowning in the open super she'd use to carry them away from the bridge.

Reaching for another of the rectangular frames she'd used for the honeycomb, Hannah glanced out the window at her pair of hives farther up the hill toward the stone barn. She didn't keep them close to the house, because *Grossmammi* Ella was scared of being stung.

The bees would start emerging soon. Nothing was blooming, so they had no work. If the rain stopped and the weather grew sunny, the bees would try to keep busy anyhow. She must make sure they had food in the hive so they wouldn't starve before they could start gathering pollen and nectar.

Looking at the frames on the table in front of her, she smiled. She'd checked each one to make sure it was in *gut* condition. If Daniel made the supers to her specifications, she could hook the pieces of comb onto the frames with rubber bands and set them in the boxes. The bees would take care of the rest, hooking the comb into place.

A piece of mesh was in the center of the table. She'd place it at the bottom of the hive, so debris could fall from the hive out onto the ground. She had everything she needed other than the supers.

Her hands stilled on the stack of frames. Had she

been a complete fool to agree to help Daniel in exchange for him teaching her about taking care of Shelby?

Give to him that asketh thee, and from him that would borrow of thee turn not thou away. The verse from Matthew echoed inside her mind.

She'd done the right thing to accept Daniel's suggestion of a barter, but it wasn't easy to see him day after day, because each conversation was another reminder of how he'd dumped her without a backward glance. She appreciated how he'd offered to help her take Shelby to the *doktorfraa*. The *kind* had screamed every time Hannah came near her yesterday until *Grossmammi* Ella had begun to complain. Tears had led to another night with no sleep. Now, her great-grandmother and the toddler were asleep, so Hannah had time to gather what she needed for the bees' removal.

A noise came from upstairs. The sound of Shelby's crib creaking against the floor. The little girl must be awake.

Gathering the frames and mesh, Hannah set them beside her sewing machine. She hurried up the stairs and into the *kind*'s room. A bed draped with a quilt was pushed against the wall to leave room in the middle for the crib Hannah had used as a *boppli*.

For once, the little girl didn't shriek at the sight of her. Instead, she cried silent sobs. Her left cheek was swollen, and she kept pulling at the side of her mouth. When the *kind* started to make her gibberish sounds, Hannah noticed a swelling on her left lower gum.

"Oh, you poor little girl," she murmured. "You're teething, ain't so?"

She cuddled Shelby close with the toddler's right cheek against her shoulder. Carrying her downstairs, she went into the kitchen. She kept Shelby balanced on her hip while opening a cupboard and taking out a bottle of honey.

"Let's try this." She dipped her finger into the open bottle and rubbed a little bit of honey on Shelby's gum.

The *kind* started to pull away, then paused as the sweet flavor soothed her. Or maybe the honey had already eased the pain. Hannah wasn't sure, but Amos Stoltzfus, Daniel's brother who owned the grocery store, had mentioned several times he'd been asked by a *mamm* for honey to help with her *boppli*'s teething.

Carrying the little girl into the living room, Hannah sat in the rocking chair and brushed Shelby's sweaty bangs off her forehead. Hannah crooned a wordless tune as the little girl faded into a deep slumber. For the first time since her arrival at the house, Shelby didn't fight going to sleep.

What a *wunderbaar* bundle the toddler was in her arms! Hannah hadn't realized, at some moment after Daniel had dumped her and her great-grandmother demanded so much of her attention, she'd relinquished the thought of having *kinder*. When she was younger, she'd dreamed of a house filled with a large family. It'd been lonely being an only *kind* when her classmates had had lots of siblings. She'd watched them together and wondered what it would be like to have sisters and brothers. Almost until the day her *mamm* had died, she'd prayed the Lord would bless her family with more *bopplin*. She'd longed to be the older sister, teaching the little ones to walk and to talk and to play.

God had brought Shelby into her life, and it was Hannah's duty to help the toddler learn to become a *gut* member of their community. This special *kind* was already a blessing.

Maybe, after this morning, the little girl would stop crying whenever Hannah was near. If only it could be that easy!

Hopes of Shelby trusting her vanished as soon as the toddler awoke and began crying the moment her eyes opened. She looked away as Hannah stood and went to the kitchen to get the honey to ease the toddler's teething pain.

"The *boppli* sounds hungry," *Grossmammi* Ella said after Hannah had spread the honey on Shelby's gum again. The old woman walked to the stove with a determination Hannah hadn't seen in months. "I'll make her some fried mush. My *kinder* loved it, and my *kinskinder* loved it more."

"We've been blessed to have you in the kitchen." Hannah stifled a yawn as she set a fussy Shelby in the high chair. The honey seemed to be doing the trick again because the toddler's screeches had eased to soft whimpers. "Do you want me to measure out the cornmeal?"

Her great-grandmother waved aside her suggestion. "If after all these years of cooking for three generations I can't figure out how to much cornmeal to put in for fried mush, I should give up my apron."

Hannah laughed hard, surprising herself. How long had it been since she'd given in to laughter, letting it surge through her and leaving her awash with happiness? She didn't want to know, because it'd been far too long.

As she worked side by side with her great-grandmother as she'd done since she was ten, she reveled in the simple joys of being with her beloved *Grossmammi* Ella when the old woman's mind was in the present instead of lost in the past. Seeing the twinkle in her great-grandmother's eyes when *Grossmammi* Ella put a piece of fried mush in front of Shelby, Hannah drizzled honey on top of the serving. Not only should the sweetness delight the *kind*, but the additional honey might coat her gum and keep her pain away.

"Look at her eat!" *Grossmammi* Ella crowed as she brought two more servings of delicious fried cornbread to the table. "I told you she was hungry."

"So you did." Hannah's smile broadened. "I appreciate your making breakfast."

"That's kind of you to say, Saloma."

As her great-grandmother began to pour honey on her fried mush, Hannah turned away. She didn't want *Grossmammi* Ella to see her smile vanish. Saloma was Hannah's *mamm*. Addressing Hannah by her *mamm*'s name was a sign the old woman was slipping away into her memories of the past.

The blessed moments of being a family, something Hannah realized she hadn't treasured enough when she was part of them, came less and less often. Her hope *Grossmammi* Ella would return to the present faded as the meal went on and her great-grandmother continued to call her Saloma.

Though the fried cornmeal probably was delicious, it tasted like grit in Hannah's mouth. Somehow, she forced it down. When her great-grandmother was finished, Hannah assisted her to the chair by the window in the living room.

A quick knock was answered, before Hannah could react, by *Grossmammi* Ella calling, "*Komm* in!"

When Daniel walked in, Hannah's breath caught. Why did he have to be so handsome? Even the cleft in his chin, which she knew he loathed, eased the stark line of his jaw. His ebony hair and bright blue eyes had held her attention from the first time she'd seen him. However, his hands fascinated her. Work-hardened, his broad fingers were gentle on the reins and one time he'd squeezed her hand out of everyone else's sight. Her skin tingled at the memory of the night when she'd dared to believe she'd found the love of her life.

The night before everything had fallen apart…

She pushed aside thoughts of the past and wondered again how her great-grandmother could prefer what had been to what was. Raising her chin, she asked, "Daniel, what are you doing here today? Shelby's appointment at the clinic isn't until tomorrow."

"I know. I came because I brought along the supers you need and—" Past the open door came the rattle of buggy wheels followed by a car door slamming.

From her chair by the window, *Grossmammi* Ella crowed, "Here comes the bishop! Hurry, Hannah! Put on the *kaffi* pot and get out some cookies. You know Reuben has a sweet tooth." She paused and asked in a sharper tone, "Who is that man with him?"

Hannah drew in a sharp breath. A car with *Paradise Springs Police Department* painted on the door was parked in front of the house.

Cold sank through her as the door opened again, but she bit her lip to keep from letting her dismay erupt. The *Englisch* chief of police entered the house with Reuben Lapp. She'd seen Steven McMurray at auctions and other events, but had never spoken to him.

After leaving his hat on the newel post at the bottom of the stairs, the chief of police greeted her and her great-grandmother with a kind smile. He was out of place in a plain home with his uniform of a dark blue shirt and black pants and shiny badge. The room abruptly seemed too full with the bishop and two tall, muscular men in it.

"I prayed on the matter," Reuben said, "and I feel the right decision is to ask for help from the police to find your *daed*. I hope you agree, Hannah."

Instead of answering, she motioned toward the kitchen. "Would you like to meet Shelby? She's finishing her breakfast."

"Do you think it'll frighten her if we all go into the kitchen?" Reuben asked.

"I don't know." Her smile wobbled. "She doesn't know us."

Her words were contradicted when Shelby gave an excited squeal and held her arms out to Daniel. She began babbling as if she believed he could understand every sound she made.

He walked over to the high chair. "Are you enjoying your breakfast, *liebling*?"

"You called her *liebling*," *Grossmammi* Ella said softly. "That's what my husband called me."

Chief McMurray smiled again at her great-grandmother before he said, "I'm assuming this is Shelby."

At her name, the little girl looked toward him with wide eyes.

"Hello there, Shelby." The big man sat beside the toddler, so he wasn't towering over her.

Hannah couldn't help being impressed at how the policeman spoke quietly and kept a smile on his face. He was making every effort to keep the little girl calm.

But why was the *kind* who might be her little sister smiling at a stranger when she recoiled from Hannah?

Shelby offered a tiny piece of the cornmeal mush to the chief of police.

He took it and pretended to eat it. *"Danki."*

Shelby tipped her head to one side in obvious bafflement.

"Thank you, Shelby," the police chief said before half turning toward Hannah. "She doesn't understand *Deitsch*?"

"I don't think so," she said. "I don't know if my *daed* speaks it to her. He didn't say in his note."

"I'd appreciate seeing that note. The basket, too."

"I'll get them." She hurried upstairs to Shelby's room and opened the closet. Checking the wrinkled note was in the basket, she carried them downstairs. She wasn't surprised *Grossmammi* Ella had joined the others in the kitchen. Her great-grandmother wouldn't want to miss the excitement.

Hannah set the basket and the note on the table before edging away as Shelby screwed her face to cry again. Why couldn't the *kind* smile at her as she did at everyone else?

Reuben sat beside the policeman as Chief McMurray examined the basket and read the note. When the policeman handed it to him, the bishop scanned it.

"I'd say your *daed*, if he wrote that note, is a man of few words." Chief McMurray watched Shelby try to unstick a dab of honey from the tray. "It'd be easier if she could tell us something." Taking a deep breath, he asked, "Are you willing to take care of her, Hannah?"

"Ja. If the note is true, she's my sister."

Grossmammi Ella snorted. "Impossible! Isaac

wouldn't treat another daughter like that." She looked at Hannah and quickly away.

"Maybe not," replied Chief McMurray, "but I'm going to act as if it's the truth. Shelby appears to be doing well, and it'd be a pity to bring social services in at this point or put the two of you through a DNA test. I assume you agree, Reuben, leaving the little girl here while we try to find Isaac Lambright is the best solution."

"I do. The *kind* has endured enough already." The bishop smiled. "And Psalm 127 tells us *kinder* are a heritage of the Lord. Shelby is a gift, and our whole community will help take care of her."

Chief McMurray stood. "I have no doubts, which is why I'm leaving her for now with the Lambrights. In the meantime, I'll start seeing what I can find out about the missing Isaac Lambright."

"So he can tell you," *Grossmammi* Ella said, "you're making a big mistake by believing he could leave another daughter behind. I know he's under the *bann*, Reuben, but my grandson is a *gut* man."

Reuben's voice was conciliatory. "I believe he is."

"Then why did you bring an *Englisch* policeman here?" She left without a further word.

Hannah started to apologize, but Chief McMurray halted her.

"I've got an eccentric grandmother myself, so I understand." He rubbed his chin and sighed. "It'd help if we had a picture of Isaac, but I know you don't have one."

"But," Hannah said, "he has to have a license to drive a car, ain't so? Don't drivers' licenses have pictures on them?"

The police chief smiled. "I keep forgetting he doesn't live a plain life now. I'll start a search in the databases. If he has—or has had—a license, he should pop up."

Not quite sure what he meant by *pop up*, Hannah didn't say anything when he offered Reuben a ride to his farm, which the bishop accepted.

Before he left, Reuben prayed with them. "Lord, bless Hannah, Ella and Daniel for opening their hearts to this lost *kind*. Let us not forget how our dear Lord said, *Suffer the little children, and forbid them not, to come unto Me: for of such is the kingdom of Heaven.* We pray that the peace and love of Your kingdom be upon this house and this family. Amen."

Hannah heard Daniel and Chief McMurray echo her "Amen" before the policeman went with the bishop to the front door. The door closed, leaving her in the kitchen with Shelby and Daniel, who'd been oddly quiet.

"How are you doing?" he asked, his eyes clouded with strong emotions.

"Tired." She sighed. "I can tell you there's nothing wrong with her lungs. They get lots of exercise whenever I'm near." Going to the sink, she drew out a clean dishcloth and soaked it. She wrung it out before carrying it to Shelby, intending to wash the *kind*'s hands.

The little girl pulled away with a plaintive cry.

"Let me," Daniel said.

Without a word, Hannah relinquished the cloth when Daniel held out his hand. As he washed Shelby's fingers, he said, "I'm sure it'll get better."

"I wish I could believe that."

"I can stop back later to play with her, if you want."

"Don't you have work on the bridge?"

He shook his head. "The road crew is going to move

barriers into place on either side of the bridge today, so we have to stay away. I'd be glad to help here."

"We'll manage," she said as she took the cloth from him and turned toward the sink.

He didn't reply, and she sensed rather than saw his hand stretch out toward her. She held her breath. As shaky as her emotions were, if his fingers settled on her shoulder, she might change her mind about being able to handle the changes in her life. If she let Daniel into her life again and came to depend on him remaining in it, even as a friend, she was opening herself to heartbreak again.

His hand drew back, and she was startled by how her relief was mixed with disappointment. Had she lost her mind? She should be grateful he hadn't touched her. If he had, she feared she would have whirled and thrown herself into his arms. She couldn't do that.

Not now.

Not ever.

Chapter Five

The Hunter's Mill Creek covered bridge sat empty between the concrete barriers that had been set into place to keep vehicles from crossing it. Water had gathered in puddles near the entrance where wooden deck boards had been dented by years of traffic.

Daniel gazed at the bridge as he drove past it. He couldn't wait to get started. Except for one guy, he'd worked with everyone on his five-man crew before and knew they'd do their best on the job. The one person he hadn't worked with was the county supervisor's son, and the teenager was using the job to fulfill his volunteering requirement for high school graduation.

A motion caught Daniel's eyes, and he looked at the Lambrights' house. As he turned his horse Taffy toward it, he realized how he'd been avoiding glancing at the house. The questions Jeremiah had asked him the night before last resonated through his head. But no answers did.

I need Your guidance to help make sure I don't hurt Hannah again, Lord.

He repeated the prayer as he drew his buggy to a stop

in front of the Lambrights' house. The door opened. He was surprised when only Hannah and an obviously angry Shelby came out. Shelby was dressed, for the first time, in at least some plain clothes. Beneath the coat she'd had with her in the basket, she wore a navy blue dress and white pinafore with her dark socks. Her shoes were still a garish pink. She looked adorable.

But Daniel frowned. Where was her—their great-grandmother?

Unlatching the door on the passenger side as they approached, he shoved it aside. He held out his hands for Shelby who beamed as she caught sight of him. Her stiffness softened when he lifted her from Hannah's arms. Murmuring to the toddler, he saw the hopelessness in her sister's eyes. He tried to imagine his younger sister Esther acting as Shelby did when she was a *boppli* and refusing to have anything to do with him. He would have been heartsick…as Hannah was.

Daniel set the toddler on his lap as Hannah climbed into the buggy and shut the door. Her black bonnet made her hair look like spun gold and her brown eyes darker. But he couldn't help noticing the gray arcs under her eyes.

"Did Shelby stay awake with teething pain?" he asked.

"No. She slept, but *Grossmammi* Ella had a tough night. She can't stop thinking about what my *daed* has done, but she refuses to believe it." She clasped her hands on her lap. "She kept me up all night insisting her grandson was a *gut* man." She grimaced. "More than you wanted to know, I'm sure."

He struggled not to smile. Her expression matched

Shelby's when the little girl tasted something she didn't like. "Is *Grossmammi* Ella coming with us?"

Hannah shook her head. "Barry Jones is here." She pointed to the small ranch house farther along the creek road. "He and his family live over there and farm the pastures across the road. He keeps an eye on *Grossmammi* Ella when I have to be away, and she doesn't want to go. He thinks she's amusing, and she thinks he's okay...for an *Englischer*." A faint laugh slipped out. "Those are her exact words, 'He's okay...for an *Englischer*.'"

"I guess I'd better not ask what your great-grandmother says about me."

Hannah's eyes began to twinkle again. "A wise decision."

"Is it so bad?"

"Possibly." She tilted her head toward him and smiled. "Or maybe it isn't bad, and you'd be in danger of a swelled head."

"Ouch!"

Shelby gasped and patted his arm, concern on her face.

Daniel tried again not to laugh, but it was impossible when Hannah was smothering a giggle behind her hand. "I'm fine, *liebling*," he assured the little girl. "I've got to remember how literally they take everything at this age."

"She seems to understand a lot."

"I agree." He shifted the toddler onto the seat between them.

"As irritable as this little one has been today, it's for the best that my great-grandmother didn't want to come along."

"Dealing with one stubborn Lambright woman at a

time is enough, ain't so?" His smile faltered when Hannah glowered at him as Shelby tried to crawl onto his lap. Now he'd done it! He'd hoped to make her feel better about Shelby's continuing antagonism toward her. Instead she must have assumed he meant Hannah was the stubborn one. In truth, she could be as obstinate as her great-grandmother or little sister, but he'd wanted to make her smile, not feel worse.

Not the best way to start the day.

"I don't mind holding her," Daniel said.

Another mistake, he realized, when the *kind* smiled and relaxed against him as soon as she sat on his knee again. Beside him, Hannah's expression went as quickly from vexed to hurt.

Help me help her, he prayed, though in his heart, he knew she'd mistrust everything he did until he proved to her that he wasn't the careless young man he'd been when they were walking out. He didn't know how to convince her.

Hannah turned the last page in the stack of papers requesting information about Shelby's health history. It hadn't taken long to fill them out because she knew nothing about Shelby's *mamm*'s pregnancy or health history. As for her *daed*'s, Hannah didn't know much about him either. She'd been too young to ask about such things before he left.

Rising to carry the clipboard to the front desk at the Paradise Springs Health Center, she glanced at Daniel and Shelby. The toddler was giggling as he played another game of peekaboo with her. She hadn't heard Shelby laugh since... Well, since the last time Daniel had come to the house.

The two of them looked as if they belonged together. How sad that after years of wishing for a sibling, she got one who despised her!

Hannah walked to the blue plastic chair that was set against the wall like the others along both sides of the waiting room. It was a comfortable space with light brown carpet and sheer curtains on the pair of windows overlooking Route 30, the road that bisected Paradise Springs. Two other people waited to see the *doktorfraa*. The elderly man was sneezing, and a younger man was coughing and blowing his nose. She hoped whatever they had wasn't contagious. The only thing she could imagine worse than having a toddler who cried whenever she came near was having a *sick* toddler who cried whenever she came near.

As she sat, Hannah picked up a magazine, shuffling the pages. Her attempts to read were stymied each time the little girl chortled with delight. She should be grateful that Daniel entertained Shelby, but she couldn't help wondering what would happen when the bridge project was finished and Daniel didn't visit any longer. She didn't want Shelby hurt as she'd been when his attention had turned from her to other young women.

"Shelby Lambright?" called a nurse from a nearby doorway.

"Here." Hannah jumped to her feet. She reached for the *kind*, but Shelby threw her arms around Daniel's neck.

"I can go with you if you don't mind," he said, glancing around the room.

Knowing he didn't want to make a scene, Hannah nodded. She followed him along a short hallway.

When the nurse went into a room to the right, she

smiled at them. "You two have an adorable little girl," the nurse said after checking Shelby's height and weight.

"Danki," Hannah said at the same time as Daniel did. When she glanced at him, he looked away, but she noticed the tops of his ears were red. She wanted to ask why. Now wasn't the time.

Following the instructions the nurse gave before leaving, he set Shelby on the paper-topped examination table. He stepped aside while Hannah undressed the *kind* until she wore only her diaper.

The door reopened, and a slender redhead walked in. Dr. Montgomery wore her stethoscope around her neck and an open white lab coat. She was carrying a manila file. Smiling, she said, "Hello, Hannah. Is this Shelby?"

"Ja," Hannah replied to the doctor who oversaw *Grossmammi* Ella's care. "She's my little sister."

The *doktorfraa* glanced at Daniel.

He cleared his throat and said, "I found Shelby on the front porch at the Lambrights' house."

Dr. Montgomery's brows arched high. "You're going to have to give me a lot more information."

Hannah shared an abridged version of the events earlier in the week. If the *doktorfraa* was shocked, no sign of it was visible on her face. She opened the file and began to read.

Dr. Montgomery's professional smile vanished when she looked up from the sheaf of papers. "Is this the only medical history you have for her? It's nothing."

"I know," Hannah said. "I don't know much about my parents because I was young when my *mamm* died and my *daed* left. And Shelby has a different *mamm*."

"Do you know whether she's been immunized?"

"No."

The *doktorfraa* sighed. "I guess the best thing to do is examine her and determine how she's doing. We'll use today as the baseline and build her medical history from this point forward. But as far as her immunizations, my recommendation is we start them all over again as if she were a newborn."

"That's safe?" Daniel asked.

"Much safer than taking the chance of her not having the full complement. This way, she won't get sick from something that can be prevented." She turned to Hannah. "Do you agree?"

Shock riveted her. The question was a stark reminder of how Shelby's life would be affected by every decision Hannah made. Hannah had to be more than sister to the little girl. In so many ways, she was going to have to be Shelby's *mamm*, too.

"I want what is best for her," she replied.

Dr. Montgomery nodded, put down the file and asked Hannah to lift Shelby to the floor. Hannah did, releasing the *kind* the moment Shelby was steady on her feet. Having the *doktorfraa* see how the toddler cried if Hannah stayed close too long would create questions she wanted to avoid answering…because she had no answer.

Shelby seemed to think the examination was a game. Dr. Montgomery pulled a dog puppet from her coat pocket and used it to talk to Shelby. The little girl giggled, excited, as she obeyed requests to walk and take a small ball from the *doktorfraa*.

Hannah set the toddler back on the table while Dr. Montgomery scribbled some notes on the page.

"I'd say your guess she's about a year-and-a-half old is accurate," said the *doktorfraa*. "Shelby can walk, though she's a bit wobbly. She recognizes her name, and it appears she's trying to repeat sounds she hears. Those are skills most children with Down syndrome should have mastered by 18 months." She pulled a hand-held computer out of her other pocket. Tapping it, she paused to read something on its screen. "Is she able to suck through a straw?"

"*Ja,*" Hannah replied.

"Does she know your names and her own?"

"She knows her own. I'm not sure about ours."

The *doktorfraa* smiled as she raised her stethoscope and blew on it. "We can't expect too much when she's been with you a few days. She recognizes people after they leave the room?"

"*Ja.*"

"Good."

The room grew silent while Dr. Montgomery listened to Shelby's heart, then let the *kind* hear her own heartbeat through the stethoscope. While Shelby was preoccupied, Dr. Montgomery checked her ears, throat and eyes. The little girl giggled when her stomach was palpitated.

"Ticklish, aren't you?" Dr. Montgomery said.

Shelby giggled more, and Hannah heard Daniel smother a chuckle from where he sat at the side of the room. She knew envy was wrong, but she couldn't help wishing again she had the connection with her little sister that he did. Except when Hannah rocked her to sleep, Shelby tolerated her if nobody else was around. Nothing more.

Straightening, the *doktorfraa* said, "Her heart sounds excellent, which is good news. So many children with Down syndrome have heart issues." She smiled at Shelby who grinned. "However, I saw some signs of frequent ear infections. Those can lead to a hearing loss. Have you noticed she's having trouble hearing?"

"She hears everything," Hannah said with a smile. "Not only in the house, but outside. Whenever a truck goes past, she rushes to look out." Hesitating, she knew it would be unwise not to share everything with the *doktorfraa*. "I think it's because *Daed* may have been driving a truck when he left her at our house."

"So she's looking for him?" Dr. Montgomery's easy smile vanished. "Poor little munchkin. It's hard enough to think of an adult being dropped into a new life without an explanation, but it's got to be more difficult for a toddler who can't understand why. I'm glad that she has you and your great-grandmother, Hannah."

"She's unsure around us." Honesty forced her to add, "Around me especially."

"Give her time. She's known you less than a week." Dr. Montgomery's smile widened. "Young children are eager to love anyone who treats them with kindness. Shelby has lost everything and everyone she's known, so she needs time to adjust. I suspect you'll see great changes in her over the next few weeks. Shelby may come to believe she was blessed the day she was left on your porch." She grinned as Shelby turned a tongue depressor over and over in her hands, examining every bit of it. "A child with Shelby's challenges is welcomed as a gift from God among you plain people."

"She *is* a gift," Hannah said, watching as Shelby began to gnaw on the wooden stick, concentrating on the area where her tooth was coming in. "A special gift."

The *doktorfraa* ran gentle fingers over Shelby's silken hair. "Her disabilities, though we can't know the scope of them at her age, can be met now with physical therapy and occupational therapy."

"Isn't she young to worry about what she'll do when she grows up?" asked Daniel.

"I'm sorry," Dr. Montgomery said, puzzled. "What did you say?"

He looked at Hannah who was glad he'd asked the question she'd been thinking. She motioned for him to go ahead, and he said, "I'm wondering why she needs to worry about an occupation when she's barely more than a *boppli*."

The *doktorfraa* smiled. "Occupational therapy isn't about getting a job. It's about helping Shelby strengthen the physical function she has. Learning fine motor skills and eye-hand coordination."

"Isn't that physical therapy?" Hannah asked, keeping a hand against Shelby's back so the little girl didn't tumble off the table.

"Physical therapy—or PT, as we call it—is used to help a patient deal with injuries or weaknesses to the muscles." She chuckled. "Don't worry. You'll learn the difference. Most patients and their families confuse the two at first. However, the therapists know their fields well, and they'll help Shelby. In addition, I'd like to have her evaluated to determine how much speech therapy she'll need. Does she speak any words?"

"No, though she makes a lot of different sounds and seems to believe we should understand what she means." Hannah chuckled. "And she's training us well because we're beginning to figure out what she means with some of the sounds."

"Excellent." The *doktorfraa* made some more notes, then said, "All that's needed is her first round of shots."

She picked up a folder from the cabinet at one side of the room. "The schedule for childhood shots is listed here as well as information on how most children react to the shots."

Hannah took it. When her little sister cried as she was given several shots, Hannah's attempts to comfort her as she re-dressed the toddler were futile. Shelby continued to cry as Dr. Montgomery handed her a sticker and told her she was a brave and *gut* girl.

The tears stopped when Daniel put the sticker on her white pinafore. Shelby kept gazing at the bright red kitten. Babbling, she giggled when he pretended to pet the cartoon cat. The toddler kept touching it while Hannah carried her to Daniel's buggy, but began to whimper and suck her thumb as soon as they were seated. Before they left the parking lot, the little girl had fallen into a fitful sleep on Hannah's lap.

"*Danki*, Daniel, for coming with us today," Hannah said beneath the rumble of rain that fell in big, oily drops that sounded like acorns dropping onto the roof of the buggy.

"I told you I'd help you when I could."

"I know, but I wanted to thank you." She let her gaze follow the stern line of his profile as he steered the buggy through the heavy rain. "Won't you accept my gratitude?"

"I don't like being obligated."

"I know, Daniel. I probably know that better than anyone."

He looked away from the road, letting his horse follow it toward the covered bridge and her house. "You do, don't you?"

Instead of the vexation she'd expected, sorrow billowed through her. "I'm trying to leave the past in the past while we work together."

"I know, and you're doing a better job than I am."

"I wouldn't say that."

The faint shadow of a grin played along his volatile lips. "Trust me, Hannah. You are. Will it be okay if I come to watch the little one's first session with the physical therapist?"

She appreciated him not using Shelby's name. That might wake the toddler. "If you want to. You don't have to feel obligated."

"Ouch!" He put his hand to the center of his chest and leaned against the side of the buggy. "I didn't realize how painful it would be to have my own words thrown back at me."

"I didn't mean—" She halted herself when he laughed quietly. Rolling her eyes, she smiled. "Let's talk about something else."

"A *wunderbaar* idea! Are you planning to move the bees tomorrow?"

"If it's not raining."

"*Gut*. I'll let my crew know they should plan to come to the bridge the following morning." He rested his elbows on his knees. "What time do you plan to move them?"

"Just before sunset. The air is chilly then, so the bees will be less active. However, I want to make sure I've got plenty of light so I can find the queen among the layers of honeycombs. Without her making the transfer, it'll be for nothing. The rest of the bees will desert their new hive."

"How long should it take?"

"If all goes well, I'll be done by dark, but I don't

want to make promises. There can be complications moving any hive."

"What can I do to help?"

"Watch Shelby and *Grossmammi* Ella while I'm at the bridge."

"I'd like to see the process of moving the bees. Not that I want to get close to them. You seem to trust them, but I don't. So I'd like to watch from a safe distance."

She shook her head. "I need you to stay away and keep everyone else away. If the bees get spooked, they'll go on the defensive. I don't want to get stung any more than necessary."

He stiffened and looked at her. "You'll get stung moving them?"

"Getting stung is always a possibility when working with bees. Even with the precautions I take, I can't be sure what might set them off. If I was afraid of being stung, I couldn't be a beekeeper." She shrugged. "Besides, I'm accustomed to it."

"I don't like the idea of you getting hurt." His hands tightened on the reins. "I shouldn't have asked you to move the bees."

"If I didn't do it, you'd have to kill the hive. That would be a real tragedy." She started to put her hand out to touch his arm to emphasize her point, but pretended she was adjusting her hold on Shelby. Touching him, even chastely, would be stupid. She needed to keep the barrier between them, the barrier made brick by brick by his betrayal and the indifference that followed.

But it was becoming more difficult every day to reconcile the man he was now with the one he'd been then.

Chapter Six

The most recent rainstorm had stopped by the time Daniel got out of his buggy at the Lambrights' house. Every day for the past week, except yesterday, there had been a downpour around midday or it'd rained all day. Not a heavy rain, but enough to make the air cold and clammy.

Taffy shook his mane, scattering water in every direction.

Patting the horse on the neck, Daniel said, "I know. I'm looking forward to a dry day, too."

The horse regarded him with a skeptical glance as if to remind Daniel that Taffy would remain out in the storm while Daniel went inside the dry house.

"I'll make it up to you, old boy," he said with a chuckle. "*Mamm* has a few apples left in the cellar."

Pricking his ears forward at the mention of his favorite treat, Taffy bowed his head in a pose of acceptance.

Again Daniel laughed as he lifted the new supers he'd built for Hannah out of the back of his buggy. The horse had a way of making himself understood without uttering a single word.

He wished it was as easy to know what Hannah was thinking. Or maybe he was trying to ignore the truth in front of him. She didn't hide that she cared about Shelby, though the toddler pulled away from her. He wished he could figure out why the little girl reacted that way. Hannah treated her with every kindness and made certain she had foods she liked.

Taking the porch steps in two leaps, Daniel set the supers down before he walked toward the door. It opened as he reached it.

Grossmammi Ella stood in the doorway, her black dress contrasting with her white *kapp*. "*Komm* in. Why are you standing on the porch, Earney?"

Daniel glanced over his shoulder, wondering if someone else stood behind him. No, he was the only one on the porch. Whom was *Grossmammi* Ella talking to? Or to whom did she *think* she was talking? Reuben had said something about the old woman losing her way. Was this what the bishop had meant? She'd acted odd before, but nothing like this.

Keeping his voice even, he began, "*Grossmammi* Ella—"

She laughed. "Don't you start calling me that, Earney. That's for our *kins-kinder*, not for old folks like us."

What was going on? She spoke as if she and he were the same age. And *Grossmammi* Ella grinned at him in a way that brought Shelby to mind. Innocent and eager and filled with delight at seeing him. It was almost as if she'd become a *kind* again.

When she urged him again to enter, he did. The hiss of a propane lamp could be heard beneath Shelby's soft singsong words from where she was playing beside her great-grandmother's chair. She had a cloth book open on her lap and was turning the pages. When Daniel moved closer to the *kind*, he realized the pictures were upside down.

Where was Hannah? She must be close. She wouldn't leave *Grossmammi* Ella and Shelby for long. But when he looked into the kitchen, he didn't see her.

He started to ask where Hannah was, but the old woman interrupted him. "Do you want some *kaffi*? I'll brew it extra strong because I know how you like it dark, Earney."

Daniel struggled to hide his uneasiness. *Grossmammi* Ella thought he was someone else. Who was Earney?

"Regular strength is fine," he replied with care. He wasn't sure which word might cause her to say something else strange. As much as the old woman's hands shook, he doubted she should be handling the *kaffi* pot. She could scald herself. "I'll get it."

"Making *kaffi* isn't a man's job. It's his wife's job and her joy," she replied, turning toward the kitchen so fast she stumbled.

He caught her arm before she could fall on Shelby. Urging her to stay where she was, he assured her that he'd changed his mind about the *kaffi*.

Where was Hannah?

The back door opened, and Hannah came in. He was astonished at the outfit she was wearing. A mesh screen beneath a broad white head cover protected her face but allowed her to see. Her loose, white coat reached over white trousers that covered her legs and vanished into boots closed with rubber bands. She carried leather gloves with extra long cuffs in one hand and her smoker in the other. Over her shoulder was a canvas bag with what looked like picture frames stuffed into it.

A long sigh emerged from *Grossmammi* Ella when Hannah walked toward them, and she seemed to shrink as he watched. She hunched over as if the weight of her years had descended on her shoulders. When she teetered, he took her thin arm and guided her to the chair by the window. She looked away from him and out at the setting sun visible beneath the thick bank of clouds.

Tiny arms grabbed his leg, and he saw Shelby grinning at him. She bounced on her bottom, every inch of her bristling with excitement.

He bent and kissed her head. "What mischief are you up to today, *liebling*?" Scooping her up, he carried her into the kitchen.

He was amazed when Hannah didn't take off the helmet as he spoke. He couldn't see her face clearly beneath the veil as he asked, "Who's Earney?"

"Earney was *Grossmammi* Ella's husband. Earnest Lambright. He died almost thirty years ago." Puzzlement filled her voice. "Why are you asking about him?"

"Your great-grandmother was talking to me as if she believed I was him."

"What?" Even with the hat and veil in place, he could hear her shock.

"She called me by his name when I came to the door. At first, I thought she was mistaken because it's cloudy and the light's not *gut*. Now I'm not sure."

"She gets mixed up sometimes. The problem is her mind is so full of memories she gets them confused."

"What does the *doktor* say?"

Instead of answering him, Hannah said, "I need to get started if I want to be done before it gets dark again."

"What can I do to help?" he asked, knowing that pressing her for more answers would be useless.

"Like I told you before, you can help me best by staying here with *Grossmammi* Ella and keeping an eye on Shelby."

He frowned. "My horse Taffy is out front. Will he be in danger?"

"Not if everything goes as it should. But if you want to bring him around back, go ahead."

He considered for a moment, then shook his head. "I'm sure you'll keep the situation under control."

"*Ja*, because before the bees would have a chance to sting Taffy, they'd be stinging me."

"That's incentive enough for anyone."

She chuckled, the sound distorted by the veiling. "Now you understand."

Though he was tempted to say he didn't understand much of what was going on in the house, he asked, "Are you sure there's nothing else I can do?"

"Knowing someone is watching over *Grossmammi* Ella and Shelby will allow me to concentrate on moving the bees." She pulled on one glove, making sure the long cuff was drawn up beneath the elastic at the hem of her sleeve. That way, he realized, no honeybee could crawl under her protective clothing. "Did you bring the supers?"

"They're on the porch. I also brought along a hand truck for you to use to get the boxes to the house once you've got the bees in them. I wasn't sure if you'd want to bring them all at once or not, but I left the hand truck by the bridge."

"Let's take it one step at a time."

"And the steps are…?"

"First I'll smoke the bees. When they're dazed, I'll cut each section of the comb out and attach it to a frame with rubber bands. The frames go into the supers, which I'll put in the cellar. I'd better get started."

When she walked past him, he caught her arm as he had her great-grandmother. He was shocked when something that felt like the buzz from a thousand bees rushed from where his fingertips touched her. It'd never happened before, not even when he was taking her home in his buggy.

He heard her sharp gasp. Had she felt the strange sensation, too?

He wanted to ask her that...and so many other things, things he couldn't put into words. *Don't be foolish again!* came the warning from his conscience. To speak of un-explored feelings could lead to her believing his priorities had changed. They hadn't. He had to focus on building his construction company.

"Daniel?" she asked, her voice trembling.

He lifted his hand off her arm. "I wanted to tell you to be careful."

"You don't have to. I know to be careful." She strode away.

He started to put Shelby in her high chair so he could give her a cookie, but halted and turned to look at the closing door. Had she been talking about the bees when she spoke of being careful? A boulder dropped through his stomach as he wondered if she'd been talking about him instead. That thought bothered him more than it should.

And that bothered him even more.

Hannah puffed smoke at the bees. Already they were quieting in the massive hive within the timbers beneath the bridge. Once they were dazed enough, she'd begin removing the layers of honeycomb and transfer them to the frames. Most of the bees would cling to the comb during the transfer. The rest would fall onto the white sheet she'd spread out next to one super. Seeing the entrance, they'd crawl in and join the rest of the members of the hive.

Once she found the queen bee, she'd put her into the bee carrier along with a couple of her worker bee attendants. The queen was vital to making the transfer a success, so when Hannah saw the bee that was a giant in comparison with the others, she smiled…and then winced.

Ach! Her left cheek ached from where *Grossmammi* Ella had struck her before breakfast. The shock of having her gentle, warmhearted great-grandmother lash out with abrupt fury hurt more than the impact of the old woman's hand.

Grossmammi Ella had been on edge since the bishop and Chief McMurray had come to the house a few days ago. She'd refused to sit at the table for meals, insisting she eat in her room where she felt safe, and she fussed every time Shelby did. Last night before bedtime, her eyes had flashed with the first sparks of a temper she'd never shown during the years Hannah was growing up. She'd been infuriated when Shelby woke in the middle of the night and had snarled at Hannah to make sure the *boppli* was quiet.

Hannah had recognized the signs of an impending storm, but she hadn't expected it to explode from her great-grandmother before they ate breakfast. Hannah had avoided the worst of the blow, but the impact had been enough to leave a red blotch on her face hours later.

She'd seen Daniel's curiosity about why she hadn't removed her hat and veil. She didn't want to answer the questions he was certain to ask if he saw the mark on her face. Those questions could lead to more, including if Hannah was capable of taking care of her great-grandmother.

Capturing the queen bee and two other bees close to her, Hannah shut them into the small plastic box built for this purpose. She then continued moving comb into the frames and sliding them into the supers, but her thoughts weren't on her work.

Would her great-grandmother be taken away if others discovered the truth of their situation? Was it safe for Shelby to be in the house with the old woman? The *Englisch* police wouldn't be willing to leave the little girl in what they deemed a dangerous place.

Should she speak with Reuben? She didn't want to think her bishop would insist she relinquish Shelby to another's care.

In spite of her determination not to, as she removed the last piece of comb and secured it, she glanced toward the house. Daniel stood by the front window with Shelby clinging again to him. His broad hand was around the *kind*, but his gaze was fixed on Hannah. Concern drew his mouth into a straight line.

She wanted to believe he was anxious for her safety. Once upon a time, when Daniel had first walked out with her—or at least, she'd believed he was walking out with her—she would have been certain his trepidation was for her. She wasn't sure what to think.

Setting one super on top of another, she put a board on the upper one. She did the same with the other supers. Noticing no bees were visible on the sheet, she picked up one pair of supers and began walking up the hill toward the road. She set them on the hand truck before collecting the others. Within minutes, she'd gathered her equipment and the sheet.

Hannah was glad, when she approached the house, that Daniel hadn't brought Shelby outside. *Gut!* Going around the house, she opened the bulkhead doors. She checked the spot in the cellar where she wanted to set the supers before hurrying up the kitchen stairs to stuff the sheet into the crack beneath the door. There mustn't be any chance of bees sneaking into the house.

With care, she carried the supers to the pair of two-by-fours that would allow for air circulation into the bottom of the hive. She brought the other two and set them beside the first set. She shut the bulkhead doors and switched on the lantern to spread light across the stone floor.

"Can I watch while you put the queen in?" Daniel asked from the top of the kitchen stairs. He stepped onto the first step without waiting for her answer.

"There's not much to see, but come ahead. Make sure you close the door and stuff that fabric under it."

Daniel did as she requested.

"There's a flashlight on the shelf up there," Hannah called. "You'd better use it so you don't fall and break your neck."

"I appreciate you worrying about me taking a tumble. I'm glad you're not still angry with me."

"If I was, all I needed to do was let you help me move the bees."

He chuckled. "You've got plenty of bees down here. You aren't going to sic them on me, are you?"

Hoping she wasn't being a fool, she put her hand

on his arm. "The past is the past, Daniel. Didn't you say that the day Shelby arrived?" She stood straighter, though she was more than six inches shorter than he was. "If you've changed your mind and want to linger in the past, fine. Just don't expect me to."

He opened his mouth to retort, but closed it. Did he want to avoid an argument, or was he unwilling to admit he agreed with her?

Knowing she couldn't keep the queen from her anxious hive, Hannah picked up the small plastic container. She set the lantern on a nearby shelf and adjusted it so the light shone on the pair of supers she'd set on top of the screen spanning the two by fours. As she stepped closer, she could hear the rapid buzzing from the uneasy bees. She lifted one corner of the uppermost super's lid and slipped the end of the plastic container under it.

She tapped the queen and other bees out and watched them crawl among the combs lashed to the frames with rubber bands. As she lowered the lid, she saw bees moving toward their queen. Nothing would calm them more than her presence.

"Will you hand me the piece of mesh over there?" Hannah asked.

"What is it?" Daniel asked as he handed it to her.

"A queen excluder." She set the simple plastic mesh on top of the supers. "It has holes worker bees can pass through, but not the queen who's larger. The queen excluder will insure she doesn't fly off while the hive is getting accustomed to their new home."

Making sure the mesh was set squarely on the box, she picked up the other supers and set them on the first ones. She took care to avoid squashing bees. Finally she looked around the cellar.

"What do you need?" Daniel asked.

"That piece of plywood. It goes on top of the supers." She pointed to the wood leaning against the shelves holding the last of the canned peaches she'd put up last summer.

They maneuvered it on the hive. On each side, it was about an inch wider than the boxes. He moved aside and watched when she took a ragged quilt from the shelf. Swinging it over the hive, she watched the quilt puddle on the floor in every direction, darkening the hive and offering no escape for the bees. However, air could sift through the fabric and reach the combs, so the bees didn't suffocate.

"And that's that," she said, walking around the hive and adjusting the quilt on each side before she set bricks on it to keep the fabric from shifting. "We'll leave them in the dark. When they come out, they'll have no idea they're not much more than a stone's throw from their old hive." She smiled. "It'll help that you're taking out the rotten board."

"I had no idea how to take care of bees. I'm glad I contacted you."

She pulled off her gloves and yanked the tabs on her protective shirt. Shrugging it off, she folded it over her arm after making sure no bees clung to it. "And I'm glad, too, that we've saved the bees."

"How long will they be here?"

"About a week or so. Maybe two. It has to be long enough for them to forget where they were before. The cold helps because they're less active, and the rain we've been having will wash away the scent trails quickly. By the time I move this hive beside my others, warmer weather should be here and the first flowers blooming.

The bees can then do what they do best, gathering nectar and spreading pollen and making honey."

"I'll be glad to help you when you're ready to move them outside, if you need help."

"I appreciate that." And she did, which surprised her. The past few days hadn't been easy, but they also hadn't been the end of the world. Daniel had shown he could be a *gut* friend by helping her with Shelby. He'd revealed he did have a heart by how gently he treated her great-grandmother. "Let's get out of here ourselves."

She walked to the cupboard where she kept her equipment and beekeeper's clothing. Putting away each piece, she made sure the kerchief she wore over her hair was in place. She turned around and gasped when she discovered Daniel standing right behind her.

He grasped her chin and tilted it so the lantern's light played across her left cheek. "What happened to you?"

How could she have forgotten the mark on her face? *Help me, Lord*, she prayed. *I can't tell the whole truth, because I don't know what will happen to us then. Help me find the right words. I have to protect my family. They're all I have.*

"Just an accident," she replied, hoping he'd leave it at that.

He didn't. "What type of accident?"

"I was down at the bridge earlier. I wanted to check on the hive once more before I moved them. It was raining, and the grass was wet." She stepped away from him. "You can guess what happened next."

Would he accept her story that was true but didn't include the part about her great-grandmother losing her temper? She held her breath.

Puzzlement dimmed his dark eyes, and she knew he

was trying to believe her. When he motioned for her to lead the way up the stairs to the kitchen, she felt relief and regret. She wished she could depend on someone else, most especially Daniel, but how could she when the one time she'd dared to trust him, he'd left her as her *daed* had?

Chapter Seven

"Gute mariye, my girls." *Grossmammi* Ella came into the kitchen with a broad smile at dawn early the next week.

"Good morning." Hannah flashed a smile over her shoulder. She stood by the stove frying eggs. She was relieved to hear her great-grandmother's happy tone. Though the elderly woman's mood could change in a split second, when *Grossmammi* Ella's voice was filled with joy, the day usually went well.

In the distance, Hannah could hear the equipment used by Daniel's crew on the Hunter's Mill Creek Bridge. They had begun tearing off the rotten boards the day after Hannah moved the bees. Behind the concrete barriers, piles of debris had been swelling, but she'd noticed this morning when she raised the shade on her bedroom window that the wood was being loaded in a beat-up truck to be carted away. Faint laughter had reached the house as the men worked together.

Smelling the eggs starting to scorch, she flipped them. At the same time, her great-grandmother announced, "I have something here."

"What is it?" She scraped at a spot where the eggs had stuck to the pan.

"It's for the *boppli*."

Hannah took the cast iron pan off the stove so she could give the older woman her complete attention. She wiped her hands on her apron to make sure there was no grease on them and then took the toy held out to her. *Grossmammi* Ella had knit its body and head before stuffing it with rags. Bright yellow and black, she guessed it was meant to be a honeybee. The old woman must have made it during the quiet times she spent in her bedroom each afternoon.

Until that moment, Hannah had wondered if her great-grandmother would accept Shelby as a member of their family. Doing that meant *Grossmammi* Ella had to admit her grandson had left the toddler behind as he had Hannah. Or perhaps her great-grandmother simply wanted to make a lonely *kind* happy.

"Don't you want to give it to Shelby?" Hannah asked.

"Ja." Walking with care to where the little girl sat in her high chair, *Grossmammi* Ella placed the knit toy on the edge of the tray. She wiggled it, catching Shelby's attention. "See, my friend, little one?"

Shelby poked one finger at the toy. When the elderly woman slid it across the high chair tray, the *kind* laughed.

Hannah was astonished when the little girl pursed her lips and made a whirring sound by blowing through them. The toddler was copying the noise Hannah had made the previous evening while reading her a picture book about a busy bee and its attempt to find a flower. Hannah hadn't been certain the *kind* had understood the story, but realized Shelby had connected the sound with the picture of a bee in the book.

What else did the toddler understand? Hannah hoped the therapists the *doktorfraa* was sending would be able to help her answer the question. And wouldn't Daniel be amazed when she told him what Shelby had done!

Hannah stared at her wooden spoon which was halfway between the pan and the plate she used for serving the eggs. She hadn't expected *that* thought. Was Daniel wheedling his way into her life—into their lives—again? The idea should have annoyed her, but all she could think of was how pleased he'd be when she told him about Shelby comprehending the story.

Things had changed—again—between her and Daniel. They hadn't been friends before, because she'd fallen so hard and fast for him. Was what they shared now friendship? A friendship could make their bargain more comfortable for them instead of being lit by the white-hot intensity of the infatuation she'd had. She wondered if any young man could have lived up to the fantasy she'd built. Especially one like Daniel who'd made no promises other than they'd have fun together.

"Sounds like she's saying buzz-buzz-buzz," said *Grossmammi* Ella, pulling Hannah from her surprising thoughts.

"Buzz-buzz would be a *gut* name," Hannah said with a smile. "*Danki*, *Grossmammi* Ella, for making her a special gift."

"A *boppli* needs toys. Soft toys to hug." Her great-grandmother sounded gruff, and Hannah guessed she was trying to hide her satisfaction at how thrilled Shelby was with her gift. "When will breakfast be ready?"

"Right away."

The rest of the morning passed as pleasantly as breakfast. Shelby continued playing with the stuffed bee much to *Grossmammi* Ella's delight. That gave Hannah time to take care of the animals, including the bees in the cellar, and to do her other chores. The two in the living room made up games together, the elderly woman in her favorite chair and the *kind* leaning against her knee as she made the bee "fly." Laughter filled the house that had been somber for too long.

During the midday meal, *Grossmammi* Ella spoke about the flowers she wanted to plant by the front steps once the weather was warm. Hannah listened while making a mental list of the annuals she'd buy for her great-grandmother at one of the greenhouses in Paradise Springs.

When the elderly woman retreated to her bedroom, Hannah tried to keep Shelby quiet. The little girl refused to nap and fussed with her sore mouth. One tooth had popped through over the weekend, but another was already giving her misery. *Grossmammi* Ella needed to rest, so Hannah put some honey on Shelby's sore gum and tried to rock her to sleep. The little girl refused to settle and continued to cry.

Hannah felt weak tears flood her eyes when she heard footfalls on the porch just as Shelby was falling asleep. The *kind* routed awake. Rising, Hannah opened the door.

Daniel stood there, his clothes dirty with the road dust ingrained in the boards on the old bridge. Her heart jumped, astonishing her. Her traitorous heart had done that in the past, but it shouldn't now. She knew better.

"I can't stay long." His lowered voice resonated through the house like the rumble of distant traffic.

Taking off his straw hat, he held it in front of him. "I wanted—" He paused as Shelby offered her new toy to him. "What do you have there, *liebling*?"

Shelby made the buzzing sound before giggling with excitement.

"She's trying to tell you," Hannah said, "the bee's name is Buzz-buzz." She quickly explained how Shelby had connected the stuffed toy with the story Hannah had read to her and the sounds she'd made for the little girl. "*Grossmammi* Ella made it for her."

When Daniel took the toy and examined it, Shelby watched him. He handed it to her, and she pretended to make it fly.

He laughed. "That's right." He winked at Hannah. "Though I doubt most bees fly upside down, do they?"

"Toy ones do." She set the little girl on the sofa. "What do you want, Daniel?"

"A couple of things. First, I hope the noise from the bridge hasn't been a bother."

"No, it's been fine. It won't go on too long, will it?"

"We need to be done in under six weeks." He turned his hat around and around by the brim, startling her because she hadn't expected him to be nervous. "The other thing I wanted to say was you should come to the supper at the Paradise Springs Fire Department tonight. We're raising money for new equipment and hoping for a big turnout. Will you come?"

"It may be too late in the day for my great-grand-mother and Shelby."

He shook his head. "Nope. The supper starts at six, and it's for a *gut* cause. In addition, it would do you *gut*, Hannah, to get out and spend the evening beyond these four walls."

Hannah hesitated. For the past couple of years, she hadn't taken her great-grandmother many places because *Grossmammi* Ella always had an excuse at the last minute not to go. It was easier to stay home. But this supper was different. Many of the volunteer firefighters in Paradise Springs were plain, and the Amish community supported the volunteers who protected their homes and other buildings. She'd heard people talking about the supper after the church service on Sunday, so there would be familiar faces there. And Daniel was right. It was for a *gut* cause.

"All I can say is maybe," she replied.

"Anything I can say or do to turn that maybe into a *ja*?" His eyes twinkled.

Again her heart did a little dance. As it had when he used to flirt with her. She'd forgotten how *gut* that felt.

"Maybe," she replied.

He grinned. "Is maybe all you can say?"

"Maybe."

Starting to laugh, he clapped his hand over his mouth so he didn't wake her great-grandmother. He winked again and ruffled Shelby's hair. "Then *maybe*, I'll see you tonight."

His easy smile sent warmth spiraling through her, even after he was gone. It should have been enough to convince her to stay away from the firehouse tonight, but she wanted to go. She couldn't remember the last time she'd gone anywhere but on errands or to attend church.

It was time to change that.

As Hannah had expected, when she suggested attending the fund-raising supper, her great-grandmother was reluctant to go. Hannah's insistence they support the firefighters convinced *Grossmammi* Ella.

Or so Hannah thought. She realized how mistaken she was when, after she'd hitched up the buggy horse, she came into the house and discovered her great-grandmother standing in the front room and watching Shelby play.

"It looks like Hannah is taking to the bee, ain't so, Saloma?" the old woman asked.

Hannah flinched. Her great-grandmother was lost in time again. The changes came without warning. *Grossmammi* Ella thought Hannah was her granddaughter-in-law and Shelby was Hannah. Last year, Hannah had paid no attention to these misconceptions, telling herself everyone mixed up names once in a while. She couldn't ignore them any longer. It was part of the sickness stealing *Grossmammi* Ella's mind.

After taking her great-grandmother to a specialist, Hannah knew how each step of the disease would progress. She also knew there was little that could halt it. The *doktor* had written a prescription for a medicine to slow the inevitable, but *Grossmammi* Ella refused to take it after the pills made her sick and dizzy.

Hannah hadn't insisted. Not after her great-grandmother in a lucid moment had said if her days on earth were numbered, she preferred not to spend them weak and nauseated. Unable to argue with that, Hannah had taken her great-grandmother to Dr. Montgomery for regular checkups. The *doktorfraa* accepted the elderly woman's determination to live her life on her terms.

"She loves it," Hannah replied to her great-grandmother's question about the stuffed toy. As long as *Grossmammi* Ella didn't do anything to hurt herself or someone else, Hannah let her keep her illusions. "She'll enjoy it while we're at the supper at the fire station."

"You're letting her take it with her?"

"Ja."

"You spoil that *kind.*" The sharp edge had returned to the old woman's voice. Her abrupt mood swings were impossible to anticipate.

"Bopplin should be spoiled." Hannah kept her voice light. "It makes them happy, and it makes us happy, too."

Her great-grandmother sniffed once at Hannah's reply and a second time while taking her cane. "Mark my words, Saloma. You're spoiling that *kind,* and who knows how she'll turn out?"

"We'll have to wait and see what the future brings, ain't so?"

Relief flooded Hannah when *Grossmammi* Ella didn't reply as they walked out to the buggy. Though it made driving difficult, Hannah made sure the toddler was sitting to her right instead of between her and her great-grandmother. There was the possibility the elderly woman would become upset and strike out at the nearest person. Hannah didn't want Shelby to be the target.

She touched her cheek where the bruise had almost faded. The *doktorfraa's* words haunted her: "If your great-grandmother gets to the point where she's a danger to herself and others, we'll have to discuss the best options for her and for you, Hannah. I know you want to keep her living with you, but you can't put both of you in peril."

Now three of them lived in the house, and Daniel was there often. She hoped *Grossmammi* Ella wouldn't get worse anytime soon.

The fire station was bright with electric lights and the flashers on the fire engines when Hannah drove the buggy into the parking lot between it and the post office. *Kinder* gathered around the trucks and firemen, calling out questions and examining the firefighting tools the volunteers held. No *kind* was allowed near the axes, but they didn't seem to mind. They were having too much fun trying on helmets and sitting behind the wheel while a fireman activated the siren.

"You came!" Daniel's voice reached her as she opened the buggy's door.

Where was he?

He grinned as he edged out of the darkness, and her breath caught. His black hair shone with blue fire beneath the powerful electric lights. Crinkled with laughter, his eyes snapped with the same blue sparks. Though dozens of voices were raised in conversation in every direction, her ears had picked out his as if it were the only one.

Before she could answer, Shelby started babbling and holding out her short arms to him. He picked up the toddler as he said, "*Komm* with me. I'll show you around."

Hannah assisted her great-grandmother from the buggy and followed him toward the firehouse. He stopped again and again to point out something to Shelby who chewed on her stuffed toy to ease her sore gums. When he reached the building, he waited for her and *Grossmammi* Ella to catch up.

She blinked when they entered the large space where the fire trucks were usually parked. Tables had been arranged in rows with baskets of rolls placed every three or four chairs. The aroma of tomato sauce and taco spices drifted from where the buffet tables were. It was a haystack dinner, and her stomach growled in eager expectancy of the flavors of beef, rice, green peppers and cheese as well as onions, olives and salsa. Everything would be piled together on their plates, each flavor enhancing the others.

Daniel walked to where a woman with graying hair was setting out stacks of cups. She smiled.

"*Grossmammi* Ella, Hannah, Shelby," he said, nodding in his head toward each of them as he spoke their names, "this is my *mamm*, Wanda Stoltzfus. *Mamm*, you remember these lovely Lambright ladies I've told you about."

Hannah appreciated Daniel introducing them to his *mamm* just in case *Grossmammi* Ella had met Wanda before and failed to remember her. There was a definite resemblance between Daniel and his *mamm*. Something about the shape of their faces and their easy smiles.

After greeting them, Wanda said, "It's so *gut* to see you again, *Grossmammi* Ella. Not that you probably remember me. It's been more than twenty years since the last time we've done more than wave while driving past each other along the road."

"I remember your husband," the older woman said.

"I'm not surprised. Paul knew everyone from the Chester County line to Harrisburg."

Grossmammi Ella gasped. "Knew? Your husband is dead?"

Hannah put her hands on her great-grandmother's arms and steered her to a nearby chair. The blunt questions had dimmed Wanda's bright eyes. Wanting to tell Daniel's *mamm* that *Grossmammi* Ella hadn't meant to say anything hurtful, Hannah stayed silent. She couldn't embarrass her great-grandmother. She handed the old woman a roll from the nearest basket.

"I need butter," her great-grandmother said.

"I'll get some. Stay here."

Hannah went to get several pats of butter from a serving table. Each person she passed smiled and welcomed her to the haystack dinner. She wondered if the prodigal son had felt like she did. Everyone acted as if they'd missed her. People she'd never met greeted her like a long-lost friend.

She took butter to *Grossmammi* Ella and helped her put it on the roll. With the old woman occupied with eating, Hannah's eyes searched the room for Wanda Stoltzfus and discovered her stacking paper napkins next to the cups.

Going to Daniel's *mamm*, Hannah said, "Wanda, I'm so sorry. *Grossmammi* Ella didn't mean—"

"I know." She put a gentle hand on Hannah's arm. "Sometimes our elders forget matters, big and small. I'd like to think it's because the *gut* Lord wants to ease their burden of carrying so many memories, letting them know He forgives past wrongs and has rejoiced with them on past joys. He lightens their hearts, making them ready to soar when their time comes to go home to Him."

Hannah blinked on sudden, scalding tears. In her isolation, she'd forgotten the comfort a kind word could bring. Wanda's words reached deep within her and loosened the thick web of futility growing there, capturing every hurt *Grossmammi* Ella didn't intend to inflict. Her great-grandmother had been a loving woman…until the past couple of years. Turning away, she hid her tears.

"If you're looking for your little girl," Wanda went

on, "Daniel is showing her the fire trucks outside. Go ahead. I'll keep an eye on your great-grandmother." She held up one finger. "Just a moment." Walking over to the desserts table, she picked up a handful of cookies and brought them to Hannah. "Why don't you take these with you? There has never been a *kind* who doesn't love my cookies." She chuckled. "Or one of my grown-up sons either."

"I wish giving her cookies would convince Shelby to like me more."

Wanda clasped Hannah's shoulder. "Do you think it's because you look so much like your *daed*?"

Shock froze her. She could barely remember what her *daed* looked like and had come to assume he resembled his *grossmammi*. "I do?"

"*Ja*. Shelby can see that, too. Do you think it's possible she's wary of you because you remind her of your *daed*, and she's afraid you'll abandon her as he did?"

She stared at Wanda in astonishment. "Really?"

"I may be way off base, but it's the only explanation that makes sense to me. You treat her with love."

"*Grossmammi* Ella tells me I spoil her."

"If loving a *kind* is spoiling her, then I agree with your great-grandmother." Wanda waved her away. "Go and spend time with the other young people. Enjoy your evening out, Hannah."

A smile tilted her lips. "I will." Without another word, she headed in the direction Wanda had indicated.

When she stepped outside, Daniel motioned for her to come over to where he had Shelby sitting on his shoulders while he spoke with several men. He introduced Hannah to the firefighters gathered there. She wished his saucy expression each time he looked at her didn't cause the butterflies inside her to take flight. Hadn't she learned her lesson? Daniel flirted with every woman, whether she was as young as Shelby or as elderly as *Grossmammi* Ella. There was, she told herself, nothing special in his grin for her.

But maybe, for this evening, she'd let the past stay in the past and enjoy herself as Wanda had suggested. She hoped she hadn't forgotten how.

Daniel felt his heart trying to do somersaults in his chest when he stood with the Lambrights in a dusky corner at the end of the evening. Until he'd seen her in the parking lot, he doubted Hannah would come tonight. She'd shut herself off from the rest of the community for two years. He admitted to himself he was relieved to know it hadn't been for three years. Then he would have blamed himself for her withdrawal. He knew his actions hadn't helped, but he guessed her great-grandmother's strange ways kept her from spending time with the rest of the residents of Paradise Springs.

Beside him, *Grossmammi* Ella was struggling to get into her coat. He helped her, but his gaze refused to leave Hannah. The bruise had faded from her face, leaving her cheek soft and pink once more. His fingers quivered at the thought of brushing them against her skin or through the rich honey of her hair.

He couldn't look away as she buttoned Shelby's coat. Did Hannah think he didn't see how she glanced at her great-grandmother to check *Grossmammi* Ella's coat was closed, too?

He'd noticed *Mamm* watching how Hannah had spent most of the meal overseeing her great-grandmother as well as the toddler. He wasn't surprised. His *mamm* cared about every member of their community almost as much as she did her *kinder*. That was why she was eager to see each of her *kinder* settled in a happy marriage. He had no doubts about her *gut* intentions, and he guessed, after tonight, she'd have several dozen questions about Hannah and her little family.

"*Danki* for asking us to attend," Hannah said as she stood and held Shelby's hand.

"Insisting, you mean." He gave her a cockeyed grin, hoping she'd respond to his teasing.

He was rewarded when she chuckled. When they were walking out together, he hadn't had to resort to jesting in order to banish her serious expression. Her eyes had brightened like twin lamps the moment her gaze met his, and her lips had offered a sweet smile. So much trust she'd invested in him. Too much for the young man he'd been.

"Everyone has been nice," she said. "I don't know why I'm surprised. Whenever I bring honey to Amos's shop, everyone says hello."

"The people of Paradise Springs are close-knit. It may be because we live so close to the highway and the *Englisch* world. That makes us appreciate each other."

"But you have *Englischers* among you." She looked across the room to where several families, who were not plain, were chatting with the Amish and Mennonite families sharing their tables.

"The fire department welcomes everyone who wants to protect Paradise Springs. Nobody cares if you're plain or not. Everyone is determined to keep a fire from taking a neighbor's house or barn. Sharing a common goal gives us common ground to build friendships upon." He grinned. "Sort of like you and me. Our goals might not have been in common, but they intersected."

She scooped up Shelby who was trying to tug away and join other youngsters running around the empty tables. "*Danki* again for inviting us, Daniel. *Grossmammi* Ella has talked so much she's hoarse, and I don't think Shelby's feet touched the floor all night."

"She's a friendly tyke."

"*Ja*, though she's leery of certain people."

"You mean you."

"Your *mamm* thinks it's because she sees too much of our *daed* in me."

His brows shot up. "I never thought of that."

"Me neither." She bid him good-night and walked with her great-grandmother and the toddler to their buggy.

He stood in the doorway, watching as they drove away. When he went into the firehouse, it seemed as if the lights were a bit duller and the conversation subdued. He helped clean up before he brought his buggy around so his *mamm* could get in.

The road leading through the village and toward their farm was deserted. He waited for *Mamm* to mention Hannah and her family, but she seemed lost in thought. He listened to Taffy's iron shoes on the road, the creak of the buggy wheels and the fine mist falling around them.

As the buggy rolled to a stop by the house, he said, "Here we are."

"*Ja*. Here we are." She half turned on the seat to look at him, her face in a silhouette against the soft glow from the kitchen windows. "After seeing you and Hannah tonight, I do want you to recall, my son, it was you who decided you didn't want to continue walking out with her." There was no censure in her voice.

"I know. I was young and foolish then."

"You aren't so young. Are you still as foolish?"

He grinned and shook his head. "I'd like to say no, but how many times have you told us that changing the past is impossible? That we must ask for forgiveness for our mistakes and move forward, making sure we never choose poorly again."

She got out of the buggy. "Remember a mistake is no longer a mistake if you remedy it in time."

"I'm not sure I can do that."

"Because you don't want to?"

"No, because the time to correct it is long past."

She regarded him for a long time, and he fought not to squirm as if he were a *kind* again. "I hope you're wrong, Daniel."

He watched as she went into the cozy *dawdi haus*. When the door closed behind her, he murmured to himself and the night and God, "I hope I am, too."

Chapter Eight

Two days after the haystack dinner at the firehouse, Hannah heard a car coming along the road before she saw it through the steady rain. A blue SUV slowed at the junction leading to the covered bridge, then began inching toward the house.

She glanced at the clock on the mantel. It was almost ten o'clock. The physical therapist's message, left on the neighbors' answering machine, was to expect her around ten this morning.

The car pulled into the driveway and parked. The driver's door opened, and a bright yellow umbrella appeared. Snapping open, it rose along with the woman emerging from the car. Hooking a large purse over her arm, she slammed the door closed and rushed toward the house, skirting the large puddles marking every depression in the yard.

Hannah threw open the door as the *Englischer* climbed the porch steps. "*Komm* in!"

"Don't mind if I do." The woman shook her umbrella and sprayed water across the porch before she closed it. "Hi, I'm Audrey Powell. Are you Hannah?"

"*Ja.*"

Audrey Powell was about as old as Hannah's *mamm* would have been, but she had a cheeky smile and was as spry as a teenager. Gray streaked the brown hair she wore in a ponytail. Her T-shirt had a big-eyed cat on the front, and her sneakers had pink-and-blue laces wound together and tied in big bows.

Those bows fascinated Shelby who couldn't take her eyes off them. Pushing herself to her feet, she waddled to Audrey and dropped to the floor in front of the sneakers. She reached out to touch the bright bows.

"Hello, Shelby," said Audrey, squatting in front of the little girl. She waved Hannah back, clearly wanting to see how the *kind* reacted to her.

Shelby made some of the sounds she used instead of words, but her gaze remained focused on the bows.

"Do you like my shoes, Shelby?" the physical therapist asked before looking up at Hannah. "Does she understand English?"

Hannah nodded. "She's been living with my *daed*— my father, and, as far as we can figure out, she's used to *Englisch*. I don't think she understands much *Deitsch*."

"That's good, because my *Deitsch* is pretty basic." She gave Hannah a reassuring smile. "I've worked with plain folk before, so I understand your children speak *Deitsch* until they begin school. I also know the Amish don't attend public schools where ongoing therapy is provided for any child requiring it. However, where she'll go to school won't make a difference in evaluating Shelby and developing an IEP for her. An Individualized Education Program." She chuckled. "We get used to talking in acronyms, so stop me whenever I use one you don't understand."

"Are you a *doktorfraa*?" demanded *Grossmammi* Ella as she walked into the room, her cane banging against the floor to emphasize her vexation at finding a stranger in her house. That she used the cane revealed she didn't want the *Englischer* to see any weakness in her.

"No, ma'am," Audrey said. "I'm a physical therapist. Dr. Montgomery asked me to come here to work with Shelby."

Hannah introduced the two women. She wished she'd had time to warn the therapist about her great-grandmother's sudden shifts in mood.

Urging the elderly woman to use a chair by the stove where she'd stay warm on the damp day, Hannah wasn't surprised when her great-grandmother asked another question as she sat, "You can help our Shelby?"

"I can make sure she gets the right help so she can become all you hope her to be." Audrey didn't seem bothered by the question.

Grossmammi Ella nodded and folded her hands on her lap. "Go ahead."

Audrey arched her brows at Hannah who struggled not to smile at her great-grandmother's regal edict.

"Where do you want to work with Shelby?" Hannah asked.

"Here on the rug will be fine." She grinned. "I find sessions go best when I'm on the children's level." Sitting cross-legged on the floor, she motioned for Hannah to join her and Shelby.

Kneeling next to the therapist, Hannah held her breath. Would Shelby cooperate with whatever Audrey had planned? Would *Grossmammi* Ella refrain from interrupting? She took a steadying breath to calm herself and sent up a prayer for serenity.

"Shelby," Audrey said with a smile, "let's play a game."

The toddler stood, ran across the room and got the knitted honeybee she'd dropped when the therapist had arrived. She held it out to Audrey.

"How cute!" the therapist gushed, earning a wide smile from Shelby and one almost as big from *Grossmammi* Ella.

"Its name is Buzz-buzz," Hannah said.

"Did Shelby give the toy that name?"

"Not exactly." She explained how Shelby had made a buzzing sound when she first saw the toy. "But she must like the name because she responds when we ask where Buzz-buzz is."

"How does she respond?"

"She points to it or goes and gets it."

Audrey smiled. "That's excellent. Some toddlers who don't have Shelby's challenges aren't able to follow even simple instructions at this age." Looking at the *kind*, she asked, "Shelby, can I hold Buzz-buzz?"

The little girl hesitated, then handed the toy to Audrey, who cooed over it. Shelby laughed, and when Audrey held out the toy, she took it and hugged it hard as she pursed her lips, making the buzzing sound.

"What other toys does she like to play with?" the therapist asked.

Before Hannah could reply, a knock came on the door. It opened, and Daniel walked in. He shrugged off his wet coat and hung it by the door. Doing so revealed the strong muscles barely hidden beneath his plain shirt and black suspenders. For a moment, as she watched his smooth motions, she seemed to have forgotten how to breathe.

"Where's my big girl?" he asked with a smile.

"Da-da!" called Shelby, waving her arms at him.

Hannah froze and saw Daniel do the same, shock on his face. Why was Shelby calling out to Daniel as if he were her *daed*? The answer came when Shelby spoke again.

"Da-dan," she called. She was trying to say Daniel rather than the *Englisch* word *daddy.* "Da-dan!" Impatience heightened her voice.

Daniel squatted beside Shelby. "How are you doing, *liebling*?" He took the knit toy and tickled her with it.

Audrey looked from him to Hannah. "I'm confused. Aren't you, Hannah, Shelby's sister?"

"I am," Hannah said.

At the same time, Daniel replied, "I'm Daniel Stoltzfus."

"But she called you *da-da*," Audrey said, bafflement threading her brow.

Hannah said, "No, she was trying to say Daniel."

Understanding crossed the therapist's face, and her smile returned. "You understand the sounds she makes better than I do. Does she use other words you recognize?"

Hannah shook her head. "She hasn't used *Da-dan* before today."

"Does she have a name for you?"

Hoping her face wasn't bright red, for heat soared through her like a wildfire, she said, "Not yet."

"That will come, I'm sure. Will Shelby be getting speech therapy, too?"

"*Ja.* Dr. Montgomery said she was contacting someone to help Shelby."

"Probably Todd Howland. You'll like him, and Shelby will, too. He's great with kids. Most likely, you'll be hearing from Keely Mattera, too. She's the occupational therapist, and the three of us work as a team with young children."

Audrey called Shelby's name and, when the little girl looked up, asked her to touch her nose as Audrey was. The toddler followed along with what she saw as a game. When the therapist took Shelby by the hand, they went to the stairs in the front hall and practiced stepping up and down off the lowest one. Shelby did, but on her hands and knees. When the therapist lifted her to her feet and urged her to try again, the *kind*'s lower lip began to tremble in a pout.

"Hannah, will you try to convince her?" Audrey asked.

Knowing it was unlikely the toddler would heed anything she said or did, Hannah stepped forward. Shelby let out a frustrated howl and sat on the step.

"Can I try?" Daniel asked.

Audrey glanced at Hannah, who nodded. If Shelby would cooperate with Daniel, they couldn't leave him out of the sessions. Even knowing that didn't make it easy for her to move aside.

"Let's go, Shelby," he said, copying Audrey's motions. "It's fun, ain't so?"

The little girl giggled and gave him a big grin before going up and down with him. When Audrey asked her to go up and down two steps, Shelby seemed eager to prove she could.

Hannah choked back her dismay. Shelby preferred anyone else to her sister. Was Wanda right? Was Shelby pushing Hannah away because of the resemblance to their *daed*? It seemed weird the toddler would avoid the one person connected to her and her parents.

Or…? Hannah didn't want to let the thought form in

her head. *Daed* had been a gentle man, but he'd been changed by his wife's death. She'd assumed he was the same loving person he'd been with her at Shelby's age. Maybe he wasn't.

She looked away from where Daniel and Shelby were traversing three steps at a time. Her distress at her unwanted thoughts vanished when she saw the chair where *Grossmammi* Ella had been sitting was empty. Where had she gone?

Dread sank through her. Wandering was another aspect of her great-grandmother's disease. How was Hannah going to watch both her and Shelby's sessions at once?

For the first time, she thought of Daniel's offer of having Shelby live with his family. His *mamm* was kind and capable, having already raised nine *kinder*. Shelby would have a *gut* home where Hannah could visit her, and *Grossmammi* Ella would be easier to keep track of when she had all of Hannah's attention. And Daniel wouldn't be coming to her house every day, looking so easy on the eyes and being so nice her resolve to avoid him was melting away.

Letting him take Shelby would be the smart thing to do, but Hannah knew she'd never say the words and end up depending on him. Not again.

"I'll be right back," she said, rushing from the front hall.

Daniel stared after Hannah in disbelief. She was leaving right in the middle of Shelby's therapy?

Audrey continued watching the toddler on the stairs, but Daniel saw her glance in the direction Hannah had gone. Torn between going after Hannah and helping

Shelby, he heard Hannah call out her great-grandmother's name just before the back door slammed shut.

Suddenly, like a clap of thunder, he realized what was going on. The chair where the old woman had been sitting was empty. Where was *Grossmammi* Ella? He'd been so focused on Shelby he hadn't noticed the elderly woman leaving.

When Audrey led Shelby into the living room, the therapist sat on the floor and began to stack blocks, motioning for Shelby to do the same.

"Will you be helping with Shelby's therapy?" Audrey asked into the silence, and Daniel guessed, though she kept her expression neutral, she was as shocked by Hannah's sudden disappearance as he'd been.

"*Ja.* At least, I hope so. Shelby likes when I play with her, and a lot of what you're doing looks like a game."

The physical therapist smiled. "We try to make it feel like that for little ones, so they're more willing to participate. I wish we could find a way to make it fun for adults, too, but they see right through our wiles."

He tried to concentrate on what the therapist was doing so he could repeat the exercises with the toddler, but he couldn't halt himself from glancing again and again toward the kitchen. When the back door opened, he buried his impulse to jump up and help Hannah guide her great-grandmother in.

Shelby shouted with excitement when her tower of blocks tumbled, but Hannah said nothing as her great-grandmother shuffled into her bedroom. When the door closed behind *Grossmammi* Ella, a long sigh drifted from Hannah. She walked toward them.

"I'm sorry I had to leave. Everything's fine," Hannah said with a strained laugh. "I wanted to make sure my great-grandmother had a warm coat while she was outside. But she decided to come in, so all's well."

A dozen questions demanded answers, but Daniel didn't ask a single one. Audrey might believe Hannah's excuse. He didn't. Her great-grandmother shouldn't have been out in the rain in the first place.

After the therapist showed Hannah the exercise she was doing with Shelby and the blocks, Audrey stood and smiled. "That's enough for today. I don't want to tire her out on our first day. I'll fill out my portion of the paperwork for her IEP. When Keely and Todd have done their sections, we'll submit it for review. Once it's complete, we'll put together a schedule that works for you and Shelby. We don't want to overwhelm you. We hope this little sweetheart will continue to cooperate with the exercises we give her."

"Danki," Hannah said. "If you need anything, let me know."

"I will. Leaving a message on your neighbor's phone is okay?"

"Ja. They'll let me know, and I'll contact you."

Slinging her bag over her shoulder, the therapist bid them and Shelby goodbye. The door closed behind her, and Daniel waited until the sound of her footsteps vanished off the porch.

"Is your great-grandmother all right?" he asked.

Hannah nodded, but she didn't meet his worried gaze. Did she think she could hide her agitation from him? Again he discovered he'd misjudged her reaction when she sat on the sofa and clasped her hands.

"Are *you* all right?" he asked as he sat beside her.

"A bit overwhelmed." She raised her eyes, and he saw she was being honest. "I'm not sure how I'm going to help Shelby with her exercises when she wants nothing to do with me."

"You'll figure out something. You always do. I admire that about you, Hannah. You don't hesitate to run in where angels fear to tread."

"Something that's foolish to do."

"Not foolish. Caring and courageous."

Astonishment softened her face, and he wondered when someone had last offered her a compliment. The Amish weren't supposed to praise one another, but it happened far more often than anyone was willing to admit. Had anyone told Hannah how pretty she was since he had…three years ago? Had anyone told her how *wunderbaar* she was since he had…three years ago? Had anyone told her how special she was? He hadn't, not even three years ago. He'd accepted the gift of her loving heart though he wasn't willing to offer his in return.

"I'm doing what I need to do," she said, lowering her eyes again.

His hand was cupping her chin, bringing her gaze to his, before he had a chance to think. "I know, but you're special, Hannah."

"You'd do the same as I am."

"I'd like to think I would, but I'm not so sure. I hope I don't have to find out."

"I hope you don't either." She shifted her head from his grip. "You're right."

"Me? Right? I never thought I'd hear Hannah Lambright say that."

Her eyes began to shine with mischief, something he'd seen too seldom since he'd found her little sister on the porch. "I'd have admitted you were right before if you'd ever been right."

He laughed, but the sound faded when Shelby walked over to them, carrying Buzz-buzz. The little girl glanced from her sister to him as if trying to figure something out. Without a word, she held up the stuffed bee. Not to him, but to Hannah. She looked at her older sister and grinned.

Tears glistened in Hannah's eyes, and Daniel found himself smiling so broadly it hurt. For the first time, the little girl was reaching out to Hannah.

Hannah took the toy and rubbed it against her cheek before doing the same to Shelby's. The little girl giggled.

"Try playing peekaboo with her," he suggested.

"That's your game."

He understood what she didn't say. Hannah wanted to have something special only she and her little sister shared. When the *kind* took the knitted toy, she held it to her face before dropping it on Hannah's apron. Shelby ran across the room to the bookshelf. Plucking a book off it, she rushed back to the sofa and set it beside the toy on Hannah's knees.

Hannah drew in a quick breath.

"What's wrong?" he asked.

"Nothing's wrong." She picked up the book and smiled at the little girl, tears of joy hanging on her lashes. "It's the book I've been reading to her. The one about bees. Would you like me to read it to you, Shelby?"

The *kind* nodded so hard her golden hair bounced around her. When she opened her arms and raised them toward Hannah, Daniel felt his own eyes sting with unexpected tears. He'd prayed for this moment when Shelby would realize the person who cared most about her in the whole world was her sister.

As Hannah lifted the toddler onto her lap and opened the book while Shelby cuddled Buzz-buzz, he stood and went to the door. He said goodbye, but neither looked toward him as they shared the story. Hannah made Shelby giggle while acting out the story with the stuffed toy. He was witnessing a family coming together, a family that didn't include him.

Three years ago, he'd made his choice to focus on building a business instead of a family. Maybe Hannah was right about him being wrong up until now, but he didn't know how to get off the path he was on when he was so close to making his dream come true. But he was beginning to see the cost of that decision. It was higher than he'd imagined.

Chapter Nine

"Today is moving day, ain't so?" Daniel asked as he walked into the backyard at the Lambright house the following week. He'd stopped by only occasionally since Shelby began trusting Hannah.

Each time he visited, he'd helped Shelby with her therapy, though the little girl wanted her sister to assist her on everything but the stairs. The exercise seemed as special to the little girl as the games of peekaboo she played with him.

That was the way it was supposed to be, but he realized how much he missed being necessary to their little family. He wondered how much longer he'd have an excuse to drop by because Hannah and Shelby now were comfortable with each other. Hannah had fulfilled her side of the bargain, too, by moving the bees.

Hannah motioned him to stay away from the two white hives. A spot was cleared to one side for the new hive. Two-by-fours were balanced on wooden legs. One side had longer legs so anything placed on the boards would be level in spite of the hill's slope.

She looked lovely in a green dress beneath her black

apron. Her beekeeper's hat was in her left hand. Her *kapp* was askew with one pin hanging out at an odd angle, and strands of her honey-gold hair fluttered around her face. Were her lips as sweet as honey? He'd often wondered when he couldn't get Hannah out of his mind and wanted her in his arms again, but kissing her three years ago when he had no intention of offering her marriage would have been all kinds of wrong.

The hushed hum of the bees' wings created an undertone for songs sung by robins somewhere nearby. He drew in a deep breath, almost disappointed when he didn't smell the rich greenness of a fresh-cut hayfield. The sounds were of spring, of days when the sunshine grew warm and *kinder* tossed aside their shoes to curl their toes in the soft, new grass. As he and Hannah had one day near the pond on his family's farm. They'd walked together and skipped stones across the still waters. That day, he'd nearly thrown aside his plans for the future and pulled her to him and kissed her.

"How are the bees doing?" he asked, pushing aside his thoughts.

"So far, they're doing well. It'll change when I bring the other hive up here. They'll be distressed because their hive is close to a strange one." She gave him a wry smile, and he was grateful she didn't sense the course of his thoughts. "You're either brave or foolish to come out here without checking first."

"I did check. Your great-grandmother was eager to tell me where you were." He arched a single brow as he thought of how excited *Grossmammi* Ella had been, believing he'd come to the house to court her great-granddaughter. He kept the conversation to himself as he did his yearning to hold Hannah close and explore her lips. *Stop thinking of that!* It was easier said than done, so he asked, "Where's Shelby?"

"She's napping. She didn't sleep well last night. She's fussy all day, but her teething pain seems worse at night. Maybe her face hurts more when she's lying down. I rubbed honey on her gums along with a teething gel your brother Amos recommended. The combination helped, and she was asleep before I put her in the crib."

He saw Hannah's exhaustion, but it didn't steal the delicate prettiness that had drawn his eyes to her from the first time he'd seen her. That sunny summer afternoon, he'd been hanging out and jesting with his twin brother…as usual. He and Micah had been having some sort of contest to see which one of them was faster or smarter or whatever…as usual. They'd been with friends who'd been talked into attending the youth gathering by someone's younger sister…as usual.

From the corner of his eye as Micah was making a joke, Daniel had seen a blonde girl in a dark blue dress leaping up to hit a volleyball over the net. She'd succeeded and was instantly surrounded by teammates who congratulated her on her *gut* play. One of the players must have noticed him and his friends approaching. The blonde girl had turned, and his gaze had locked with hers.

He knew nothing would be as usual again.

And it hadn't been. That evening was the first time he'd asked Hannah if he could drive her home. When she'd said *ja*, he'd wondered if he'd ever been so happy. They'd talked about everything and nothing, getting to know each other and feeling—at least in his case—as if he'd known her his whole life. She'd laughed at his humorous stories, and he'd been fascinated by her sparkling brown eyes. In fact, he'd been immersed in joy until the demanding voice of his determination to be his own boss sounded in his mind after he'd dropped Hannah off and continued home.

Today wasn't the first time—nor would it be the last, he was certain—when he wondered what might have happened if he'd ignored the strident voice and instead listened to his heart. He'd tried, asking her again and again to let him take her home, but the dream of owning a construction company refused to be silenced.

"Poor little tyke," Daniel said when he realized he'd become mired again in his thoughts of the past. "She must have most of her teeth, ain't so?"

"If I counted right, she's got five more to come in." She yawned, putting her hand up to her mouth. "Sorry. When Shelby doesn't sleep, nobody sleeps." Glancing at her hives shadowed by the barn farther up the hill, she sighed. "I know a lot about taking care of bees. I wish I knew as much about taking care of a toddler."

"You didn't plan to become a *mamm* now."

"No, but God has surprises for us." She gave him another crooked grin. "Some more than others."

"You're doing a great job, Hannah."

For a moment, he thought she might protest or demur, but instead she said, "*Danki.* I'm trying to make a home for the three of us."

"Don't you want more?" Maybe if she'd talk about her dreams, she could understand his and why he'd done what he had. Maybe then she'd forgive him…and he'd be able to forgive himself.

"I'm not sure I can handle more, Daniel." She ran her fingers along the mesh on the front of her mask. "Sometimes being surrounded by peace and quiet so

I can be in the moment is the most *wunderbaar* thing I can imagine."

"Do you mean like in Psalm 46? 'Be still, and know that I am God.'"

"*Ja*. I try to surrender up the problems of the day because God knows how to resolve them better than I do."

Her faith wasn't gentle as he'd once thought, but a fierce force propelling her through the challenges of her life. He wished he could be as willing to hand his problems to the Lord. He wanted to, but his impatience got in the way, and he believed he had to move his dreams forward himself. *Mamm* had hinted more than once he should let life unfold as it was meant to in God's plan instead of Daniel trying to make it happen as he wanted it to.

"So what can I do for you, Daniel?" Hannah asked.

"Can't I stop by to see how moving the bees is going?"

"Can you?"

He chuckled. "I guess not. I came to ask a favor. I promise you, if you agree, it won't cost you any more sleep."

"Not losing more sleep sounds lovely. What's the favor?"

"Until today, I don't remember the last time we had a rain-free day." He glanced at the clouds building over the western hills. "And it doesn't look as if it's going to change any time soon. I was wondering if I could put my horse in your barn on rainy days while I'm working on the bridge."

Her eyes widened, and he couldn't help wondering what she'd thought he intended to ask. Maybe it was better he didn't know.

"Of course," she replied. "There's no reason for the

poor creature to stand out in the rain. What about the rest of your crew's horses?"

"Two of the men working with us are *Englischers*, and one gives the Amish men on the crew a ride every morning in his truck. Taffy is the only horse at the bridge most of the time."

With a smile, she wagged a finger at him as if he were no older than Shelby. "Make sure you close the barn door. Since it's been raining every day, I've kept the chickens and our two cows in the barn, and I don't want them to wander away."

"I know better than to leave the door open. Just imagine how my big brother Ezra would react. He'd have my hide if I let his prize Brown Swiss cows out." He chuckled. "He watches over them as closely as you do Shelby."

When she laughed, he let the lyrical sound wash over him like a cleansing wave. It swept away the debris left after the decisions he'd made. The dubiousness as he second-guessed himself, the regrets at his mistakes and the invisible scars of hurtful words. Ones he'd spoken and ones spoken to him. Both had been unintentional, but the wound endured nonetheless. And then there was how he'd treated Hannah…

Suddenly he wanted to follow his own advice and leave the past in the past. The best way to do that was to be in the present and look to the future.

"How can I help with moving your bees?"

"I have to do this slowly. If you've got to get to the bridge—"

"We're waiting on an inspection from the county before we can continue. It won't be until tomorrow morning. I sent the other men home. We've got some long days ahead of us to meet our schedule, so they're glad to have a couple hours off this afternoon."

She frowned. "Don't you want to take the afternoon off, too?"

"I am. I'm not working on the bridge. I'm here to help you." He hesitated, then added, "If you can use my help."

His heart threatened to stop beating as he held his breath, waiting for her answer. She had every right to tell him to get lost. Again, he wished he could find the right words to apologize after three years and ask her forgiveness for being a *dummkopf* because he'd been afraid to be honest with her.

"*Danki*, Daniel," she said again. "I could use your help. Shelby won't nap long, I'm sure. I'd like to have this done before she wakes up."

While they walked to the bulkhead, he listened as she outlined what they needed to do. She'd carry a pair of supers to the platform she'd built and set them in place.

"I'll take them out through the bulkhead," she said, "so there's less chance of them escaping into the house."

"So what can I do?"

"Hold the bulkhead door open. I don't want it to fall when I'm coming up. It wouldn't be *gut* for the bees."

"Or for you either." He ran his finger along the thick slab. "This door is heavy. Having it fall on your head would be something you'd notice."

"Even with my hard head?"

He laughed. "I don't know about your head, but even *my* hard head would notice a door crashing on it."

When she giggled, sounding as young and carefree as her little sister, he wanted to capture the sound so he could enjoy it over and over. He'd squandered her musical joy years ago, not realizing how precious it was until her laugh vanished from his life.

He wanted to chastise himself again for being so *dumm*, but it was useless to keep rehashing the past. He couldn't change the man he'd been, the man so focused on his ambitions he couldn't see anything else. So, instead, he helped her remove the quilt and the plywood on top of the supers. Hurrying up the stairs as she donned her veiled hat and plugged the entrances to the supers with some twisted grass, he held on to the heavy door while she brought them into the yard.

She settled the last box filled with honeycomb, the one holding the queen, on top of the other supers. She unplugged the entrances so the bees could fly in and out. Removing her veiled hat again, she smiled. "Having a third hive will mean extra work, but it'll also mean more honey to sell."

"You enjoy working with bees, don't you?"

"I do, and it's partly because I like being my own boss." She sat on the steps by the kitchen door.

"I'd like to be my own boss, too." He sighed and glanced toward the covered bridge. "And if this job goes well, I may be. Finally!"

Hannah was startled by the wistfulness in Daniel's voice. She'd never heard him speak with such honest and deep feelings. While they were walking out together, he'd kept her laughing. She couldn't recall a time when he'd talked about anything important to him or asked her about what mattered to her.

She'd considered him fun to be around and was pleased he'd selected her to take home week after week.

Several times, she'd tried to discuss her concerns about how oddly her great-grandmother was acting, but he changed the subject. Only in retrospect had she noticed that. At the time, she'd thought he was trying to tease away her worry. When he'd started flirting with other girls, she'd wondered if she was too serious for someone who loved to laugh as much as he did.

Had she known the real Daniel when they were courting?

That was an unsettling thought. Had Daniel changed, or had she failed to see the real person behind the endless jests?

"I didn't know you wanted to be your own boss," she said when she realized he was waiting for her to respond.

"It's been my goal since I finished school. I'm surprised you're surprised, Hannah."

"Why shouldn't I be surprised? You never mentioned anything about this…before."

He gave her a wry grin. "When a young man is walking out with a young woman, his attention should be on her. Not his hopes for the future."

"That's maybe the dumbest thing you've ever said to me, Daniel Stoltzfus."

"Really?" His eyes widened in astonishment. "The dumbest?"

She laughed in spite of herself. "If not the dumbest, then close. Why would you think I wouldn't have wanted to know about your hopes and dreams? They're part of you. Isn't that what walking out together is for? To get to know someone well enough to decide if you want to spend the rest of your life with him or her?"

"I thought it was a chance to get a girl alone and maybe steal a kiss."

"You're a rogue!"

"I *was* a rogue. I'm not that guy any longer."

She wasn't sure how to answer. Now wasn't the time to speak of the many rumors she'd heard of his numerous girlfriends who, like her, had believed he was serious and then, after being dropped by him, had married someone else. Not everything shared through the Amish grapevine was true.

"You don't believe me," he said with a grimace. He walked to the bulkhead and lowered the door.

"I didn't say that!"

"You didn't say anything." He sat beside her on the steps. "Sometimes silence speaks louder than words."

"And actions speak louder than words, too." She wished she hadn't spoken the words as soon as they left her lips.

Beside her, Daniel's face blanched beneath his deep tan. If she'd meant to wound him, she'd succeeded. That hadn't been her aim. Or had it been? Had she intended to hurt him as he'd hurt her years ago? She wanted to take back the words, but wasn't sure how.

Daniel stood and walked away without saying anything else. She got up, too, but didn't follow. What could she say? That what she said wasn't true? It was.

You could apologize, her conscience whispered in her mind.

She took a single step to go after him and ask his forgiveness, but paused when the back door opened.

Grossmammi Ella looked out and called, "Saloma, I can hear your Hannah crying upstairs. She needs her *mamm* with her."

Hannah was tempted to weep right there as her great-grandmother's words warned the old woman was lost in time again. She couldn't leave *Grossmammi* Ella alone with Shelby. Maybe if Hannah ran upstairs, got her little sister and went after Daniel, she could...

The sound of buggy wheels rolling away into the distance warned her it was too late. She sighed, hoping she'd have a chance to say she was sorry. She didn't want their friendship to end again before it'd barely begun.

Chapter Ten

Daniel listened to the rain tapping against the roof of the covered bridge. Was the rain ever going to stop? During the past week, except on the day Hannah had moved her bees, it'd stormed for four days, and it'd been overcast and drizzled the rest. The wind remained as chilly as it'd been a month ago, and the creek beneath the bridge was rising and running faster each day. He'd heard his crew say, half-joking, that they needed to start building an ark.

He was tired of having to rework his schedule around tasks they could accomplish while rain fell. If it sprinkled, he took a chance on running the power tools off the portable generator he'd set on the side of the bridge farther away from the Lambright house. It wasn't the best location, but the bridge, even stripped of the boards on its deck and side walls, muted the generator's noise. He didn't want the racket to intrude on either Shelby's or *Grossmammi* Ella's afternoon rest.

That none of his crew had mentioned the inconvenience of the generator's position warned him that they'd guessed why he'd made the decision. He wasn't going to ask why they weren't curious. He was just grateful they hadn't questioned him.

He drove the nail into the thick beam which would support the new deck. Working kept him from thinking too much about Hannah and the harsh words she'd thrown at him four days ago. That what she said was true had added to their sting. His actions *had* spoken louder than his words three years ago, because he hadn't said a single word.

"There she goes again! I wonder why she's always in such a hurry when she heads out at this time of day." Phil Botti leaned back to give himself a better view of the road leading out to the old mill which had given the bridge its name. The young man, the son of Jake Botti, the man who'd asked Daniel to supervise the project, was a hard worker, but distracted by every vehicle passing by.

"Who?" Daniel asked as he calculated the proper angle for the next board he should cut to support the bridge's right arch. Each one must be the exact length so each portion of the arch could handle its proper share of the weight of the bridge deck as well as the walls and roof.

"Hannah Lambright."

His head snapped up. What was Hannah doing out on the inclement day? The cold would bother her great-grandmother.

Hearing muffled chuckles, Daniel ignored his crew. Since they'd begun work on the bridge, the Amish men and the *Englischers* had made several comments loud enough so he couldn't miss them. Comments about the amount of time he'd spent at the Lambrights' house and how he had a lighter step when Hannah brought the toddler and her great-grandmother to visit the men working on the bridge. Many of the comments were appreciative of the *kaffi* she shared along with cookies or biscuits dripping with honey from her hives, but he couldn't look past the glances his crew shared while their heads bent toward each other.

There was no need for whispers. He knew what they were talking about. They thought he was courting Hannah. If they had any idea how far it was from the truth, maybe they'd stop. But he wouldn't discuss Hannah with anyone, not even his brothers, though Jeremiah had given him an opening several times since their conversation in Daniel's almost finished house.

Hannah's buggy disappeared along the road at her horse's fastest pace. She was headed upstream along the creek and the dead end near the ruins of the mill that hadn't been in use since before he was born. Maybe since before his *daed* had been born.

Why was Hannah going there? The asphalt road changed to gravel and then to dirt less than a half mile beyond the Jones farm. The dirt must have turned into mire after so much rain. She could get stuck out there.

He'd seen her rush away in her buggy at least four times in the last two weeks. It was, he realized, always about three in the afternoon. Right around the time when Hannah's great-grandmother finished her nap and came out of her bedroom. Each time when Hannah had sped away, the buggy had returned to the house less than fifteen minutes later.

His brows dropped into a frown as he stood. "I'll be right back."

He ran after the buggy. It would take too long to hitch his horse, and he wanted answers.

Now.

* * *

She should be used to this nonsense, Hannah told herself, but she couldn't become accustomed to discovering her great-grandmother had wandered away from the house again without saying where she was going. Not that there was any need. *Grossmammi* Ella went only two places on her own. Either to the barn where she called for cows that hadn't been there in a decade, or she headed toward the old mill. Hannah had no idea why her great-grandmother went there, and the elderly woman couldn't explain.

Grossmammi Ella always acted baffled when they returned to the house, and Hannah wasn't sure if her great-grandmother knew why she was outside. Each time she became lost in her memories seemed to go on longer. Would her great-grandmother eventually have an episode when she never returned to the present? Hannah didn't know what she'd do then. Would she have to pretend to be her *mamm* for the rest of her life?

Beside her on the buggy seat, Shelby played with Buzz-buzz. Oh, how Hannah wished she could be like her little sister, caught up in the joys of being a *kind*! Sudden tears rushed into her eyes as she realized, if *Grossmammi* Ella's past continued to overwhelm her, Shelby might never know their real great-grandmother. That was so sad because unless *Daed* returned, the little girl wouldn't have memories of him either.

Was it worse to have someone in your life and lose them, or never to have a single memory of them? Though she tried to halt her thoughts, Daniel appeared in her mind. If she had the choice, would she prefer to have had a crush on him and lost him or to have never known him at all?

She was being preposterous. He'd walked away from her *again* just a few days ago. Exactly as she'd expected, but it didn't make the pain of him leaving any easier.

Hannah saw her great-grandmother standing under a tree and looking along the creek that was higher than it'd been the last time they'd come along the road. What was *Grossmammi* Ella staring at? Nothing was out there but the tumbledown walls of the old mill and the dam built to collect water to make the wheel turn.

Pulling gently on Thunder's reins, Hannah waited for the black horse to halt. Like Hannah, the horse was growing accustomed to these wild drives.

She jumped out, leaving the door open so she could keep an eye on Shelby, and walked through the rain to where the elderly woman stood. "*Grossmammi* Ella?"

Hannah repeated her great-grandmother's name several times before *Grossmammi* Ella turned to face her. As her eyes focused, bafflement filled them.

"I think you've walked far enough today." Hannah didn't let her smile slide away. "Let's go home. I'll make tea, and I've got your favorite cookies."

Her great-grandmother didn't answer. She kept staring at Hannah as if she didn't recognize her.

"*Grossmammi* Ella," she pleaded, "we need to get out of the rain. You'll catch a cold. You don't want to get a cold, do you?"

The old woman remained silent.

Hannah wasn't sure what to do. Touching her great-grandmother when she was lost in the past could bring on her uncontrollable temper. That was how Hannah got struck the day before yesterday. Her ear still hurt from the blow.

But they couldn't stand out in the rain, getting

drenched. Shelby must be getting chilled, too. They needed to go home.

Calling the old woman's name again was futile. *Grossmammi* Ella didn't respond or move.

"Da-dan!" cried Shelby with excitement.

When Hannah saw Daniel coming around the buggy, she was torn between being relieved he'd chased after her and dismay that he was witnessing how out-of-control her life had become. She wasn't making any progress persuading her great-grandmother to get in the buggy now that it had stopped raining. Maybe he could. She couldn't allow her frustration to prevent her from accepting help.

Greeting Shelby with a laugh and tickling the little girl who adored him, he turned to Hannah and *Grossmammi* Ella. "You're going to get stuck if you let the buggy sit there much longer. The wheels are already sinking into the mud."

"I know." Exasperation sharpened Hannah's voice, and she took a steadying breath to calm herself. Her great-grandmother became unreasonable if Hannah showed aggravation. "We're leaving."

Grossmammi Ella startled her by saying, "I'm not going." Her great-grandmother crossed her arms over her chest and glared at her and Daniel.

Stepping past Hannah, he went to the elderly woman. He was smiling as if none of them had a care in the world. "*Grossmammi* Ella," he said in his charming voice that seemed to work with women of every age, "you know it's time for Hannah to start getting supper ready. What will we do if we don't have anything to eat after a hard day's work?"

"We? You're coming to supper at our house?" The

old woman turned to scowl at Hannah. "Why didn't you tell me you'd invited him?"

"I…" She refused to lie to her great-grandmother, but saying *Grossmammi* Ella was confused would make the situation worse.

"Oh, I shouldn't have said anything," Daniel said with his easy grin. "I guess Hannah wanted it to be a surprise."

"For all of us."

"Let me help you into the buggy, *Grossmammi* Ella." Before turning to her great-grandmother, Daniel whispered, "I'm sorry, Hannah."

Shocked at the words she'd come to doubt that she'd ever hear from him, she watched as he assisted the elderly woman to step into the buggy. He made sure she had a blanket over her knees before he closed the door.

When he faced her, Hannah made sure her astonishment was well hidden.

"*Danki* for convincing her to get into the buggy."

"I wasn't sure I could when she knew who I was. It helps when she believes I'm her late husband." He grimaced. "That sounds pretty lousy, but you know what I mean."

"I do."

"Does she always know who you are?"

Instead of answering, because she didn't want to raise his suspicions further given that her great-grandmother was barely holding on to her mind, she said, "Like you said, we need to move the buggy before it settles farther into the mud."

"Avoiding my questions isn't going to change anything, Hannah."

"Can't we discuss this some other time? I want to get

my great-grandmother and my little sister home before it starts raining again."

"All right." His reluctance laced through the two words. As he walked with her around the buggy to the driver's side, he glanced over at the old stone mill which had lost its roof in a long-forgotten storm. "What does *Grossmammi* Ella find so interesting about the mill?"

"I don't have any idea, and she won't tell me." She shuddered. "I wish I knew, because maybe I could convince her not to come out here. It's dangerous with the slippery banks around the mill pond. The old dam should have washed out long ago."

He nodded as he opened the buggy door. "When I was over at Jake Botti's office, he talked about other projects that need to be done in the county. The dam is high on the list of priority repairs, but I don't know when the county supervisors plan to get to it. Look how bad the bridge had to get before they decided to fix it." He motioned for her to climb in. "I wasn't joking. You'd better get the buggy moving before it's stuck here until the road dries out."

Hannah didn't hesitate. Getting in, she left the door open as she slapped the reins on Thunder's back and gave him the order to start. He pulled, but the buggy didn't move. Straining again, he tried to walk forward. She halted him, not wanting the horse to hurt himself. She frowned when she felt the wheels drop more deeply into the thick mud.

"You're definitely stuck." Daniel put one foot on the buggy's step. "I hate to ask this, but you need to get out."

He was right. She was so frustrated she wanted to cry. Now she had to persuade *Grossmammi* Ella to get out.

Again Daniel succeeded where she couldn't. Hannah

held Shelby close as he talked the old woman into stepping down. When she stood beside Hannah, he went to Thunder. He gripped the reins and spoke to the horse.

Thunder shook his mane as if agreeing with whatever Daniel said, then stepped forward. One step. A second one. The mud released the buggy's wheels with a sucking sound. Once the wheels emerged from the mud, Thunder moved quickly a few more paces. It was as if the black horse knew how important it was not to let the buggy wheels get bogged again.

"Let's go!" Daniel waved for them to get into the buggy before it sank into the mire again.

Hannah got in and held Shelby on her lap as he assisted her great-grandmother. *Grossmammi* Ella stared at Thunder as if the horse was the most fascinating thing she'd ever seen. Daniel grabbed the reins and gave the horse the command to go.

The drive to the house would have been silent except for Shelby's "talking." She kept patting Daniel's arm, and Hannah realized the little girl had missed him.

As Hannah had.

What's wrong with me? He acts outrageously, so I should be glad he's not at the house every day. But her days had seemed emptier and longer and flavorless since he'd stormed off after helping her move the bees.

At the house, Hannah helped her great-grandmother inside while Daniel unhitched the horse and put him in the barn. *Grossmammi* Ella sat in her favorite chair as if nothing had happened. Shelby toddled to the box of toys in a corner of the kitchen. Sitting on the floor, she took Buzz-buzz out and hugged the stuffed bee.

Everything was as it should be, but Hannah's nerves were on edge. She wrapped her arms around herself when she heard the back door open and Daniel enter. Going into the kitchen, she thanked him for helping with her great-grandmother.

"I'm here every workday, Hannah." He was as serious and appeared as uncomfortable as she did. "My buggy is here, and, if you let me know when she's gone roaming again, I can go and bring her back faster than you can get Shelby and give chase."

"I can't ask you to do that. You've got your job to do."

"The foreman has the right to a *kaffi* break each day."

"It's supposed to be your time to relax so you can finish the rest of the day's work. It's not your time to be running off after my great-grandmother."

He folded his arms over his chest, drawing her gaze to its breadth. She looked away because she didn't want to be distracted by that enticing sight. It brought reminders of her cheek resting against the spot where his chest and shoulder met.

"You make it sound," he said in a taut voice, "as if you sit around doing nothing. I know as the weather gets warmer, you'll be busier with your bees as well as other chores. I may not have time to go after your great-grandmother, but neither do you."

"But she's *my* responsibility."

"If you don't want my help…" His words trailed away.

She knew what she should say. *Of course, I'd appreciate your help.* That was what plain folk did for each other. They lent a helping hand so nobody's burden was too great. The silence stretched between them, becoming almost painful, as she sought the right words to say.

Again she didn't have a chance because he reached

for the knob on the door. "I thought we could be friends."

"I thought so, too." Why were words failing her? Maybe because she couldn't say what she wanted to. She shouldn't speak of how, after breaking her heart, he'd started to help it heal. That would reveal too much. He'd think she was crazy when he'd made it clear—over and over—his dreams of the future didn't include her. "Maybe it's impossible for us to be friends, Daniel."

His brows rose, and she knew her blunt words had shocked him. But to tiptoe around the truth would only hurt them again. She couldn't risk that.

Twisting the knob, he yanked the door open. "Well, if you need me, Hannah, you know where I am."

Then he was gone again, and she was left there by herself...again.

Chapter Eleven

From where he stood by the covered bridge, Daniel recognized the small red car heading away from Hannah's house. It belonged to Todd Howland, the speech therapist who came twice a week to work with Shelby. Unlike with physical therapy and occupational therapy, there weren't exercises Daniel could help with, so there was no need for him to go to the house.

Even if he was sure Hannah wouldn't slam the door in his face.

Why had he made such a muddle of everything with her? She'd agreed to be his friend, and he should be glad she had. Instead, he seemed to be doing everything he could to irritate her.

Why?

It didn't make sense, especially when he'd been enjoying time with her and Shelby. So why had he said things he knew would upset her?

He pulled his gaze from the car as it turned a corner and disappeared from sight. All last night, rain had poured through the openings in the bridge roof that had been made wider by the storm's strong winds. Tomorrow morning, sheets of plywood were being delivered from the lumberyard. He'd hoped they could get the boards to him today, but it'd been impossible. Once the wood arrived, he and his crew would get up on the rotting roof and tack on the sheets to stop the leaks until they had time to replace the shingles. It was beyond the scope of the job he'd been hired to do, but he hoped the project still could be done on time. That was important, so he could use Jake Botti as a reference for a couple of other jobs he wanted to bid on.

Before he could think of fixing the whole roof, however, more of the bridge's deck must be finished. There wasn't any place to put a ladder now with the whole deck removed.

Crossing his arms, he sighed. Nothing had gone as he'd planned. The weather refused to cooperate, and it seemed for every day they managed to work, two were lost to rain. As soon as the first half dozen boards were back in place on the deck, the saw used to cut the planks could be set up out of the rain.

No rain tomorrow, Lord. He almost laughed at his prayer. No doubt the farmers in the county were praying the rain returned to water the seeds they sowed today.

Or were they able to get out in their wet fields to work? He looked at the swollen creek. Like others near Paradise Springs, it was running too fast, too high, and was the color of *kaffi* with too much milk.

He wasn't going to get any more work done today. He might as well spend the time finishing the baseboard molding at his house. He was astonished to realize he hadn't gone to the house in over a week. Longer, because the last time he'd spent time there was before he'd helped Hannah move her bees. He needed to get back to it because his twin brother had mentioned a youth gathering tonight, and how he planned to ask a special girl if he could take her home.

A prickle of envy spurred Daniel off the bridge. His brother's relationship with Katie Kay, nebulous as it might be, was simpler than his with Hannah. After three years of convincing himself he'd done the right thing by not getting serious with her, he was the one having trouble being just friends. His thoughts kept urging him to draw her into his arms.

"Your dream is to have your own company," he chided himself as he walked to the Lambrights' barn where he stabled Taffy every day.

Stuffing his hands in his coat pockets, he felt the crackle of the piece of paper he'd shoved in there before he left home. *Mamm* had given him a message for Hannah and her great-grandmother. She'd written it down because she'd said she didn't want him to forget the details while his mind was on boards and nails for the covered bridge. That was what she'd said, but her laughter-filled eyes suggested she thought he'd lose every thought in his head the moment he spoke to Hannah.

If Hannah was surprised to see him at her front door, she gave no sign. Daniel couldn't guess if she was pleased or annoyed he'd come to the house. She wiped her hands on a dish towel as she stepped aside to let him in. Past her, he saw her little sister and her great-grandmother looking at a cloth book together in the kitchen.

For the first time, Shelby hadn't come running to him. That startled him and made him sad. It was for the best, he told himself, that Shelby was feeling comfortable with her family. Still, he missed her enthusiastic greetings and her contralto laughter.

The aroma of chocolate swept over him, and he wondered if Hannah was baking that special chocolate chip cake she'd brought to youth events while they'd walked out together. The rich cake with its peanut butter icing had been a favorite with the young people, and Hannah had made sure she saved an extra piece for him to enjoy on the way home. She'd made a whole chocolate chip cake for him for his twenty-second birthday that year.

The week before he turned his back on her.

Shame rushed through him, but how could he ask for her forgiveness when he'd told everyone—including himself—over and over that the past was in the past and they needed to focus on the future?

Pride, warned his conscience. He was being prideful.

"I came by," he said, ignoring his conscience, "because *Mamm* asked me to invite you and *Grossmammi* Ella to a quilting frolic the day after tomorrow at our place. She says she remembers your great-grandmother used to be one of the finest quilters in the county."

"Tell her *danki*, but I doubt we'll be able to go." She kept wiping her hands on the towel, and he knew she was nervous and wanted the conversation over.

He frowned. "You don't have to turn down the invitation because of how you feel about me. *Mamm* is asking you."

"I realize that."

"So go if you want to."

"Go where?" asked *Grossmammi* Ella as she came into the living room. Her eyes lit up.

Did she see him today as Daniel Stoltzfus or as her late husband?

He got his answer when the elderly woman went

on, "Daniel, have you come to ask our Hannah to walk out with you?"

"No, *Grossmammi* Ella. *Mamm* wanted me to stop by with an invitation for you and Hannah to come to a quilt frolic at our house the day after tomorrow."

"A quilt frolic?"

For a moment, Daniel thought the old woman wasn't sure what he meant, that she'd forgotten how, when the Amish gathered to work together, they called it a frolic. He sought the right words to explain without insulting her.

Before he could, *Grossmammi* Ella turned to Hannah. "Do you know where my sewing box is?"

"*Ja,*" she answered. "Do you want me to get it?"

"Not now, but I'll need it for the frolic. And my reading glasses? Do you know where they are?"

Hannah looked as stunned as if someone had announced Amish women were expected to drive bright red Ferraris. She gulped before replying, "*Ja.* I know where they are. On the table by your bed, but we aren't going—"

"Of course, we're going." *Grossmammi* Ella's brows lowered. "I thought I'd taught you better, Hannah! When a neighbor announces a frolic, it's our chance to offer assistance to them. And we'll learn the latest news in the district."

"It's not today," Hannah said when her great-grandmother paused to take a breath. "That's what I was going to say."

"Well, you should have said it then." The old woman walked from the living room, her head held high.

Daniel put his hand over his mouth to hide his smile.

He was glad he did because *Grossmammi* Ella paused and turned to him.

"What are you waiting for?" the old woman asked.

"Me?" He glanced at Hannah and saw she was as puzzled as he was.

"*Ja.* You! Are all young men as dense as you are? They weren't when I was a girl. They could see it's a nice day, just right for taking a young woman for a walk. So why aren't you asking our Hannah to go for a walk? She's a kind young woman who takes *gut* care of her old great-grandmother. What more could you ask for than our Hannah's company on this pretty day the *gut* Lord has made, Daniel Stoltzfus?"

He wasn't sure which question to answer first, except he knew it wouldn't be the last one. Without looking at Hannah, he knew her cheeks had become the adorable pink painted by her strongest emotions.

"Hannah is busy with her bees." It was a lame answer, but it was the best he could manage.

Grossmammi Ella wrinkled her nose. "The bees can take care of themselves for an hour, and so can I. You should take our Hannah out in the sunshine and enjoy the day. So what are you waiting for?"

Hannah wished she could blame *Grossmammi* Ella's questions on dementia, but it was clear the elderly woman knew where and when she was and what she was asking. Poor Daniel! He hadn't anticipated any matchmaking when he came to deliver his *mamm*'s invitation. Hannah was still irritated with him, but she had to pity him when he confronted her great-grandmother.

"*Grossmammi* Ella," she said, "I can't go for a walk. I need to watch Shelby."

A frustrated yelp came from the kitchen. Whirling, Hannah stared at little Shelby trying to get her hair unstuck from her fingers. Strands clung to her cheeks. The front of her pinafore was covered with globs of honey.

"Like you've been doing now?" Her great-grandmother sniffed. "Take the *boppli* with you. She could use some sunshine, too. I don't know what's going on with youngsters nowadays. In my day, we enjoyed a spring stroll."

The old woman walked away, going into her bedroom and shutting the door so neither Hannah nor Daniel had a chance to reply.

Hannah looked at Daniel's shocked expression and burst into laughter. She clamped her hands over her mouth to keep her great-grandmother from hearing, but her shoulders shook with mirth. Soon Daniel was trying to restrain himself, too.

Deciding the best way to stop laughing was to do something, Hannah went to where Shelby sat. The little girl had pulled herself up onto the chair before digging into the bottle of honey, spreading it everywhere.

Daniel stepped past her and picked up the *kind*. He held her out straight-armed, so her sticky clothes and fingers couldn't reach him. "Time for a bath, my girl."

Hannah hurried ahead of them into the bathroom and began to run water into the tub. As she got a washcloth and soap, Daniel undressed her little sister. He asked where Hannah wanted the honey-coated clothes, and she pointed to a bucket near the door.

"My mop bucket will do," she said.

Lifting Shelby high in the air, Daniel set her in the water and began washing the sticky streaks off her hands and arms. Hannah sat on her heels and watched.

So much had changed since the first time she and Daniel had put the *kind* in the tub. Shelby didn't cringe away when Hannah touched her. Maybe it was because Hannah felt confident around the little girl. She no longer feared she would do something wrong and hurt the toddler.

However, one thing—one important thing—hadn't changed. Shelby adored Daniel. She babbled her version of his name as he shampooed her hair. Slapping her hands in the water, she giggled when Daniel pretended to be horrified to get wet.

Her lingering anger faded as Hannah watched them. She couldn't act as if Daniel was a horrible person who thought only of himself. For too long, she'd focused on a single selfish act and refused to think about the *gut* things he'd done. She'd been as self-centered as she'd accused him of being.

But if she didn't have her anger as a bulwark against him, how could she protect her heart from being hurt again? There must be a way. *Dearest Lord, help me discover it, so I no longer harbor this animosity within me. I don't want to tote around this burden any longer.*

Hannah toweled off the clean *kind* and then redressed her. Brushing out Shelby's soft, golden hair, she braided it.

"Ready?" asked Daniel as she folded the damp towel over the side of the tub.

"For what?"

"Our walk."

Again, heat soared up her face. "You don't have to go for a walk with me because *Grossmammi* Ella told you to."

"She didn't tell me to. She asked me why I wasn't

asking you to go. I'm asking you *and* Shelby if you'd like to go for a walk. We may find some early flowers along the road."

"We will."

"You sound sure."

"No, I sound like a beekeeper. I've seen my bees working hard for the past couple of days."

He winked at Shelby before asking, "Shall we follow the *beezzzz*?" He stretched out the sound until the little girl giggled and made the buzzing sound that made them all laugh.

"How can I say no to both of you?" Hannah asked.

"That was the idea." This time, his wink was for her.

Something quivered deep in her heart, and, for the first time in too long, she didn't try to silence a pulse of honest joy. She did want to call Daniel her friend. No, she wanted far more than friendship with him, but she wasn't going to make the same mistake of letting her heart overrule her head.

She continued to savor her happiness as she pulled on her coat and bonnet while Daniel helped her little sister into her coat. Shelby kept her fingers in her mouth, a sign that her gums hurt. Hannah dabbed honey and teething gel on them. Shelby's last new tooth couldn't come in soon enough.

When the three of them stepped out into the backyard, the hives were alive with the sound of bees. Shelby began copying the sound and giggling.

"It's astonishing how much noise those little wings can make," Daniel said. "I can hear it in my bones as well as my ears."

"There are a lot of little wings," Hannah replied with

a smile. "One hive can hold as many as fifty thousand bees."

He whistled a long, steady note before saying, "I had no idea that many lived in a single hive. But they've got the right idea. Let's not waste this sunny day. We haven't had many lately."

Hannah held Shelby's right hand as they walked down the sloping yard. The little girl reached for Daniel, but her arms were too short. When they got to the road, he picked her up. Setting her on his shoulders, he clasped her hands and bounced along the road like a runaway pony. Shelby squealed with delight.

Following at a more sedate pace, Hannah watched how careful Daniel was with the little girl. He didn't jostle her too hard, but kept her laughing. Someday, when he decided to settle down, he would be a *gut* father.

Halfway between her home and her neighbor's, where a small thicket of blackberry bushes and saplings grew, she paused and bent to look at clumps of snowdrops perched atop their green stems. The blossoms drooped toward the ground, making the ground beneath the bushes look as if there had been a fresh fall of snow. She called to Daniel to bring Shelby to look at them.

The little girl was delighted. Hannah convinced her to pick only a couple, telling her the bees would want the rest.

"I'm not sure how much she understands," Hannah said, glancing at Daniel who was squatting beside the *kind*.

Shelby looked at her and made the buzzing sound. When Hannah smiled, the little girl grinned, showing off her newest tooth.

"I'd say she knows what you're saying." Daniel stood and brushed his hands against this trousers. "Do you think there was a house here at one time and someone planted these flowers?"

"Maybe. Or the seeds were scattered here by birds."

"Look here." He reached deeper into the bushes. "Bloodroot." He pulled up one, and the sap burst out onto his fingers, turning them red. "My brothers and I used to use these to paint the trees. It takes a lot of them to write Daniel Paul Stoltzfus on bark."

"They're too pretty to yank from the ground. Look at the yellow in the center."

When he walked into the thicket, where the shadows draped the ground in cool dampness, Hannah took her little sister's hand and went, too. They had to stop every few steps as they climbed the slope so Shelby could collect another blossom. Hannah doubted there would be much left of the flowers by the time they returned to the house because the toddler clutched the stems tightly, and her bouquet already sagged over her tiny fingers.

The sound of trickling water reached Hannah's ears before she saw a spring half-hidden by thick moss. Daniel paused and then dropped to sit by the narrow stream of water drifting beneath the bare roots of the nearby trees.

Drawing Shelby onto his lap, he handed her a leaf that had fallen last autumn. He laughed when the little girl tossed it toward the water. She missed, so he stretched to retrieve it. On her second try, it landed in the small stream. She clapped her hands in glee as the leaf twirled and spun on the current before disappearing beyond the roots.

Hannah smiled when Daniel stood, and she took

Shelby's hand again. They walked out of the shadows into the sunshine. When Shelby held up her arms and teased, he put the little girl on his shoulders again.

"You're going to spoil her," Hannah said with a laugh.

"I hope so." He winked before galloping across the open field.

Again she watched the two of them and couldn't help smiling. She was glad she hadn't accepted Daniel's offer to take Shelby to live at his house, but she was happy he'd helped during the rough times until her little sister began to trust her.

When Daniel bent, he set Shelby on her feet. He plucked a long piece of grass. "Listen to this." He blew on it. Hard.

An awkward sounding squeak emerged.

Shelby clapped her hands before holding them out. He squatted beside her again and helped her put her fingers around the piece of grass. Holding it close to her mouth, he urged her to blow on it. The little girl did, and the faintest sound emerged.

Hannah cheered before picking another piece of grass. When she held it to her lips, a lovely note rippled through the air.

Daniel stared at her wide-eyed, then applauded. Shelby did, too.

Bowing, Hannah tossed the grass aside and hugged Shelby as her little sister ran to throw her arms around Hannah's legs. She didn't look in Daniel's direction, not wanting him to see how much she wished she could embrace him, too.

"Hey! Look!" He pointed toward the sky that was littered with thickening clouds. "There's a bald eagle."

Hannah held her breath as she watched the magnificent bird soar overhead. Its motions looked effortless while it drifted, letting the winds high above them carry it.

"It's beautiful," she whispered.

"I'm glad whenever I see an eagle." He walked over to stand by her and Shelby. "We almost lost them."

"But people wised up in time to bring them back from extinction."

"Too bad being smart doesn't happen more often. We don't realize our mistakes until we look back at our lives and know we should have chosen better."

When his gaze caught hers, she couldn't look away from the powerful emotions within it. He wasn't talking about birds. He was talking about him and her.

She searched his face, her gaze lingering on the cleft in his chin he despised and she thought made his face interesting. Again the longing to step into his embrace and let his arms close around her was so strong she had to fight herself.

She didn't want to talk about the past. It was dangerous territory. As the future was. That was why she preferred to think about the here and now. Except as his blue eyes regarded her, the moment itself held the potential for disaster.

Picking up Shelby, she set the *kind* on her hip. "*Grossmammi* Ella will get worried if we stay out past the time she gets up. We need to go."

"Hannah—"

She didn't let him finish. She left with Shelby. She was being a coward, turning away from the problem instead of facing it. But she knew where courage would lead.

To her heart being broken all over again.

Chapter Twelve

Hannah was amazed two days later when *Grossmammi* Ella asked her when they'd be leaving for the Stoltzfus farm.

"As soon as breakfast is done," Hannah replied, hoping her shock wasn't visible. For the past six months, she'd had to insist every church Sunday that her great-grandmother leave the house and attend services. A few times, *Grossmammi* Ella had been so stubborn neither she nor Hannah had been able to go.

But the elderly woman acted as excited as Shelby did when she had a cookie. *Grossmammi* Ella talked about the many quilting frolics she'd attended and spoke of people Hannah had never met. Hoping her great-grandmother continued to focus on the present, Hannah packed their sewing boxes in the buggy and made sure Shelby had Buzz-buzz with her.

As they drove onto the creek road, Hannah heard shouts and the whir of power tools from the covered bridge. Knowing she should pay no attention to the men working on it, she couldn't keep from looking in that direction. Men were cutting boards and nailing them in place to create a new deck. She picked out Daniel as if a flashlight focused on him. Her breath caught when he began to climb a ladder, balancing a large sheet of plywood on his back.

Don't fall. Don't fall. Don't fall. The words resonated through her mind as she drew in the reins to watch while he climbed through a hole in the bridge's roof and set the plywood down.

She released her breath and urged Thunder to continue along the road. She should be grateful that Daniel would be occupied at the bridge so she didn't have to see him at his family's farm. Since their walk through the woods and meadow, she hadn't been able to get his easy grin and warm gaze out of her mind. He'd slipped into her dreams again.

Her hands tightened on the reins until the leather cut into her palms. She was close to making the same mistake. Friendship! That was all they could share, and she must not pray for more.

Hannah was relieved when traffic demanded her attention as she reached the center of Paradise Springs. It kept her from thinking of anything else. They had to wait several minutes to cross Route 30 because cars and tractor-trailers rushed by at a speed far over the posted speed limit in the village.

"Is that where Daniel works?" asked *Grossmammi* Ella when they passed a low building with the sign Stoltzfus Family Shops in the parking lot.

"I don't know."

Her great-grandmother gave her a baffled glance, and Hannah kept her gaze on the road and the cars passing them. Why didn't she know more about the man who'd infiltrated her dreams? Did he work there with his brothers? She'd never gone to any of the shops except the grocery store.

Hannah was relieved when they reached the Stoltzfus farmhouse. It was set off a long lane. A half dozen buggies were parked under the trees that would give the house cooling shade in the summer. The house, like the barns, was painted white. In a nearby field, a team of five mules pulled a plow. *Englisch* farmers had to wait for the ground to dry out so their tractors didn't get mired in the fields, but plain farmers who used horses and mules were already at work getting ready for planting.

Wanda Stoltzfus met them at the kitchen door and ushered them in as if they were special guests. She introduced them to her current daughters-in-law and her future one. Finding *Grossmammi* Ella a seat at the middle of the quilting frame where she'd be able to hear what everyone said as they worked, she urged Hannah to sit beside her great-grandmother. Shelby was bundled away to play with the other *kinder* who were too young for school and were being overseen by Daniel's younger sister Esther who showed the earliest signs of being pregnant.

Hannah didn't mention it, but others weren't so circumspect. The young woman, who'd been the district's schoolteacher until her marriage, was congratulated and teased by the other women. Everyone had an opinion on whether the *boppli* would be a boy or a girl. Esther smiled as she went into the other room to entertain the *kinder*.

The day passed quickly as Hannah worked with eight other women on the large Sunshine and Shadow quilt stretched between them on the quilt frame. She tried to match her great-grandmother's tiny stitches. The small squares in light and dark shades of blue, purple and green created a large diamond in the middle of the quilt. The border, which was more than a foot wide, was dark green and edged with a narrow strip of navy blue fabric.

As she listened to the conversations around her, she wondered again why she'd let *Grossmammi* Ella's condition keep them from spending time with their neighbors. Her great-grandmother seemed more alive than she had in months as news from the district was shared. Hannah heard the names of several friends from her school years. Shelby joined them when the quilters took a break for a lunch of salads and sandwiches and pies of every description made by their hostess and her family. Hannah hoped it wouldn't be long before the Lambright family could become a vital part of the community again.

Weaving his way through the crowd of women getting ready to go home and make the evening meal for their families, Daniel saw Hannah moving toward the kitchen door. He didn't want her to leave yet. He'd cleaned up in the barn, keeping an eye on the house to make sure she didn't go before he'd washed off the sweat of working on the bridge.

"Hannah?"

She glanced over her shoulder and smiled. "Hi, Daniel!"

His heart thudded like a nail gun. He hadn't been sure if she'd talk to him after she'd taken off like a shingle in a high wind the other day. Aware of the women around him, including those from his family, he made sure no tremor tainted his voice as he asked, "Would you like to come and see the project I've been working on for the past year?"

"Where is it?"

"A short walk from here. Get Shelby, and we'll head over. It shouldn't take more than a few minutes." He didn't add he hoped she'd stay longer.

Conflicting emotions flitted through her eyes, and he wasn't sure what she'd decide until she nodded. "Let me get Shelby and her coat. I'll tell *Grossmammi* Ella we'll be right back."

He watched as she did and kissed her great-grandmother on the cheek. *Grossmammi* Ella was so enthralled in telling a story, she didn't seem to notice. Buttoning her coat as well as the *kind*'s, Hannah walked out the door with him.

"You don't need a coat," Daniel said. "It's warmer today than I expected."

"That's what we get when the sky isn't filled with rain clouds." Hannah settled Shelby in her arms, then relinquished her when the toddler held out her arms to Daniel.

He led the way toward the barn. "Watch where you step. Ezra's been trying out some goats to see if they'll eat the weeds along the fence. They've been wandering free."

"The weeds?"

Laughing, he said, "I'm not going to dignify that with an answer. I'm going to enjoy the nice weather."

"The nice weather is frustrating my bees. The weather is warm, but, except for the earliest flowers, most buds haven't burst yet. The bees visit bushes and hedgerows, but come back without much nectar."

"At least, they've got last year's honey to eat." He held the gate open for her and followed her into the field.

She smiled as Shelby bopped her on the head with Buzz-buzz. "Adult bees don't eat honey. They make honey to feed their larvae. Adult bees eat pollen and nectar from blossoms. They store food for themselves, but it seems that as we prefer vegetables from the garden to what we freeze and can, they're eager to get fresh food." With a laugh, she said, "Probably more than you want to know."

"You find it fascinating, and when you talk about it, you make it fascinating for everyone else, too."

"Not everyone. I've encountered plenty of people whose eyes glaze over with boredom when I start prattling on and on about my bees."

With a chuckle, he said, "I've seen the same thing when I start talking about trusses and foundations and sheetrock."

"Well, I can understand that. Nobody in their right mind should get excited about sheetrock."

"*I* get excited about it."

When she arched her brows, he wanted to put his arm around her shoulders and squeeze her. Usually Hannah was the epitome of a proper Amish woman, but he preferred when, like tonight, she was sassy and matched him jest for jest.

"Okay," he said. "Point taken. You wouldn't be the first one to tell me I'm *ab in kopp*. Not even the first today."

"Who called you crazy?"

"Some of the men on my crew. They think I'm crazy to want to replace the whole roof of the Hunter's Mill Creek Bridge when we weren't hired to do that."

She became serious. "But you were hired to fix the bridge, and you can't fix the bridge if the roof's leaking, ain't so?"

"Why do you get it and they don't?"

"Because I'm not the one having to get on the roof?" Her smile returned.

He grinned at her. "Point taken again." Taking a deep breath, he said, "This way."

The woods were dim because the trees blocked the last rays of the early sunset. It would be weeks before the sun was above the horizon after supper. When the *Englischers* went to daylight savings time, he must remember the difference between it and what the Amish called slow time. He wasn't sure why the *Englischers* moved their clocks one hour ahead each spring. He was as impatient for summer to come each year as they were, but the shift didn't make sense to him.

A short distance later, he stepped from the woods and into the clearing. He swept one arm toward the house he'd been working on for so long, but his gaze was focused on Hannah as he asked, "What do you think?"

His heart seemed to stop in midbeat as he waited for her answer. Until that moment, he hadn't realized how important her opinion was to him. More important than anyone else's. He didn't want to think why, so he watched her face, looking for any sign of what she'd say.

Hannah didn't answer right away. Instead she admired the white house in front of her. It was smaller than the rambling farmhouse where his family lived. However, it was freshly painted, and the setting among the trees was idyllic. A pair of large windows flanked the simple wood door. Upstairs, two more windows were set into identical dormers.

"Whose house is this?" she asked.

"Mine. I'm building it."

"Why?" She couldn't ask the next question burning on her tongue. A man usually built a house when he planned to marry. Had she misread everything? Was Daniel planning to marry another woman?

"I want to use it with prospective clients as an example of the work I—and my construction company—can do."

Relief flooded her. "What a *gut* idea! Can I see inside?"

"I'd hoped you'd want to." He grinned like a kid with a new scooter.

Hannah followed him onto the porch. It was wider than hers, wide enough for chairs where someone could sit and listen to the birds singing good-night.

When he opened the door, he gestured for her to go in first. She did and stared about in astonishment. It was a plain house with no extra ornamentation, but that made it easier for her to see the quality of Daniel's work. Not a single gap showed along the woodwork or the stones on the fireplace. The wood floors glistened and were so smooth they looked like an ice-coated pond.

Daniel set Shelby down, and the toddler headed for the kitchen. Following her, because she wasn't sure what tools might be out there, Hannah stopped as she saw that room. The cabinets were beautiful, and light poured into the room, making the pale yellow walls glow.

"I added skylights for the kitchen and upstairs bathroom," Daniel said in a whisper, "because the trees block much of the sunshine early in the morning and during the later afternoon." He gave her a tentative smile, and she realized he was anxious to know if she liked the house he'd built. "I didn't want to cut more trees than I had to."

"I agree," she said as she watched his shoulders lose their rigid line. "You did this all yourself?"

"*Ja*. While I was working with plumbers and sheet-rockers and painters on other jobs, I watched what they did. I asked questions. Lots of them, and I learned their tricks of the trade. What I learned I put to use here." He leaned against the doorframe. "I'll use it until my twin brother, Micah, gets married."

"You'd give your brother a *house* as a wedding gift?" She wondered how she could have considered Daniel selfish and self-centered.

"He'll need it. Why wouldn't I give it to him?"

Walking away and pretending to be fascinated by an arch leading from the kitchen to the laundry room, she asked in what she hoped was a casual voice, "So you don't plan on marrying?"

"I told you, Hannah, I needed to concentrate on starting my business. It wouldn't be fair to spend all my time on that if I were a husband and *daed*."

"*Ja*, you told me that." *But I don't want to believe it.* That was her problem, not his, and she needed a way to deal with her ridiculous heart which kept believing Daniel would change his dreams to make hers come true.

He cleared his throat, as uncomfortable with the turn the conversation had taken as she was. "I've got something for Shelby." He opened one of the cupboard doors and pulled out a piece of wood about a foot long and eight inches wide. It'd been smoothed and polished, glinting beneath the skylight. "I spoke to Keely about this, because it might help Shelby with her occupational therapy." He held it out.

Hannah took it. Her eyes widened as she examined it. Into the board were set a variety of large wooden pegs and screws. Each had been painted a bright color. The pegs had been glued into place, so no amount of hammering would push them through the wood. The screws had been inserted so they could turn a few times, but couldn't be removed.

"What is it?" she asked.

"A toy that doubles as a therapy tool. Keely wanted Shelby to have some small objects to grip, and the pegs are the right size." He tapped one of the screws. "Turning these will strengthen Shelby's fingers and wrists."

She blinked back sudden tears. She wondered if she'd ever figure out Daniel. One minute, he was all business, talking about the company he wanted to establish and how he never would be a family man. The next, he was showing the depth of his heart by planning to give the beautiful house to his brother and by making such a *wunderbaar* gift for Shelby.

"You give it to her," Hannah choked out, so overwhelmed she could hardly speak. "Then she'll know it's from you."

Daniel called the toddler over to him. Setting the board on the floor, he said, "This is for you, *liebling*."

"Da-dan!" cried Shelby in delight as she dropped with a plop to sit on the floor. Tossing Buzz-buzz aside, she reached for the red peg. Her fingers closed in front of it, but instead of getting frustrated as she often was during her therapy sessions, she tried again.

And again and again.

Hannah lost count of the number of times the little

girl tried to grab the peg. She watched, holding her breath. When Shelby grasped the peg and chortled her deep laugh, Hannah clapped her hands and cheered.

Daniel came to his feet while Shelby tried to grasp the blue peg and was successful on her first try.

Through happy tears racing down her face, Hannah said, "*Danki*, Daniel!"

"I'm glad it makes you happy." His hand curved along her face, his thumb brushing away her tears.

She gazed at him, unable to speak as his arm slid around her waist, drawing her to him. He ran his fingers along her cheek, and she feared her trembling legs would forget how to hold her. She wanted to forget everything except for the yearning in his eyes. He whispered her name in the moment before his lips captured hers. When he tugged her to him, she curved her arms around his shoulders. Her hands clenched on his wool coat that couldn't disguise the work-hardened muscles beneath it.

Slowly he lifted his mouth from hers after grazing her lips with another swift kiss. His blue eyes glowed like a calm pond, but there was nothing serene about them. Emotions collided within them, and she couldn't help wondering if he was feeling the same joy she was. She hoped so because this moment was everything she'd dreamed of.

Before…

Hannah gasped and stepped away. Now wasn't before, and she'd learned something in the past three years about letting her heart lead the way. She seized Shelby who yelped a protest as her new toy clattered against the floor.

"*Danki* for showing us your house, Daniel, but we have to go."

He frowned. "Are you going to run away every time you let me a little bit past the walls you've raised to keep me away?"

"It's better I leave than wait for you to go without saying goodbye." The bitter words spilled from her mouth, erasing the pleasure she'd found in his kiss.

He flinched as if she'd struck him.

"I'm sorry," she whispered, cuddling Shelby close. "I shouldn't have said that."

"No." He stuffed his hands into his coat pockets and looked bleak. "You have every right to say that, because it's true. I messed up three years ago."

She took one step away, then another. He watched her until she reached the door. Bending, he picked up the toy he'd made for Shelby. He handed it and Buzz-buzz to Hannah. She thanked him and waited for him to say something.

But he didn't.

Neither did she as she opened the door and left. She hurried across the clearing and hoped he'd call her back.

But he didn't.

How foolish she'd been to kiss him! She'd dared to believe he'd come to love her as much as she'd loved him for so long.

But he didn't.

Chapter Thirteen

Hannah dropped a canning jar. It broke into a half dozen pieces, sliding across the bare floor. Leaving the shards where they were, she set Shelby in her high chair before her little sister could touch the broken glass. Hannah selected an apple oatmeal muffin from the ones cooling on the counter. Checking it wasn't too hot, she peeled off the paper and set the sweet muffin on the tray. The little girl took a big bite, scattering crumbs down the front of her.

Going to the laundry room, Hannah got the broom and dustpan. She began to sweep up the broken glass.

"That's the fourth thing you've broken since the quilting frolic," *Grossmammi* Ella said as she came into the kitchen. Counting on her fingers, she said, "A cup, a glass, the sugar bowl and the canning jar."

"I'll be more careful," she said like an obedient *kind*. It was easier to agree because she didn't have to think about it. She didn't want to think about anything when too many of her thoughts led to Daniel.

"Sit," her great-grandmother said, pointing to the table.

"I need to—"

"Shelby is in the high chair, and you and I have enough *gut* sense to step around the glass. Sit."

Hannah obeyed. Again it was easier than explaining she had too many chores to do this morning to sit and be scolded for being clumsy.

As soon as she sat across from her great-grandmother, *Grossmammi* Ella said, "I know I miss a lot, Hannah, and I'm sure I've forgotten more, but there are some things I can see. You're attracted to your Daniel."

Don't call him my *Daniel!* She silenced the thought which sounded petulant even in her head.

"*Grossmammi* Ella, you know I made a mistake trusting Daniel Stoltzfus once," she said. "I'd be a fool to do so again."

"Bah!" Her great-grandmother waved aside her words as if they were annoying gnats. "So you made a mistake? What was it? Two years ago?"

"Three."

"So you made a mistake three years ago. Everyone makes mistakes. The important thing is to learn from them. Learn what you did wrong and learn how with God's help, you can avoid the mistake again."

Hannah sighed. "So much easier said than done. I've been asking God to guide me in what I should do. I need to make sure I listen to Him instead of anyone else."

"Like the *gut*-looking young man who glows with joy when he visits?" *Grossmammi* Ella folded her thin arms on the table. "Your Daniel has the look my Earney had when he came to court me. And I see the happiness in your eyes when Daniel is at our door. It's like what I felt in my heart when Earney smiled at me. I tell you, Hannah, he's a *gut* man."

"*Ja, Grossdawdi* was—"

"Not my Earney. I'm talking about your Daniel. He's a *gut* man."

Looking away, she didn't want to admit she agreed. Daniel was a *gut* man, not the villain she'd created and nurtured in her imagination for the past three years. He was a hardworking man in pursuit of what he'd wanted.

The memory of Daniel's laugh rumbled through her head. His laugh—his real one, not the polite one he'd used when he first came to the house—was like the sound of distant thunder against the rolling hills. It resonated within her, slipping past the guard she'd put in place to keep her heart from being touched again. His joking had stripped away her anger.

"The *gut* Lord has given you three years to heal," her great-grandmother said, "and He has brought your Daniel back into your life. God has a reason for these things. If it's not to give you two a chance to reconsider, what else could it be?"

Hannah blinked on tears as her great-grandmother continued in a logical manner. This was the woman she remembered from fifteen years ago, before the Alzheimer's disease had begun to rob her of what she'd been.

Reaching across the table, Hannah cradled *Grossmammi* Ella's fragile hand. Her great-grandmother stretched to take Shelby's right hand while Hannah clasped her little sister's left. When her great-grandmother bowed her head in silent prayer, Hannah did the same, grateful for her family circle that was the perfect haven from the yearnings and fears in her heart.

Had anyone ever been as stupid as Daniel had been yesterday when he'd kissed Hannah? When he'd been walking out with her, he'd known better than to kiss her and let her think he was ready to offer her the future she wanted. He hadn't planned to kiss her yesterday either, but when he'd seen the joy on her face and knew he'd brought it to her, his longing to hold her had silenced his *gut* sense.

He glanced at her house through the rain which had returned at dawn. Hannah must know he was at the bridge. His crew had just gone home, leaving silence in their wake after a long day of cutting boards and nailing them in place. One more board needed to be cut; then Daniel could call it a day, too. The only sounds were the thud of the rain on the repaired roof and his conscience urging him to go to the Lambrights' house and apologize for what he'd done.

Which would be fine if he were sorry he'd kissed her. He wasn't. Not a bit. For years, he wondered if her lips would be as luscious and sweet as her honey, and he had his answer. They were. But instead of satisfying his curiosity and putting the idea of kissing her out of his head, the caress of her lips against his had whetted his longing for another kiss...and another...and another.

Irritated at his thoughts, he pounded the hammer against the board to wedge into the narrow curve so it would support that section of the arch. The hammer grazed his thumb. He yelped and dropped the hammer. Shaking his hand as if he could make the pain fall out, he surged to his feet.

He grimaced. He hadn't hit a finger since he was an apprentice learning how to wield a hammer. That was what he got for not paying attention to his work.

At a loud roar, Daniel looked up. A black sports car came to a stop by the barriers on the far end of the bridge. Its engine cut out, and the noise vanished. The door opened and out stepped a man with bright red hair and tattered blue jeans tucked into work boots that looked newer than Daniel's. He wore a leather jacket over a white shirt.

Coming to the concrete barrier, the *Englischer* waved.

"Can I help you?" Daniel called.

"You're Daniel Stoltzfus, right?" the *Englischer* asked in an odd accent Daniel had never heard.

"Ja." Hanging his hammer on his tool belt, he asked, "What can I do for you?"

"I was hoping to talk to you."

"Sure." Daniel walked with care on the thick stringers where the planks of the deck hadn't been secured into place. In the past two weeks, he'd had to traverse them often enough so he didn't have to watch every step he took, but he knew better than to get too overconfident. Not paying attention could lead to an accident far more serious than a throbbing thumb; then there wouldn't be any chance of finishing the bridge on time.

Stepping onto the asphalt, he strode to the barrier curving across the road from one set of guardrails to the other. He greeted the *Englischer* and waited for the man to state his business.

"I'm Liam O'Neill." The redhead hooked a thumb behind him toward the south. "I bought the McClellan farm near Strasburg. Do you know it?"

Daniel was intrigued by the lilt of the man's accent. *"Ja,* but not well."

"The barn and the house need work. Since my wife and I purchased the farm last month, I've been asking around for someone who could do the work. Your name has come up a lot. Would you be willing to stop by and take a look and see if you're interested in the project?"

"*Ja*, I'd be interested in seeing what you want done."

"We want what you're doing here." He gestured toward the bridge. "I've driven past a few times, and I like how you're updating the bridge without the changes being obvious. That's what my wife wants with the farmhouse. It's an old stone-end house like the one over there." He pointed to the Lambrights' house. "She wants what she calls a sympathetic renovation. Do you know what that is?"

"*Ja*. A house that lives like it's new and looks like it's old."

The *Englischer* grinned. "Exactly. When can you stop by?"

"With the rain, we're having to work whenever there's a break and plenty of light. How about tomorrow night around six?"

"Perfect." Liam offered his hand.

Daniel shook it as he said, "If you've got a list of projects you want done, that would help us get started."

"I'll have my wife pull her lists together into one." He chuckled, then turned to leave. He paused and said, "You know, you're the first Amish man I've ever spoken with."

"And you're the first I've ever spoken with from…"

"Ireland. Dublin."

That explained his accent and his name, and Daniel grinned. "So let's hope this project has no more firsts for either of us."

"By the way, will you need transportation?"

"My horse and buggy will be fine, but *danki*." He added, "Thanks."

"I figured that out," Liam said. "Okay, it sounds as if we've got a plan for tomorrow night. You can look around and see what you think is possible and what isn't. I should warn you. My wife wants to open up the small rooms."

"You'll need a structural engineer to determine how best to support any load-bearing walls."

"I don't know any in the area."

"I know a *gut* one, and I'll be glad to give you his name and phone number whether you and I work together or not."

"That's generous of you, Mr. Stoltzfus."

"Call me Daniel. Plain folk don't put weight in titles."

Liam nodded and walked to his car. The engine awoke with another mighty growl.

Daniel watched it drive away. He'd had his dream handed to him after years of waiting and hoping and saving to buy the equipment he needed and making contacts in the construction business throughout Lancaster County. He'd just been offered a job where he could be the boss and work with the best artisans he knew.

His dream was coming true.

So why wasn't he excited?

He glanced again toward the Lambrights' house. Maybe he wasn't as thrilled as he'd expected because he didn't have anyone special to share the news with. But how could he bring Hannah into his life when he could see the long, long days and nights of work ahead if Liam hired him? Time he wouldn't be able to spend with her and her family. It wouldn't be right.

Or so he'd thought. All of the sudden, he wasn't too sure.

Of anything.

* * *

Daniel was halfway to Paradise Springs when he turned his buggy around and headed back toward Hannah's house. Why was he making himself miserable? Hannah had said several times she wanted to be his friend, and shouldn't he share his *gut* news with his *gut* friend? More than anyone else, she'd paid the price for his ambition. It seemed only right she should be the first one he told about the opportunity to make his dream come true.

Hoping he wasn't trying to fool himself again, he rode through the thickening twilight which had come earlier with the rain. He wasn't sure, but it seemed to be raining harder than it'd been earlier. Or maybe he was, like everyone else, tired of day after day of rain.

He heard the raised voices and Shelby's crying as he reached the door of the Lambrights' house. No, not raised *voices*. Just a single one even louder than the toddler's frantic cries. A woman's voice at a furious pitch. He opened the door and heard a hand slap hard against someone's skin.

As he watched in disbelief, Hannah recoiled away from her great-grandmother. Hannah was trying to reason with her, but *Grossmammi* Ella's eyes snapped with fury as the old woman raised her hand again. Beyond them, Shelby clung to a chair and her stuffed honeybee and sobbed.

Daniel stepped between Hannah and *Grossmammi* Ella who snarled at him to get out of the way so she could teach that horrible woman not to flirt with her husband. Gently he caught the elderly woman's birdlike wrist and lowered her arm to her side. When she cried out and tried to break free, he held her easily.

"Now, now," he said as if she were no older than Shelby, "you don't want to do that, *Grossmammi* Ella. You don't want to hurt Hannah."

"I wouldn't hurt Hannah," the old woman retorted. "But Mima needs to get her own husband."

"Mima?" he mouthed in Hannah's direction.

She replied, "Later." Out loud, she added, "*Grossmammi* Ella, let me get you a cup of chamomile tea. It'll make you feel better, ain't so?"

Daniel watched the old woman's face and saw it alter from rage to bewilderment. He released her wrist but kept his hand beneath her elbow as he steered her toward the chair by the living room window. Draping a quilt over her knees, he sighed. *Lost.* The word burst into his mind. *Grossmammi* Ella was lost.

Picking up Shelby, he soothed her by making faces and playing peekaboo. He kept at it while Hannah made tea and took it to her great-grandmother. Not once did she look in his direction, but he could see she was blushing. Why? She couldn't be embarrassed, could she, that he'd halted the old woman's rampage?

She was, he realized, when she wouldn't meet his eyes as she returned to the kitchen. He took her elbow, as he had *Grossmammi* Ella's, and urged her to come with him out onto the front porch. She paused long enough to collect her coat and Shelby's.

He closed the door behind them, so their voices wouldn't reach into the house. While she pulled on her coat, he slipped Shelby's arms into hers. He sat on the top step where the rain didn't reach, bouncing the little girl on his knee. When Hannah perched beside him, he ached to put his arm around her shoulders. He resisted, not wanting to do anything to upset her more.

"Are you okay?" he asked as she stared at the rushing creek across the road.

"*Ja. Danki* for helping."

"Does she get like this often?"

"Not often, but often enough." Her smile appeared and fled in a heartbeat. "Usually I can calm her, but sometimes I can't."

He was about to answer, but paused when he realized the enormity of what she'd said. His voice cracked as he asked, "She's hit you before?"

Not meeting his gaze, she nodded. "I know she doesn't mean to hurt me. She gets mired in her memories."

"She could hurt you badly." He frowned. "She'd hit you the day you removed the bees from the bridge, hadn't she? That's why you kept your beekeeper's hat on as long as you could. Why did you let me think you fell?"

Flinging out her hands, she said, "Because I knew you'd react like this."

"Being angry that she hit you? Of course, I'm going to react like this." He caught one of her hands as he turned her face toward him. "Why didn't you tell me the truth?"

"I was honest with you."

"But you said—"

"I slipped on the wet grass and bumped against the bridge." Tears glistened in her luminous eyes. "It happened, Daniel, as I said. I told you the truth, but not all of it."

"The bruise was from your great-grandmother striking you." He didn't make it a question.

"*Ja.*"

He pretended to recoil when Shelby bopped him on the chin with Buzz-buzz, but he didn't look away from Hannah. How could she be so calm? The Amish believed in nonresistance, he knew well, but that didn't mean she had to endure her great-grandmother's blows.

When he said as much, Hannah gave him a sad smile. "Daniel, you didn't get upset when Shelby hit you just now with her toy, did you?"

"She's not much more than a *boppli*. She doesn't know what she's doing."

"*Grossmammi* Ella is the same. She doesn't know what she's doing. So how can I get mad at *Grossmammi* Ella if I don't get mad at Shelby?"

He opened his mouth to reply; then he realized he didn't have anything to say. Hannah was right. With each passing day, her great-grandmother's mind was wandering further and further into the past. The sudden shifts in mood from happy to furious and frustrated no longer startled him as much as they had at the beginning.

"But you can't have her here with you if she's going to hurt you and Shelby," he said.

"She hasn't raised her hand to Shelby."

"Not yet."

"She won't. Each time she's hit me, she's believed I was someone else, someone who was trying to keep her from her beloved Earney. If she knew me, she never would have swung her hand. She's scared of what she can't remember and uncertain of what she can."

"But if she thinks Shelby is someone else…"

"When she's confused, she thinks Shelby is me. She'd never hurt a toddler." She took his hand, startling him. "Daniel, she's my family. Until Shelby came, she was my only family. I can't turn my back on her because it's not easy to take care of her. She took care of me during times when I'm sure I wasn't easy to be around."

"She never struck you, though."

Putting her fingers to her cheek, she said, "Each time, the bruise heals. My heart wouldn't heal if I put her into some sort of nursing home. I need you to understand."

"I do understand," he replied as he tried to imagine having to make that same choice for his *mamm.* "You should seek Reuben's advice."

"I have." She met his gaze. "He urged me to do two things. One was to love my great-grandmother, even if I despise her condition. The other was to remember none of us is alone if we trust God is with us. Knowing that has gotten me through the toughest times so I can enjoy the happy ones. I know it won't be long until she's called home, and I don't want to miss a minute we've got together."

When tears fell down her cheeks, he tilted her head on his shoulder and held her without saying anything else. He didn't want to let her go. Not ever.

He looked over her head toward the bridge where he'd been offered a chance to make his dreams come true. Could he be the man Hannah needed? Until he knew the answer, he mustn't say anything else either.

Chapter Fourteen

When a knock came just as Hannah was about to turn off the propane light in the kitchen, she stiffened. Who was calling at this late hour?

Her wish that Daniel was at the door was absurd. There wasn't any reason for him to come from the far side of Paradise Springs at this hour, but she missed him holding her as he had earlier when he comforted her.

It'd been a tough day. Her great-grandmother had been on edge until she went to bed right after supper. She hadn't lost her temper again, but each time Shelby made a sound, the old woman flinched and glared in the *kind*'s direction.

Had Daniel been right? Would the time come when *Grossmammi* Ella was a danger to the toddler?

The thought added another layer of pain to Hannah's headache that had plagued her since her great-grandmother struck her. She hoped a *gut* night's sleep would ease the ache, and she would wake up feeling well.

But first she needed to see who was knocking. She didn't want either Shelby or *Grossmammi* Ella to be routed up, because it might take a long time to get them back to sleep.

Opening the door, Hannah gasped when she saw Chief McMurray standing on her porch. Why was he there?

"May I come in?" he asked, his face giving no clue to his thoughts.

Her legs were stiff as she backed away to let him in. He took off his cap with its insignia. She wasn't sure if she should offer to take it or not. She led the way into the living room and motioned for him to sit.

He did on the sofa and, as soon as she was perched on her great-grandmother's favorite chair, he said, "There's no way to say this gently. Hannah, your father and his wife were killed in a highway accident last night."

"Oh…" She should feel something. Sorrow, regret, anger…something, but she'd become numb. Maybe her feelings had been burned away already after the horrible day. But it was her *daed* the chief of police was talking about. She should feel something.

"The state police in Nebraska contacted me."

"My *daed* was in Nebraska?" She couldn't guess why he'd been so far away.

"Yes, and the state police told me that there had been a sudden snow squall on the highway last night. A complete whiteout. A couple of big semis skidded and caused a chain reaction."

"Was one of them my *daed*'s?" She'd guessed he was a truck driver from the multiple places he'd sent postcards from, but she'd never been sure.

"He wasn't driving either of the ones that caused the accident, but your father's rig was caught in it." He leaned forward, and his kind gaze caught and held hers as he added, "Hannah, you need to know something important. The officer I spoke with said witnesses told him that your father swerved to miss a school bus and a couple of SUVs. If he hadn't turned to avoid them, his truck wouldn't have rolled as it did. But, by doing so, he saved those people's lives."

She knew Chief McMurray expected her to be proud of her *daed*, but the numbness smothered her. "*Danki* for coming to tell me," she whispered.

"Is there someone I can contact for you?"

Daniel, her heart cried, but she said, "If you'll let the bishop know, I'd appreciate it."

"I will." Coming to his feet, he added, "I'm sorry for your loss, Hannah."

She thanked him again, but didn't add she'd lost her *daed* over fifteen years before. What had been lost tonight was her dream of seeing him again and discovering why he'd abandoned her and Shelby. The chance to learn the truth was gone forever.

Daniel frowned when he walked toward Hannah's house the next morning. It was the day the occupational therapist came to work with Shelby. The sessions with Keely were in the morning when the toddler was most alert and amiable to play "the games" the therapist had devised to help her.

But the road in front of the Lambrights' house was empty. Keely's black pickup wasn't in the driveway either. Curiosity propelled him toward the house, not only to discover why the therapist hadn't come but to learn how Hannah fared in the wake of yesterday's uproar.

When the front door opened and *Grossmammi* Ella

stood there, he was so startled that he mumbled his greeting.

"What are you doing here?" she asked as if he were a naughty *kind*.

He had no idea how to answer the old woman's question. Was she in the present day or had her mind wandered again into the past? Had she tried to hit Hannah again?

"I come to work with Shelby and Keely at this time."

Grossmammi Ella's nose wrinkled. "That *Englisch* woman has many squirrelly ideas." Her answer told him she was aware of what was currently going on.

"She's trying to help Shelby." He glanced around the room. "Where's Shelby? Did she and Hannah go somewhere?" He couldn't imagine anything that would compel Hannah to leave her great-grandmother alone.

As if he'd said that aloud, an elderly man strode in from the kitchen. He was almost bald and had a round, cheerful face. His clothes and thick black mustache identified him as an *Englischer*.

"Hi! I'm Barry Jones."

Daniel introduced himself and glanced from the old man to Hannah's great-grandmother. "So you're here to keep *Grossmammi* Ella company?" he asked, not wanting to insult the elderly woman.

"Yep. We've been talking about how soon we can plant our gardens," Barry replied. "Do you garden, young man?"

"No. I'm a carpenter."

"The one working on our covered bridge?"

"Ja." Hoping he didn't seem rude, he asked, "Where are Hannah and Shelby?"

Instead of answering his question, *Grossmammi* Ella

wagged a finger under his nose. "Why are you here? You should be with Hannah. She needs someone with her, and she wouldn't let me go with her."

"Where?"

"Into the village. She's seeing some *Englisch* lawyer." *Grossmammi* Ella's mouth twisted with distaste. "Trust my foolish grandson to do something else stupid. Not only did he jump the fence and leave his daughter behind without a second thought, but he shared his business with an *Englischer*. That's not our way." She glanced at Barry, who shrugged at her words.

Daniel didn't argue with the elderly woman either, though he knew many Amish folks sought out the help and advice of an attorney with business or family matters, especially with incorporation of businesses or probate issues.

"Hannah's *daed* has contacted her?" he asked.

Barry answered after glancing at the old woman, who'd turned and walked toward her chair, "Isaac and his wife were killed in an accident in Nebraska. The police came to let the family know last night." He glanced at *Grossmammi* Ella. "I'm not sure if she comprehends the news yet."

Weight pressed onto Daniel's chest, making it impossible to breathe. Hannah's *daed* was dead? Suddenly he couldn't think of anything other than finding Hannah and comforting her, but he somehow managed to ask, "Do you know which attorney she's seeing?"

"Some peculiar *Englisch* name," *Grossmammi* Ella said as she sat in her favorite chair. "How can I be expected to remember it?"

"Didn't you say it was on the letter delivered to Hannah this morning, Ella?" asked her neighbor.

"Ja." She frowned at Daniel. "I suppose you want to see it."

"I'd like to, if you don't mind." He chafed at the delay. Hannah shouldn't be alone after receiving such news.

She made a sniffing sound as if he'd made an impertinent reply. "It's on the table in the kitchen."

Daniel half-ran to get the white envelope. He glanced at the return address and smiled when he saw the Marianelli and Loggins logo. Quentin Marianelli handled legal matters for many plain families around Paradise Springs. Daniel should have guessed Isaac Lambright had used his services.

"What are you waiting for?" Hannah's great-grandmother asked. "She shouldn't have gone alone. You should be there with her."

Daniel agreed. He spun on his heel, crossed the room and yanked the door open. Calling a goodbye over his shoulder, he crossed the porch in a single step and then jumped onto the grass. His feet almost slid out from beneath him, but he regained his balance and climbed into his buggy that he'd left by the bridge. He shouted to the men working there to let them know he'd be back when he could. He didn't wait for their response.

As soon as he arrived at the lawyer's office in a pleasant house along Route 30 in the heart of Paradise Springs, Daniel saw Hannah sitting stiffly with Shelby on her lap. Her eyes widened as he entered, and he saw her relief she wasn't alone. As she'd been too long because he'd walked away.

Taking a chair beside her, he said, "Your great-grandmother told me where you'd gone, and I thought you'd like some company."

"Ja," she said in a whisper.

He started to tell her how sorry he was about her *daed*, but a man in a dark suit came over to where they were sitting.

"Hannah Lambright?" When she nodded, he said, "I'm Quentin Marianelli. Thank you for coming today. I'm sorry for your loss."

"Danki," she replied. "This is my little sister, Shelby, and Daniel Stoltzfus."

The attorney greeted them before asking them to come with him to his office.

"Do you want me to come?" he asked when Hannah stood.

"Ja." She didn't add anything else.

He followed her and the lawyer down a short hall to an office dominated by a large desk and a wall of bookshelves. The attorney sat behind the desk and motioned for them to take the two chairs in front of it.

"I'm glad you're here, Daniel," the lawyer said as soon as they were settled in their places. "You can help us with one procedural step before we can proceed. I know you don't carry identification, so will you vouch this woman is, indeed, Hannah Lambright, a woman you have known for…?"

"Almost five years," Daniel supplied.

"A woman you have known for over four years," the attorney said as he scribbled on the form waiting on his desk. "Do you vouch for her identity?" He gave them a brief smile. "All you need to do, Daniel, is say yes or no."

"Ja. I mean, yes."

"Either works fine." Scrawling something across the bottom of the page, he pushed the page toward Daniel. "Will you sign at the bottom, too? By signing, you're acknowledging your statement about Hannah is the truth."

What had he said? That he'd known her for years. True, but there were depths to Hannah he hadn't realized existed until the past few weeks. She was a woman who stood strong against the storms of life and, despite what she'd experienced—or maybe *because* of it—she offered every bit of her strength to others as she held them up to God in action and in prayer. He wondered if he'd ever met another person who so embodied God's grace, giving everything she had and expecting nothing in return.

The attorney slipped the paper into a folder, then looked again at Hannah. "Do you wish the rest of our conversation to be private?"

"Having Daniel here is fine." Her voice was so dull she sounded as if a large part of her had died along with her *daed*.

"All right." Opening the folder, he said, "Your father left detailed instructions for his funeral." He looked uncomfortable as he went on, "He did not want his remains to be brought to Paradise Springs. He wanted to be buried in Michigan where he lived when he wasn't on the road. He told me he found it too painful even to think of returning here after your mother died."

Daniel looked at the toddler who was wiggling on Hannah's lap. Isaac had returned long enough to leave Shelby on the porch.

"Usually we wait until after the funeral to read the will," the attorney said.

"My *daed* had a will?" Hannah asked as she set Shelby on the floor.

"Yes." Mr. Marianelli tapped the folder. "He prepared it after your mother died and left it with me. It's straightforward with his estate divided between his children. There is some insurance money, and we'll deal with that when the funds are disbursed." He tapped the folder on the desk. "Why I wanted you to come here today was I received two letters from your father. He wanted you to have them after his death. He gave the first one to me about three years ago."

"He was here three years ago?" Betrayal rang through her question.

"Yes," said the attorney. "He was pleased you were making yourself a future with a good man, Hannah. Those were his exact words. He didn't want to do anything to ruin your happiness with your young man."

Sickness clawed at Daniel's gut. Three years ago, Hannah had been walking out with him. Isaac must have chanced to see them together or heard they were courting. Because he was under the *bann*, Isaac had assumed speaking with his daughter might cause trouble between her and her admirer.

Hannah reached over and took his hand as she had on the porch yesterday. Only yesterday? It seemed like a lifetime ago. He squeezed her hand, not surprised she was offering *him* comfort.

Mr. Marianelli took an unmarked envelope from the file and held it out.

Daniel held his breath as he saw the last remnants of color fall away from her face as she stared at the letter that contained the final words her *daed* would ever have for her.

* * *

As she stared at the envelope, Hannah wanted to flee, but she must read what her *daed* had wanted her to read, for herself and for Shelby. She was grateful Daniel had arrived before she was called in to talk with the attorney. She'd wanted Daniel to stay because too much of the conversations around her sounded like Shelby's gibberish.

Her fingers trembled as she reached for the envelope. "Should I read it now?"

"If you don't mind," the lawyer said.

When Daniel put a steadying hand on her arm, she didn't glance at him. She opened the envelope and lifted out a single folded page. She opened it.

Her *daed* had printed the four lines, but the letters were smudged as if he'd erased some words several times. She began reading aloud,

"Dearest Hannah,
"Forgive me. I can't stay. Each time I see you, I see your *mamm*. I am weak, I know, but you'll have a better life without me.
"Your *Daed*"

That was it. *Daed* had left because he couldn't bear to look at her because she reminded him too much of her *mamm*. How ironic Shelby had been fearful of her at first because everyone said Hannah had grown to resemble him.

"That's all it says." She folded the page and put it into its envelope. She placed it on Mr. Marianelli's desk.

The attorney shuffled pages in the file, then drew out another envelope. It had printing in the upper left-hand corner. When he handed it to Hannah, he said, "This arrived a few weeks ago. On the back, you can see the date it was delivered."

She turned over the envelope imprinted with the name of a hotel chain. With a gasp, she stared at the date. "It's two days after Shelby was left at our house."

She ripped the envelope getting it open and pulled out another sheet with writing on both sides. Seeing her name on the top on one side, she began reading,

"Dearest Hannah,
"You must have many questions after finding a little girl on the front porch of *Grossmammi* Ella's house, but I have space to answer only the important ones. Shelby is your little sister. Karen tells me she's actually your half-sister. That's Shelby's *mamm*. Karen. She and I know a special child like Shelby needs a stable home, and we can't give her that. She shouldn't be living in a big rig. She needs extra help, and she needs someone she can depend on to get her help. That's you, Hannah. We would have kept her with us awhile longer, but a new job has come up in Alaska, and we're going to head that way once we've finished the other jobs we have scheduled. It's a good job, and it pays well. I'll send money to you and Shelby when I can. I should have sent you money before, but somehow the rig always needed repairs or times were lean. I could afford to send postcards, and I hope you thought of me when you received them and knew I was thinking of you.

"I know you think I'm abandoning Shelby as I did you, but no matter how much distance has separated us, nothing could remove you from my heart, Hannah. Your *mamm* and I loved you. I still love you, and I miss you, just as I'll miss Shelby. But I thank God my daughters will be safe with each other.

"Your *Daed*"

No one spoke as Hannah lowered the letter to her lap. Her *daed* loved her. The pain she'd expected when told her *daed* had died rushed over her like a fierce storm. She'd never hear him say those words again.

"May I take this with me?" she asked, struggling to hold in the tears stinging her eyes.

Mr. Marianelli smiled sadly. "Of course. The letters are yours. I want you to know there's no hurry to go over your father's last will and testament. We can arrange a meeting in a week or two at a time convenient for you."

Coming to her feet, she thanked him as she put the letters in her bag. She went to where Shelby had been paging through magazines, looking for pictures. Several were scattered on the floor by the table. Putting them back, she picked up the toddler. She went with Daniel from the office and to where his buggy was parked beside hers.

So many thoughts were ricocheting through her mind she was surprised her head could hold them. Everything she'd come to believe had been turned upside down. She wasn't unlovable. Her *daed* loved her as did her great-grandmother and her adorable little sister. No half about it. Shelby was her sister.

"Hannah?" asked Daniel as she put Shelby in the buggy. "Do you want me to go back to the house with you?"

She shook her head. "No, I need time to think about this and to share it with *Grossmammi* Ella."

"Are you sure? I know this has to be tough for you."

"It is."

"Isn't there anything I can do to help?"

Climbing into her buggy, she shook her head. "I appreciate your offer, Daniel, but the truth is I can manage with God's help." She looked into his handsome face, fighting her fingers that wanted to push the ebony hair from his brow. "*Danki* for being here today. I know you've got to get going to meet with a potential client."

He stared at her in disbelief. "How did you hear that?"

"The *Englischer* who is looking to hire you heard about you from our neighbor, Barry Jones. Barry told *Grossmammi* Ella, and I saw you talking to a stranger at the bridge yesterday. I put one and one together." It took all her strength to smile. "I'm happy for you, Daniel. It's what you've wanted for so long."

"I meant to tell you, but I couldn't when you were upset. I could come over to your house after—"

"I don't think you should come by as often as you have."

His dark brows lowered as he frowned. "You mean you don't want me to help with Shelby's therapy?"

"You're going to make me say it, aren't you?"

"Say what?"

She forced herself to meet his eyes. What she had to say was going to be hurtful, but it had to be better to say it than to be heartbroken again. "I don't want to think I can depend on you, Daniel, and then realize I can't."

"You can depend on me." He frowned, his brows knitting together. "Haven't I been here to help you?"

"*Ja*, you have been. But you've got a chance to have the work you've been waiting for. I'm afraid it will be like before when—"

Realization of what she was trying not to say must have hit him because the color washed from his face. He looked as horrified as if she'd told him to jump off the bridge.

"I've told you I'm not that man any longer," he said.

"I know."

"But you can't believe me."

Her heart cramped when he didn't make it a question. "I want to, but I believed you before. I can't risk that again, so you should focus on your new job instead of us."

"By us, you mean you, don't you?"

"I mean me, and I mean us. I don't want Shelby to believe you'll be there for her and then have your job keep you from coming to see her as you've promised." She looked from him to her little sister who was yawning and cuddling her stuffed honeybee. "Really, Daniel, I'm glad this opportunity has come along for you. I want you to be happy."

He opened his mouth, then shut it. Swallowing hard, he squared his shoulders. "Can I come and see Shelby?"

"Of course. She likes to do her therapy games with you." Every instinct urged her to put her hand on his arm to comfort him. She didn't. As he turned away, she added, "Daniel?"

"What?"

"I'm sorry."

As he got into his buggy, she thought she heard him say, "I am, too." Then he was gone.

And her heart broke again. Her efforts to protect it had been for nothing as she realized the one truth she'd tried to ignore: she'd fallen in love with him again as hard and deeply as the first time. Only this time she'd pushed him away before he could do the same to her.

She put her hands over her face as sobs ripped through her.

A tiny hand patted her cheek. She looked into Shelby's dark eyes.

"Han-han," the little girl murmured, throwing her arms around Hannah's neck and burying her face against her shoulder.

Hannah wrapped her arms around the little girl. Shelby had never spoken her name before, and the *kind*'s message was clear. She didn't want Hannah to cry. Holding the toddler close, Hannah wept for everything she'd lost and everything she'd found…and everything she'd lost again.

Chapter Fifteen

The rain had been falling hard all night, and it'd become heavier as Daniel pulled into the parking lot for the Stoltzfus Family Shops. If he were the fanciful type, he would have said the weather reflected his bleak state of mind.

Puddles, poked by raindrops, marked lower spots in front of the shops. He didn't have to steer Taffy around them. The horse hated puddles, so he maneuvered the buggy without guidance from Daniel. Just as well, because Daniel's attention wasn't on driving.

The parking lot was deserted. Nobody, not even *Englischers* in their cars, wanted to be out on such a miserable day. He wouldn't be out himself if he didn't want to get advice from his brothers.

Every prayer he'd sent up in the long hours since he'd last spoken with Hannah had led him to the truth. He needed help. He'd been trying to figure out his uneven relationship with Hannah by himself for too long... and failing.

He'd known she'd find out about the possible job with Liam O'Neill sooner or later. He'd been going to tell her himself before the appalling scene with her great-grandmother and then the news of her *daed*'s tragic death. Not once had he imagined she'd congratulate him on the job and then tell him it'd be better if they didn't see each other so often.

Parking in front of Joshua's buggy shop, he jumped out and bent his head as the rain pelted him like a hundred tiny needles. He hurried onto the covered area in front of the shops and shook water off his straw hat and shoulders. He walked into the vast room that was filled to overflowing with equipment and buggy parts on the other side of a half wall. Five of Daniel's six brothers were there. His oldest brother, Joshua, had brewed *kaffi*, and Amos had brought some cookies and muffins from the grocery store. Isaiah's hands were ingrained with black soot from his work in the smithy behind the shops, but he held a chocolate chip cookie with a big bite out of it. Jeremiah sat to one side, rubbing varnish into a small box he must have been working on before he came to Joshua's shop. Joining them was Ezra, who soon would be so busy with spring chores he wouldn't have time for enjoying a cup of *kaffi* with his brothers.

They all looked toward the door as Daniel entered. He saw the glances they exchanged before putting on innocent expressions. They'd been talking about him. Had word already gone through the Amish grapevine about Hannah dumping him yesterday?

"Kaffi?" asked Joshua with a strained smile.

"Getting something to warm me after that cold rain sounds like a *gut* idea," he replied, following his oldest brother's lead of pretending as if everything was normal.

Daniel took the steaming cup. All the chairs had been claimed, so he sat on the half wall dividing the shop. Holding the cup to his face, he appreciated the heat billowing from it.

"The rain is going to turn to sleet or snow if it gets much colder," he said after taking a sip.

"We had enough snow already during the winter." Ezra gave an emoted shudder. "I didn't think it'd ever stop."

"It did when it turned to rain."

His brothers chuckled, and Daniel relaxed. He liked making his brothers laugh, and having them do so made the tension tightening his shoulders ease.

"Where's Micah?" he asked as he took a cookie from the plate Joshua held out to him. Among the cookies from the grocery store, he saw a few of the delicious date-nut cookies his oldest brother's wife, Rebekah, baked. With a cockeyed grin, he snatched two of those before Joshua offered the plate to the others.

"He said something about taking *Mamm* out to Reuben's house." Amos winked at him. "I'm not sure why *Mamm* decided she needed to go on such a lousy day, but it's easy to guess why Micah was eager to take her."

"Unless he's willing to talk to Katie Kay, there's no reason for him to go," Daniel said.

Joshua began, "His spirit is willing—"

"But his courage is weak," said Ezra with a chuckle.

"I seem to remember," Jeremiah said as he looked up, "how we had to intervene for you and Leah when your courage was weak, Ezra."

The brothers hooted with laughter.

"How's the work coming at the bridge?" asked Amos.

"It'd go better if the rain would stop," Daniel replied and took another bite of a cookie. He knew what was on his brothers' minds. How long before they asked about Hannah?

Ezra chuckled, but with little humor. "The same thing I said about getting the corn in the field. As wet as it is, though I could get the planting started with my team, the seed will rot before it has a chance to grow."

"If we could get two days without rain, we'd be finished out at the bridge."

"I hear you're taking a job with an *Englischer* in Strasburg next." Isaiah held out his cup for a refill.

Tilting the pot over it, Daniel said, "It's not for sure. And don't call Liam O'Neill an *Englischer*. When I went over to talk to him about his project, he told me that it's an insult to *gut* Irishmen everywhere to be labeled *Englisch*." He kept his tone light because he didn't want anyone to know how hard it'd been for him to have that meeting after his strained conversation with Hannah outside the attorney's office.

It'd taken all his determination to be able to act as if he only cared about helping Liam and his wife renovate the old farmhouse that was close to falling in. He'd answered their questions and proposed an idea or two to make the project work, but his thoughts had constantly veered to Hannah. How could he fault her for trying to protect herself and her family after how he'd treated her? He should be grateful she hadn't spoken of how her *daed* might have sought her out if Isaac hadn't believed her future was set with Daniel. That thought shadowed him, making sleep impossible.

Joshua didn't look at him. "Once you're done at the bridge, you won't have many chances to spend time with Hannah, ain't so?"

"Ja." So much for his appearance of not having a

care in the world. He should have known he couldn't fool his older brothers.

"Unless you ask her to walk out with you," Isaiah said.

"Not likely. I ruined everything last time with her." *And this time.*

"You did," Joshua said as his other brothers nodded. "I have to admit I was surprised she wanted anything to do with you once she removed the bees from the bridge."

"I don't know if she would have if it hadn't been for Shelby. The *kind* preferred me at first."

"You know what the *Englischers* say, don't you?" asked Ezra as he reached for another chocolate chip cookie.

"What's that?" he asked, though the twinkle in his brother's eye warned he wouldn't like hearing what Ezra had to say.

"There's no accounting for taste." Ezra's retort brought more howls of laughter from his brothers.

Daniel accepted the teasing with a wry grin. The Stoltzfus brothers ribbed one another, but also stood behind one another in trying times. They'd come together to support their *mamm* and each other when *Daed* died, and they'd done the same when two of the brothers had lost their wives. Joshua was married again, and Daniel hoped Isaiah would eventually as well.

"Speaking of Hannah," he said, "let me ask you a question."

Again his brothers exchanged a glance. He wished he understood what they were signaling to each other, but, for once, he wasn't part of the silent discussion.

"Go ahead." Amos leaned forward, clasping his hands between his knees.

He did, before he lost his nerve. "I've been wondering how you do it. Except for Jeremiah, Micah and me, you've been married or are getting married. What's the secret to owning a business and having a wife and a family? How do you have everything at the same time?"

"You're kidding, ain't so?" asked Joshua.

Ezra shook his head. "It's impossible to do everything. Have a wife, have a family, have a job."

"But you do it!" Daniel exclaimed.

"*Ja*, we do it." Ezra sighed. "We do it, but no matter how hard we try, something or someone gets too little attention."

"It's like trying to roll a log," added Joshua. "You have to adjust to keep from falling in the water, and sometimes, no matter how hard you try, you get dunked."

"Only you can decide what's your priority." Isaiah sighed, a sure sign the conversation wasn't easy for him because his beloved Rose had died less than a year before. "And then, there are times when you have no hope of keeping things in balance. Something has to give."

Daniel ate the cookies and two more as he listened to his brothers talk about the occasions when their jobs had intruded on their family time and other times when family had to take a back seat to their work obligations. His spirits fell lower and lower. Before he got depressed, he stood and thanked his brothers for their advice.

As he went outside, he heard his name from behind him. Amos walked out of the shop and clapped him on the shoulder. Together they stood on the covered porch and stared at the rain.

"You can't say when love is going to come into your life." Amos shrugged, then sighed. "Look at me! I didn't expect to fall in love when I decided to halt a miniature thief before Christmas. Now *Mamm* and Belinda are discussing wedding plans, though we won't be married until October or November."

"But you were smart enough to hold on to love once you had it."

"After learning the hard way that you need to be sure it's truly love. If you want my advice, Daniel, here it is. Once you know it's love, don't let it go. You've been blessed with a second chance to accept God's most precious gift. You blew it once. Why would you risk doing so again? You may never have a third chance."

"But, after listening to you, I don't know how I can keep everything in balance."

"You can't. Not by yourself. You have to bring God into it, Daniel. Hand over the things to Him that you can't do by yourself. Not that he's going to borrow a hammer and work beside you."

"I wasn't expecting that!" He chuckled, glad his older brother was being honest with him.

Amos didn't smile as he put his hand on Daniel's shoulder again and looked him square in the eyes. "What God can do for you, if you'll let Him, is reach into you and lift the weight of your obligations from your heart. The obligations will still be there, but you'll know no matter what happens, you never have to handle them alone. Going to God should be your first choice, Daniel, not your last resort."

Daniel stared at him as the words struck a chord deep within him. Hannah had said much the same thing, but he'd thought what worked for her wouldn't work for him. God had more important things to do than listen to Daniel go on and on about his dreams.

Didn't He?

"Think about it," Amos said before walking away as a car pulled into the lot and parked in front of his shop. He waved to the two women scurrying through the rain. He held the door open for them, then followed them into the store.

As Daniel climbed into his buggy and turned Taffy along the road leading toward the covered bridge, he couldn't think of anything but Amos's advice. Go to God first with his problems?

Is that what I should do, Father? As he asked the question, he heard the answer in his heart. Who had Daniel gone to with his worries as a child? To his *daed*, who helped him find a way to ease his concerns and solve his problems. Why hadn't Daniel considered before that his relationship with his heavenly Father should be the same as with his *daed*?

By the time he reached the covered bridge, Daniel's head hurt with the thoughts rushing through it. He had a lot to sort out while he worked on nailing the last remaining boards into place on the deck. Once the rain eased, he and his crew could finish the sides of the bridge and paint them. After that, he could start the work at the O'Neills', and he'd have no excuse to come to the creek.

He glanced along it toward Hannah's house. Nobody was visible there, which was no surprise with the clatter of rain on the buggy's roof. He looked away, knowing he needed to figure out a lot before he tried to insert himself into the lives of Hannah and her family again.

Stopping the buggy by the bridge, he apologized to

Taffy for leaving the horse out in the rain. He could take the horse to Hannah's barn, but he wasn't ready to face her.

He walked into the bridge and found it deserted. He'd told his crew not to bother to come if the rain continued today because they needed a dry day to work on the exterior. Moving to the far end, he stood by the thick board that was ready to be put into place.

Daniel bit back a gasp as he looked down. Hunter's Mill Creek had risen so high it was a foot or less from the bottom of the bridge. It had swallowed large sections of its banks and was crawling toward the road. Lost in his thoughts while he drove to the bridge, he'd missed how high and fast the creek was running.

Leaving the shelter of the covered bridge and walking out into the storm, Daniel ducked his head. The wind blew rain hard into his face, and he pulled up the collar of his work coat to protect his cheeks. The rain was falling faster by the minute. It was as if someone had turned on a faucet in the sky and left it running. None of the previous storms had been this bad.

He leaned out over the abutment and watched the water race under the bridge. The current of the usually sleepy creek was so swift that foam was splashing into the air whenever the water hit a submerged stone. Branches and other debris rushed past, disappearing beneath the water and then reappearing farther downstream.

Would the bridge hold?

He climbed over the guardrail and balanced a moment on the top of the stone abutment. Sliding on his feet and hands down the steep hill, he took care to go slow. If he tumbled into the creek, he might not get out alive. He braced his feet on the hillside and held his hand to his forehead. That kept the rain from his eyes while he appraised the work he and his crew had done over the past month.

The braces along the arch connecting one side of the bridge support to the other remained in place. The rotted boards had been replaced beneath the trusses and along the roadbed. Wind-driven raindrops splattered against the arched skeleton walls and the roof, but the bridge didn't shudder as the gusts struck it. If the water didn't rise farther, the old bridge should be able to survive the flood.

He almost laughed at the thought. At the rate the rain was coming down, even if it stopped that very second, the water would continue to rise for days. Sandbags wouldn't help. There was no place to put them to divert the water away from the bridge. Its future was in God's hands. There was nothing else Daniel could do to protect it.

Going to God should be your first choice, Daniel, not your last resort. His brother's voice echoed through his head as he glanced toward Hannah's house again.

Shock struck him anew. He'd known, of course, that the house was close to the creek, but now he noticed how it was on the same level above the water as the deck of the bridge. If the creek kept rising, her home was going to flood. The barn behind it should be fine, because it was set on higher ground.

Glancing once at the bridge, he prayed, *God, I'm leaving the bridge in Your hands, but please keep Hannah and her family safe in Your hands as well. Help me help them because I'm not sure I can do it alone.*

He ran to his buggy, knowing he couldn't hesitate.

Hannah needed to evacuate along with her great-grandmother and Shelby.

Taffy shivered with fear as Daniel reached him.

"Let's go," Daniel urged, stroking the horse's nose.

The horse shifted his weight, and Daniel tugged on the bearing rein. He kept talking to Taffy as they walked into the storm, unsure if the horse was comforted by his voice. Or if the horse could hear it. Between the wind and the pounding rain, Daniel could barely hear his own voice.

He froze as he led a reluctant Taffy toward the Lambrights' house. Had he heard someone call his name? It must have been his imagination.

Then he heard it again. "Daniel, is that you?"

Hannah!

Tugging Taffy after him, he rushed up the muddy driveway. He saw her standing on the porch, waving. He left the horse and crossed the yard, leaping onto the porch. "You need to get out of here."

"I know." Her bonnet was a black, soggy mass around her face. Strands of her hair fell and stuck to her cheek. She shoved them back. "The Joneses have already left. They stopped to ask us to go with them."

"Why didn't you?"

"I tried to get *Grossmammi* Ella to go, but…" Her shrug said it all. Her great-grandmother had been too stubborn to leave.

"Let's get her and Shelby and go."

"Take them and go. I can't leave!"

"Hannah, I know things aren't right with us, but—"

"Daniel, it's the bees." Her eyes were frantic. "The bees are going to drown."

"Drown?"

"*Ja.* If the hives fill with water, they'll drown."

"Then let's move them."

She threw open the door and motioned for him to follow her. As he did, he was praying God would be merciful and save all of them.

Hannah retrieved her beekeeper's clothing. When it'd begun to rain hard last night, she'd brought it upstairs. Just to be prepared if the worst happened. Now it was.

While Shelby danced around them, excited, Hannah gave Daniel several pieces of the protective clothing for his use. His hands were too big for her gloves, but he pulled them on as best as he could. Taking rubber bands, he wrapped them around the long ends and the sleeves of his coat. The rain would keep most of the bees in the hive, but a few might dare the storm to protect their hive when it was moved. She insisted he wear her hat and veil.

"No, Hannah, you need it," he argued.

"I've got the smoker. If they panic and come toward me, I'll use it. You won't have anything to protect you. I can't have you flinch when you're carrying the hive. If it tumbles over, it could kill the queen bee and destroy the whole hive."

"But—"

"They most likely won't budge from the hive. I'll be fine." Not giving him time to reply, she turned to her great-grandmother who was sitting by the window and staring at the rising creek. "*Grossmammi* Ella," she said, making sure her voice remained calm, "we'll be in the backyard. Shelby has her toys, so she'll be fine until we get back."

"Be careful." The old woman's gaze went to Daniel. "Please be careful, Earney."

He didn't miss a beat as he said, "I will. Keep an eye on the creek and the covered bridge for me, won't you?"

"Ja." Her great-grandmother straightened in her chair. "I will."

"Danki." He tossed aside his straw hat. Pulling on the beekeeper's helmet, he didn't lower the veil over his face. "Let's get this over with."

When Hannah stepped outside, the rain seemed to be coming faster. She hadn't guessed that was possible. Her soaked bonnet clung to her hair like a deflated balloon.

She explained the easiest and safest way to move them was to lift the boards the hives sat on. They'd carry each hive into the barn as if it were on a litter.

When Daniel nodded he was ready and pulled down the veil, she smoked the closest of the three hives. The rain tore apart the smoke, so she wasn't sure how much reached the bees.

Keep them calm, she prayed as she set the smoker on the wet grass and bent to lift the hive.

It was heavier than she remembered, even with Daniel taking most of the weight on his side. They inched up the hill toward the barn. She saw bees gathering near the hive's entrance, but few ventured out. They were knocked to the ground by the rain, and she promised herself she'd try to find them once the hives were safe.

Setting the hive far enough inside the barn so it would stay dry, she hurried with Daniel to get the second one. When she asked him if he was all right, he nodded but said nothing.

They repeated the task twice, losing a few bees each time. Leaving Daniel to throw bright blue tarps over the hives to protect them further, she ran into the rain to collect the lost bees in her apron. They struggled as she set them on the floor near the hives. Each one must find its way to its own hive.

"Those are all I could find." She straightened and leaned against the low wall between the front of the barn and the stalls. Checking the tarps over the hives to make sure air could get to the bees, she listened to the hammering rain. Each drop sounded as if it were trying to pierce the roof.

The animals were restless, but she wasn't sure if the storm bothered them or the low hum of the bees. But they should be safe in the barn.

Wiping her wet hair from her eyes, she turned to Daniel who had taken off the beekeeper's helmet. He looked as soaked as she felt, but also incredibly handsome. His dark hair caught the faint light and glistened like his bright blue eyes. She wanted to stand there and drink in the sight of this man whom she'd loved almost from the moment they met.

She halted herself before she flung herself into his arms. Staring at the hives beneath the bright blue tarps, she said, "I couldn't have done it without you. *Danki*."

"I'm glad to help." He undid the rubber bands and handed them and the gloves to her. "Once the storm is past, I'll help you move them back."

"You don't have to."

"You can't move them alone. I'll help…though I'd rather go to the dentist."

She laughed. "That's obvious. You should have seen your face. You looked like you were about to grab a poisonous snake."

"I'm leery of bees. That's no secret."

"And that's why I'm so grateful for your help. Not

everyone would be able to get past their fears to touch the hives."

He put a hand on the wall behind her, standing closer than he had since they were in his house. He didn't touch her as he bent so their eyes were level. "With God's love, everything is possible. I believe that, and I've come to realize I need to live my belief every day." Each word brushed her damp face and touched her battered heart. "If I don't take the opportunities God makes available to me, I'm ignoring His blessings."

"You believe that? Really?" What a turnabout from his assumption he could handle everything on his own.

Lightning flashed and thunder crashed overhead, shaking the barn like a dog coming in from the rain.

"That was close." Daniel stepped away from her. "Let's go and get Shelby and your great-grandmother and get out of here."

She nodded. With one last check of the bees and the other animals, she ran with him out into the rain. She was drenched and cold by the time they reached the kitchen door.

"You get what you need for them," Daniel said, "while I help them put on their coats."

She nodded and hurried into the living room. It was empty.

"*Grossmammi* Ella! Shelby!" She ran to the bottom of the stairs, though her great-grandmother had not climbed them in a year. Had *Grossmammi* Ella decided to take Shelby up for her nap? The old woman wasn't steady enough to lift the toddler into her crib.

Taking the steps two at a time, she reached the top and called her great-grandmother's name and then her little sister's. Her voice echoed along the hallway. She pushed aside the nursery door, hoping *Grossmammi* Ella would be there and unharmed.

The room was as deserted as the first floor. Spinning, she ran down the stairs and collided with Daniel.

"Their coats are gone," he told her, his face pale.

"So are they! Where could they have gone in this storm?"

Chapter Sixteen

Hannah struggled to breathe. Had her great-grandmother wandered away, lost again in the past? She'd called Daniel by her late husband's name. Had she gone to find Earney? But why had her great-grandmother taken Shelby with her? That had never happened before.

"Oh, no!" groaned Daniel.

She whirled to look at him. "What?"

"I told *Grossmammi* Ella to watch the rising water and the bridge. Do you think she thought I meant she should watch the creek *from* the bridge?"

Horror sank through her. She scanned the room again as if she could find her great-grandmother on a second look. "I don't know what she'll do anymore."

"Hannah." His voice was so heavy she looked at him and discovered his face had turned gray. "I never would have said that if I'd guessed—"

"I know you didn't. But we don't have time to discuss this. We need to find them!"

"C'mon!" He grabbed his hat and took her hand.

She raced with him from the house to where his horse stood in the unrelenting storm. The creek roared like a wounded beast was clawing its way onto the banks. The water level rose as she watched, pools gathering and combining on the road and along the creek. The new boards beneath the bridge were less than three inches above the rushing water.

When he turned toward the bridge, she grasped his sleeve. He didn't slow and almost jerked her off her feet.

"No!" she shouted over the din from the rushing water.

When he spoke, she had to guess what he was saying because his words were swallowed by the cacophony from the creek. He was asking why she was slowing him down. Or that's what she thought he'd said.

She tugged him toward the buggy. He looked at her as if she'd lost her mind. Standing on tiptoe, she knocked aside his hat so she could say into his ear, "We need to get the buggy."

He pointed at the covered bridge.

Hannah shook her head. Pulling on his arm again, she sent up a prayer of gratitude when he came with her. She threw open the buggy door and climbed in. Daniel did the same on the other side. The two doors shut at the same time, rocking the buggy, but the sound was lost beneath the rain striking the roof.

When he turned to her, she grimaced as rain sprayed off his hat's brim. She shook it off her face as she said, "*Grossmammi* Ella wouldn't have gone to the bridge. She hasn't gone to the bridge since the day you showed me where the bees are. She hates bees."

"Then where do you think they've gone?" Abrupt understanding burst into his eyes, followed an instant later by fear. "You think she took Shelby out to the old mill, ain't so?" He grasped the reins and slapped them on his horse to send the buggy along the flooded road.

Hannah clenched her hands. If she was wrong, they could be marooned out near the mill, and nobody else knew her great-grandmother and the toddler were missing.

Lord, guide us to them in time. The prayer resonated through her mind over and over in tempo with the horse's hooves.

Watching the road, Hannah leaned forward as if she could make the buggy move faster. Daniel guided Taffy around the biggest puddles, not wanting to mire the wheels, but each detour, no matter how small, seemed to lengthen the journey by miles instead of inches.

A hand settled over hers on the seat, and she tore her gaze from the road. Looking down, she saw Daniel's broad, workworn fingers atop hers. He squeezed her hand. The motion said more than words could have about how he shared her trepidation.

Tears welled in her eyes. If someone had told her yesterday that Daniel Stoltzfus would gauge her feelings accurately and care so much, she would have laughed with derision. What he'd said yesterday was true. The young, callous man he'd been, a man focused only on his dreams and ambitions...that man was gone. He'd been replaced by the Daniel sitting beside her, a warmhearted man who had told her that he'd changed.

And, though she'd tried to deny the truth, he *had* changed.

A lot.

As she had, because she wasn't the uncertain, desperate girl she'd been, wondering if anyone would love her after her *daed* abandoned her. She'd wondered if her great-grandmother saw her as anything other than an unwanted obligation dropped on her in her later years. How wrong she'd been! Discounting *Grossmammi* Ella's love as nothing but a duty had been her first mistake. Believing she was unlovable was her second. Her *daed* had loved her, Shelby loved her, and…

Raising her eyes, she traced Daniel's profile. Was it possible he loved her, too? She loved him. She knew that as surely as she knew rain was falling.

Hannah rocked forward when the buggy came to a sudden stop. The road ahead was beneath water.

"We'll have to walk the rest of the way." Daniel threw open his door.

She jumped out and winced when the rain battered her. The wind tried to rock her off her feet as lightning flashed and thunder exploded around them. She was grateful when Daniel seized her hand and led her onto the side of the road so they could keep going.

As the old mill came into sight, it looked nothing as it had the last time she'd come out there. The crumbling walls were surrounded by water. The dam on the mill pond must be holding, though she wondered how long it could stand against the raging current.

She glanced toward it and pressed her hand to her mouth to silence her cry of alarm.

Her great-grandmother and Shelby stood hand-in-hand on top of the rickety dam. Waves splashed over it, and the whole structure trembled with the onslaught against it. Seeing Daniel looking in the other direction, she groaned. Farther up the creek, a tree slanted toward the water that had carved the earth away from its roots. If it toppled in, it would race like an arrow at the unstable dam.

Hannah ran as close as she could to the dam. She stood in ankle-high water, bracing herself to keep from being pulled in. Cupping her hands over her mouth, she shouted, "Shelby, come and see. Daniel's here."

The little girl's mouth moved, but the crash of the water stole the sound. She clutched her stuffed honey-bee to her chest. Hannah wasn't sure if tears or the rain coursed down her round face.

"*Grossmammi* Ella, send Shelby to us. Please!"

For a moment, her great-grandmother's eyes focused on her and Daniel. Her gnarled fingers loosened on the toddler's hand.

Shelby teetered on the dam. When the little girl tumbled off her feet, Hannah's heart jumped into her throat. Somehow, the *kind* landed in the center of the top of the dam and held on to Buzz-buzz.

Hannah felt Daniel tense, but he kept her from moving forward as Shelby began crawling toward them.

"Don't spook your great-grandmother," he said close to her ear.

The moment Shelby reached the edge of the dam, Hannah held out her hands to the toddler. The little girl threw herself into Hannah's arms.

"Han-han!" she cried.

Hannah pressed her face against the *kind*'s soaked hair. Lifting her into her arms, she wept as the little girl wrapped her arms around her neck and clung to her. She moved backward, Daniel's hand gripping her arm to keep her feet from sliding out from under her on the slick slope.

"Get Shelby to the buggy," he said. "I'll get your great-grandmother."

"I need to—"

"You need to let me do this."

She shook her head, but didn't answer as a crack came from farther up the creek. The tree slipped closer to the water.

He took her by the shoulders. "Don't argue, Hannah. You've let others depend on you, but you've never been willing to depend on others. Why? Do you think it makes you powerless if you allow someone else to help you?"

"No, it's not that."

"Then what is it?"

She didn't have an answer for him, because having him come into her life again had led her to question how she lived her life as well as her expectations of herself and others.

"Hannah." He framed her face with his hands, tilting it so she could look into his eyes without having rain splash along her face. "You, of all people, should know how important it is for everyone to depend on each other. Your bees rely on each other to build their hive. If one fails, they all fail. That kind of dependence isn't weakness—it's strength."

He was right, but could she trust *Grossmammi* Ella's life to him? The answer came quickly. *Ja!* Even when he'd broken her heart, he'd been trying to do what was best for her. He'd helped her move the hives even though he hated being near bees. He'd won her heart…twice. How could she *not* trust him?

More important, she knew she could depend on him. He wasn't running away, torn between his conflicting dreams for his future. Her heart, no longer willing to be silent, called out she must give him another chance.

This chance.

She must depend on him to do what she couldn't: save her great-grandmother's life.

Shifting Shelby in her arms, she stepped toward the buggy. "Do what you can, Daniel, to save my great-grandmother."

* * *

Daniel was staggered by the strength of Hannah's belief in him. It shone from her eyes and flowed from her fingers as she clasped his arm. *Dear God, be with me so I don't disappoint Hannah again. Help me find the right words and do the right things to reach* Grossmammi *Ella.*

A sense of peace draped over him like an umbrella. Only this umbrella quieted a storm that had raged within him so long he'd learned to ignore it. In its wake seeped the warmth of knowing he wasn't alone. What had he told Hannah in the barn? With God's love, everything was possible. It was time for him to take his own words to heart.

He pulled his gaze from her great-grandmother. "Take Shelby and get in the buggy. Be ready to flee if the dam goes."

"Be careful." Her voice sounded like a whisper, but he guessed she was shouting as he was.

He nodded as Hannah hurried to the buggy. He didn't wait to see if she got in. No time for anything but getting her great-grandmother to safety.

His heart stopped in midbeat when he saw the tree topple into the creek, caught in an eddy. Once it escaped, it was going to hit the dam.

"*Grossmammi* Ella!" he called.

She ignored him.

He had to think of a way to reach her. He could run out and force her off, but he wasn't sure the dam could hold two adults. And there wasn't time to argue as she did except when she thought he was her late husband.

That was the answer!

"Ella!" he shouted. "Ella, *liebling*!"

The old woman's head snapped around like a marionette's. She stared at him and said something. Her words were lost in the noise, but he saw her lips form her husband's name.

"Ja!" He yelled louder. "Ella, *liebling*, come here to me. I know how much you miss your Earney." He chose his words carefully. He didn't want to lie to her.

"I've been waiting for you right here." She moved toward him. Slowly. Too slowly. "Right here where we used to watch the stars when we were courting."

He understood at last why she'd kept coming here. He'd share that with Hannah…later. For now, he had to chance going out to the old woman. As he put his foot on the dam, it seemed to sway beneath him. *Lord, I put our lives in Your hands.*

Running, he reached *Grossmammi* Ella. The dam was shaking with the current. He glanced to his right. The tree was on a collision course with the dam.

"Earney! I knew you'd come. I knew it!" The desperate cry came from deep within the old woman's heart as she collapsed in his arms.

He scooped her up and pulled his open coat around her to protect her from the storm. She couldn't weigh a hundred pounds. Shifting her so he didn't put pressure on her ancient bones, he turned to get off the dam.

He gasped when the windblown rain blinded him. He blinked, trying to see. When a hand grasped his elbow, pulling him to his left, he followed Hannah onto solid ground. He kept blinking hard, and his eyes cleared in time to see the buggy right in front of him.

He put *Grossmammi* Ella in next to Shelby who was watching with her thumb in her mouth, a sure sign the little girl was afraid. Motioning to Hannah to get in, he ran around to the other side. He jumped in and grabbed the reins, slapping them on the horse as soon as Hannah was inside.

Later, there would be time to thank her for guiding him to the buggy. Later, after they were safe. He shouted to the horse to go at its top speed.

Taffy must have understood the danger because the horse ran along the road, splashing water into the buggy through the open doors. He yanked his door closed and, from the corner of his eye, saw Hannah do the same on the other side.

"We've got to get up the hill," said *Grossmammi* Ella in a matter-of-fact tone.

He knew that, but a fence edged the road. They could climb over, but he didn't want to leave Taffy behind.

"Over there!" Hannah pointed to an open gate barely visible in the rain.

"Take the reins! I'll help Taffy." He was out of the buggy before she could answer. As he slammed the door shut, he saw her grope for the reins.

Fighting his way through the fast-moving water, he grasped the horse's bridle. "Let's go, Taffy."

The water rose higher and higher as he led the horse toward the open gate. He watched, appalled, when the buggy slid sideways. He gritted his teeth and tried to move faster.

As soon as they reached the gate, Daniel slapped Taffy's rear to send the horse racing up the hill. He ran alongside and jumped in when Hannah threw the door open. He took the reins from her, fighting to keep the buggy upright as they bounced over the uneven ground.

At the top, he drew in the horse. Silence filled the buggy for the length of a single heartbeat.

He didn't hear the crash when the tree struck, but the

dam collapsing was as loud as the thunder overhead. Shrieks came from the toddler and *Grossmammi* Ella. Hannah hushed them before she scrambled out of the buggy.

Daniel jumped out and came around to where she stood. He grasped her shoulders and spun her so her back was to the scene of destruction below them.

"Look at Taffy." He clasped her face between his hands to keep her from seeing the maddened creek. "Or better yet, look at me, Hannah. Look at me, and don't look away."

"I don't want to look anywhere else."

"*Gut!* Look at me, and I'll look at you. Nowhere else."

Crashes came from below, and she shuddered. "Don't you want to see what's happening to the bridge?"

He shook his head. "We fixed it once. We can fix it again."

"*Danki* for saving us." She rested her head against his chest, and he knew she must be able to hear his heart thud with the joy of holding her close.

"*Danki* for trusting me." He leaned his cheek against the top of her ruined bonnet.

"I always will." She raised her gaze to his. "Always."

"And I'll never give you a reason to believe you can't depend on me again."

She tightened her hold around him as he claimed her lips. As crashes heralded damage along the creek, he held her close as he found everything he wanted in her kiss.

Chapter Seventeen

"Excellent work, Daniel." Liam O'Neill's booming voice echoed in the covered bridge like the metal buggy wheels of an Amish buggy on the deck. "I didn't know if this old bridge would still be standing, but it seems you saved it."

"The *gut* Lord did," Daniel replied, giving credit where it was due.

"By giving you and your crew the skills to strengthen it in time for the flood." The Irishman glanced at the tools and scrap wood piled on the deck. The debris had been swept out yesterday. "When will you be done here?"

"It's going to take us another few weeks. The flood did enough damage that we have to check each bridge support and replace the missing ones as well as those that were weakened." He glanced along the bridge and tried to quell the pulse of pride that nearly all the repairs had survived the flood.

The repairs hadn't been just his work. They'd been his and his crew's work. It'd taken him long enough to see one man couldn't do the work alone. A leader's job was to find the best men for the job and let them do it.

More than a week had passed before the waters retreated enough for him to assess the full damage. The waterline inside the bridge was almost two feet above the deck, but the reinforced bridge had stood. The days had been fair and warm, a gift from God in the wake of the month of rain and floods. During that time, Liam had offered him the project he wanted Stoltzfus Brothers Construction to oversee.

Stoltzfus Brothers Construction. The name seemed perfect, because he intended to use his brothers' skills whenever a job required them. Primarily his twin, since he'd asked Micah if he'd like to become his partner in the business. Micah told him he needed time to consider the offer, surprising Daniel. That sounded like their cautious brother Jeremiah instead of his twin who usually looked while he was leaping.

"After you've checked out the bridge, you plan to start on my project?" asked Liam.

"Ja."

"Excellent." He glanced past Daniel. "You've got some people waiting to talk to you."

Looking over his shoulder, Daniel smiled when he saw Hannah standing on the other side of the concrete barrier. Shelby clung to her as the *kind* had since they fled the flood. He hoped the toddler would soon forget the experience, though he knew he never would. Every night since that harrowing escape, he'd had nightmares about the waters overtaking them after he'd asked Hannah to depend on him—truly depend on him for the first time.

Thanking Liam, Daniel walked over to where Hannah stood by their buggy. "Where's *Grossmammi* Ella?"

"At the time we left your family's house, she was trying to teach your *mamm* to make *snitz* pie."

"My *mamm* makes the best *snitz* pie in the county." He grinned. "Maybe the whole world."

"You know that. I know that. Wanda knows that, though she'd never be so prideful as to admit it. But my great-grandmother doesn't know that, and she's sure Wanda can learn a lot from her."

"We all can."

"And we'll have the time to do that, thanks to you saving her."

He tapped her nose as if she were no older than Shelby. "Don't you remember what I've said so often? Let's leave the past in the past?"

"I agree. I'd rather look to the future, too." She glanced at her home which was leaning from where the strong current had pushed it off its foundation. A tree trunk had impaled itself in the center of the porch, and branches and other debris tumbled out the front door.

But the three hives had escaped the flood in the barn along with the other animals. The chickens hadn't left their roosts under the roof. Judging by their hoofprints, the two cows had gone no farther than the field beyond the barn. Both had returned by the time Hannah was able to check on them.

"Do you want to look in the windows?" he asked.

"I already did. There's nothing left inside worth saving. Everything either washed away or is ruined beyond repair." She set Shelby on the buggy seat and smiled as her little sister cuddled her stuffed bumblebee. "I'm so grateful Shelby had Buzz-buzz with her when *Grossmammi* Ella took her to the mill."

"*Grossmammi* Ella saved our lives." He rested

his elbow on the side of the door. "If your great-grandmother hadn't rushed off so we had to give chase, we could have been in the house and never known what was coming at us until it was too late to escape."

"I've thanked her, but I don't think she understands why. And I've thanked God for keeping us safe."

"As I have." He slipped his arm around her waist. "You know, I've been thinking."

"Uh-oh, that could mean trouble."

He chuckled. "Usually, but this time you'll like what I'm thinking. The house is cramped with your family living with mine, so you and Shelby and your great-grandmother should move to my house."

"Didn't you build it for your brother and his future wife?"

"That wife is further in the future every day because he can't get up the nerve to talk to her." He curved his hand along her face. "Hannah, I built the house for a family. So why don't you move in? I'll join you after we get married."

"Married?" she gasped.

"Isn't that what people in love do? Get married?" He leaned into the buggy. "I love you, Hannah Lambright. I always have. I was too young and foolish and proud to admit it three years ago."

"But your business—"

"Will always be secondary to my wife and our family. I believed owning a business was my dream, but I never realized the best reason for having my own company was being able to provide a *gut* home for the ones I love. You and Shelby and *Grossmammi* Ella. We'll take care of each other and watch over each other. Will you marry me, Hannah?"

"*Ja*, because I love you, too, Daniel," she whispered as she stood on tiptoe and pressed her lips to his.

He swept his arms around her and kissed her, knowing *all* his dreams were finally coming true.

* * * * *

Love Inspired®

Save $1.00

on the purchase of any
Love Inspired®,
Love Inspired® Suspense or
Love Inspired® Historical book.

Available wherever books are sold,
including most bookstores, supermarkets,
drugstores and discount stores.

Save $1.00

on the purchase of any Love Inspired®, Love Inspired® Suspense
or Love Inspired® Historical book.

Coupon valid until April 30, 2018. Redeemable at participating retail outlets in the
U.S. and Canada only. Limit one coupon per customer.

52615519

5 65373 00076 2   (8100)0 12342

® and ™ are trademarks owned and used by the trademark owner and/or its licensee.

© 2018 Harlequin Enterprises Limited

LIINCICOUP0118

*He'll help fix up her home for her and her four amazing
kids, but after leaving her at the altar years ago,
can Luke Wheeler earn Amish widow Honor King's
forgiveness—and love—once more?*

*Read on for a sneak preview of
A MAN FOR HONOR
by Emma Miller,
available February 2018 from Love Inspired!*

Leaving the cellar door open, Luke came down the stairs
and settled on one of the lower steps. "I suppose Sara is
trying to match us up. It is what she does for a living. And
from what I hear, she knows what she's doing."

Honor pursed her lips, but the look in her eyes didn't
appear to be disapproving.

Luke took it as a positive sign and forged ahead. "I
already know we'd be a good fit. Perfect, in fact, if it
wasn't for what happened last time you agreed to marry
me. We have to talk about it someday," he insisted.

"Maybe, maybe not." She shrugged. "But definitely
not today. I'm having a wonderful time, and I don't want
anything to ruin it."

"Sit with me? Unless you think you'd better go up and
check on the children."

Honor regarded him for a long moment, then lowered
herself onto the step beside him. "*Ne*, I don't want to
check on the children. There are enough pairs of eyes to
watch them and, truthfully, I'm enjoying having someone

else do it." She glanced away and he noticed a slight rosy tint on her cheeks. "Now I've said it," she murmured. "You'll think me a terrible mother."

"I think you're a wonderful mother," he said. "An amazing person who never deserved what I did to you."

Her eyes narrowed. "Didn't we agree we weren't going to discuss this?"

"Not really. You said we weren't. I never agreed. Thinking back, I wonder if we'd just—"

The door at the top of the cellar steps abruptly slammed shut. Then they heard the latch slide into place and the sound of a child's laughter.

Luke got to his feet. "What's going on?" He reached the top of the steps and tried the door. "Locked." He glanced down at Honor. "Sorry."

"Not your fault." She pressed her lips together. "Unless I miss my guess, one of my little troublemakers is at it again."

He chuckled. "When you think about it, it is pretty funny."

She flashed him a smile so full of life and hope that it nearly brought tears to his eyes, a smile he'd been praying for all these years.

Don't miss
A MAN FOR HONOR by Emma Miller,
available February 2018 wherever
Love Inspired® books and ebooks are sold.

www.LoveInspired.com

LIEXP0118

Reward the book lover in you!

Earn points from all your Harlequin book purchases from wherever you shop.

Turn your points into *FREE BOOKS* of your choice
OR
EXCLUSIVE GIFTS from your favorite authors or series.

Join for FREE today at
www.HarlequinMyRewards.com.

Harlequin My Rewards is a free program (no fees) without any commitments or obligations.

MYR17